37

A THOMAS IRONCUTTER NOVEL

DAVID ACHORD

SEVERED PRESS
HOBART TASMANIA

37: A THOMAS IRONCUTTER NOVEL

CHAPTER 1

February

"Dude, at least roll down the window," Jason chastised.

Charlie gestured with his vape. "It's just water vapor. Besides, it's cold out."

"Yeah, but you have it filled with that sativa shit. Crack it open a little," Jason said.

Charlie scoffed, but obliged and opened the passenger window a couple of inches. "You weren't so sensitive back when you were straight."

Benny, who was sitting in the backseat, laughed, and then motioned with his hand. "Don't be stingy, puff-puff-pass."

Jason laughed along with them. When he had made the announcement on Facebook, he'd lost a few friends, but these two had stuck with him, even if they joked about it a little too much. Soon, the three young men were taking the exit to Manchester, Tennessee and followed the directions to the fight.

"This is going to be great," he said. "I've been looking on the internet, Wolf is undefeated."

"Black Thunder is no slouch either," Charlie added. "I wonder if they've ever fought each other."

Jason shook his head. "Different weight divisions, but they probably spar and train together."

"What's his real name?" Benny asked and then clarified. "Wolf, what's his real name?"

"I have no idea," Jason answered. In fact, he couldn't even find Wolf's real name or his MMA history, no matter how much he researched. The only thing he found was a poorly recorded YouTube video of one of his matches and a comment saying he was undefeated.

When they drove into the parking lot, they could see a crowd already lined up, waiting to get in. They parked and the three of them hurried to get in line. Two girls were in front of them. Jason saw them checking them out as they walked up but ignored them. Even if he were into girls, those two were trashy.

"Where are you guys from?" the heavier one asked almost immediately when they got into line.

"Nashville," Charlie said with a grin. He was always grinning.

"Nashville, huh? Did you bring any party favors?" the other girl asked.

Both of them were giving flirtatious smiles, exposing nicotine-stained teeth. Jason saw Charlie give Benny a subtle nudge.

"It's highly possible," Charlie said. "But we don't share with just anybody."

"We don't share with just anybody either," the first girl replied and emphasized her statement with a wink. She then draped her arm around her friend and gave one of her breasts a playful squeeze. "But we come as a package." Her friend responded by kissing her on the cheek and smiling seductively.

Charlie glanced at Benny. Benny's grin was bigger than Charlie's.

"If you two want to hang out with us, that'd be cool," Benny said. "We'll share."

Jason rolled his eyes and scanned the crowd. It was the usual mix, a few more rednecks than he cared for, but that was okay, and then he spotted him. The man was at the far back of the wall, scanning the crowd as well. The two of them locked eyes and Jason stirred. It was Wolf. He was ruggedly handsome, and even from afar Jason could feel the electricity.

Jason gave him a head nod. Wolf gave him a slow nod back, which caused Jason to grin. *Maybe this was going to be a good night,* Jason thought.

CHAPTER 2

April

Personally, I never thought blood smelled like copper. I'd read that descriptor many times in thriller novels and had even heard it mentioned in a few cop movies. Frankly, it was bullshit.

If it were true, it would've smelled like a copper mine in here. There was blood everywhere. There was a metallic odor, sure, but there was no way a blindfolded person would have walked in, took a sniff, and say, "Hey, I smell copper!"

So, there I was, no longer a cop, but nevertheless standing in the doorway of a million-dollar home nestled in the middle of a gated community known as the Governor's Club. There were two people lying on the floor of the den. Both surrounded in blood. Both deader than Grandpa's Johnson on a Sunday night.

I was loading up the car with my golf clubs when Sherman called me. He had an urgent tone in his voice when he told me he needed me. Sherman was a close personal friend, almost like a father to me. He once kept me out of prison for a murder I did not commit. I never turned down Sherman when he asked for my assistance.

He filled me in as I hopped in my car and sped down the road.

"I'm sure you remember Lou Habinger," he said.

I did. Lou was a doctor, an orthopedic surgeon to be specific, and a close personal friend of Sherman's. They went to the same synagogue and moved in the same social circles.

"I don't know if you remember, his youngest daughter married a couple of years ago to an investment trader."

I remembered him too. He was a snarky, arrogant prick who cheated at golf.

"I seem to recall reading in the news about his investment company being under investigation by the Feds," I said.

"Yes. He was informed yesterday that indictments were forthcoming," Sherman replied. "And, it would seem the marriage has been rather tumultuous. He was arrested on a domestic violence charge recently. Lou tried calling his daughter this morning, but when she did not answer, he decided to go to their home and check up on her. He found them both deceased in the den of the home. He believes it is a murder-suicide."

"Did he call 911?" I immediately asked.

"I am not certain, Thomas. He seems to think he needs an attorney present," Sherman replied. "Perhaps he is scared. Perhaps there is more to it than he is saying."

"Sounds sketchy," I remarked.

"Indeed. That's why I need you to check things out. Make sure everything is kosher, no pun intended."

I knew what he meant. He was wondering the same thing I was, and that was, perhaps Lou's son-in-law had killed his daughter and Lou killed him in retaliation.

So, that is how I found myself on a pleasant Sunday morning; looking at a crime scene.

Lou's daughter, I think she was about twenty-five, was on her stomach. Her corpse was surrounded in a pool of drying blood. Her husband was nearby, lying on his back, a revolver clenched tightly in his right hand and a bloody steak knife lying by his side.

I stepped carefully into the house, crouched by the bodies, and scrutinized everything. Under the right circumstances, blood spatter could tell you everything you needed to know about the crime.

After studying the spatter, cast-off, and the general state of the den, I then made my way through the house. I inspected one room at a time, not an easy task. Even so, it only took me thirty minutes. When I was through, I walked outside and toward Sherman's Mercedes. Sherman rolled down his window as I approached.

"You can go ahead and call 911," I said.

Sherman nodded and did so. I walked a little down the driveway and took several slow, deep breaths, a technique I had found was the best way to get the stench out of my nose. Sherman joined me a minute later.

"I'm going to have a dandy of a time explaining the delay in calling the authorities," he said. "So, what do you think happened?"

"They were both dressed and the blood is coagulated, so I think it happened last night, dinner time would be my guess. There are still dishes with food on the kitchen table and a couple of glasses of wine. They got into some type of argument. A steak knife was used on her. It started in the kitchen and ended with her collapsing in the den. At some point, he felt remorse. He went into the master bedroom, retrieved a handgun from the nightstand, came back in the den, and shot himself in the head."

Sherman's face darkened and he slowly shook his head. "So very sad."

"Yeah," I replied. "So, when they get around to asking why he called you instead of calling 911, what are you going to say?"

"I'll tell them when my client called, he was too upset to specify the nature of the emergency, which is mostly true, so you and I rushed over here. I'll bullshit my way through the rest. I'm an old hand at bullshitting," he said with his cherubic trademark grin.

I nodded. Sherman knew what to say and do in situations like these. We walked back to his car as the sounds of sirens grew closer.

The first officer, a young rookie who did not look like he needed to shave yet, was the first on the scene. He left his siren on a little too long after he parked before springing from his car with his gun drawn. Sherman and I watched in a mixture of fascination and disdain. He had his weapon gripped tightly in both hands. Thankfully, he had it at the low-ready position and not aimed at us.

"Where is the suspect?" he demanded. I pointed toward the open door. Oh, sure, I could have told him the suspect was dead and there was no emergency, but why bother?

"Stay here," he ordered and rushed to the door. To his credit, once he approached the door, he made a tactical entry.

Neighbors were already coming out of their oversized homes as two other police cars turned into the driveway. Thankfully, they had their lights and sirens turned off. I recognized the older of the two as he got out of the car. The other one jogged inside while the older walked over to us.

"Hey, Thomas," he said and shook my hand. "I'm assuming there is no emergency, otherwise you wouldn't be standing around here looking like you've just come off the golf course."

He was referring to my attire. I had a tee time in a couple of hours and was wearing a new Tiger Woods signature shirt with matching pants. I gestured toward Sherman.

"This is Sherman Goldman. He is the attorney for Lou Habinger. Lou is the father of the female decedent."

"Officer Ted Iorio," he said. He did not offer to shake hands. Sherman noticed. Most officers avoided shaking hands; it was nothing personal. I kept going.

"Mister Habinger's daughter had recently been assaulted by her husband. She had him arrested three days ago..."

"Yes, I was the one who arrested him," Officer Iorio said.

I glanced at Sherman. "You're aware of the situation then, good." He nodded. "So, her father came by to check on her this morning and found the two of them inside, deceased. I don't want to sound presumptuous, but to me it appears to be a murder-suicide."

Our conversation was interrupted by what sounded like a heated exchange from inside the house. A few seconds later, the two officers emerged. The rookie officer had blood on his hands. I could only imagine what happened, but one thing was for certain, he violated one of the cardinal rules of crime scene preservation—don't touch anything.

"So much for preserving the scene," I remarked.

Iorio's jaw muscles tightened, but he didn't respond. The rookie officer focused on us, squared his shoulders, and pointedly walked toward us.

"Which one of you called this in?" he demanded.

"I did, young man," Sherman answered.

"Alright, I'm going to need a statement from you." He seemed to notice me for the first time. "Who are you?"

"My name is Thomas Ironcutter, and the gentlemen sitting inside the car is Lou Habinger. He is the father of the deceased woman and father-in-law of the deceased man."

"I'm going to need IDs from all of you," he demanded.

I scowled at the rookie like I was looking at dog shit on the bottom of my shoe before turning to Officer Iorio. "I assume a detective or two is on the way?"

He nodded.

"Good. We'll wait for them," I said.

The rookie officer stepped closer to within inches of me. "I don't know who you think you are, but you are not the one to give orders at my crime scene. You're not in charge here."

"You're right, I'm not in charge here. If I were, I'd have you fired for your buffoonery." I pointed toward the house and then at his hands. "You contaminated the crime scene. A smart officer would have known better."

The young officer scowled and started to say something, but Iorio cut him off.

"Streeter, let's wait for the detectives."

I glanced at my watch. I hoped I could make my tee time.

CHAPTER 3

While the young officer continued blustering and posturing, an unmarked car carrying a man and woman parked by the curb. I did not know either one, but they seemed to be all business. The young officer saw his chance to shine.

"We have two deceased people inside the home. Both appear to be victims of a brutal homicide."

The woman listened to the young officer while the older man glanced over at us. He made a subtle nod to his partner and walked over to us.

"Good morning, gents," he greeted.

I led off with the introductions and gave him a brief synopsis of the circumstances. I may have mentioned I peeked into the doorway, saw blood, and backed out. It may not have been totally factual, but if I had been, they might have insisted I stay with them and eventually give a formal statement.

There was no telling how long that would take, and the end result would have been the same. Nope, I had no time for that. When the two detectives were occupied, I hopped in my car and took off. I managed to get away with plenty of time to spare and drove directly to Mick's, my favorite cigar bar.

My fat Irish buddy, Mick O'Hara, was sitting in front of his business, kicked back in one of his ornamental iron chairs, smoking a cigar like he hadn't a care in the world. I frowned as I parked. He was wearing a faded pair of jeans, an orange UT jersey, and matching ball cap which was tattered and frayed. I helped him put his clubs in the back and waited until he got in the car before jumping on him.

"I just looked at the weather report. Sunny all day with a high in the sixties. Great golf weather."

"Yeah, great weather. Let me ask you something, did you drink a big glass of stupid juice this morning?" I asked.

"What the hell are you going on about?" he retorted with a scowl.

"We're not playing at a municipal golf course, bub. It's a country club. They have a strict dress code."

"They do?"

I sighed in exasperation and glanced at my watch. "Do you have a change of clothes inside?"

"Nope," he replied as he relit his cigar and puffed on it with feigned indignity.

"Figures," I muttered and made a beeline to a nearby Target store.

It took a little bit of scolding before he agreed to go in. Thirty minutes later, I had him clothed in a light blue golf shirt and khaki slacks. He refused to ditch the hat though. When we got to the checkout line, he couldn't help but embarrass me. He leaned toward the cashier and gave her a sidelong look.

"Say, I think one of those he-she transveratite things was in the men's room watching me change. I felt very uncomfortable."

Both the cashier and another customer gave him a withering stare. I hurried him out of there.

"Do us both a favor, refrain from any crass remarks while we're at the country club," I said.

Mick looked at me in mock confusion. "What do you mean? I am the personification of sensitivity."

"Of course you are," I said. He changed the subject.

"Alright, let's talk business. I'm counting on you to be on your A-game today. I'm tired of hearing Wally flapping his gums about what a great golfer he is."

I nodded in agreement. "I need you on your game too, no screwing around. Do you know anything about this partner of his?" I asked.

"Not much," Mick said. "He's been in a couple of times with Wally. His name's Hiram something and Wally says he's a retired CIA secret agent. Oh, and Wally said he has a twelve handicap, but it all sounds like horseshit to me."

I had to chuckle. Mick often liked to express his disdain in terms of animal excrement.

"Are you really going to join this high-brow country club?"

"I'm thinking about it," I said.

His only reply was a, "Humph."

The previous day, I'd bumped into a busty brunette at a local Starbucks. She was wearing a blouse that showed a lot of cleavage and I had to admit I gave her assets a thorough appraisal. She caught me looking, gave a flirtatious grin and before I knew it, we were sitting at a table chatting like old friends. She introduced herself as Debbie Cart. She told me she was the membership recruiter for Davidson Hills Country Club and asked if I would be interested in joining. Before I knew it, she'd given me a pass for a free round of golf and told me I could even invite friends.

Unfortunately, when I went to Mick's later that evening, I made the mistake of showing the passes and telling the story of how I got them. Mick immediately invited himself to play and Wally eagerly joined in. Honestly, I planned on playing alone, or inviting Sherman to join me, but I gave in and set up a tee time.

I should have listened to my intuition. It didn't matter that it was a beautiful day and the course was in immaculate condition, the antics of my three so-called friends made for a long, excruciating round of golf.

Wally was a pleasant enough guy in small doses, but the problem with him was he was lost in his own fantasy world. When he was a young man, he had dropped out of college in order to pursue the dream of being a professional golfer. Fame and fortune and all that. Suffice it to say, it did not work out for him. But you wouldn't know it by the frequent stories he told. According to him, he was a living legend in the golfing world. Now in his sixties, he occasionally gave lessons, but mostly he hung out at Mick's. His only income I knew of was Social Security and an inheritance from his deceased mother.

His partner, Hiram, was so much like him they may as well have been brothers. More than once, he let us know he was a former super-secret agent man for the CIA. The two of them spent the entire day telling wild stories and it was downright annoying. Mick was one of my best friends, but he was also an irritating curmudgeon who often took great joy in pushing my buttons.

All I wanted was a peaceful round of golf, but it wasn't happening. In addition to the asinine prattle, these guys sucked at golf. Even Wally, who was supposed to be a pro. They hooked, sliced, topped, chunked, bladed, whiffed, you name it. As a result, our pace of play was abysmally slow. Oh, and yeah, they cheated. The foot wedge and unlimited mulligans were constantly in use. Even for Mick.

After what seemed like an eternity, we finished the round. I thought it was over, but then Mick and Wally began bickering over the score. I tried to ignore them, but my patience was at an end.

"For the love of God, knock it off!" I said it a little louder than I intended and immediately regretted it. "C'mon, let's go try the restaurant here."

"They better have cheeseburgers and beer," Mick grumbled.

"Lunch sounds wonderful, I'm famished," Wally said.

"Here, here," Hiram added.

I did not intend for Wally and Hiram to join us, but I guess it was my own fault for mentioning it in front of them. I motioned for them to follow and hopped in our golf cart.

The waitress was on us as soon as we sat and we all ordered beers. I looked around as the three stooges prattled on. I'd done a little research and knew the place had been in business since the sixties. It was obvious from the style of architecture, but the interior had been redecorated into a modern motif with a nice blend of pastel colors and scenic pictures hanging on the walls. I could almost see myself as a frequent patron.

"What are you going to order, Dago?" Mick asked.

"Good question. May I ask that everyone order something different? I want to see if the cook staff is on the ball."

"No problem. I'm getting a cheeseburger and fries," Mick quickly said.

"But I wanted a cheeseburger," Wally grumbled.

It took some wheedling, but I finally got them all in agreement. Wally ordered a turkey club, Hiram got chicken tenders, and I got an Italian beef sandwich. I could make one blindfolded and would readily be able to tell if the cook was any good. The beers came within a minute. Mick took a big slurp.

"The course is in nice shape," he remarked.

"Yes, it is," I agreed. "They do a good job of maintaining it." They'd put down fresh sod in spots that did not survive the winter and I could smell a fresh application of fertilizer on the greens.

"It reminds me of the Albany golf course," Wally said. "I placed second there on three different occasions. I never could pull off a win though. Too much wind for my playing style."

Mick rolled his eyes and drank another slurpy swallow. Wally was prone to telling tall tales in regards to his professional golfing career. Mick and I looked him up on the PGA website once and he'd only played in two pro events, failing to make the cut in each tournament. Mick finished his beer, waved the glass at the waitress, and wiped his face.

"Well, Mister Pro-Golfer, let's see what the final score is," he said and pulled the scorecard out of his back pocket. "It looks like we tied the front nine, won the back nine, and had the best overall score. That means you two owe us twenty dollars, each."

"No, no, and no," Wally rejoined. "I tied Thomas, therefore we tied the back nine and tied overall."

Mick gave him the stink eye. "What world are you living in? We're not counting those mulligans you kept taking. Thomas beat you by seven strokes, and that's without a single mulligan."

Wally let out a condescending sigh. "Mick, Mick, Mick. I noticed you took a mulligan or two as well."

"Thomas didn't. He smoked you like a cheap cigar and you know it," Mick retorted.

It didn't take a genius to see this petty bickering was going to start back, so I decided to quash it. "Guys, can we please knock it off and enjoy lunch? You can squabble all you want back at Mick's."

Wally grumbled some more, but they reluctantly agreed. Mick occasionally threw out a smart-assed remark, but he stayed mostly civil. Soon enough, the food arrived and everyone dug in.

"That sandwich looks delicious, Thomas," Hiram said.

I mumbled an agreement and took a bite. I noticed he'd had been paying a lot of attention to me throughout the day. He'd go out of his way to compliment me whenever I made a good shot, or even when I made an average shot. Now, he was eyeing me again, causing me to be suspicious. It wasn't until I'd finished my first beer that I began to get an inkling of what he was up to.

"Say, Thomas, Wally says you're a private investigator," he said as the waitress brought us a fresh round.

"I am."

"A highly successful PI," Mick said, and punctuated it with a belch.

The waitress had been clearing away our plates and when she heard Mick, she stared at me oddly before hurrying away. I caught Wally and Hiram exchange a tacit glance. Here it comes, I thought.

"You know, Thomas, Hiram's work as a spy is very similar to PI work," Wally said.

"Indeed," Hiram added. "On a higher, more complex level of course, but yes, there are many similarities."

"Sure," I agreed, although I didn't. Hiram was a gangly man, with the exception of a paunch the size of a basketball sticking out of his shirt. If that wasn't bad enough, he had long stringy hair that was currently braided into a long tail down the back like he was some kind of hippy, or perhaps a Dick Marcinko wannabe. He was probably in his early fifties, which meant to me if he had in fact worked for the CIA, he did not retire like he claimed, but instead left the agency early, if in fact he had ever worked there at all. He missed my sarcasm and kept talking.

"Yeah, I was deep undercover and got into some serious ka-ka over the years. The last year was a doozy and I had to get out of the business. I have a bounty on my head in three different countries, but don't ask me the details." He punctuated his story with a smug grin and what he would probably call a conspiratorial wink.

I caught Mick gawking at him like he was looking at someone who walked into his business and asked if he sold water bongs. "So, you're like James Bond or something," he said in mock seriousness.

I agreed with Mick's skepticism. I had no reason to doubt the man, but yeah, I doubted him. I doubted his credibility and I doubted his sincerity. He was up to something, but I didn't care. I motioned at the waitress with my empty beer glass and gestured at Mick and myself.

Hiram gave a deprecating laugh. "Something like that, I suppose. These days, I outsource for The Company," he said and used air quotes when he said it.

"Company?" Mick asked. "Like Mary Kay cosmetics? That kind of company?"

Hiram cocked his head. "Sorry, I'm so used to shop talk it's become second nature to me. The Company is how we refer to the CIA."

"Oh," Mick drawled.

"Yeah, my specialty is international espionage, but during the course of my career, I've pretty much done it all." He looked around and made a politician's gesture with his hand. "Nashville is a nice place. For years, I've thought about relocating down here and setting up shop."

He then looked up like he had an epiphany and snapped his fingers. "You know, I can't believe I haven't thought of this sooner."

Wally took his cue. "What's that, Hiram?"

Mick and I exchanged a glance. I looked back at Hiram, who was staring at me with what I'm sure he believed to be an earnest expression.

"You know, Thomas, even though the majority of my work these days involves international consultation work, we should explore going into partnership together. With my experience and your local connections, we'd have a formidable PI business."

I didn't answer. After all, I thought he was full of horseshit, as Mick would say.

"Once we've established ourselves, we could make a fortune," he added. He then arched an eyebrow. "Thoughts?"

"I have a thought. What do you have to bring to the table?" Mick asked.

Hiram looked at Mick and gave a pained smile, as if he were dealing with a feebleminded child.

"You don't understand, Mick. I have a distinctive set of skills. I have international connections. I am intimately acquainted with the inner sanctum of the ABC agencies and the off-the-books operations the black ops guys run. This partnership would be a unique, one of a kind operation." He looked pointedly at me. "The potential here is unlimited. We need to have a sit-down, Thomas, and talk about this. You know, get into each other's heads. This could be a once in a lifetime opportunity."

I set my beer down. He thought he was fooling me, but I was onto him. Spy or not, he was a scammer. He was unemployed and looking for a meal wagon to latch onto. I could've been acerbic in my response, but I chose pleasant bluntness instead.

"Frankly, Hiram, I have no need to expand. My current business model is fine." In fact, it was better than fine. I'd been turning away work and could use one or two extra employees, but there was no way in hell I was going to put him on the payroll.

Mick looked shocked. "What's wrong, Dago? Don't you want to be a secret agent?"

Hiram ignored Mick and leaned forward on his forearms. "No offense, Thomas, but that's rather shortsighted. A one-man operation is limited both in scope and profit potential. I can get exclusive contracts with some of the biggest conglomerates in the world."

A wicked look flashed across Mick's face for a split second. "Yeah, Dago, you think too small. You ain't ever going to make millions the way you're operating." He gestured at Hiram with his beer. "The secret agent here could show you a thing or two."

Wally seemed to feel the need to add his opinion.

"You should give Hiram's proposition serious thought, Thomas. You don't want him coming into town and setting up his own PI business. The competition would be too much for you."

Hiram gave another smile. This smile was pompous rather than patronizing. "Ah, Wally, it wouldn't be like that. I consider Thomas a friend and wouldn't tread on his turf. But if a potential client were to come along…"

He finished his sentence by holding his hands up, like he was implying he would not turn away business that I would have potentially picked up. I would have laughed if he wasn't so serious. He made a few more attempts to fuel my interest in his plan but eventually gave up. At least, for now. I suspected I had not heard the last of this.

Soon, the two men made some excuses and scurried off. They somehow forgot they had an outstanding bet to pay off and even worse, they neglected to leave a tip for the waitress. The welshing on the bet I could understand, but people in the food service industry relied on tips; they certainly weren't doing it for the pleasure of waiting on sweaty old men.

"Can you believe that?" Mick said while I paid the bill and left a generous tip.

"Are you surprised?" I asked.

"No, but it's still a weasel-shit thing to do."

Ah, yes, another category of animal poo. I added it to my mental list.

I took us on a slow tour of the pro shop, checking things out, but mostly hoping to see Debbie. She was nowhere around though. Satisfied I'd seen enough, I motioned to my fat Irish friend.

"Let's get out of here," I said and led Mick toward the parking lot.

"You know we'll never get a dime out of them," he said, seemingly forgetting I had paid for his lunch as well.

I chuckled. "I don't know about the secret agent, but Wally's going to pay up sooner than you think."

"Why's that, Dago?" Mick asked.

"You know that new driver he's been bragging about?"

"Yeah, the Callaway one. What about it?"

I pointed toward my Cadi. "While you two were arguing on the eighteenth hole, I slipped it out of his bag and put it in mine. Watch this."

I pulled out my phone and began typing a text message.

Hey Dumbass, if you want your driver back, pay up!

Mick watched as I typed and erupted in a belly laugh.

"That's a good one, Dago. Let's get going. I'm out of cigars," he said.

"Sure."

As we started to get into my car, a man's voice called out. "Excuse me!"

I turned to see a younger man jogging toward us. I guessed him to be in his early twenties, easily fifty pounds overweight, an untrimmed beard, a tattoo on the side of his neck, and wearing a chef's jacket that had more than a few food stains.

"Can I help you?" I asked.

He took a moment to catch his breath before speaking. "Hi, my girlfriend was your waitress. She said you're a private investigator."

"I am," I said. "What's on your mind?"

"I've been thinking about hiring someone like you, and if you have a minute, I'd like to talk to you about it."

"Sure, what kind of issue are you having?" I asked.

"My little brother is missing and I'm pretty sure he's been murdered."

CHAPTER 4

He wiped his hand and stuck it out. "My name's Joseph, Joseph Belew. I'm a sous chef here."

"I'm pleased to meet you," I said. "I'm Thomas Ironcutter and this is my golf partner, Mick."

Handshakes were exchanged and then the young man stared like he didn't know what to do next. I knew this was not going to be a short conversation, so I pointed at some benches at the edge of the parking lot.

"Why don't we sit down and you can tell me about your brother."

He eagerly nodded. Once seated, I got the ball rolling.

"Why don't you tell me about your brother?" I suggested.

"Yeah, um, wait a sec." He pulled out his cellphone and showed me a picture. "That's him, Jason Belew. Well, Jason LeClaire Belew. Both of us have the same middle name. That was our mother's maiden name."

I looked at the photo. It was a selfie of the two of them grinning like kids. His little brother was actually an inch taller than Joseph, more muscle, a lot less fat.

"Yeah, he's bigger than me, but I'm still the older brother," Joseph said.

"What are the circumstances of his disappearance?" I said.

"Jason has it in his head he wants to be a professional martial arts fighter. Back in February, he went to watch a tournament in Manchester, Tennessee with a couple of his friends and hasn't been seen since."

"What'd his friends say?" I asked.

Joseph shrugged. "Not much. They only said they went down there together, met some girls, and they lost track of him."

"Did you file a police report?" I asked.

"Yes, sir, me and my mother did, but they don't seem to be doing anything. I had to leave four messages before anyone would even call me back." He shook his head. "Four messages. Ridiculous. That's why I think I need to hire a private investigator."

"Have you talked to his friends, his girlfriend, any of that?"

He began nodding before I'd even finished the question. "I have." He then looked a little uncomfortable. "My brother's gay and he recently came out, but he doesn't have a boyfriend."

"How'd that go?" I asked.

"Alright, I guess," he said with a slight shrug. "Mom was fine with it, and most of his friends were cool with it too."

"Most?"

"Yeah, there were a couple of guys at the dojo he trains at who were assholes about it, but Jason didn't let it bother him."

I let him talk. His expression would alternate between happiness and pride when describing his brother to somberness when he talked about the last time he had seen him. I paid diligent attention and made mental notes. I also thought about Joseph. The man was a sous chef on a sous chef's salary and I sincerely doubted he could afford me. I decided I was going to let him down gently. When he had run out of things to say, I cleared my throat.

"First, let me say, I sincerely hope your brother is okay and that he simply felt the need to get away for a while."

"I don't think so, Mister Ironcutter. Jason and I were close. If he needed to get away, as you say, he would have called or texted me. We didn't have any secrets between us."

"Okay, I understand." I paused for a moment. "It's good that you've contacted the police. Unlike what you see on TV, they have a lot of resources at their disposal that private investigators don't. Also, they don't cost you anything. I, however, am not free."

"How much do you charge?" he asked.

"A thousand a week, plus reasonable expenses."

Upon hearing this, his long face took a nose dive into the depths of Gloomville. I'd seen this happen before. I was used to it by now. Joseph stared at his feet and a single tear fell to the ground. He wiped his face with the back of his hand.

"Some people think that's too much, and don't take this the wrong way, but you're not one of these rich country club members; you're a working man who doesn't have money to throw around."

"No, sir," he said.

"I know I'm not cheap and I make no apologies for it. I also have to tell you, I've been burned in the past, so I always require payment up front."

"I understand," Joseph replied.

"Alright, give this some thought. If you hire me, you'll be spending hard-earned money and I cannot guarantee positive results."

I ended the conversation by giving him a business card and repeated my admonition to think it over.

"What were those things in his ears?" Mick asked as we rode.

"They call them gauges, I think."

"They look stupid," Mick said. "It's like he's saying, look at me, I'm stupid and I eat Tide pods."

I couldn't help but chuckle.

"Are you going to take his case?" he asked.

"He can't afford me," I said. "I sympathize, but he can't afford me."

Mick was quiet for a solid two minutes, which was highly unusual for him, but then he said something that surprised me.

"I had a little brother."

I glanced over at him. "I didn't know that. You said had, as in past tense."

"Yeah, he died when he was nine. Leukemia."

I stopped for a traffic light and stared at my friend, who was now looking out of the window, lost in his thoughts. In all of the time the two of us had been friends, he had never once mentioned his dead brother. It must have been difficult for him to talk about.

"If you were me, what would you do?" I asked him.

He did not answer. Instead, he rolled down the window and stared out at the passing scenery until we arrived back at his cigar bar. When we walked in, he went directly to his office. His wife, Kim, looked at me questioningly.

"He just told me about his brother," I whispered. I didn't know if he'd told any of the other patrons and did not want to be the one who blabbed. Kim's expression darkened.

"It still bothers him," she said and gave a worried glance at the closed office door. "He'll be okay. I've learned to just give him some space and he's back to his normal self in no time. You want a beer?"

"Certainly. How about a Nashville Lager?" I said and gave a casual glance around the bar. There was the usual afternoon crowd in the place, a mixture of retired men who had nothing else to do and businessmen who wanted to unwind a little before going home to their families. Mick O'Hara was a foul-mouthed curmudgeon, but likeable enough where he had a strong following who regularly patronized his place.

"Hey, Thomas, come join us," one of the regulars said.

"Maybe later," I replied. "I'm meeting someone."

Most of the regulars were likable guys, but they were always getting into silly debates about sports, politics, religion, or some other stupidity. A couple of days ago, a couple of them got into a heated argument over the proper method to peel a banana. When the adult beverages were flowing, silly arguments happened frequently.

None of that for me today. I decided on a cigar, my second of the day, and sat at a table at the far end of the bar. I pulled my laptop out of my briefcase, plugged in, turned it on, and lit my cigar as I waited for it to boot up.

"Hey, Thomas, one day you really should think about getting an office," one of the regulars said.

"Yeah, one day, Ebbie, one day," I replied and then promptly ignored him.

When I first got into PI work, money was tight. I simply could not afford to rent an office space. I soon found I did not actually need one. A computer and a cell phone were sufficient for the work I did. Any time I needed to meet with someone, I could always find a location.

I sent a text to Hal, informing him I was at Mick's. He responded he was stuck in traffic and it would be approximately another thirty minutes. So, I filled the time by checking my emails. I scanned for familiar names and opened those first. The only one of note was from Sherman. He'd talked me into going in with him and a couple of others on a real estate investment trust, more commonly known as a REIT. His email informed me there were some issues and had scheduled a meeting. It was two days from now. I checked the calendar and responded I'd try to be there and went on to rest of the emails.

I was halfway through my cigar before my client drove into the parking lot. Hal Garrison was a criminal defense attorney who had been practicing law for the past thirty-something years. Hal had an easygoing, smart-assed personality outside of the courtroom, but in the courtroom, he was a tiger. He was highly skilled and unrelenting when cross-examining prosecution witnesses, especially cops. We'd had more than one courtroom encounter back in the day. In spite of that, or maybe because of it, we'd become friends. Sort of. He greeted me warmly as he sat down.

"Whatta ya' say, asshole."

"Not much, dickhead," I replied.

Now in his late sixties, Hal had somehow managed to stay slim and trim throughout the years, but, male pattern baldness had attacked at an early age. Since the only hair he had left now was a little peach fuzz on each side, he preferred to completely shave it. It looked better that way, but the first time I saw him with a shaved head I told him he looked like a dick with ears.

Currently, he had two independent cases involving murder. One was charged with murdering two prostitutes in a massage parlor over twenty years ago. The other was a man charged with murdering his estranged wife. Most attorneys would never have two murder cases going at the same time, but Hal wasn't like most attorneys.

"Alright, enough of the idle chitchat. I hope you're not going to hit me up for more money. I know how you private dicks are," he said as he clipped and lit a cigar.

"Do you want the good news or the bad news?" I asked, ignoring the jibe.

"Surprise me."

"Alright, I'll start with the Jackson case," I said.

Last year, Allen Jackson, no relation to the country music superstar, had laid in wait for his estranged wife to come home from a late-night assignation with her lover. He shot her twice as soon as she parked her Jaguar in the garage of their home. As he was leaving the scene, a neighbor happened to be walking his dog and encountered Allen exiting his driveway. Instead of stopping to say hello, or simply waving, Allen sped out in his customized Corvette, leaving a fresh line of tire tracks in his wake. The neighbor, sensing something amiss, went to investigate and found Mrs. Jackson.

"Unless they're hiding something from you, it appears they searched and processed the Jackson home without a search warrant and without the consent of your client," I said. "As you know, even though they were separated, he was still paying the mortgage."

Hal grinned. "And if they weren't going to bother with a search warrant, they needed his consent. Nice catch. Now all of that other shit can be suppressed."

The "other shit" he was referring to were numerous pieces of documentary evidence the detectives seized which contained a mélange of incriminating evidence regarding Allen's ongoing criminal enterprises. The mafia did not have a strong presence in Nashville, but there were organized crime figures here nonetheless. Allen Jackson was one of them.

"But the murder charge will stick," I said. "When he was arrested, he was placed in the back of a patrol car, whereupon he asked the officer if he could use his cell phone, to which the officer gladly accommodated him."

I watched as Hal started chewing on his cigar in thought for several seconds before he spoke. "What happened?"

"It'll come out in discovery, but the patrol officer had his backseat wired. He was able to record a conversation of your client talking about the murder.

According to my source, during the conversation he said, and I quote, I killed the bitch."

"Shit," he muttered. "Are you sure?"

"That's what I was told. If it's true, it's admissible, you know that, right?"

He gave me a look and blew a waft of blue smoke in my direction. "Of course, I know that. I've been doing this stuff since you were a kid."

I was making a dig at him. In Tennessee, the absence of a reasonable expectation of privacy while in police custody allowed the police to surreptitiously record an arrestee. Any criminal attorney worth their salt knew this. For that matter, any criminal worth their salt knew it as well.

Hal digested the information with no overt signs of consternation and moved on to the other murder case. "Alright, what about Vancouver?"

Javonte Vancouver was Hal's other client. His high school sweetheart was a cute nineteen-year-old who had been seduced by the excitement of parties and drugs. For some reason, she got herself a job at a massage parlor, which was nothing more than a front for prostitution. Vancouver had joined the Marines after high school and found out about her new lifestyle while he was home on leave.

The two girls had been stabbed well over a hundred times, a classic indicator of a rage murder. He soon emerged as a possible suspect, but there was not enough to arrest him, as far as the detectives knew. The case languished for years. There were no witnesses, no murder weapon was recovered, and there was no surveillance video.

Eventually, the cold case detectives took over. One of them reviewed the case and spotted an error; the medical examiner had taken fingernail scrapings from both of the girls, but nobody had ever submitted the scrapings for DNA analysis. This case had already been through the judicial process known as the preliminary hearing, which allowed Hal to file discovery. He promptly hired me and tasked me to analyze the evidence.

"It's winnable," I said reluctantly.

Hal arched his furry eyebrows. "You're serious?"

"Yes."

"How so?" he asked.

"It's all in my report," I replied and tapped the three-ring binder lying on the table.

"Well give me an overview, asshole. I'll read your report later."

I cleared my throat. "Okay, starting from when the victims were first discovered, the scene was overrun with police personnel. Here, I'll show you." I inserted a USB drive into my laptop and opened a file. A friend of mine who worked for one of the local new stations searched the archives and found some video. I played it for Hal.

"Look at all of those officers and detectives wandering in and out of the business. I know all of them, and only one still works for the department. The rest are either retired or dead. Now, you can review it later, but out of all of those officers, only three of them wrote a supplement report detailing their actions in the scene."

I clicked on another file. "Here's all of the detective's reports. They did a lot, but there are a lot of things they didn't do."

"Like what, for instance?" Hal asked.

"I know from personal experience that several of the businesses up and down this street had exterior surveillance cameras, yet nobody had bothered checking them or downloading videos during the time frame of the murder."

"No video, got it. What else?"

I went to another set of reports.

"When they decided your client was a person of interest, he was back at Parris Island. A couple of detectives went there five days later and interviewed him. It was a superficial interview, recorded on a microcassette tape, which was stupid."

"I've got one of those, what's wrong with them?" Hal asked.

"A microcassette tape is not meant to be played over and over, which is what I believe has been done with this one. The sound quality has deteriorated somewhat. So much so, the stenographer had a hard time transcribing it. There are several indecipherable words. In legal terms, it's going to be worthless for the prosecution. The only real thing that's clear is your client denying being involved in the murder."

"Okay, good. Anything else?"

"Yes. At some point, they shifted the focus of the investigation away from Vancouver. They decided the murders were the work of a serial killer that was operating in Nashville at that time and abandoned the investigation on your client."

"Who was the serial killer?"

"A knucklehead by the name of Paul Reid. They expended a lot of man-hours trying to link him to the murders, but never came up with anything. Incidentally, Paul Reid died while on death row and at least one member of the command staff wanted to write up the case with Reid being the suspect and then close it."

"Interesting," Hal said. "Have you spoken with any of those retired cops?"

"I've gotten in touch with most of them. One is living in Belize and he told me to piss off. Six of them are dead. The others claim amnesia, which means they aren't interested in wasting their time sitting court without being paid. The only detective who was actually on the scene and is still with the department is Paul Parton."

"I've cross examined him before," Hal said. "He seems to know his onions."

"He's a sawed-off little runt who'll lie at the drop of hat," I replied. "He claims to have a photographic memory."

"Hell, everyone lies," he said with a chuckle. "I take it there's a history between you two."

"Yeah, you might say that."

In fact, there were two people still employed with the department who I considered enemies, the kind of enemies that, if I ever bumped into them in a dark alley, I'd give them a beating they'd never forget. Parton was one of them. I didn't bother telling Hal the story; it was old news.

"There are other issues with the case which you can use in court. It's all in my report."

"Did he do it?" Hal asked.

I looked at him with a frown. "Isn't it one of those unwritten rules a defense attorney never questions the guilt of their client?"

He made a flippant wave with his cigar. "It's just you and me talking here. If it was your case, would you have arrested him?"

I answered without hesitating. "Yes."

"Wait, why weren't you involved in the case?"

"It happened before I transferred into homicide," I replied.

"Oh." He puffed on his cigar and thought a minute. "Winnable, huh?"

"The man belongs in prison, but yeah, with your courtroom skills, it's winnable."

"And Jackson?" he asked.

"If you ask me, file a motion to suppress all of the evidence they recovered from the house and then see what kind of deal they'll offer. But, you're already considering that, aren't you."

He grinned. "Yeah, I am. The only problem I'm going to have is with my client. He believes he can skate on this. You didn't hear it from me, but he's an arrogant prick of galactic proportions. If the DA offers six to twelve, which would be a damn good offer, I have no doubt he'll reject it."

"I hope you're getting a good paycheck out of it," I remarked.

"You better believe it. I've been called a lot of things, Thomas, most of them may be true, but stupid isn't one of them."

I couldn't help but grin. He grinned in return, took a large swallow of beer, and set the glass down.

"Alright, I've got to go. The wife has some people from church coming over for dinner, I better get home." He stood. "Always a pleasure. See you later, asshole."

"You too, dickhead," I replied.

My cellphone buzzed. I glanced down at the screen and saw it was from Anna.

Where are you?

I'm at Mick's.

Stay there. OMW.

I ordered another beer and joined the regulars as they watched the evening news. A busty redhead was on the scene where some skeletal remains were found at a construction site in the bottom of a cistern well.

"What do you think about that, Thomas?" one of them asked.

I gave a noncommittal shrug. "It's a true mystery."

"They think he was a Civil War soldier," another one said. "I've no doubt I'll be called in to consult on this."

The one who made that somber declaration was Ebbie, and he was once a professor of history at a local university. He, not unlike a couple of other regulars, had an exaggerated sense of self-importance. Businesses that served alcohol often attracted these types.

I listened as they conversed. A couple of them had opinions on how the person died and ended up in the well, which led to an all-out discussion which soon segued into unsolved murders and the Civil War. I gave a few hmms and yesses at the appropriate times, but mostly stayed out of it. Trying to have an intellectual debate with a bunch of drunks was seldom fun.

Anna arrived several minutes later in her blue Nissan Cube. She had her stereo turned up so loud I could hear it from inside the bar. She walked in with another woman her age, a petite blonde with ample breasts which were being shown off with a tight-fitting, low-cut top. Anna was wearing a plain blue T-shirt with some kind of logo on it, and both were wearing what those silly looking skinny jeans.

"Hey," I greeted and motioned toward two empty barstools.

"You girls want something to drink?" Kim asked after they had gotten seated. She'd lived in Tennessee for the last forty years, but she still had a distinct native Korean accent.

"Yes," Anna said with a slight amount of eagerness. They ordered two Black Abbeys, I ordered another Nashville Lager.

"This is Marti," Anna said. "I don't know if you remember her."

"I believe I do. You two used to be roommates, right?"

In fact, the two of them were strippers at the Red Lynx together. That was Anna's place of employment back when I first met her. When it burned down, it was probably one of the better things that happened to Nashville.

I never thought of Anna as the stripper type, but Marti was a textbook definition of one. She had the body, the big boobs, the tattoos, and that sultry yet trashy look about her. I bet she made a lot of money.

"Good memory," Marti said with a smile and stuck out her hand. "My real name is Martina, but everyone calls me Marti." The handshake lingered a little bit longer than normal, which was discomforting, but I gave a friendly smile.

"Nice to meet you," I said. "What are you girls up to?"

"Just hanging out. What've you been doing?" Anna asked.

"I played a round of golf with Mick and a couple of others," I said.

"And we kicked their ass," Mick said. He'd walked up with our beers and set them down with a grin. He then gave Anna a sweaty hug, but she didn't seem to mind.

"So, you won?" she asked him.

"You bet your ass we did. The Dago here struggled a little bit, but I managed to carry him and pull it out."

Obviously, he was back to his normal self. He looked over at Wally, who was sitting at his usual spot at the end of the bar. At the moment, he was unabashedly leering at the girls. Mick noticed and continued.

"And, the two losers still haven't paid up," he said loud enough for everyone in the bar to hear, which elicited a few knowing chuckles from the regulars.

Marti unexpectedly reached out and put her hand on my arm. "I'd love to learn how to play, maybe you can give me lessons some time." She emphasized it with a flirty smile and I wasn't sure if she was intentionally making a double entendre.

"We'll have to have an outing one day," I said, smiling back. I caught Anna looking at me and then she casually reached for her phone. I knew she was about to text me.

"Excuse me for a moment," I said and went to the restroom. Sure enough, my phone buzzed within seconds.

Careful, she knows you have money and is looking for a sugar daddy!

I scoffed. Sugar daddy, right. Drying my hands, I stared at the mirror above the sink. The gray seemed to be a little more pronounced these days. I looked closer. Could anyone see those hints of sadness peeking out? Ever since Simone's death, I was having a hard time keeping a positive mindset. I thought of her often and when I did, I'd become sad. A therapist would say I was experiencing grief and perhaps some unresolved issues from my past. Then said therapist would ask me how I felt about that statement while holding their notepad and pencil at the ready. The hell with therapy.

"Work it out, Hoss," I whispered to my reflection.

I took a few slow, deep breaths, ran my fingers through my hair one more time, and straightened. I sighed at the thought of Marti. She was a looker, no denying it, but I knew immediately she was not for me. Nope, I was going to keep it in my pants for a change.

Heading back to the bar, I wasn't all that surprised to see Wally standing close beside Marti. He was laying it on thick.

"As Mick and Thomas can tell you, I am a certified PGA pro instructor. If you want lessons, there is nobody better to teach you."

Mick scoffed and rolled his eyes. I squeezed past Wally and sat back on my stool. Wally continued with his sales pitch while Marti smiled in amusement.

"Isn't golf expensive?" she asked him.

Wally's grin widened. "I suppose it is with people who have a tight budget. With me, I play at all of the finest golf courses in the world. Nothing but the best for me."

"So, you live lavishly," Marti remarked with a slight hint of a smirk.

"That I do," Wally replied, beaming, and then he tried to set the hook. "And, any lady who is in my company can expect the same."

"But, if you live such a lavish lifestyle, why do you buy your clothes at Walmart?"

Mick howled in laughter as Wally's grin faltered.

"I don't buy my clothes at Walmart," he stammered.

Marti giggled and then patted Wally on the arm. "Oh, I'm teasing you, Mister Wally. You're a sweet old man. You remind me of my grandfather."

Whether she knew it or not, implying Wally was old enough to be her grandfather cut deeper than the crack about his clothes. He lingered there a moment longer, his brain trying to figure out whether or not she was interested. It would not have done any good for me to tell him any woman who was forty years his junior would not have any romantic interest in him. He finally gave her shoulder a rub.

"We'll talk later," he said with a wink before going back to his bar stool. Anna and Marti looked at each other and rolled their eyes in unison. Anna then focused on me.

"Guess what I did this morning?" she asked. She loved to play the "guess what" game, even when I gave smart-assed answers.

I acted surprised. "You washed and waxed my cars?"

"You wish," Anna said in mock annoyance. "I had a meeting with Ms. Braxton. She wants to hire me to do some work."

Ah yes, Esther Braxton. She was what they called old money. Not too long ago, she hired me to prove her husband had fathered a child from another woman. I let Anna run with the case and she did splendidly. Ms. Braxton was pleased with her work and she'd been a partner in my PI business ever since.

"Ms. Braxton, huh? What kind of work?" I asked.

"She wants me to help her research her family tree."

"Oh, that sounds interesting," I said. "I would have thought a woman of Ms. Braxton's status would have done that already."

"She's done some, but there are gaps she wants filled in. She says it needs some good old-fashioned legwork done and she wants to hire me to do it."

"Did you discuss the fee, or does she expect you to do this for free?" I asked. As rich as Ms. Braxton was, she'd make a penny bleed if she could.

Anna's expression tightened slightly. "We've worked out a salary."

I could have reminded her that she was now on my payroll and therefore needed to stick with the fixed rates, but I let it go.

"Well, it'll be an interesting learning process for you," I said. "Is there any way you can put it on hold for a couple of months?"

Anna blinked. "Um, I told her I'd get started on it right away, why?"

"The Goldman firm has a job for us," I said. "One of their attorneys is representing a kidney dialysis corporation in a lawsuit. I'm surprised William hasn't mentioned it."

Her lips tightened slightly. "No, he hasn't. What kind of case is it?"

I paused a few seconds. Talking specifics in front of someone like Marti, while harmless, could be considered unprofessional. I decided to keep it rather vague.

"A health insurance company is claiming their client has manipulated certain terms of the contract they have. The Goldman client contends everything has been above board and the management of the insurance company was well aware of the terms they are now disputing."

"Sounds complicated," she said. "What will our job be? Conduct surveillance or something?"

"Nothing like that. No, we've been hired to read through several thousand emails and look for specific correspondence that would validate the client's claim."

Now, her eyes widened. "Thousands?"

"Some are only a couple of sentences long, some are longer, much longer." I let it sink in as I drank my beer. "And, this is a case where we charge by billable hours, which will have a cap. We will be tasked with reading these emails in a specific amount of time."

My phone buzzed during this discussion. It was Wally. Rather than speaking to me in person, he texted me, begging me to give his driver back. He agreed to pay up, so I went to the trunk of my car and came back inside with his driver.

Wouldn't you know it, he followed me back to the girls. I could tell by the look on his face he had regrouped and was now ready to throw out a fresh round of bullshit. He started as soon as he got within three feet of Anna and Marti.

"Hey girls, check this out. Callaway gave this to me as a part of their sponsorship," he said, holding up his driver.

This immediately led into another one of his long-winded tales. Anna and Marti seemed amused, so I didn't run him off. I tuned out his prattle and instead watched the first round of the NHL playoffs on one of the big screens that surrounded the bar.

I finished my beer, and even though there was a pleasant crowd, I was not feeling sociable. When Simone and her daughter were murdered, I fell into a deep depression, exacerbated by self-medicating with copious amounts of alcohol.

I'd been doing better; lots of exercise, eating healthy, drinking only in moderation, etcetera. But I still had bouts of melancholy and all of the associated side-effects to go along with it. So, before I slipped back into that previous lifestyle, I paid my tab and left.

Tommy Boy was yammering for my attention as soon as I walked in the door, but before I could pet him, my phone began ringing.

"Hi, it's Debbie."

Ah, yes, Debbie Cart. I could almost close my eyes and imagine what she looked like without clothes. I focused and tried to keep the lust out of my voice.

"Hi, Debbie. What are you up to?" I asked.

"I was calling to see if you enjoyed your round of golf," she said.

"I did," I replied. "That is a beautiful course. Kudos to the greenskeeper." There was no need boring her by describing the antics of the three stooges and instead focused on the positive.

I sat in my easy chair. Tommy Boy immediately jumped up on my lap and made himself comfortable.

"Excellent, so I can sign you up," she said with a lilting laugh. I laughed along with her.

"I admit it's a nice place but, I'm not completely sure it's the venue for me."

"How so?" she asked.

"I got the impression that it's a family environment. As you know, I'm not married."

She gave another lighthearted laugh. "Oh, don't be silly. There are members who are single. I tell you what. We have a get together once a month for our single and divorced members. The next one is Saturday. Why don't you come with me? You can be my date."

I thought about it a long moment. So long, she thought I'd hung up on her.

"Are you there?"

"Oh, yeah. I was just trying to think if I had any previous plans, but I don't and I'd love to be your date," I said.

I thought it was a nice recovery. To be honest, I was not sure whether or not I was emotionally ready to go out on a date. We talked some more before she told me she couldn't wait to see me Saturday before hanging up. I'd debated on if I wanted another beer when my phone rang again.

"Mister Ironcutter, this is Joseph Belew."

"Hi, Joseph. How are you?" I asked.

"I'm okay. Listen, I hope I didn't call too late," he said.

"Not at all. What's on your mind?"

"I've talked it over with my mother and girlfriend, and I want to hire you."

I thought for a moment. "I'll be glad to take on the case, but I want to tell you now, there is probably not a lot I can do that the police have not already done."

"I still want to hire you, and I have your fee ready."

The mention of money caused my expression to light up. "Okay. Well then, if you're certain about this, we need to meet and sign a contract."

We agreed to meet in the morning. After hanging up, I got on the internet and typed in Jason's name. Other than a link to his Facebook page, I received zero hits. Same with his brother, Joseph.

I decided against another beer and fixed a large glass of ice water before logging onto Jason's page. There was nothing remarkable about it, other than the fact that there was no mention of a girlfriend, or boyfriend. He had several friends, but there was no mention of any type of romance. There was no grand proclamation of him coming out as gay either. There were a few pictures of friends, a few pics of him in a karate Gi, but again, nothing special.

Since Joseph had not heard anything from his brother and there was a police report on file, I assumed he was not in jail somewhere. Even so, I checked with the Davidson County Sheriff's Department. There was nobody named Jason Belew currently in their jail.

I pulled out an A4 pad and jotted down some of the questions I was going to ask Joseph, including employment, cell number, and any bank accounts or credit cards. I then created a new file, named it Joseph LeClaire Belew, and copied everything from his Facebook Page.

I also found an Instagram account, but like his Facebook account, there was nothing remarkable on it. I knew there were many other types of social media accounts that were popular among younger people, but I was done searching and would go over it with Joseph tomorrow.

Jotting a few more notes, I finished with it and changed locations to my bedroom. I made myself comfortable, turned off the overhead, and turned on the lamp on my nightstand. I then settled into a book I'd been reading. Tommy Boy meandered in, sat on the floor, and stared up at me.

"What? This is what old single men do for excitement."

He stared a moment longer and then began licking himself.

CHAPTER 5

I met with Joseph at ten the next morning in the lobby of the Davidson Hills Country Club. We shook hands and I followed him to the kitchen and through a back door which led outdoors where there was a picnic table and a few folding chairs, all hidden from view by untrimmed hedges. A five-gallon plastic bucket was sitting beside the table, filled with sand and cigarette butts.

"This is our designated break area," he explained. "We're not allowed to loiter anywhere the members might be hanging out."

I nodded in understanding as I set my briefcase on the table.

"Do you enjoy working here?" I asked. "I'm thinking of joining as a member."

He shrugged. "It's okay, I guess. We're shorthanded, we're always shorthanded, and so I've been putting in a lot of hours. It gets old but I need the money."

A girl walked out and joined us. I recognized her as our waitress from yesterday. "This is my girlfriend, Jenna."

"Hi," she said with an outstretched hand. "I'm Jenna Copeland."

She was the same age as Joseph, a little plump around the middle but cute. "Would you like some coffee or something?" she asked.

"It's too hot for coffee, but if it wouldn't be too much trouble, a glass of iced tea would be wonderful," I said.

"We have iced coffee, if you'd like some," she suggested.

I scoffed. "Iced tea, please. No self-respecting southern man puts ice in his coffee."

She gave a patient smile and disappeared through the door as I sat and opened my briefcase. A moment later, she returned with a glass and sat beside Joseph. The two of them gazed at me expectantly. I got a sense they were not sure how to proceed, so I started it off.

"After speaking with you last night, I went ahead and worked up a contract. The language is pretty standard. It outlines the work I will do for your money and the standard disclaimer clauses."

"Like what?" he asked.

"I specifically notate that I am not going to do anything illegal, nor do I guarantee I will be able to locate your brother. There are also clauses written in that are designed for your benefit. Why don't you read it over? If you find any issues, we can work it out, okay? Also, if you want to add something, we can certainly do so."

I slid the contract across the table. Joseph looked at it like it was written in a foreign language. I took pity.

"Why don't I go over it with you two," I suggested, retrieved the contract, and read it aloud to them. I explained each clause as simplistically as I could, which took all of three minutes to go over. When I was finished, they looked at each other and then at me.

"Any questions?" I asked.

"No, sir, I guess you've got everything covered," Joseph said.

Satisfied he understood the terms of the contract, we took turns signing and Jenna acted as the witness. Before I could say anything, Joseph reached into his pocket and counted out a thousand in twenty-dollar bills.

We spent the next thirty minutes talking about Jason. I didn't need his life story, but Joseph told me anyway. That was okay; it gave me an idea of who Jason was. I've always been a good listener, mostly because of my childhood. If my father thought I wasn't paying attention whenever he spoke, I'd get a smack with his calloused hand. Sometimes it was only hard enough to sting, sometimes he drew blood. I don't know what B.F. Skinner thought about this form of behavior modification, but it certainly worked on me. I listened attentively and waited until he was finished before speaking.

"Alright, tell me about Jason's drug use," I said offhandedly.

Joseph was momentarily taken aback and then vigorously shook his head. "No, sir. Jason doesn't do drugs. Not any. He doesn't even drink or smoke." He gestured back and forth to Jenna and himself. "We drink, and we smoke weed, but that's it. Jason has it in his head he wants to get into professional fighting one day, so he doesn't do any of that."

I noted that he referred to his brother in the present tense, which indicated a sense of hope. I kept pushing it.

"Does he sell?" I asked.

"No, sir. He never has," he said.

"Who are his enemies?"

This time, Joseph slowly shook his head. "I've thought long and hard over that question, and as far as I know, he doesn't have any. His friends say the same thing. Like I told you before, he recently came out. We have mostly the same friends. Most of them were cool with it, some weren't, but there wasn't any bad blood."

I asked a few more questions, and then had him jot down Jason's bank account information, along with all of his social media info. Eventually, I closed my briefcase and stood.

"Alright, I'm going to give the detective a call and see if he'll meet with me."

"Do you think he will?" Joseph asked.

I shrugged. "I'll give it a try."

Some detectives will accommodate to PIs poking into their case, some won't. Those that won't could either be pleasant in their refusal or they could be assholes. I had to deal with one such asshole not long ago in which he had incorrectly ruled a homicide as a suicide. He was an arrogant, lazy man and honestly had no business in law enforcement.

We spoke a minute more before shaking hands and parting company. As I headed to my car, someone called out to me.

"Thomas!"

I turned to the voice. It was Debbie. She walked across the parking lot with her usual radiant smile and a bounce in her step which reverberated all the way up to her breasts. She was wearing high-heeled shoes, a plaid skirt that showed a lot of leg, and a white blouse. Her dark hair flowed down over it, like it had been freshly brushed.

"Hi," she said.

"Hi," I replied. "You look nice."

"I'm trying for the naughty Catholic schoolgirl look."

I smiled, which probably looked more like a lecherous leer. "I'd say you nailed it."

"Are you looking the place over some more?" she asked.

"Actually, one of the employees hired me and I was meeting with him."

"Ooh, it sounds like some juicy gossip. Tell me all about it," she said.

I gave another smile, not so lascivious this time. "I'm afraid it's confidential."

Her smile faltered slightly, but then she recovered. "Oh, like a lawyer-client kind of secret."

"Yeah, something like that. I have a confidentiality clause in the contract."

She gave a scoff, which she somehow made a sound like a prelude to an orgasm. "Nobody can keep a secret from me around here; I'll find out."

"I'm sure you're right, as long as you don't find out from me."

"So, please tell me you're still considering joining?" she asked.

"I am," I answered with another polite smile, not at all sure I was telling the truth. She must have sensed my reticence.

"And?" she drawled while twirling a tress of hair.

"I'm still on the fence, but I must admit, you make it hard to say no." Did I just say hard? Did I just see her make a quick glance downward? I checked my watch. "I have to go, but I'll see you Saturday, okay?"

"I would hope you call me once or twice before Saturday." She maintained eye contact this time.

I nodded. "Absolutely."

I hadn't thought of making any phone calls before our date. Obviously, I'd been out of the game far too long, or maybe I wasn't as interested in her as I thought I was—I didn't know. She stepped forward and gave me a light peck on the cheek before we said our goodbyes.

One of the differences between the police and a private investigator is expediency. A police detective usually has a dozen or more investigations going on at the same time. And, that did not include court time or doing busy work for your boss. Nope, none of that for a PI. As a PI, I could control my caseload, I did not have a boss to answer to, and a subpoena to court was only honored if it was convenient to me. Therefore, once I was hired, I could begin investigating the case immediately.

Once seated in my car, I gave Ronald a call.

"I've got some info on a young man I need you to investigate."

"What kind of info?" he asked.

"Bank account, cell phone number, social media accounts. Do your thing on them and see what you find out."

"What kind of case is it?" Ronald asked.

"Missing person. He went down to Manchester to watch a martial arts tournament back in February and hasn't been seen since."

"Oh, man, do you think he's been abducted or did he take off?"

"I don't know. I'm heading down to Manchester right now. Do you want to go with me?"

"Oh, hell no," Ronald immediately answered.

"Are you sure? It's a beautiful day, it'll be good for you to get out of the house for a little while. Besides, have you ever even been to Manchester?"

Ronald stammered a moment before responding. "It's just that, well, I need to get the house cleaned up. I have a date tonight."

"You have a date?" I asked in surprise.

"Um, yeah, but don't worry, I'm going to get on this right now. Give me thirty minutes or so," he said, and then promptly hung up.

I chuckled at his embarrassment. Ronald was probably the most socially awkward person I knew, so for him to actually have a date was a positive step. Honestly, I don't think Ronald is in touch with his sexuality. A few months ago, he had a male acquaintance over for dinner. I never asked if it was two buds hanging out or if there were something more to it. For that matter, I had no idea if this 'date' was with a boy or a girl. Whoever it was, I hoped the best for him.

After speaking with Ronald, I called ahead to the Coffee County Sheriff's Department, which was the agency handling the case. I was put on hold for several minutes before being connected with a man who identified himself as Detective Walter Brannigan. He was friendly enough and agreed to meet with me.

I maneuvered through the heavy Nashville traffic and soon was driving east on I-24. I was in my Mustang this morning. I had not driven her in several days and felt the need to show her some attention. When I accelerated onto the interstate, the throaty growl of the exhaust was like her telling me she wanted to stretch her legs, so I opened her up. I was ten miles outside of the Coffee County line when Ronald called back.

"On February twenty-first, your boy made an ATM withdrawal of a hundred bucks and he also filled up with gas at a Delta market in Nashville. He made a phone call an hour later. I'll send you the coordinates of the tower that was pinged. That was the last time the phone was used."

"Have you tried to ping the phone?" I asked.

"Yeah, but either the battery is dead or it's been disabled," Ronald said. "Alright, that's all I have for now. Give me a little time and I'll research his social media."

"Thanks, Ronald. Have fun on your date. Take her somewhere nice."

Ronald giggled before hanging up.

The Coffee County Sheriff's Department was in a brown brick building located on Hillsboro Boulevard less than a mile from I-24. I was using my Google app for directions, but I could have found it easily. I drove into the parking lot and parked. I noticed a man about my age standing outside, smoking a cigarette and watching me curiously.

"Are you Ironcutter?" he asked as I approached.

"I am. You must be Detective Brannigan."

"Walter," he said and stuck out his hand. He was six feet, average build, short-cropped brown hair with a touch of gray in it and wearing wire-framed glasses. He dropped his cigarette and stepped on it.

"Alright, let's go inside." He motioned for me to follow him through the security door and back to a simple office that was cluttered with files. A solitary picture was on the desk of him and a teenage boy, both holding up fish and grinning.

"What can I do for you?" he asked once we got seated.

"As I said on the phone, Joseph Belew has hired me to try to locate his brother. Would it be too much trouble for a briefing on the case?" I asked. He knew why I was there, so I was uncertain why he asked.

He shrugged and pointed at one of the many case files cluttering his desk. "There's not much to tell you. He's still missing." He paused a moment, apparently thinking something over before speaking.

"Your name rang a bell with me, so I did some Googling. You used to be a cop with Nashville."

"Yes, I was," I said.

"Alright, that makes this a little easier. The victim's vehicle was found at the location of the fight, which is an abandoned business located on McMinnville Highway. It was processed, and we found nothing. There's been no activity on his bank account or cell phone. There are no John Does in the area hospitals or morgue. I have him entered into NCIC, but so far, no hits. So, I am currently at a dead end."

He then held up a finger and looked pointedly at me. "What I'm about to say next is off the record."

I gave a slight nod. "Of course."

"We're not a high-tech police department. All of our reports are still done the old-fashioned way, by hand. When a report is written out, it's handed over to a sergeant. He reads them over, approves them, and then puts them in an in-basket where a sweet, motherly lady name Lucy takes the reports, compiles the data for the TIBRS stats, and then hands them over to my boss who decides which cases are filed and which cases are investigated."

"Did something happen?" I asked.

He nodded and gave a slight, rueful smile. "On March tenth, she came to work, took her clothes off, sat down, and began reading scripture like she was preaching to the dead." He shrugged. "They think she had a stroke or something. Anyway, we found several reports crammed in her purse, along with Joseph Belew's missing person report."

"I'm curious why she did that," I remarked.

"The sheriff was curious as well and asked her why. She looked at him all serious like and said, and I quote, donkey balls."

"Donkey balls? I asked.

"Yep," Walter answered. "She was asked to elaborate, but it was futile. She's currently in an assisted care facility. So, anyway, as you can surmise, there was no investigative work done until yours truly got assigned the case. I'm also under the impression you are unaware of the missing girl."

I absently frowned. "No, I'm not."

He nodded somberly, then reached into a manila folder sitting on his desk and pulled out a picture. It was an eight-by-ten of a pale, plain-looking girl who appeared to be in her late teens. Walter confirmed it.

"Her name is Telisha Thompkins. She's seventeen and according to her mother, she's in her full-blown rebellion stage. Typical teen. Goes to the local high school, poor grades and close to dropping out, mother is an alcoholic and father is not in the picture. She doesn't have a car, so she caught a ride from a friend who lived in the neighborhood."

"She went to the fight alone?" I asked.

"It appears so. The young man who gave her the ride said she told him she was meeting someone there. She gave him two bucks for gas and he dropped her off in front."

"I take it he was interviewed."

"Extensively," Walter replied. "We even took him to the TBI for a polygraph, which he passed with flying colors. Oh, I almost forgot, he told us she had a knapsack that was crammed full. He asked her about it and she said if everything worked out, she wasn't going back home. We're treating her as a runaway, therefore no Amber alert was issued." He said it and then waited.

"Do you believe she ran away with Jason Belew?" I asked.

"It's possible, right? I mean, two horny teenage kids. They're probably in Florida right now and will come home when they get bored with each other and the money runs out, right?"

"There is one problem with your scenario," I said. "Jason Belew is gay."

Walter stared in puzzlement and reached for a coffee cup. He tried to take a drink and found the contents cold.

"Well, this may change things," he said. "We subpoenaed her phone records. During the last two weeks, she had multiple conversations to a specific phone number. Turns out it's a burner phone and is no longer in service."

I nodded. "I don't think it's Jason, but I suppose it's possible. I'll ask his brother if he had a burner. Once the report was found on Jason, what was done?"

"The deputy who took the initial report found his car immediately, looked around, but didn't find anything. He put the info in the report thinking it'd be followed up on."

"I understand it was an underground fight event," I said.

"Yeah," he said. "Unsanctioned. There were supposed to be eight fights, but they ended up only having four. Afterward, they had a rave party that lasted all night."

"Where was this event at?" I asked.

"About ten minutes from here at an abandoned business on McMinnville Highway. The property owner was told it was going to be an amateur boxing event. Admission was twenty-five a person. It's my understanding a lot of side bets were going on and a lot of drugs were being bought and sold."

"You guys didn't know about it?" I asked.

"Again, we were told it was an amateur boxing contest. I imagine a couple of our younger deputies might have known about it and didn't say anything." He glanced out of his open door and lowered his voice. "Besides, the property is owned by a county commissioner who has more than one business in this town. He's good friends with certain people. Elected people."

I read between the lines and deduced he was talking about his boss, the sheriff. Walter paused and rubbed his chin.

"Google had some interesting information about you," he remarked.

I nodded but didn't answer. I can't say I liked getting Googled, but I suppose if I were in his shoes, I would've done the same.

"A rogue FBI agent killed your wife and a corrupt assistant chief tried to frame you for the murder. That's straight out of some crazy-ass Lifetime movie," he said with a grin. "The part where you caught those two killer cops was the most interesting story though. Do you know why?"

"Why's that?" I asked, not at all sure I wanted to hear his answer.

"Because it tells me you have good detective skills."

His statement surprised me. It took me a moment to acknowledge the compliment. "I appreciate that," I said.

"So, humor me here, what would you have done differently?" he asked.

"Have you interviewed the two men who he went to the fight with?"

He tapped a three-ring notebook on his desk. "Benny Newton and Charlie Thomas. They rode down together with the Belew kid. The two of them hooked up with two local girls and went home with them. They said the last time they saw Belew, he was gushing over one of the fighters. I've also gotten copies of a couple of cell phone videos of both the fight and the rave party. He's easily spotted at the fight. I also managed to get some cell phone video of the party, but I didn't see Belew in it. That doesn't mean he wasn't there though."

"How did those two boys get home?" I asked.

"They advised they tried calling Belew the next morning, couldn't get ahold of him, so one of the girls drove them home. I obtained copies of Newton's cell phone record and it confirms he made a couple of calls to the victim. Oh, I also got Belew's phone records. Belew had sent a text to his brother shortly before midnight. At that time, his phone pinged a tower near the location of the fight, but it's off now."

I took a moment to jot a couple of notes. Detective Brannigan waited patiently.

"Did I hear you correctly, Jason's car has been located?" I asked.

"Yeah, in the parking lot. We towed it here. It's parked out back. Our tech checked for prints. Two sets of prints match the two men who rode down here with the victim. There is an unidentified set in various places in the car, mostly on the driver's side, so it is assumed they belong to the victim. He's never been arrested, so we have nothing to compare them to.

"Our tech even squirted Luminol all over it, but it yielded nothing. By the way, I've left a message with the mother to come down here and get it, but she hasn't done it yet. Do you think you can expedite that for me?"

"Yeah, I'll make sure of it," I said and jotted a reminder. "Detective, I'll have to say, you seem to be on top of it and I apologize for wasting your time. I'll relay all of this information to Jason's brother; it might help his state of mind."

He gave a small nod at the compliment. "It's no problem." He thought for a couple of seconds and gestured at the notebook again. "If you want, I can get you an electronic copy of the case file. I just need an email or a flash drive."

I looked at him in surprise. "Yeah, that'll be great."

I always kept a flash drive with me for occasions like this. I retrieved it out of my pocket and handed it over. He got on his computer and a couple of minutes later handed it back to me.

"I certainly appreciate it. You guys are on top of the computer stuff," I said.

He let out a small chuckle. "No, we're still stuck in the twentieth century, but my son is awesome with computers. He scans all of my case files for me. He wants to be a cop one day, but I've already told him he's going to do better than that."

I gave a polite smile and absently wondered what kind of father I might have been. "I'm sure he'll do the right thing. Would you happen to know the address in question off of the top of your head?"

He arched an eyebrow. "Are you going there?"

"I thought I'd have a look around and take a few pictures. I hope you don't mind."

He nodded thoughtfully. Up until now, Detective Walter Brannigan had been both professional and polite. But this was the part where he was probably going to tell me to butt out of his investigation, and if he did so, I had to decide whether or not I was going to ignore his directive.

"Since that event, the real estate company has fenced off entry to the parking lot." He paused and looked at his watch. "I'm taking the afternoon off, but if you want, you can follow me out there."

I readily agreed. It was only a ten-minute drive to the location, which was three prefab metal buildings. There was a chain-link fence and gate blocking the entrance and a big for sale sign erected. Walter stopped, got out, and unlocked the padlock. He opened the double gates and motioned me to follow him. After we parked, he saw my questioning look and pointed to the real estate sign. The surname of the realtor was, coincidentally, Brannigan. Walter sensed what I was thinking.

"She's my sister-in-law," he explained.

"What kind of business was this?" I asked.

"Kind of a cross between a farmer's co-op and a home improvement center. It was a vibrant business for several years, but I have no idea why it closed. Since then, they occasionally have yard sales or church revivals here."

"So, a county commissioner owns it," I remarked.

"Yeah, his nephew hooked up with some two-bit hustler and they put it all together. I had to practically beg to put out a statement to the media about Belew's disappearance. They didn't want the bad publicity."

I scoffed. This county commissioner was worried more about his reputation than Jason Belew's welfare.

"Do you have any idea who this two-bit hustler is?" I asked.

"He goes by the nickname Candy-Man. He's black and in his thirties. That's all I know. According to my son, he has a social media account on Snapchat. How familiar are you with it?"

"Not very," I said.

"Me neither. Young people love it though. The way I understand it, if I were to send you a message, after you read it, it disappears. If that's true, if I were to find his account and then put a subpoena on it, I would not be able to retrieve any data."

"That'd make it hard to get evidence on him," I said.

"Yep. I think he lives somewhere in Tennessee, but that's only because he's done three other promotions like this within a two-hundred-mile radius of here. He's always paid the property owners cash up front, so there's no paper trail."

"Do you think he has something to do with Jason's disappearance?" I asked.

He gave a slight shrug. "I have no idea, but I'd certainly want to question him about it."

I nodded in understanding and I saw him look at his watch.

"In the meantime, I've got to go to some kind of school function my wife volunteered me for. I'll call my sister-in-law and let her know you're here with my blessing. Do me a favor and lock the gate back when you're through."

"You got it," I said.

We shook hands and Walter sped off. I fetched a cigar and got it going before standing there, looking things over. There were four buildings. One was the main building and three prefab metal buildings behind it. I assumed the building in front, which was the largest, was the main showroom and the others were for storage or side businesses, but it was hard to tell. There was a large parking lot in front, easily capable of handling fifty or more cars and it was surrounded by land that'd recently been plowed up and ready for planting. If I had a farming background, I could have probably guessed which crop, but it was irrelevant to the case.

According to Detective Walter Brannigan, Jason and his two friends, Benny Newton and Charlie Thomas rode down here together from Nashville. They attended the fight together, and then Jason's two friends hooked up with the two girls. They were probably drunk and high by the time the party started, so they weren't concerned when they lost contact with Jason. After all, he was an aspiring martial artist and could take care of himself. I wondered if Jason's recently coming out had anything to do with their lack of sticking together.

I used my phone, opened the case PDF, and read Benny and Charlie's statements. They both said everyone was having a good time and there were absolutely no problems. I could only guess how wild the rave party was. I'd never been to one, but I've heard stories.

I smoked and scanned the rest of the file. Joseph had filed the report two days later. I saw where Detective Brannigan had contacted Jason's employer, a man who ran a martial arts gym in south Nashville. He had confirmed Jason had not shown up for work nor had he heard from him.

I finished reading, put my phone away, and went to my trunk. I had what I called a detective's kit consisting of a Pelican case packed with various goodies. I pulled out a small flashlight and a digital camera. After taking a couple of panorama pictures, I went to the first building. It was unlocked, and I had no problem going inside. Walter was right, there was nothing but debris on the floor and a few overflowing trashcans. Same with the other two buildings. Nevertheless, I explored every nook and cranny and took pictures of it all.

Eventually, my investigation of the buildings, such that it was, was complete. I suppose I could have gone to the extreme of spraying each building with something like Luminol, but it would have taken a couple of gallons and a lot of time. No, that wasn't a viable option. Not yet, anyway.

I walked around outside and took more photographs, but frankly, there was nothing here. Not even a note posted on the wall telling me where I could find Jason. I continued taking pictures as I walked around, but eventually, I ran out of things to photograph.

It was a nice day and my work had produced a few beads of sweat on my forehead. I looked around as I smoked, wondering if there was nothing here or I simply wasn't seeing it. I wandered around some more and found myself standing by one of the smaller buildings and gazed at the back of the property. I noted old railroad tracks and a spur line that led directly to the northeast corner of the lot. Three rusty boxcars splattered with nonsensical graffiti sat silently on the spur line some fifty yards away.

I stared at them for several minutes as I smoked my cigar down to the stub. My thoughts drifted as I wondered what kind of stories they could've told, all the places they'd been, what they had seen. It seemed odd in a way. Those boxcars could not have been cheap to manufacture, yet here they were, abandoned.

I stood there in the sunshine, staring at nothing in particular, and decided to light a fresh cigar. I started to go back to my car to get one when I stopped and looked back over my shoulder to the boxcars. Something happened. An epiphany, a firing of a neuron, something, I don't know, but I forgot all about the cigar.

"No way," I muttered to myself and began walking toward them.

The doors were over five feet above the ground and they were closed. I had seen a step ladder back in one of the buildings, which was several yards away. Cussing to myself at my silly notions, I walked back and retrieved the ladder. It was old and rickety. Hell, it was in such bad shape I wasn't sure it'd even hold my weight. And, it was grimy. I tried to hold it away from my custom-tailored suit as I walked back to the boxcars.

I took my jacket off, gently laid it in the weeds, and started with the first car. The doors weren't locked, but they were rusty and needed a little muscle to get them to slide open. The bright sunlight affected my vision, causing me to use my flashlight.

The first two were mostly empty, only some trash. When I opened the third boxcar, I caught a slight whiff of something unpleasant.

Decomposition.

CHAPTER 6

The third boxcar was more of the same, a scattering of trash, some crinkled water bottles, and a stack of wood pallets on one end. I would not have even searched inside, if not for the distinctive odor.

I took a photo before stepping inside and waiting for my eyes to adjust. The pallets, a stack of eight of them, were positioned at an angle to the walls of the boxcar, effectively hiding a triangular space between the pallets and the corner. I took another photograph, then walked over and squatted down. The smell was stronger now.

"Here goes nothing," I muttered, got a handhold on the bottom pallet, and pulled.

The stack made an unpleasant grating noise as I pulled. When I had enough room to get a good look at that hidden space, I stopped and stood. I wouldn't admit it to anyone, but I had to stretch my back a little before bracing myself for what I knew I was going to discover. Peering around the pallets, I saw a crumpled tarpaulin lying there, covering something.

It was not the first body I'd seen up close and personal, but when I lifted the tarp, I was hit with a wave of rancid odor. I fought off the nausea and took several pictures before lowering the tarp and backing out of the car. I tried to be careful, but almost busted my ass as I climbed down the ladder. And, wouldn't you know it, I snagged my pants leg on one solitary exposed screw.

Landing on the ground, I inspected the new tear. It was small, but these were expensive slacks and it irritated me to no end. I brushed myself off before straightening, and when I did, the first thing I saw was a muscular black man in a deputy's uniform staring intently at me. He saw my Springfield Armory 45 holstered on my hip at about the same time I thought of it and his hand dropped to his duty weapon. I hastily raised my hands to shoulder level.

"I have a carry permit," I said.

"Alright, we'll get to that in a moment. Who are you and what are you doing?"

I identified myself and explained. He had me interlace my fingers behind my head, disarmed me, which I didn't like, and then had me show him my identification.

"And you say there's a dead body in there?" he asked.

"Yes, sir, there is," I replied. "Help yourself if you want to have a look, but I have to warn you, it doesn't smell too good in there."

The deputy, his nametag said Pickney, scowled as he eyed the open door.

"I can smell it from here," he said.

"Here, this is even better." I held up the camera and showed him the pictures I'd taken. He stared at them with interest before holding up a hand.

"Wait a minute, is this the boy who was reported missing a while back?" he asked.

"I believe it is. I'm going to give Detective Brannigan a call," I said.

"Don't worry, I'll have the dispatcher get ahold of him."

Even though he'd checked my bona fides, he took no chances and checked my jacket before handing it to me. He radioed the dispatcher and we walked back to our cars. His patrol car was parked behind mine, and he gently insisted on securing my handgun in the trunk of my car. Technically, I could have balked at this, but he'd been professional and there was no need to complain. At least, not yet.

"What caused you to drive in here and check me out? Did somebody see me and call it in?" I asked.

"No, but I've been keeping an eye on this business ever since that damn party," he said. "We had a DUI fatality at about four in the morning. The person who caused the wreck had been at that party and they ran head-on into an old buddy of mine who was on his way to work."

Deputy Pickney's cell phone rang as another deputy drove into the parking lot. From the conversation, I could tell he was speaking with Detective Brannigan. After a moment, he hung up.

"That was Brannigan, he's on his way. Him and probably the rest of the department, including the sheriff."

I nodded in agreement. This was no doubt going to be a big dog and pony show, especially if anyone from the media shows up.

"Walter said you used to be a homicide detective in Nashville."

"Yeah, I used to be. I'm going to get a cigar. Do you want one?" I asked.

He declined with a shake of his head. That was fine with me; the only cigars I had retailed for ten dollars a stick and I wasn't the kind of guy who gave money away. I clipped and lit one and then leaned against my car watching the circus begin.

When Detective Brannigan parked, he got out of his car, walked directly toward me, and got right to the point.

"Is it Belew?" he asked.

"I couldn't get a facial recognition without moving the body, not to mention the decomposition, but the corpse was wearing a number thirty-five Preds Jersey. Just like Jason was wearing."

Walter gave a small, rueful shake of his head. "Yeah, alright. Why don't you show me what you found?"

We walked back to the boxcars and I pointed out the third car. "He's in there."

I handed him my Streamlight and stood by while Walter used the ladder and entered the boxcar. A moment later, he reappeared and hastily stepped down from the ladder like I had.

"No sign of the girl, I'm assuming."

I shook my head.

"Did you alter anything?" he asked.

"Yeah. The doors were closed and the pallets were stacked in a way to hide the body. I lifted the tarp only to confirm there was a body under there and placed it back the way I found it. You'll find my prints on the doors and my DNA on the bottom pallet. Sorry about that."

He nodded in understanding and then made a comment. "His pants were off."

He was right. A pair of jeans and underwear were lying off to the side of the corpse. Detective Brannigan was thinking the same thing I was—Belew may have been sexually assaulted. He stared at the ground, working his jaw.

"He was here the whole time," he said. "Right under our noses."

I didn't respond. There wasn't anything to say that would make him feel any better.

"I guess right about now you're thinking we're a bunch of country bumpkins who don't know how to investigate a case."

"No, not at all," I said. He fixed me with a disbelieving stare for a moment.

"Alright, the TBI are on their way. They're going to process the scene and they'll want to interview you. While I'm standing around here waiting, I'd normally go ahead and take a statement from you, but we may as well wait until they get here and then you can tell us all at once," Walter said.

"Yeah, I appreciate that."

"So, what are you going to say?" he asked. I glanced at him as I smoked my cigar. I sensed he had something in mind.

"I'm open to suggestions," I replied.

Deputy Pickney had walked up and was listening in silence. The two men exchanged glances.

"I'm not suggesting you say anything that isn't true," Walter said. "But I know how the sheriff is going to react. When he gets me alone, the first thing he's going to say is some city slicker from Nashville came down here and did what we couldn't do and how inept it's going to make the department look."

I understood immediately. Walter had shown me courtesy and professionalism. What I said in my statement could cast him in a dim light. For that matter, it might cast his entire department in a dim light. I took a drag off of my cigar.

"I'm not so sure he should say that," I said.

"Oh? Why's that?" Walter asked.

"Because, the way I remember it, I was looking around when Deputy Pickney drove up." I then made a thoughtful frown. "In fact, when the two of us discussed the details of the case, I believe he was the one who suggested we look in the boxcars." I looked at Pickney, who looked at Walter, who gave a subtle nod.

"I appreciate it, Thomas," Walter said.

I committed a small taboo in the world of auto restoration buffs, and that is I leaned against my car while I watched the dog and pony show begin. There was no danger of me scuffing the paint, but enthusiasts would pull their hair out if someone leaned up against a car in which they had painstakingly refinished.

The sheriff was the first to arrive on the scene, soon followed by other deputies and the TBI. Everyone insisted on having a look inside the boxcar. All except Pickney, who was sitting in his patrol car diligently completing a report. He occasionally looked around, and by the look on his face, I guessed he was probably wondering what he'd got himself into.

The TBI mobile forensics lab drove into the parking lot an hour later. Within seconds, two techs scurried around like worker ants setting up the lab and even stringing lights to the boxcar. They knew they were going to be there for many hours. Walter walked up with another man following him.

"Thomas, this is Sheriff Cooperman," he said.

The sheriff extended his hand. "Walter speaks highly of you," he said, clasping my hand firmly. He was a nondescript man in his late forties with square shoulders and an affable smile. We talked for a minute before he excused himself and walked over to a television news crew who had arrived on the scene. I understood. The sheriff was an elected position after all and he needed good publicity whenever he could get it.

Eventually, they got around to taking a formal statement from me. I gave them the facts, downplaying my role and complimenting Deputy Pickney's keen eye and professionalism. When they'd asked me every conceivable question they could think of, they decided they were done with me and let me go.

I motioned to Walter and had him follow me away from the group.

"If you don't mind, I'm going to go pay a visit to Jason's brother," I said.

"I should be the one to make the notification," he countered.

We discussed it and decided to do it together. The sheriff gave his okay and soon we were on I-24 heading to Nashville. I called ahead to the Davidson Hills Country Club and confirmed Joseph was still working. When we arrived, the two of us walked in together. The hostess got the manager and we informed him of the purpose of our visit. He gave me the once over, noting my dirty slacks and sweat-stained shirt, but said nothing and led us to his office. He left, and a moment later brought Joseph in. When he saw us, the blood drained from his face.

"You found him, didn't you," he said.

The two of us nodded grimly. We sat him down and calmly explained everything while he sobbed.

"Now, keep in mind, he has not yet been positively identified," I said.

"I know it's him," he said with tears flowing freely down his face.

I looked at Walter, who cleared his throat.

"It's a strong possibility, but we will not know for certain until the autopsy," he said.

The manager, who had been sitting quietly and listening, raised his hand.

"Yes, sir?" I asked.

"What happens now?" he asked.

I waited for Walter to respond, but when he hesitated, I spoke up.

"The autopsy will be performed within the next couple of days. They will confirm his identity and attempt to determine the cause of death."

Joseph looked at me like a lost puppy dog. "Do you think he was murdered?"

I thought for a moment, and I knew Walter was looking at me, perhaps tacitly telling me to hold off. Nevertheless, I answered honestly.

"Yes, I do."

He nodded somberly and wiped away some more tears. We talked some more and then I told him we had to leave. Walter walked with me to the parking lot.

"How does it work with you? Is the TBI going to take over the case?" I asked.

"It'll be a joint investigation. It sounds good in theory. Sometimes it works, sometimes it doesn't," he answered.

"Well, good luck with it."

"Are you done with your investigation?" he asked.

I sighed. "I am, I suppose, but I'd be lying if I said I was done sticking my nose into it."

Walter grunted. "Well, let's not be adversarial. I'll call you if anything comes up and I expect you to do the same."

"Certainly," I said. We shook hands before departing company.

I got home at almost midnight. Anna and Marti were sitting on the couch watching TV. Tommy Boy was curled up contentedly between them.

"Hi, girls," I said.

Anna looked me up and down. "You're a mess. Did you get into a fight or something?"

"No, no fighting," I replied and walked into the kitchen. I poured myself a healthy dose of Balvenie Caribbean Cask single malt and sat in my easy chair, whereupon I gave them the ten-minute version. They listened in stunned silence.

"That is so sad," Anna said when I'd finished. "What happens now?"

"The cops have a murder investigation on their hands," I said.

"But what are you going to do next?" she pressed.

I shrugged and sipped my Scotch. "Technically, I've fulfilled the terms of the contract. Besides, the man can't afford me."

"You think he was murdered though."

I nodded. "Yes."

"It seems like you could help him," she said.

I shrugged and didn't answer. Standing, I motioned her to follow me to my bedroom.

"What's up?" she asked.

"I've been thinking about your situation."

"What situation is that?"

"Your education, or lack thereof."

"Nooo, I don't want to get into that tonight," she said.

"Hear me out," I pleaded. "I was thinking you should go to college."

Anna scoffed. "Bad idea."

"Why?" I asked.

"Because I'm too old, I don't have the money, and I'm too stupid."

"I disagree on all three of those. First off, you're not stupid. In fact, I think you're rather intelligent, you simply lack a formal education to talk about things like Plato and other nonsense. Second, you're not too old. Hell, you're only what, twenty-three?"

"You're forgetting about money," she pointed out.

"No, I'm not. I'll pay for it."

Anna looked at me like I was playing a cruel joke on her. "Stop messing with me."

"I'm being serious," I said.

Now, her eyes widened. "Why would you do something like that, Thomas?" she asked quietly.

"Oh, that part's easy. It's a given that I'll never have kids, so, when I get old, I'm going to need somebody to be a live-in caregiver. You know, feed me and change my diaper. So, I look at this as an investment."

She tried not to but couldn't help herself and burst out into laughter. "You're an ass sometimes."

I smiled. "Yeah, sometimes." I finished my drink and handed her my empty glass. "Think about it. Now, get out of here, I'm going to bed."

CHAPTER 7

I took a relaxing hot shower before going to bed, but even so, I tossed and turned all night. I found myself continually waking up and looking over at the digital clock on the nightstand before trying to will myself back to sleep. Finally, when the clock read five, I gave up and threw the covers off.

I walked over to the window and opened the blinds. The sky was starting to turn gray. It looked like we were going to have a pleasant, sunny day. I decided a morning jog in the crisp air might do me some good.

I snuck by Marti, who was sleeping on the couch, went outside, and after a couple of minutes of stretching, started off at a slow gait, an old man's pace. It got the blood going and gave me time to think about things and try to work out the stress. One would think I didn't have a care in the world. With the recent settlement of the lawsuit against the city of Nashville, I was financially secure for the rest of my natural life, and I'm the first to admit, after all of the troubles last year, my life was good. More than good. But that wasn't how my brain worked.

I had a bad habit of overly worrying about things. I know, a shrink would have a heyday with me, but that's how I was. I worried about Ronald. I worried about Anna. Sometimes I even worried about myself. Now, I was worrying about Joseph and the mysterious death of his brother. It was pure luck that I found Jason. At least, I kept telling myself that. Ever since the senseless murder of Simone and her daughter, I had lost a lot of faith in God. Even so, there was that nagging feeling, borne of a Catholic upbringing, that God had perhaps nudged me in the right direction, leading me to find Jason when others had failed.

My breathing was good and the muscles had loosened up, so I decided to push myself and quickened my pace. The cool morning air felt good and there was a not unpleasant burn in my lungs. I imagined my body expelling accumulated cigar smoke. I was currently running easterly, which gave me a scenic view of a beautiful sunrise. It was invigorating and helped me focus, mostly on Jason's case. I went through a long list of questions about the case and what role, if any, I had in pursuing the investigation.

I also thought about my business. I'd had more than a couple phone calls and emails from prospective clients. One of them even had the potential for a lucrative payday, but they wanted me to jump on the case immediately. It'd be easy to end my investigation on Jason's murder and move on.

The increase of my caseload also made me think about Mister CIA agent's offer. Should I hire more people? I turned my head and spit. If I were to hire anyone, it would not be him. Even if half of what he bragged about were true, he would not be a good fit for my little group of sleuths.

I finished my run at the head of my driveway and did a slow cool-down walk. The run had had the desired effect and I had reached a decision. I finished up by knocking out pushups until my arms became wobbly. After some stretching, I went inside, found my phone, and texted Joseph Belew.

I hope you're holding up okay. I have not committed a full week on your case and you are due a partial refund. Send me a text of a date and time of your convenience where I can meet with you. And, if you need to talk, I'm available.

I hit send, set the phone down, and quietly prepped the coffee pot. My phone buzzed within a minute. The table amplified the noise, causing Marti to stir. She sat up, saw me, and gave a tired smile. Even though I thought Anna was prettier, I had to admit, Marti was nothing to scoff at.

"Good morning," I said. "The coffee's almost ready."

She stretched, purposely straining her breasts against her shirt. "What time is it?"

"A little after six," I replied.

"Holy shit, you get up early," she said and pulled the blanket off her. I couldn't help but notice she had stripped out of her pants and was only wearing a pair of panties that hardly hid anything. I quickly looked away and walked over to the coffee pot.

"Can I use your restroom?" she asked. "I don't want to wake Anna."

"Sure," I said, hoping she didn't help herself to my toothbrush. She got her purse off the coffee table and disappeared into my bedroom.

I poured myself a steaming mug and heard the sound of an incoming text. I grabbed my phone and stared at the screen.

This is Jenna. Joe had a rough night and he's finally sleeping. Thank you for everything you've done. When he wakes up, I'll relay the message, but I think he'd like you to stick with it and try to solve his brother's murder.

So, there it was. I was kind of hoping for this response. If I walked away from this case, it would bother me for years to come. I texted back immediately.

I'll gladly do so, if this is what he wants. Please have him call or text with his decision. Thanks.

As soon as I hit send, my phone pinged, indicating someone was coming up the driveway. Activating my camera, I saw Percy's Toyota. I had a mug of coffee waiting for him when he walked in the back door.

"I figured you'd be awake," he said. He was wearing khaki slacks, a dark blue Polo shirt which was tight in the shoulders and loose in the waist, and brushed suede loafers. I grunted. The man could wear anything and still ooze machismo.

"Are you working today?" I asked.

"Nope, I have a rare weekend off. Thought I'd come visit my buddies." He then added a little wistfully. "The house is mostly empty these days."

"You're always welcome. Anna is still asleep, but she'll be up soon. How's it going at work?" I asked when he'd sat.

"Same old, same old," he said and sipped some coffee. "At the moment, I'm still Bartlett's golden boy, so I guess I'm doing okay. At the moment, he's assigned me to a few cold cases and some missing person cases. He told me to work diligently on them, but keep myself available in case he needed me for something hot."

I grunted in understanding. Sory Bartlett was the commander of the Office of Professional Accountability up until six months ago when he was transferred to run the Criminal Investigations Division. While leading the rat squad, he'd directed more than one internal investigation against Percy. When he was transferred to CID, he became Percy's boss, which, as one can imagine, did not sit well with Percy.

However, after my incident with the rogue officers, Bartlett got an inside look at his skills and decided Detective Percy Trotter was an asset rather than a problem child. Percy was not completely convinced of whether Bartlett was sincere or if he had ulterior motives and remained suspicious. Either way, I was happy for Percy. He was finally being recognized for his investigative acumen and no longer being spied upon. At least, not as far as I knew.

While we were sitting at the kitchen table, Marti walked out of my bedroom, still clad in nothing but a T-shirt and panties and stopped short when she saw Percy.

"Marti, this is Percy. Percy, this is Anna's friend, Marti," I said, wondering if he was inferring something when he saw her emerge from my bedroom.

"Holy shit, you're even bigger than Thomas," she said, looking him up and down.

"I'm pleased to meet you," he said while trying hard not to stare.

Anna soon walked out of her bedroom wearing her oversized bathrobe and headed straight for her tea kettle. Filling it with water and placing it on the stove eye, she gave us all a baleful look.

"Why are we up so early?" she asked.

"Because it's a beautiful day out," I replied with a grin.

She responded by shaking her head in mock disgust and looked at Marti.

"Put some pants on," she admonished and disappeared back into her bedroom. Marti grinned at us before following Anna.

"How's your daughter?" I asked. Percy had recently reunited with a long-lost daughter he did not know existed.

"She's fine. She prefers texting instead of actually talking. Typical teenager, I guess. We've discussed the idea of her coming here to live."

"Oh, yeah? That'd be awesome," I said.

Percy gave a combination of a slight grin and frown. "I have no idea how to be a dad to a teenage girl, so your idea of awesome is subjective."

We were on our second cup of coffee when Anna walked out. She was freshly showered, wearing jeans and a Preds jersey. The same style of jersey Jason had been wearing the night he was killed. It even had the same player's name on the back. She sat down, took a sip of tea, and began brushing her damp hair.

"Marti thinks you're handsome," she said to Percy. Percy glanced at me. I quickly replied.

"Nope, she and I are not an item. She slept on the couch last night. When you saw her coming out of my bedroom, she didn't want to wake up Anna, so she used my restroom."

"Oh," Percy said.

"She's also got it in her head she'd like to be a PI," Anna said.

I responded with a, "Hmm."

"What does that mean?" Anna asked.

"I've been thinking it over lately, and we could probably use another person. We've turned away more than one case because we were working other cases."

"Is that something you want to do?" she asked.

I shrugged. "I've been mentally crunching the numbers. It's doable, I think."

Anna nodded thoughtfully and then a smile crept across her face.

"How do you think Ronald would react if you hired her?"

I chuckled, but then I realized something. "Speaking of Ronald, I haven't talked to him in a couple of days. Have you?"

Anna's brow furrowed. "No. You two talk every day, don't you?"

"More or less." I picked up my phone and called him. It went to voicemail. "Hmm. I wonder if he's engrossed in one of his online games. I'll go pay him a visit later." I turned to Percy. "Say, I'm glad you're here. What do you know of underground fight rings operating around here?" I asked.

He thought about it a moment as he drank his coffee. "There used to be a professional wrestling promoter who occasionally had what they called tough guy tournaments. He knew everyone in the racket, but that was several years back and he's retired. Hell, he might even be dead, but I can try to look him up if you'd like. What've you got going on?"

He listened quietly as I laid out Jason Belew's case.

"Do you know who was running the fight?" he asked.

"Somebody who goes by the nickname of Candy-Man."

"Hmm," he said. "I'm not familiar with that name, but let's check."

Percy stood and went to his car. He returned a moment later carrying his department-issued laptop. He resumed his seat, booted it up, and logged on to the police website.

"Something tells me Ronald has the ability to hack into our police portal," he remarked as he typed.

"I can neither deny nor affirm," I said.

Percy gave a small grunt. "There are different databases within the portal which require additional passwords that have to be a minimum sixteen characters. This one is linked to the Integrated Criminal Justice Portal, which is also linked to a portal called DI3."

"I remember the name of that one...let's see, the Tennessee Drug Intelligence Integration System," I said.

"Yep, you always did have a pretty good memory," Percy said and then paused. "Did you know Poston has been going around telling everyone he has a photographic memory?"

"Yeah, I'd heard that," I said. "I'm calling bullshit."

"Me too." Percy didn't like Poston either. He did some typing and then dragged his finger along the touchscreen a couple of times, and then pointed at a list of names on the screen. After a couple of minutes, he gestured at the screen.

"You have six individuals on the database who live in the mid-state area with the nickname of either Candy or Candy-Man," he said and pointed at each line. "Those are their real names, but I'm afraid I cannot go any further."

"Why not?" Anna asked.

"If I click on a specific name, I have to associate it with an active investigation, and if they ask, I must be able to show the corroborating case.

They perform random audits and if I cannot show a reason for searching a specific person's information, I could face disciplinary action, including possible criminal charges. Sorry."

"Oh," she said. "Well, we can't have that."

"No problem," I said, pulled out a pen, and wrote the names on the palm of my hand. I then called Ronald again, but once again only got his voicemail. I left him a message and then texted him the information.

"Does he really have access to these databases?" Percy asked.

"I'm not sure about those specific portals, but the good thing about people under forty these days, almost all of them are active on social media. Ronald will search those first. He says it's much easier."

"And legal," Percy added. "Good."

I sipped my coffee and waited for Ronald to call back. After ten minutes, I became concerned and tried calling him again. Once again, it went straight to voicemail. It was unlike him. Even when he was sound asleep or playing one of his games, he always answered or called back within minutes. Always. Damned odd. Anna must have seen the consternation on my face.

"What's wrong?" she asked.

"Ronald didn't answer." I couldn't say why, but my gut told me something was wrong. I stood. "I think I'm going to go over to his house and see what's going on."

Percy stood as well. "I've never seen the boy-wonder's computer set up, do you think he'd mind showing it to me?"

"Of course, he likes you, even though he's a little intimidated by you," I said.

"I want to go too," Anna instantly said.

"Sure. Marti, do you want to go too?" I asked.

She smiled. "I'd love to, but I'm opening today and have to be there at eleven. I'm working at Edgefield bar now," she said. "It sucks, but it's a job until I find something better."

"Alright, I'm going to grab a shower," I said.

When I'd cleaned up, I walked out to find Percy and Anna were still on the porch, engaging in quiet conversation. They stopped and stared curiously when I walked outside.

"I'm ready if you guys are," I said. They stood in unison.

"Which car are we taking?" Anna asked, and then grinned. "I know, let's take your new car. I want to drive."

The three of us loaded up in my Explorer. I was apprehensive about Anna driving, especially when she adjusted the seat and mirrors. I said as much.

"You know the position of the seat, mirrors, and steering wheel are programmable to individual drivers," she said. "You can set it to your specifications and change it back after someone else has driven it."

I glanced back at Percy, who nodded in agreement. I spent the rest of the ride reading that particular section in the owner's manual.

There was a strange car parked in Ronald's driveway. It was a rough-looking, older model Ford Taurus, and I noticed it had out-of-state tags.

"He's got company," Anna observed. "That's unusual."

Ronald answered after we'd rang the doorbell several times, but he only partially opened the door and peeked out.

"Hi cutie," Anna said and started to walk in, but Ronald did not open the door. Instead, he kept her from entering. She took a step back and frowned.

"What's wrong, Ronald?" I asked.

"Uh, nothing," he stammered.

Anna gasped in mock surprise. "Do you have a woman in there?"

I expected him to blush in embarrassment, but instead, he looked down at his shoes and refused to answer or make eye contact. Percy gave me a questioning stare, which activated my brain.

"What's going on here, Ronald?" I asked.

When he didn't answer, I pushed past him and walked in. There were three of them sitting in the den, two men and a woman. They all had that rough, trailer park trash kind of look. Instead of saying hello or asking who we were, they stared at us sullenly. I guess they either forgot about the glass pipe sitting on the coffee table or they didn't care.

"Who the hell are you people?" I demanded.

One of the men was a few years older than the other two. He was also bigger and harder looking. He had a pockmarked face and lots of shitty tattoos, including a couple of teardrops along the side of his cheek.

"Who the hell are you?" he retorted.

"Yeah, okay. You three have ten seconds to get the hell out of here."

"Fuck you, asshole. We're not going anywhere," the girl said. She was sitting lazily in a chair without a care in the world.

I stared in growing anger. She couldn't have been any older than eighteen, stringy hair, acne, and a petulant scowl of her own. She was wearing dirty jeans and a T-shirt with a heavy metal band logo on it and I wondered when the last time either had been laundered. The second man wasn't much older. He was rail thin and also had a face full of acne. Neither of them concerned me. It was the big one who was going to be trouble. He leaned forward and stood. He was almost as tall as me and had some muscle to him. Prison muscle, most likely. I guessed him in his late twenties. He puffed up his chest and fixed me with a challenging stare.

"Who the hell are you?" he asked again. "You don't live here."

"It doesn't matter who I am. You three are leaving."

"We ain't going anywhere," he declared. We locked eyes and stared each other down.

"You'll leave," I said in a calm tone. "The question you should be asking yourself is whether you're going to leave in one piece or not."

His facial expression turned to disbelief, and then a small smirk crept onto his face. "What, you want some, old man?"

I saw Percy stir out of the corner of my eye. I waved him off with a flick of my hand. The tough guy saw it too and thought he had his chance, his opening.

"C'mon, old man," he barked and tried to give me a forceful push. I think he might have been a little surprised when his push failed to move me. He then stepped back slightly and started to bring a fist up.

I wasted no time and responded with a flurry of punches. The first one crushed his nose, and the second one caused his eyes to roll back in his head. That was enough; his knees were wobbling and he was going down, but I wasn't through. I stepped in and finished with a right uppercut, knocking him off his feet. I jumped on top of him and unmercifully began pounding him. I was in a rage, and, looking back, if it wasn't for Percy, I'm not certain I would have stopped until he was dead.

"Easy, big guy," he said in my ear as he wrapped his arms around me and pulled me back.

I locked eyes with Anna as I got my breathing back to normal. She had a look of surprise on her face. The girl started to stand, but Percy wouldn't have it.

"Sit your ass down!" he barked. She sat quickly. Her smirk was replaced with worry.

When Percy felt like I'd calmed myself, he let go and walked over to the now unconscious bruiser and frisked him. He found a snub-nose revolver shoved down in his crotch.

He opened the cylinder and dropped the bullets to the floor. Closing the cylinder back, he stuck it in his waistband and pulled a wallet from the man's hip pocket. I focused on the younger man and stepped over to him. He was visibly shaking and staring at me in mortal fright.

"I didn't do nothing," he squeaked.

"Stand up," I ordered. He was reluctant to do so, so I grabbed him by the shoulder and hoisted him to his feet.

"Do you have any needles on you or anything else that's going to stick me?" I asked.

"Uh, no," he said, his eyes jumping back and forth between his unconscious friend, Percy, and me.

"I'm going to search you, and if I get stuck by something, I'm going to take whatever it is and jam it in your eye, do you understand?"

"I don't have any needles, man, I swear," he said anxiously.

He was telling the truth. All I found was a wallet with three dollars in it and an expired driver's license. Anna took my lead and searched the woman. She started to protest, but one look from me and she closed her mouth. As an afterthought, I pulled out my phone and snapped a few photos of all three of them.

"Whose car is that outside?" I asked.

"It's mine," the young man said.

"What's your name?"

"B-B-B-Bobby," he stammered. I pointed at his unconscious friend. "Uh, he goes by Steel Willie."

"And her?"

"Uh, Barb. She's my sister."

I stared down at the girl. Her fear was mostly gone and she fixed me with a sullen glare, like we'd committed an egregious offense against her.

"Alright, Bobby and Barb, here's how this is going to go. You three pieces of shit are going to get in your car and go back to wherever you came from and never come back."

I emphasized the point by turning and kicking Steel Willie in the side. He exhaled a painful groan.

"If I ever see any of you again, if you even drive down the street in front of this house, I'll kill him, but I'm going to take a knife to you two. When I get finished, you won't even recognize each other. Understand?" I growled.

Bobby nodded vigorously. Barb continued to look at me like she wanted to kill me. I felt like it was time to put the fear of God into her and pulled out my lock blade knife.

"I guess you don't believe me," I said, opened it, and took a step toward her. Her angry stare instantly turned to fear. She threw her hands out.

"Okay, okay," she said.

I stared at her a long moment before slowly closing my knife and putting it away. I then pointed toward the door. Percy and I carried Steel Willie out and unceremoniously tossed him into the passenger seat of the small car. We then motioned for the two younger ones to get in.

"Uh, sir?" Bobby asked.

"What?" I growled.

"We have some clothes and stuff inside."

I looked over and nodded at Anna.

"I'll get it," she said and went back inside.

Percy took the opportunity to look through their car. He took his own photo of the vehicle registration before pocketing a checkbook and some credit cards he found in the glove box. He then found some paperwork that he stared at curiously before sticking everything in his pocket.

"Where are you two from, Bobby?" I asked.

"Mayfield, Kentucky, sir," he said.

"What about numbnuts over there?" I asked, referring to Willie, who was now conscious and tenderly touching his bleeding nose. He looked around and made eye contact with me, but the fight was gone from him. Instead, he used his shirt to try to staunch the blood.

"Barb met him online and we went and picked him up when he got out of prison. That was two weeks ago. We've kind of been on our own since then. Like nomads, I guess you'd say."

"Nomads, huh? It sounds like a shitty life you've got yourself into, Bobby," I said.

He hung his head and didn't respond. I looked over at Barb, who was staring out of the backseat window with one of those pissed off at the world expressions. I knew there was no hope for her. If Bobby was smart, he'd get himself far away from her.

After five minutes, Anna emerged carrying two stuffed trash bags.

"Nothing but clothes," she said. "They have a couple of cell phones, but they're probably stolen."

I took the bags and threw them on top of the tough guy. He flashed a brief angry stare at me but said nothing.

"Alright, get out of here, and don't think for a minute I'm not serious." I then leaned in closer and whispered in Bobby's ear, "You three thought Ronald was easy prey, and I guess he is, but I can assure you if we see you again, you three will go down hard."

"You guys are cops, aren't you?" Bobby asked. "I've heard police departments have their own goon squads, that's what you guys are."

"You're smarter than you look, Bobby," I said. "Alright, get out of here and don't come back." I pointed at Steel Willie. "Especially you."

He stared back for a moment before turning and staring blankly out of the window. When they got about fifty yards down the road, Barb held her middle finger up through the back window.

Anna scoffed. "I should've slapped the taste out of her mouth when I had the chance. Okay, I've got Ronald in the bedroom. He's pretty upset, so give me a few minutes to talk to him."

We walked in and looked around. The place was a disaster. I started to pick up some trash, but Percy stopped me.

"You might want to go clean up your hands first," he said. "Remember what happened to Roger that time."

I looked down to see my knuckles skinned up. Percy was referring to a co-worker named Roger. A few years back, he had to fight a DUI suspect. One hard punch to the mouth was all it took to subdue the guy, but Roger had skinned up his knuckles, much like mine were. He got an infection and his hand ballooned up like a cantaloupe. It was touch and go for a while, and the doctors were actually considering amputation at one point. I hurried into the restroom and washed up.

When I walked back into the den, Anna emerged from the back bedroom. She sighed and shook her head.

"It was a setup. He met her on a dating website. He met up with her, took her to dinner, and they seemed to hit it off. She suggested they go back to his place, slept with him, and when he woke up the next morning, the other two were here. He said he tried to call, but the big one took his phone and they wouldn't let him go out."

"How long have they been here?" Percy asked.

"Four days," Anna said. I started to walk into the room where Ronald was, but Anna put a hand on my arm.

"He's embarrassed and humiliated. Also, they've apparently pawned all of his computers and used the money for their meth habit. He's pretty tore up about that."

Percy pulled the papers out of his pocket. "That would explain these pawn receipts."

"Shit," I muttered and rushed down into the basement where Ronald ran his cyber domain. There was nothing but empty tables where his computers and monitors once sat; nothing but a few cables were left and dusty outlines on the tables. Ronald kept fastidious files in some file cabinets off in the corner. It did not take much of an effort to find an inventory sheet which included all of the serial numbers of his beloved computers. I walked back upstairs and showed

Percy the list. He started making comparisons with the pawn receipts and nodded when he started finding matches.

"If you'll stay here and keep an eye on things, I'll go try and get them back," I said.

"No," he said. "Stay here with your boy. He needs you. I'll take care of it."

I started to protest but he held up a hand, silencing me. I don't know why I thought I'd have more success in getting the computers back; he was as good a detective as anybody. Better than most, actually. I nodded gratefully and handed him my keys.

I watched him leave and then went into the bedroom. Ronald was curled up on the bed in the fetal position. His eyes were red and puffy.

"They're gone and won't be back," I said.

"Okay," he replied meekly.

"Did they get into your bank account?"

Ronald shook his head. "Well, sort of. I only had a couple of hundred in my checking account. They used my debit account to drain that and I told them that's all I had. They didn't know about my other accounts. I thought they'd leave then, but then Barb suggested they pawn my computers."

"Okay, I guess that's good. Did they get into your stocks and bonds?"

Ronald shook his head. I nodded gratefully. Ronald was a hobbyist investor, but he'd made some decent investments over the past years. I stood and motioned Anna out into the hallway.

"Percy's going to hit these pawnshops and get his computers back. In the meantime, let's get this place cleaned up. Ronald has a thing about cleanliness."

"Okay."

Those crackheads had sure done a number on his house. It was trashed. Anna and I spent the rest of the day cleaning up while Ronald sat on the couch, watching us in silence and rocking himself. When we'd finished, we joined him on the couch. Anna put her arms around him.

"Ronald, sweetie, it's going to be okay," she told him.

Ronald glanced at her and then at me. "I can't live without my computers," he lamented and his eyes started watering up again. I patted him on the leg.

"Don't worry about that. Percy is going to get them back. If he doesn't, we'll get you some new ones."

He shook his head. "It's not that simple. I've got them all specially modified." An unbidden sob came out and I joined Anna in putting my arm around him. He ranted on. "I've upgraded them and they have my own personal programming. They're unique. They're my babies."

"Don't worry, we'll figure something out," I said, to which Ronald sobbed some more.

Percy parked in the driveway at five and honked the horn. Ronald, who had not moved from the couch, literally jumped up and ran outside. When he saw his computers lined up in the backseat, his face took on an expression of joy that was hard to describe. It took us another hour to get his computers unloaded and set up in his basement. His face lit up in joy as he began powering them up.

"Did you have any trouble?" I asked Percy.

He shrugged. "They pawned them at six different pawn shops. It took a while, but I got them all. Oh, by the way, you owe me five hundred."

I groaned in acknowledgment and pulled out my wallet. My phone gave a two-toned beep, signaling a memo reminder. I groaned again.

"What?" Anna asked.

"I forgot, I have a date tonight. I guess I'll cancel." I started to dial, but Percy put one of his big paws on my hand.

"When is the last time you've been on an actual date?" he asked.

"Um, well, it's been a while."

"Then by all means, go," he said.

I made a face and shook my head. "I can't leave him alone," I whispered as I gestured at Ronald, who was engrossed in some type of computer language being displayed on one of the monitors.

"I'll stay," Anna said.

"I'll stay too," Percy added. "I don't have anything else to do."

I saw a look pass between Anna and him. I tried to argue, but in the end, they convinced me everything would be okay. Anna rode with me and I hurried home. She gave me a kiss on the cheek before leaving in Percy's car.

"Have fun, and don't worry. We'll take care of him. Oh, and take the Cadi, it's sexy," she said with a grin.

CHAPTER 8

I texted ahead to Debbie to let her know I was running late and expected some flak, but she responded with a text full of smiley-face emoticons, which I assume meant she wasn't upset. A teenage girl answered the door, and there was no mistaking this was Debbie's daughter. Debbie rushed to the door wearing a black dress with a plunging neckline that looked stunning on her. She was one of those women who was no doubt a knockout during college. She'd added a few pounds as the years went by, but she was still a fine-looking woman and was smart enough not to deceive herself in believing she could wear the same dress size from fifteen years ago. She gave me a warm smile and gestured at the young girl.

"This is my daughter, Missy," she said.

"Hi, I'm pleased to meet you," I said.

"Whatever," Missy replied.

Her mother scolded her, but then hugged her and told her not to stay up too late.

"You'll need a coat," her daughter admonished. "It's going to be chilly tonight."

Debbie looked at me for confirmation.

"She's right," I said.

Missy opened the coat closet in the foyer and handed her mother a full-length coat that looked like it once belonged to her grandmother. Debbie looked at her daughter with an arched eyebrow but didn't say anything.

"Is Missy your only child?" I asked as I drove.

"I have another daughter who is with her father this weekend. Missy's father currently lives in California. That's where I'm originally from."

I silently added one plus one and deduced she'd been married twice. Well, that could've been incorrect. She had two kids by two different men, but that did not necessarily mean she'd been married twice. Not everyone got married when they were pregnant these days. Not that I was judging. But I didn't think it would be appropriate to ask the details and instead listened attentively when she changed the subject and began talking about the virtues of the country club. Traffic was about what you'd expect in Nashville these days and what once would have been a ten-minute drive was now twice as long. Even so, I liked listening to Debbie. She liked to gossip, but she made it a pleasant conversation rather than spending the twenty minutes badmouthing people.

"When there is a big event, we have valet parking, but not tonight," she said and pointed at an empty spot near the front. "Park in my spot." It wasn't necessary—there were plenty of empty spots—but I nodded and parked where she directed.

"You'll love the events we have, and we're always having golf tournaments when the weather permits. I'm going to have to introduce you to our pro, he's a neat guy."

She continued with the sales pitch as she led us inside and directly to the bar. She hung her coat and then led the way. I could not help but check out her backside as we walked. It was obvious she had on nothing underneath her dress, which caused more than one dirty thought. Surprisingly, they had Nashville Lager on tap. I ordered a glass and she ordered a glass of chardonnay.

"Do you have any kids?" she asked.

I thought about the answer for a moment. "I guess I'd have to say I have two adopted kids, a son and a daughter."

She looked at me in surprise. "Unmarried with two adopted kids? Impressive."

I chuckled. "I think I should explain." I then told her about Ronald and Anna and the circumstances in which I'd met the two of them.

"That's quite the story," she said after I finished. I don't know if she was impressed or not.

"So, you're a private investigator?" she asked.

"I am."

She nodded thoughtfully, and I could almost read her mind.

"Let me guess. You are now wondering what kind of salary a private investigator earns and if I can afford the membership dues of this place."

She grinned. "Touché. I guess I should have asked sooner. You've never asked what it'll cost. That's usually the first question I get."

"How do you usually answer?"

"We offer different membership packages. The silver membership is the cheapest but I never use words like that."

"Let me guess, after you assess someone's income, you tell them the silver is the most economical," I said.

She gave a flirtatious laugh. "Yes, I do, and it is. It runs four hundred a month with a ten thousand initiation fee. That includes all of the amenities, but you must spend a minimum amount every month in either the restaurant or bar."

"Does that include unlimited rounds of golf?" I asked.

Her grin faltered slightly.

"A silver member's package includes one free round a week. If you want to play more, we have what is called the sports package, which includes sixteen rounds of golf a month and two guests a month, for a slightly higher monthly fee and also a minimum spending requirement in the restaurant or bar. That's the package I was going to try to sell you. You also get unlimited use of the pool and tennis courts. Unless there is a special event, of course. It's pretty standard among most country clubs. What do you think so far?"

"Well, I don't play tennis but having access to a pool is appealing. Is it always full of kids?"

She snickered. "At times it can be a little crowded, but remember, whenever there are kids, there are also moms. Some are divorced, some are married but looking, if you know what I mean."

I ignored the innuendo and asked a few questions about club rules, how many members they had, things like that, if only to keep her interested in me. The truth be told, I was not an overly social person, so I sincerely doubted I'd spend much time here. If I joined at all, it would only be for the golf. And perhaps the bar.

Looking around, I saw there were only a dozen people mingling around. I'd never been a fan of big crowds, but this seemed a little slim for a party. Debbie noticed.

"We're a little early; most of the crowd won't start trickling in for another hour."

"What other types of events do you guys have?" I asked.

Her face brightened. "We have all kinds. There are golf tournaments of course, special events, holiday parties, and even theme parties."

I peered closer to see if she was bullshitting me. "Theme parties?"

Debbie laughed. "Yes, theme parties. Last October we had a Halloween costume party."

"What did you dress up as?" I asked.

"Raven," she said, and then saw my questioning expression. "The comic book heroine."

"Ah, did you win the best costume award?" I asked.

"You bet your ass I did," she said, grinning at the memory. "That was one wild night. We try to have several theme parties every year. What do you like to do for excitement?" Her grin morphed into a hint of a mischievous sexual undertone. I was about to disappoint her.

"That's easy. I go home, fix a glass of Scotch, get comfortable in my easy chair, and read a good book."

She laughed again. "Oh, you definitely need to join then. It'll get you out of your rut."

I arched an eyebrow. "I'm in a rut?"

She laughed and on impulse, or maybe it was planned, she reached up and caressed my cheek. I won't say it bothered me. In fact, it felt kind of nice, but it also made me slightly uncomfortable. I think Debbie sensed it and pulled her hand away. She gazed at me a moment longer and then switched gears.

"Do you see that older man over there?" she asked with a slight head nod.

I looked over and saw a middle-aged man doing his best impression of a wallflower.

"Yeah, he looks decidedly uncomfortable," I said. "And lonely."

"He was referred by a member. So, I hope you don't get jealous, but I need to go over there and flirt and get him to mingle. Would that be alright?"

"Of course," I said. "I believe I am in the perfect spot to hang out, right here by the bar."

She gave me that radiant smile of hers again. "You're the greatest. Give me thirty minutes, and then we'll do some dancing."

"Hang on now, I don't dance."

"Not even slow dancing?" she asked.

I cocked my head. "Oh, yeah, I can slow dance."

She smiled again, reached up, pulled me down by the neck and gave me another kiss, on the lips this time, before walking over to the man. I watched his face light up when she approached. I couldn't help but smile, but the old man caused me to think about myself. I hoped I'd never be as lonely as he obviously was, but it was looking that way more and more. When it came to relationships, I seemed to be jinxed somehow. Debbie was being friendly, flirtatious even, but I knew she was only looking for that signing commission. She was the kind of woman who would flirt with a man even if she had no romantic interest. Sighing, I ordered another beer.

I leaned against the bar and enjoyed my beer. The crowd had grown to almost thirty people now, about twenty men and a dozen women, including Debbie. Poor odds for a single man desiring companionship. The music cranked up and soon a few couples went out to the dance floor. I casually spoke to a few men as they came up and ordered drinks, but mostly I was left alone, which was fine.

I amused myself by people watching. There were a few who had dates and were genuinely having a good time. There were a couple of men who were already drunk and acting like they were still in college and making fools of themselves. During all of this, I somehow picked up a bar buddy. He had walked up, ordered a drink, and leaned up against the bar no more than a foot from me.

"What a bunch of pretentious assholes," he said loud enough so I could hear him over the music.

I gave a noncommittal shrug. I was pretty sure I knew his type; he was one of those people who was always in a foul mood about something. He was looking for a brother in arms to share in his disgust, but I wasn't interested. I spotted Debbie in the crowd and watched her as she introduced Gloomy Gus to a buxom woman close to his age. She looked over, saw me watching, and gave a wink.

"Well, you certainly look a lot better since the last time I saw you."

I turned to see a gorgeous blonde standing to my right. Even in the dim light, I could see her pale blue eyes and I recognized her immediately.

"I remember you," I said.

She was the paramedic. The first time I met her, I had found a man who had been brutally beaten and left to die on some railroad tracks. Our second encounter happened when the psychopath, Officer Ben Smith, attacked me and nearly beat me to death.

"Do you remember my name?" she asked.

I thought hard but drew a blank and offered an apologetic smile. "I'm sorry, I don't."

"Allison, but everyone calls me Al," she said and then smiled. I'm certain she'd never smiled during either of our previous encounters.

I stuck out my hand. "I'm pleased to finally meet you, Al. I've never thanked you for treating me."

Instead of a formal handshake, she took my hand in both of hers and held it gently. "How have you been?"

I gave a shrug and a pleasant smile. "It was a hard road back the first month, but I'm doing great these days. How about you?"

She glanced down and her smile vanished when she saw my scraped knuckles. "Still getting into fights, I see."

I pulled my hand back. "Oh, no. I was working on one of my cars today and the wrench slipped."

"Right," she drawled. She clearly did not believe me, but it didn't matter. She changed the subject. "You said cars, as in plural."

"Yeah, I have a couple of old cars. They require work from time to time."

The man who had been leaning against the bar was listening to us. "Is that your old Cadillac in the parking lot?"

"The black one, yes."

"That is a beautiful car. My grandfather had one just like it," he said.

"Yeah, I think she's my favorite." I refocused on Al. "Are you a member here?"

"No, he is," she said, pointing to the man still perched against the bar. He was a good enough looking guy, longer hair than I thought was necessary for a man, about the same age as Al, which I guessed to be late thirties. He was wearing an off-white button-down shirt which was untucked, khaki slacks, and Berkley penny loafers. Something told me if I were to look, he wouldn't be wearing socks. When you belonged to a country club, you never wore socks with leather shoes unless you were over seventy.

"Are you a member?" Al asked.

"No, my date is the membership recruiter. She's trying to get me to join."

"Ah, you mean Debbie," the man said.

"Yes, Debbie," I replied.

He smirked, erected himself off of the bar and stuck his hand out. "I'm Eddie Barker."

"Thomas Ironcutter," I replied, shaking his hand. I couldn't say why, but I instantly disliked him. His smarmy personality was off-putting.

"So, you're thinking of joining?" he asked.

"Yeah, thinking about it. I'll be honest though, I'm not sure it's a good fit for me. You know, pretentious assholes and all that."

He smiled at my remark. "What do you do for a living?" he asked. He didn't ask it because he was genuinely curious about me; he was gauging how much money I made based on my job.

"I'm a private investigator, and you?" I asked in feigned interest. In truth, I didn't care what he did.

He gave an exaggerated scoff with a corresponding facial expression. "Work is overrated," he proclaimed.

"So, you don't work. It must be nice," I replied. I suspected he was a trust fund baby but kept my opinion to myself. I glanced over at Al, who was staring with a knowing smile.

"We've known each other since high school," she said. "He's a conceited pain in the ass sometimes, but otherwise he's a decent guy."

Eddie held his arms out slightly, trying to appear self-deprecating. "What can I say. I am who I am. So, you and Debbie?"

"We're here together, yes. Is she an old girlfriend of yours or something?" I asked.

Eddie smirked. "Or something."

"Have you two been dating long?" Al asked.

I was quickly becoming tired of the interrogation. I looked over at Debbie, who was still being a social butterfly.

"It's our first date, although I'm not sure it's exactly a date. Speaking of Debbie, I better rejoin her. It was nice seeing you again, Al."

I gave Al a pleasant smile, ignored Eddie, and walked over to Debbie. She smiled when she saw me approaching and patted the empty chair beside her. She introduced me to the couple she was talking to and the four of us engaged in pleasant conversation for the next hour.

Eventually, I needed to hit the head. After washing up, I stood outside of the men's restroom and texted Anna.

How's it going?

She replied quickly.

Great. Ronald has been showing Percy everything about his computers. He's happy as hell that he has a new friend.

I responded.

That's good.

Anna texted back with one of those silly emoticons and then asked me how my date was going. I gave her the usual, "everything's wonderful" spiel and told her I'd see her later. Putting my phone away, I looked up to see Al walking over.

"I want to apologize for the twenty questions," she said.

I made light of it. "Yeah, what's up with that?" I asked with a smile.

"I wanted to know if you and that woman are dating."

I glanced at Debbie again. "It's our first date, although I think I'd have to call it a friend date. She's trying to recruit me to buy a membership." I doubted there was anything else to it, but with a woman like Debbie, anything was possible.

"Are you seeing anyone else?" she asked.

"Not at the moment," I said, wondering why I was getting asked so many questions.

She smiled slightly. "Good." She then stepped closer and stuck something into my pocket. "Give me a call sometime." She finished it off by standing on her tiptoes and giving me a kiss on the cheek before walking away.

I pushed the scrap of paper deeper into my pocket as I did what men are known for doing, staring at her backside as she walked off. It was a nice sight. She was wearing snug-fitting slacks and a chartreuse blouse, both of which accentuated her figure nicely. It was a nice, athletic figure with broad shoulders that tapered down to a trim waist. It led me to believe she worked out regularly.

"Who was that?" Debbie asked when I sat back down.

"Her name's Al. She's Eddie's date," I said.

"Do you know her?"

"Yeah, she's a paramedic. I've bumped into her a couple of times," I said.

"Oh. I mean, you two seemed chummy."

I looked at her, wondering what she meant, but she dropped it and started talking about something else. I suppose I could have asked her what kind of history she had with Eddie, but I didn't care and it was probably none of my business anyway.

We stayed until almost midnight. I took her home, walked her to her door, and gave her a kiss goodnight. I don't know if she was hinting for me to come in. She did not outright ask, and I did not invite myself in, and maybe it was nothing more than my ego making me believe she was into me but was being coy about it. We kissed once more before saying our goodbyes. I waited until I was down the road before pulling the scrap of paper out of my pocket. It was a phone number with a heart and smiley face drawn beside it.

CHAPTER 9

I went to Ronald's house early the next morning. Percy had spent the night, which seemed uncharacteristic of him, but I didn't say anything. In fact, I was glad he did. If those knuckleheads decided to come back, Percy would have made short work of them. He met me at the front door.

"The man has no coffee and the only breakfast he has is Frosted Flakes," he said.

"Well, let's wake them up and go eat somewhere," I suggested.

Percy shrugged. "Yeah, okay."

It took almost an hour to get the two of them going. During that time, Percy and I sat in the den, watching the morning news and talking.

"Did you have any visitors while I was gone?" I asked.

Percy shook his head. "I seriously doubt they'll come back here. Besides, as far as they know, they've already gotten everything out of Ronald that they can. By the way, the kid found Candy-Man last night," he said.

"He did?" I asked.

Percy nodded. "You're right, he's a whiz with those computers. He has some kind of software program he created that searches all of the popular social media sites. All he did was plug in the names and let the program do the work. Within a couple of minutes, we had some good data."

My eyes lit up. "Do tell."

Percy gave a small smile. "I won't steal Ronald's thunder. He's excited to tell you all about it." He then looked down the hallway and cleared his throat. "By the way, even though I spent the night, Anna and I did not do anything. I just want you to know that."

I nodded, but his statement gave me pause. Why would he say something like that? Did something really happen? Not sex, Percy would not lie to me, but did something else happen? Before I could ask anything, Ronald and Anna walked into the den.

"How're you doing, big guy?" I asked him.

"Fine," he said. "I'm hungry. Do you guys want some cereal?"

The three of us exchanged glances. It took some work, but we coaxed him into going to a nearby Waffle House. All of us had a hearty breakfast, with the exception of Ronald, who insisted on white toast and a soda.

The conversation was lighthearted and I heartily joined in, but the entire time I watched the interaction between Anna and Percy for any telltale clues. Was there a romantic connection? I thought I saw a little spark, perhaps a lingering smile from Anna when Percy said something witty, but hell it could've been nothing more than my overactive imagination.

"How was your date?" Anna asked.

"Huh?"

"Your date. You went on your date, right?" she pressed.

"Oh, yeah. We had an enjoyable evening," I said.

"Enjoyable evening? That doesn't sound exciting, Thomas. What did you two do?"

I told them about the party and how Debbie was the hostess so we did not spend a great amount of time together. And, I started to tell them about Al slipping her number in my pocket, but I had no doubt I'd get some ribbing about it, so I kept that part to myself.

"Are you two going to go out again?" Anna asked. She was giving me one of her smartass grins, but I was onto her game.

"I'm not sure, but it's possible. What about you? Any new love interest in your life?"

She blew a tuft of hair out of her left eye and broke eye contact. "Nobody I know of," she said. She quickly changed the subject. "Oh, Ronald has some good news for you. Tell him, Ronald."

He looked up from his toast. There were only a few people he would make eye contact with and I was one of them. "I found Candy-Man," he said smugly.

"Oh yeah? Tell me about it," I encouraged.

He broke eye contact and looked back down at the edges of his toast. "The address the cops had is years old. I'm pretty sure he lives in La Vergne. I've got it all at home on a file I created. I'll email it to you. Can I have some more toast?"

I got the waitress to fix another couple of pieces of toast with the edges cut off this time and a fresh refill of coke. Once we got back to Ronald's house, he quickly disappeared into his basement.

I gestured at the open basement door. "I'm going to spend some time with him. Why don't you two get out of here."

"Are you sure?" Anna asked.

"Certainly." I lowered my voice. "I think he and I are overdue for a talk."

Anna hesitated. "Percy has already talked to him."

"No," Percy said. "He looks up to Thomas as a father figure. What Thomas says to him will have far more meaning. We'll get out of your hair."

Once they'd left, I went downstairs and stood beside him. He had the file titled Candy-Man open and there were more than a few documents in it. As much as I wanted to look over what he had, it could wait.

"Alright, get your attention off of those computers for now. You and I are going upstairs and have a talk."

"But, I'm busy here," he protested.

"I'm not asking, I'm telling," I said and went back up the stairs. Ronald reluctantly followed and sat with me on the den couch.

"So, you got on a dating site, huh?" I asked.

"Yeah." He spoke in a voice barely above a whisper and kept his gaze fixed on the coffee table.

"That's a positive step; you know I want you to be more sociable. Did you check out her bona fides before going out with her?" I asked. "You are perfectly able to run a background check."

"No," he said, giving his head a slight shake back and forth.

"Why not, Hoss?" I asked in a gentle voice.

"She seemed nice and, um, I thought she liked me."

"She beguiled you," I said.

He looked at me funny. "What?"

"Beguiled, bewitched, bamboozled, inveigled. They all mean the same thing. She used her charm and her sex to deceive you and take advantage of you."

"Oh," he said, nodding. "Yeah, I guess she did."

"There are a lot of people like her in this world. Don't get me wrong, there are nice girls out there, but there are girls like her as well. Did you use protection when you slept with her?"

His face turned beet red and didn't answer, which caused me to let out a long sigh.

"Alright, let's get you an appointment with your doctor. The sooner you find out whether or not you caught something, the better."

"Caught something?" he asked.

"Yeah, you know, a sexually transmitted disease, commonly called an STD. Messing around with girls like that is risky."

Ronald paled. "Oh."

I called the doctor for him and made an appointment for next week. We talked some more about the birds and the bees and the ways of the world before we changed the subject to the Candy-Man. We went back down to the basement where he excitedly showed me everything he had found.

"I started with the names you gave me and researched all of them on my social media search program. I won't bother telling you how I eliminated the other names, unless you want me to."

"No, that's not necessary. Tell me what you've got," I said.

"So, according to the drug intel website, Candy-Man number two is also known as Raymondo Calendar. He had only one major drug charge as an adult—felony cultivating of marijuana."

"So, he had a grow operation that got busted. Does it say how much?" I asked.

"It just says it's a Class-B felony," Ronald said.

I searched my memory. "That's something like over a hundred plants. A pretty significant amount. Did you find out how much time he served?"

"It doesn't really say, but three years after the conviction he was posting on social media."

I nodded in thought. A Class-B felony in Tennessee was punishable by eight to thirty years imprisonment, so he had a good lawyer who got him a decent deal, or he did some snitch work for the cops in exchange for a lighter sentence.

"Anyway, he's on parole until next year," Ronald added.

"How did you find out where he lives?"

"I haven't, at least, not his exact address. Look at this." He did some clicking and a picture filled one of his monitors. It was a picture of a Candy standing beside a shiny red corvette and grinning broadly.

"He posted it on Facebook. Now, watch."

I watched as Ronald started manipulating the photograph. He focused on a section of the picture over Candy's shoulder and enlarged it. The picture became slightly pixelated but I could see a street sign identifying an intersection and a house in the background.

"I actually used Microsoft Maps, plugged the intersection into the directions, and voila," he said and clicked on a screenshot. "This is in La Vergne."

I nodded thoughtfully. La Vergne was a dent in the road for many years until the population exploded in Nashville and all of the surrounding counties. Now, La Vergne was a thriving bedroom community.

"What are you thinking?" Ronald asked.

"I'm thinking of heading down there and introducing myself. Do you want to go?"

"Oh, no," Ronald quickly answered. He looked at me like I'd asked him to participate in a ritual goat fuck.

"Come on, buddy. I could use some help with this. Besides, you need to start learning more about PI work."

Ronald protested, but I gently persuaded him and convinced him it would be fun. He finally agreed, but only if I went to the grocery store for him after we were done.

Traffic was surprisingly light and we made it to La Vergne with ease. With the assistance of Google, we had no trouble locating the street in question. I'd gone a couple of blocks when Ronald gestured excitedly.

"That's the street sign," he said. "And, look at that house, that's the same house in the picture. This is definitely the street."

After that, it was easy to find Candy's house. Even so, when Ronald spotted it, he gave out a hoot. "There it is!"

As casually as I could, I drove a half block and parked in front of a townhouse that had a for sale sign in the front yard. I took a moment to look it over, like I was a prospective buyer. At the same time, I'd glance back behind us, checking out Candy's townhouse. His was a two-story townhouse affair, sand-colored paint, and brown trim. And, there were actually a few potted flowers on the small porch. Most importantly, there was the red Corvette parked under the carport along the side of the house.

"Act like you're playing with your laptop and take a few pictures," I said. Ronald did so without complaint. In fact, there was a hint of a smile on his face. He was enjoying himself.

"Uh-oh, somebody's coming outside," he said.

We watched as a man exited the front door and locked it behind him.

"Is that Candy-Man?" Ronald asked.

There was no mistaking it: the man currently walking toward the Corvette was the same man in the phone video Detective Brannigan showed me.

"Yes, it is."

"Aren't you going to talk to him?" Ronald asked.

"I believe I have a better idea," I replied. Ronald was confused for a moment, but then his eyes widened.

"Are you going to sneak into his house?"

"I am."

Ronald took a sharp breath. "Oh, shit."

When Candy drove by us, he made direct eye contact, which caused Ronald to become flustered.

"He saw us!"

"Don't worry. For all he knows, we're simply looking at the house for sale," I said.

"We shouldn't do this," Ronald moaned. "It's illegal."

I gave him a withering stare. I mean, Ronald's favorite hobby was to hack into the seemingly secure websites of various businesses and government entities, simply to prove that he could.

"Do you remember that flash drive you gave me?" I asked. "The one with the special software?"

"The keylogger software?" he asked.

"Yeah. We've never used your latest version. I figure we might be able to try it out on Candy. If he has a computer in there, I'll try it out."

Ronald was nervous, but a slow grin crept across his face, like I told him we were going to wait for the parents to go to bed and sneak a look at the Christmas presents.

"What if we get caught?" he asked.

"*You* won't get caught. If I do, drive away and call Percy. He'll know to do."

Ronald muttered out an okay. He was nervous, but I could tell it excited him as well.

I waited until the Corvette drove out of sight, got out, and went to the back of my SUV. Opening my kit, I retrieved a few items, including the flash drive Ronald had programmed.

"Alright, have you got the city police frequency?" I asked. Ronald nodded.

"Good. I don't see any alarm signs or decals, but listen close and call if a police officer is dispatched. Or if Candy comes back. Or if a neighbor comes snooping. Or any other signs of trouble."

"Like what?" Ronald asked. His nervousness was growing, but there was nothing I could do about it now.

I casually walked down the sidewalk, holding a clipboard in my hand and studying the papers intently. I paused in front of Candy's home and made a show of confirming the address before walking to the front door. I rang the doorbell and then knocked loudly several times. As I waited, I took note of the door. It had an old lock of a common brand, along with an equally old deadbolt of the same brand. That was good.

I rang and knocked one more time to ensure nobody was home, and then pulled out a special-made key along with my lead sap. Back in the day, I'd used the sap a few times on unruly drunks. One shot to the part of the jawbone located immediately below the ear and they were down for the count. It was too bad officers were no longer allowed to use them.

The key was what is known as a bump key. I had placed a small O-ring at the base of it. I inserted the key, applied a slight amount of twist, and then began thumping it with my sap. Both locks opened within seconds.

I pushed the door open, the hinges squeaked slightly, and I waited for either someone to start screaming, or for an alarm to go off. Neither happened. I walked in and closed the door behind me.

"Hey, Candy, it's me, Tommy!" I bellowed. I was met with silence, which I hoped was also a good sign.

The door entered into a small foyer, which immediately opened up into the den. I stood there a moment, making a visual assessment while I waited to see if anyone appeared. After a minute, I made a quick search of the ground floor. Den, kitchen, closets, half-bath. The place was neat, tastefully decorated, a few African-American prints adorned the walls, along with some photos of a cute little girl. I estimated the square footage at twelve hundred, which in the Nashville area meant this was an economy home, lower to middle class.

The only item catching my attention was a laptop sitting on the kitchen table. I took a look at it and saw Candy was still logged in. Perfect.

I had a lot of items in my PI kit, most of which I'd probably never use. I thought I'd never have the opportunity to use the flash drive, but now here I was. Pulling it out, I plugged it into the USB port. In a couple of seconds, the screen went blank, and then the command prompt came up. I typed in the command line that Ronald made me memorize. A bar graph appeared, along with a timer. It was going to take between five and ten minutes. I made my way upstairs.

Once reaching the upper floor, I paused at the head of the stairs and listened for any movement. The stairs ended in a small hallway that ran perpendicular. On each end was a bedroom. Directly ahead was a full bathroom. The bedroom to the left had children's clothes and bed sheets with cartoon characters on them. I started with the other bedroom.

This room was obviously decorated by a single man. There was a queen-sized bed fitted with maroon satin sheets and there were lava lamps on each nightstand, along with an incense burner. The nightstands' drawers contained condoms, lubricants, and what not. He also had a couple of vapes along with what smelled like honey oil.

The closet was neatly organized and there was a stack of shoeboxes. I performed a quick but thorough search. I did not find anything illegal, nor did I find the body of Telisha Thompkins stuffed in a suitcase, but three of the shoeboxes were full of money. I guessed about a hundred grand, to be precise.

To claim I was not tempted would be a lie. I looked at the money a little longer than I should have before I placed the tops back on the shoeboxes and put them back in place. I was a lot of things, but I wasn't a thief. I mean, I was in this man's house illegally, and if I was caught, I'd be charged with burglary, true enough. But I wasn't a thief.

I double checked a few more hiding spots before heading back downstairs. The bar graph indicated seventy-five percent was downloaded. Ronald texted me, wondering if I'd been shot or arrested. I responded all was good and I'd be out in the next five minutes. I used the time to check the cupboards and plastic containers in the freezer, but came up with nothing.

There was a beep from the laptop. I looked over and saw the homepage back on the screen. Ronald's imaging program was complete. I put the flash drive in my pocket, went to the front door, and opened it slightly. I looked through the crack, and seeing nothing wrong, I exited, closing the door behind me. I locked the doorknob, but couldn't do anything about the deadbolt. I only hoped Candy-Man wasn't overly suspicious.

Ronald was paler than normal and wide-eyed when I got back into my SUV.

"How'd it go?" he asked anxiously. I explained everything as I started up and drove away.

"Oh, wow, you really did it," he said.

"I hope so. Let me ask you something. I didn't see any surveillance cameras, but if he had one or two hidden, it'd make sense he could access them from his laptop, correct?"

"Um, yeah, and his cell phone if he has a setup like you do," he said, and seemed to have a thought. "Give me the flash drive."

Ronald plugged the flash drive into his laptop as I drove. I hit a pothole, which caused him to flash me a look of annoyance. I got the hint and stopped in the parking lot of a local Burger King. Ronald's fingers flew across the keyboard.

"Uh-oh. Yeah, he has a camera covering the front and back doors," he said. I watched as he brought my image up on the screen.

"Well, it's a good thing I'm wearing a fedora," I said. I had it pulled down at an angle, effectively hiding my face.

"What should I do?" Ronald asked.

"Can you delete it?"

He nodded. "Yeah, but he'll be able to tell some footage was deleted."

"Who cares, he won't know it was us, right? Delete it." It took him less than thirty seconds. I pointed at the restaurant.

"I'm a little hungry. Do you want a burger or something?" I asked.

Ronald made a face. "I don't eat hamburgers. I'll take a coke though."

"So, what exactly does that software do?" I asked. I held off on ordering a burger and instead got us both a large coke. I wanted to go sit at a table, but Ronald adamantly refused, citing a well-known lack of hygiene in all fast food restaurants. So, we sat in my car.

"It's a type of spyware. Me and a couple of online friends created it. As long as he has Wi-Fi, I can access everything on his computer. Plus, it has a keylogger program. We can access everything he has on his hard drive and whatever he types."

He took a sip of coke and looked at me in awe. Like I was a bigger than life hero or something. "I can't believe you actually broke into his home."

"That's between you and me only, right?" I warned.

"Oh, of course, but man, that's incredible. I could never do anything like that. You know, you've done things I only dream of," he said.

"Like what?" I asked.

"Dang, Thomas, don't you know? You've been in gunfights, you've arrested dangerous criminals, you sneak into a stranger's home like it's no big deal. Is that the first black bag job you've done?"

"I've done a couple," I admitted.

Ronald nodded, like he already knew it. "And you were in a war when you were in the Army. Desert Storm, right?"

"I was in the ass end of it. Not a lot of combat at that point." I didn't mention a shit-hole city called Fallujah where I nearly got killed a couple of times.

"But you still saw combat," he said. "And, you got a silver star or something."

I gave a reluctant nod. "Or something."

"And there's stuff about you I don't even know about, I'm betting. You're like a regular James Bond, or something."

I chuckled. "I wouldn't go that far."

He glanced up at me from his computer. "How many people have you killed?"

I gave him a look. "Ronald, do you want to know what my greatest achievement was when I was on the force?"

"What?" he asked.

"It has nothing to do with how many people I might have killed. Nope. Something altogether different. One night, I had the task of delivering a death notice to a young man who was scared to death of interacting with the outside world except when he was online. When I told him that his parents had been killed by a drunk driver, he had an anxiety attack and locked himself in a closet."

Ronald broke eye contact and hung his head.

"I could have walked out of that house and left him there, but I didn't."

"No, you didn't," Ronald said in almost a whisper.

"No, I didn't. I sat on the other side of that door and talked to you the rest of the night. Do you know what happened?"

Ronald looked up. "I finally came out."

"You did, but more than that happened."

"What?" he asked.

"I found the best friend I've ever had," I answered.

Ronald looked surprised. "I'm your best friend?"

"Absolutely."

"But I thought Percy and Mick are your best friends."

"They are close friends, sure, but you're my best friend."

His expression was a combination of surprise and adoration. I held up a fist, and after a moment, a childlike grin emerged and he gave me a fist bump.

"I hope your spyware works," I remarked as I finished my coke.

"You should know by now to never doubt me when it comes to computers." He clicked on something and pointed. "He has a Tor account. That should be interesting."

"What's a Tor account?" I asked.

"It's an ISP for accessing the dark web."

"I've heard of the dark web, but I'm not so sure what it's all about. What's so special about it?"

"You can operate in virtual anonymity through it, although it's rumored the NSA actually runs it. He's probably a member of some online drug sites. He's a drug dealer, right?"

"Yeah, probably," I said, thinking back to those shoeboxes full of money.

"He might sell drugs online, or something like that. I'll work on it," he said. I looked over. He was lost in his computer and I knew any further meaningful conversation was futile. I started my vehicle and drove us back to Nashville. When I exited the interstate, I got Ronald's attention.

"Alright, what do you need from the store?"

He needed a lot; those three vagabonds had eaten everything he had, although it mostly consisted of soup, bread, snacks, and coke. After getting him stocked up, I found myself with a growling stomach. I should've ordered a Whopper combo like I wanted to in the first place, but decided to go to a steakhouse located only a few miles from my home. I liked it so much I dined there once or twice a week.

After parking, I bellied up to the bar and said hello to Jude, the bartender. He had a Sam Adams poured into a chilled glass before I'd even taken a seat.

"How's it going this evening?" I asked him.

"This is my last night," he replied. "I'm starting a new job at a bar on Music Row."

Jude confided in me one night he dreamed of being the next country music superstar. He wasn't the only one. This city was full of aspiring artists.

"Good for you, bad for me," I said. "I hope they pay better."

He grinned. "Yep."

After placing my order, a filet mignon with a loaded sweet potato and broccoli, I sipped my beer and thought over the events of the day. Like Ronald guessed, Candy's home was not my first black bag job. When I'd resigned from the Metropolitan Nashville Police Department, I was dead broke and had a lot of overdue bills.

An old friend, who at the time was a county sheriff, called me one day and said he had a special job for me. We met at a restaurant in Murfreesboro, and after buying me lunch, he asked me point blank if I wanted to do some off-the-record work for a friend of his. It turned out the friend in question suspected his wife was having an affair with his business partner. He wanted proof. Undeniable proof. He was willing to pay top dollar for that kind of proof.

I broke into the business partner's house while he was at work and installed a couple of surveillance cameras, complete with audio. Highly illegal. I did it anyway. He got his proof and I got a sizeable cash payment. The videos were like sleazy porn movies with the actors being middle-aged and overweight. He could never use them in court, but that was not his intention. Instead, he used them to blackmail his partner, who was also married.

My thoughts then drifted to my date with Debbie. I had a good time with her, and the goodnight kisses consisted of her probing deeply with her tongue to see if I still had my tonsils. I had to admit I was aroused, and she no doubt felt it. She had smiled naughtily at me before going inside and leaving me on the front porch, alone with my turgidity.

Yeah, I enjoyed her company, but if I had to be honest with myself, I was not so sure my attraction to her extended beyond the physical level. I was intrigued by Al, though. She was beautiful, with a quiet yet intense demeanor.

I was still hurting over the death of Simone. She was the first woman since my wife's death that I'd had feelings for. After her death, I was lost when it came to any kind of romantic feelings.

But, nothing ventured, nothing gained. I pulled my phone out, dialed the number from memory, and began typing.

Hi, it's Thomas. Social decorum dictates I wait two days before calling, but I thought I'd text you and tell you it was nice running into you last night. So, please expect the follow-up phone call at the appropriate time.

I'd no sooner finished my beer when there was a response.

I'll eagerly await the call - maybe :)

I smiled broadly at the thought, and then remembered I'd made a promise to Detective Brannigan. Reluctantly, I gave him a call. It went to voicemail, no surprise there, so I left him a message telling him I had identified Candy-Man and found where he lived. I omitted everything else.

When I was done, I ordered a fresh beer. It arrived at the same time as my meal. I held the waitress while I cut into the steak, ensuring it had been cooked properly. It had. I gave her a nod of approval before digging in.

CHAPTER 10

It was two days before Detective Brannigan called me back. I had almost given up on him and this morning I had made the decision to go have a talk with Candy-Man myself when Walter finally called.

"I'm sorry I didn't get back to you sooner; my dumbass son was in a car wreck."

"Oh, shit. Is he okay?" I asked.

"He will be, eventually. He was going too fast, went off of the road, and rolled the car. He's got a fractured vertebra in his neck. It was touch and go for a little bit, but the doctors are confident he'll make a full recovery."

"That's good news," I said.

"Yeah, but my insurance is going to skyrocket, not to mention the things they won't cover. My out-of-pocket expenses are going to be awful." I thought I could hear him rubbing the stubble on his face. "Alright, enough talk about that, just thinking about it sends my blood pressure through the roof. So, tell me about Candy-Man."

I told a story about how we'd found him on Facebook and put it together from there. It goes without saying I left out the part where I black-bagged his house and we were drawing information off of his laptop. Unfortunately, all he had been doing was socializing with women. I could only assume he conducted his drug deals through his cell phone.

"Damn, that's good work. I must say, I'm impressed," he said when I'd finished.

"I was going to have a chat with him, but I don't want to interfere with your investigation," I said.

"I'm definitely going to question him. I'm guessing you want to be there when I do it," Walter said.

"I would and I'm hoping that won't be a problem."

Walter readily agreed and we worked out the details. An hour later, we met at a Waffle House located at the Waldron Road exit off of I-24. I was the first one there, so I sat at a booth and ordered coffee. Checking the clock on my phone, I decided it wasn't too early and gave Al a call. After several rings, it went to voicemail. I wondered if I'd screwed up by waiting too long, but decided to leave a message anyway.

"Hi Al, this is Thomas. I was calling to see if perhaps you'd like to get together for dinner sometime, or we don't have to do dinner. We can meet for a drink. Or even coffee. Your choice. Give me a call back. Take care."

I hung up, wondering both how awkward I sounded and if she was going to even bother calling back.

"Oh, well," I murmured and drank my coffee.

Detective Walter Brannigan drove into the parking lot while I was on my second cup. Another car followed him in. It was one of the TBI detectives from the other night. I gave them a wave through the plate glass windows.

"You remember Agent Meeks, right?" Walter asked.

"Yes, I do," I said, shaking the two men's hands. As soon as they sat, Agent Meeks piped up.

"My boss does not want you to participate in the interview," he said.

"On account that I'm a civilian, I'm guessing," I responded.

"Yes, but Walter intervened and told him you're the one who found him and put us onto him."

It was true. I didn't say it, but I doubted they would have identified Candy-Man without my help. And, on the off chance they'd conduct the interview without me, I didn't give them Candy's real name and address. Hence, the agreement to meet me. I'm sure they knew this, but they played along.

"I informed them of your background as well, so it's not like you're a numb-nuts civilian," Walter said with a small grin.

"I'll be perfectly content to stay in the background and let you two do all of the talking, but all I ask is you prepare how you're going to conduct the interview ahead of time instead of simply winging it. I worked with people who always did that and they were seldom successful."

The two men looked at each other. I gathered they did not care to be lectured by me. I took the hint. "Just saying," I said, shut up, and drank my coffee. I didn't tell them I was going to secretly record it.

I rode with Walter and directed him to Candy-Man's townhouse. When we knocked, Candy himself opened the door. I got a much better look at him in the daylight. With the exception of a stupid-looking soul patch, he was not a bad-looking man. I guessed him to be in his early thirties, six feet tall, and a medium skin tone. Currently, he was wearing a brand name warm-up outfit. There was only a microsecond of surprise, and then he put on his best poker face.

"You gentlemen look like you're trying to recruit me to join your church," he said with a used car salesman's smile, revealing a gold grill. I thought those things went out of style ten years ago. I guess he didn't get the memo.

"My grand mama wouldn't care too much for me doing that. I've been going to her church since I was a little baby," he said.

When Agent Meeks produced his badge, Candy squinted and peered closely at it like it was something he'd never seen before.

"T-B-I? What's that?"

"You know exactly what it is," Agent Meeks replied and brushed by Candy. Walter followed him in. Candy watched them walk by in a mixture of annoyance and concern before focusing on me. I held out the extra Waffle House cup.

"I brought you coffee," I said with a friendly grin.

Candy looked at it like it might have poison in it and slowly took it from my hand. He stepped back so I could walk in without bumping him. He stuck his head outside and looked around before shutting the door. I guess he was wondering if his yard was full of SWAT officers. I paused in the foyer and took a sip. Nothing was different from my recent visit, with the exception of a plastic bin of children's toys sitting beside the coffee table.

"Nice place," I said. "Very clean. Your wife must run a tight ship."

"I'm not married," Candy replied. "I live here by myself."

He saw me glance over at the bin of toys.

"I have a daughter. Normally, I get her every other weekend, but today she's sick and can't go to school. Her mother is dropping her off and will be here any minute. So, you gentlemen go ahead and tell me what you want."

I had to hand it to him, the man was calm, cool, and collected. Meeks sat on the couch. Walter joined him. Candy remained standing, as did I. Walter got the ball rolling.

"Raymondo Calendar, also known as Candy-Man, correct?"

"If you say so," Candy said.

"Tell us about your underground fight and rave party promotions," Agent Meeks said.

"I don't know what you're talking about," he replied. "Should I have an attorney here with me?"

Both men were silent, but I would call it more of a pregnant pause before Walter gestured at a file folder he was holding.

"It's totally up to you, Raymondo, but, let me show you this." He produced a photograph of the late Jason Belew. It was a screenshot from a phone video. Walter had told me about it. Somehow, he'd obtained someone's cell phone video of one of the fights, and when he had played it, he spotted Jason in the background.

"Our only purpose of this visit is to allow you the opportunity to help us with this murder."

Candy frowned as he peered closer at the picture. "What is this?"

Walter produced another picture. This one was a screenshot of Jason cheering on the fight.

"His name is Jason LeClaire Belew. He was at the underground fight you organized down in Manchester on the night of February twenty-first. This photograph was the last time he was seen alive.

"And, this photograph..." Walter paused and pulled out a picture of the decomposing remains of Jason. "This is a photograph showing how he looked when we found him. By the way, he was found at the same location where the party was held."

Candy stared at the photo a moment longer. He was on guard, but he was calm. Too calm. He knew he was in some kind of predicament, but he wasn't sure how deep in the doo-doo he was. Candy was about to say something but Walter interrupted him.

"Now, don't get us wrong, we don't think you killed him, but we think you may have information about this young man's murder and we would like your cooperation."

"I don't know anything about this dude," he said. "And, I don't know anything about this so-called, whatever you called it, underground fight. Now, I've been to a rave party or two, but I couldn't tell you anything about them; they're all a blur, if you know what I mean."

Walter responded by pulling another still photo and laid it on the table with the others. It was a screenshot from the same phone video. It showed Candy, standing in the background. It looked to me like he was making a drug deal but I kept my opinion to myself. Candy glanced at it only momentarily.

"I admit, whoever that is looks a little bit like me, but I'm definitely more handsome than that guy," Candy said with a slight grin.

Agent Meeks leaned forward and tapped the photo with his finger. "That's you. You know it and we know it. We are in the process of having other people who were at the event picking you out of a photo lineup. Once they identify you, it will be the first in a long line of investigations in which you will be charged with racketeering."

Walter jumped in. "So, you may be asking yourself, if we're investigating you on racketeering charges, why are we even here? The answer is, we would rather solve this murder case. Simple as that."

Candy's eyes lingered on the photographs for several seconds before looking up at the two detectives. Then, he recalled I was there and looked over at me.

"You never said who you are," he said.

"My name is Thomas Ironcutter. I'm a private investigator who has been hired by Jason's brother."

"You're not po-lice?" he asked.

"No, I'm not," I answered.

"There is one other thing," Walter said. He reached into the file and retrieved an 8x10 photo of Telisha. It looked like her senior high school picture.

"She went missing the same night of the fight. We believe she was there."

He stared at the picture a moment. For the first time, I saw a look of concern on his face. He started at it for a few more seconds before making pointed eye contact with Meeks and Brannigan.

"I never laid eyes on that man, I didn't murder him, and I don't know who murdered him. And, I've never seen that girl."

The two detectives asked a few questions which didn't lead anywhere and before they could get into the meat of it, they were interrupted by a car horn giving a rat-a-tat. Raymondo looked out of the front window.

"That would be my daughter and her mother. I'm going to stop answering all of these questions and speak with an attorney. Now, I'd rather spend the day with my little girl and not you men, so…" He held a hand out toward the front door.

We were done here. Walter gathered his photographs. The two detectives stood, whereupon Candy ushered us out.

"Thanks for the coffee," Candy said as I walked past. I paused, reached into my pocket, and proffered a business card.

"Perhaps you can pay me back sometime," I said.

He responded with a smirk, but at least he took my card.

Walter grumbled the entire way back to the Waffle House.

"Meeks and his people wanted to hold off on any follow-up interview with Mister Candy-Man." He saw my questioning expression and explained. "They want to put him under surveillance and develop a racketeering case against him. I talked them into making the murder a priority. I'm afraid we might've blown it, and I'm the one who'll be blamed for it."

I nodded in understanding. I sympathized, but the truth was, I was going to talk to Candy with or without them and he would have been tipped off either way.

Walter dropped me off at my car and I started back toward Nashville. There were a lot of things going on in my mind, but honestly, I felt like I was stuck with the case. But then I had an idea, exited the interstate, and then hopped back on it going the opposite direction. Soon, with the help of my smartphone, I was parking at a set of apartments in Manchester. This was a cold call, but I was wearing one of my new suits and I looked resplendent, if I do say so myself.

After a polite knock, a twenty-something girl opened the door partially. She could have been attractive under normal circumstances, but today she looked like she'd been ridden hard and hung up wet. Her brown hair was in disarray and her matching brown eyes were bloodshot and puffy. She was wearing sweatpants and a wrinkled T-shirt that made her figure indistinguishable. I suppose the worst thing was her smell, a combination of cigarette smoke and stale sweat emanating off of her. I kept my expression friendly.

"Hi, are you LaDonna Pitts?" I asked.

"No, she's in bed. Who are you?"

"Ah, you must be Carla. My name is Thomas Ironcutter. Could I talk to you a minute about the fighting match you two went to back in February?"

She looked at me in confusion. "That was like, months ago."

"Yes, almost three months ago," I said. "You two met a couple of guys at that match and I'd like to talk about it."

She frowned and rubbed the sleep out of her eyes. Obviously, I'd woken her up, even though it was after eleven. She finally turned and walked inside. Assuming this meant she was going to talk, I followed her in.

It was a small apartment. There was no fancy foyer; the entrance led directly into the den, which had some cheap furniture with an oversized TV on the far wall. Carla walked toward the kitchen, which was separated from the den by a bar counter. She looked around in confusion before plopping down and sitting on one of the stools.

"I'm hungry, but I don't feel like fixing anything. Have you ever felt like that?"

"Many times," I said and walked into the kitchen. There were dirty dishes everywhere, but I saw a coffeemaker and one of those red plastic Folger coffee containers. I gestured at the percolator.

"Would you like me to get a pot of coffee going?" I asked.

She yawned and looked up. "Sure, if you want to. I have to pee."

She slid off of the stool and walked through the den to a hallway, scratching her behind as she disappeared through a door at the end of the hall.

I found some dishwashing liquid under the sink and washed out the carafe before prepping the coffeemaker. I heard the muted sound of a toilet flushing running water. A moment later, Carla reappeared, planted herself back in the same stool, and rested her head on the counter. I needed her to talk to me and decided a little flirting might help.

"How about I cook you some breakfast?" I asked with a warm grin.

"Sure," she said, never looking up. So much for my attempts at being a lady-killer.

I opened the refrigerator and surprisingly, it was stocked. I think she fell back asleep, but that was okay. I had to wash a skillet and some plates, but I soon had a cheese omelet, toast, bacon, and a hot cup of coffee in front of her. The aromas roused her and she lifted her head.

"Holy shit," she muttered.

"Get it while it's hot," I proclaimed. I fixed myself a cup and leaned against the counter, watching her eat.

"Holy shit, this is good," she said with more vigor.

"I'm a halfway decent cook. Tell me about the fight and the rave party," I urged as I set a paper towel in front of her. She picked it up and dabbed at some bacon juice running down her chin before answering.

"It was okay. I mean, there was one kickass fight, but there were only like four matches, so that part was pretty lame. So, me and LaDonna met these two guys and they had brought a bottle of tequila and some other party favors."

"Like what?" I asked.

"Molly," she said and made eye contact. "Have you ever done Molly?"

"I have not," I answered. She snickered.

"Yeah, I figured as much. You're too old for Molly. You ought to try it sometime. Sex is incredible when you're rolling," she said with a mischievous smile. It might have even been a little on the flirtatious side, but she had a mouth full of food.

"I'll keep that in mind," I said with a forced smile. "So, you and LaDonna hooked up with two men?"

"Yeah."

"Do you recall their names?"

She shrugged and shoveled in another mouthful of food before answering. "The guy I was with is named Benny…" she stopped in mid-sentence, searching her memory for Benny's last name. She then gave up with a shrug.

"Benny," she repeated.

"Benny Newton?" I prodded as I refreshed her cup of coffee.

She shrugged again. I pulled out my phone and scrolled to a picture that Joseph had sent to me. It was a group picture of Joseph, Jason, and a couple of their friends. I showed it to her. She looked and pointed.

"That one's Benny, and that's the guy LaDonna was with." She then pointed at Jason. "He was there with them."

"So, what did you guys do?" I asked.

"After the fights were over, they fired up the music and everybody partied. It lasted until about five, then we came back here."

"Who? All of the guys?"

She shook her head. "Just Benny and the other guy."

"Which one?" I asked.

"Charlie."

Carla wasn't the one who said it. I looked up to see her roommate, LaDonna, walking down the hall. She was wearing gym shorts and a wrinkled green T-shirt. Her hair was blonde and she was overdue to get her roots touched up. She looked as rough as Carla, and at least forty pounds heavier. She was not a woman I would have ever wanted to wake up next to. She plopped down on the stool beside Carla and rubbed her face. At some point, she smelled the cooking aromas.

"Coffee?" I asked her.

"Sure," she said. "Lots of sugar. Are you a cop?"

"No. My name's Thomas Ironcutter. I'm a private investigator who was hired to find Jason."

She looked over at Carla, who shrugged.

"I thought he was a cop," she said.

LaDonna stared at her a long moment before focusing back on me.

"Who is Jason?" she asked. I picked up my phone and pointed him out in the picture.

"Oh, him. I remember him. He's cute but he's a fag," she said and made a back and forth hand motion to her mouth for emphasis. I noticed she mentioned him in the present tense.

"Did he do anything once he came back home with you guys?" I asked.

LaDonna quickly shook her head. "He didn't come home with us. Only Charlie and Benny."

"What happened to him?"

LaDonna held up two open hands and shrugged. "Beats me." She looked over at Carla, who looked like she was about to fall asleep again. It took her a moment to realize we were both waiting on her to say something.

"Look, uh, Thomas. We were all pretty wasted that night and it was so long ago. All I know is Jason didn't come home with us."

"The three of them rode down here together and Jason drove. So, how did Charlie and Benny get back home?"

"I took them," LaDonna said. "We slept until around six that evening. Charlie offered to fill up my gas tank if I took them home, so I did. I asked them what happened to their ride, but all they said was the fag left without them."

"Do you have an issue with gay people?" I asked her.

She shook her head and picked up a pack of cigarettes lying on the counter. "I don't care one way or another, but Charlie was pissed at Jason for turning into a fag."

"How so?"

"He kept saying things about him all night," she said. "You know, fag stuff."

She looked around for a lighter. I pulled out mine and lit it. She thanked me by taking a deep drag and then blowing it in the direction of my face. A real classy girl, this one.

"You know, the cops already asked us about this stuff," she said in seeming irritation.

"Yes, ma'am. I'm simply following up in case you two might have remembered something. Have either of you seen or spoken with Charlie or Benny since?"

LaDonna shook her head, but Carla spoke up.

"Benny and I have texted a few times, but that's it. Have they ever found that dude?" she asked. "Jason, I mean?"

I stared pointedly. "Yeah, he was murdered."

CHAPTER 11

The two women feigned shock at the news, but I don't think they were too terribly concerned. Carla asked me if I wanted to hang out with them, but I declined. I gave a polite smile when I did, but honestly, these two girls were far too rough for my taste. I believe skanky was the correct descriptor and I didn't do skanky.

I tried calling Detective Brannigan, but it went to voicemail. Reviewing the file, I realized I had not spoken to Telisha's parents. Finding the address, I plugged it into Google and headed that way.

The Thompkins house was one of those cheaply built houses from the sixties and had never been well maintained. Hell, it still had asbestos siding on the exterior. When I knocked, I could hear a chorus of barking emanating from within. A deflated-looking forty-something woman shaped like a pear with stubby legs answered the door.

"Hello, my name is Thomas Ironcutter. I'm a private investigator. Are you Telisha's mother?"

"I'm Danita Thompkins. What do you want?"

"I'd like to talk to you about Telisha and the circumstances of her disappearance, if you don't mind."

"Has she been found?"

"No, ma'am, she hasn't," I said.

"Then why are you here?" she asked, her voice cracking.

"I was hoping to speak to you in the hopes of gaining some insight about Telisha."

She stared at my feet a moment before opening the door and turning her back to me. I interpreted it as an invitation and followed her inside. She led me to the den, a moderately furnished room that had the distinctive odor of stinky dogs. That's probably because she had three little mongrels running around and barking incessantly. If I closed my eyes, I would've sworn I was in an ill-maintained kennel. I wondered how Telisha felt about it when her friends visited. Ms. Thompkins motioned me over to a sofa that looked straight out of the eighties and covered with dog hair.

"I need to stand a little while and stretch my back, if you don't mind," I said.

"Suit yourself," she replied and sat in a chair covered with a hair-infested afghan. Two of the dogs immediately jumped in her lap while the third dog warily sniffed my ankles.

"I've spoken to Detective Brannigan about the disappearance of your daughter. He said she's an only child, is that correct?"

"She had an older, half-brother, but he's living out on the west coast somewhere with his cousin. Those two never got along anyway." She seemed to suddenly remember a picture sitting on top of a dusty upright piano and pointed at it. "That's her on her first birthday."

It was a family photo, I guess. Baby Telisha was dressed in some kind of silly birthday outfit. She was being held by her mother, who was several pounds lighter and had a lighter shade of brown hair. The old man had stringy brown hair as well. He looked drunk. Standing beside him was a young acne-faced teenage boy with a surly expression.

"That's us, in happier times," she said. I looked again. Telisha seemed to be the only one smiling. Of course, she may have simply had gone boom-boom in her diaper.

"May I ask where Telisha's father is?"

She gave a slight shrug of a rounded shoulder. "I came home from work one day and his stuff was gone. No note, no nothing. Just gone. Telisha was ten when that happened."

I nodded somberly. "My mother did the same when I was ten. She took my little sister with her when she left."

She stared at me through bloodshot eyes. "My little Telisha changed then. She was a happy little girl up until then, but she changed. She grew into an angry teenager. Did you change too?"

I found myself biting my lip. "Yeah, I guess I did in some ways. Sometimes, when I thought about it, I blamed myself for her leaving. I convinced myself it was all my fault and it tore me up inside."

"Guilt," she said.

"Yeah, guilt."

"Did you ever see your mother again?"

"No, she died of cancer a while back. I saw my little sister not too long ago, but it wasn't a happy family reunion, you know?"

She nodded like in fact she did know.

"Has Telisha seen her father since he left?"

She shook her head and stroked one of the dogs. "She tried and tried to find him. One time, she even wrote to one of those daytime talk shows, asking them to reunite the two of them, but they couldn't find him either. He's probably living under a bridge somewhere."

"Do you know who she was supposed to meet that night, Ms. Thompkins? Where she might have disappeared to?"

She could not, or would not answer. Instead, she kept stroking those stinky dogs.

"Ms. Thompkins, is there anyone you think I could talk to who may have information? Anyone at all?"

She slowly looked up at me and spoke in a pained rasp. "She's never coming back."

CHAPTER 12

I left Ms. Thompkins and her malodorous dogs and walked back to my car, hoping the outdoor air would dissipate any lingering smell. As I sat in my car, a sense of deep sadness washed over me. Based on my own recent experiences, I had a sense of the depths of her sorrow. She'd lost a husband, stepson, and now her only real blood kin. All she had left were those dogs.

Telisha's name went on my mental list, right next to Jason's. If there was any way I could do this, I was going to find her and solve Jason's murder.

My brain was running a hundred miles an hour, intensely trying to think up ideas for this case, but it was only going in circles. The only thing I could think of at the moment was to follow up with Jason's two friends, Benny and Charlie. I did not have to bother with the case file; I already had their address committed to memory. I found my way back to I-24 and headed back to Nashville. Anna called as I crossed into Rutherford County.

"Ms. Braxton wants me to research baptism records," she said. "And she only knows the name of an old church where her great grandparents went, but it's been gone for years. I don't think we'll be able to do any good with this one."

"Perhaps, but sometimes baptismal records are passed along to another church, or the county archives might have them."

"Really? How do we find them?" she asked.

I gave a tired laugh. "What's this *we* shit, Kemosabe?"

"Kemosabe is right. We're partners and you've done this stuff before, I haven't," she lamented.

"Okay, sure. But you're going to need to tell her we'll have to delay her case for a week or two. The email logs for the Reavis case are due to arrive tomorrow or the next day. Ronald has everything set up and ready for us. That job is time sensitive and we need to jump right on it."

"I'm glad you brought that up. I have a great idea."

"Oh, yeah? What's that?" I asked.

"The case involves reading the emails, right?"

"Yeah, that's our role in the case for now. There are going to be a lot of emails to wade through, which means we're going to spend a lot of hours sitting in front of computers, reading and analyzing."

"Well, I think we should hire Marti to help out," she declared. "I've already talked it over with her and she said she'd do it. She could use the extra money."

I felt myself frowning. "Anna, this is a sensitive job. If we had a case where we needed a honey trap, sure, she'd be perfect, but this job requires reading comprehension skills."

"We don't do infidelity cases, you said so yourself," she said.

"You are so right. That means we don't need her."

"Yes, we do. You said yourself it's a big job, right?"

"I did," I conceded. "But…"

"But nothing," she retorted. "I've already told her it would be temporary and I happen to know she's plenty smart. The ditzy blonde routine is just an act. She always pulled in a shitload of tips at the club acting like that. She's actually pretty smart and she has a great work ethic."

"I don't know, Anna. Like I said, this job is very sensitive..."

"Discretion is paramount," Anna said, interrupting me yet again. "I've already explained all of that to her and warned her she would have to sign an NDA. She's agreed to all of it."

I thought about it some more. The truth was, I wasn't looking forward to the Reavis case. Sure, the money was going to be good, but the last thing I wanted to do was sit in front of a computer all day reading emails. Besides, if we hired Marti, it would free me up to work on Jason's case.

"Yeah, let me have a talk with her, but I think it may be doable."

Anna squealed in delight and I heard her talking to someone. "She's sitting right there, isn't she?"

"Yep," Anna answered and I heard Marti in the background saying hi to me.

"Alright, when I get home, I'll work up the paperwork. We'll hire her as an independent contractor, which means she only gets paid. No benefits."

"I'm already one step ahead of you," she said cheerily. "The paperwork is done and awaiting your signature."

"Okay. We'll talk more when I get home."

I disconnected, but did not even have a chance to put my phone down when it immediately rang again.

"Hello, Thomas. Reuben Chandler here."

Reuben Chandler, G-Man. FBI. The last time I saw him was at Simone's funeral visitation.

"Hello, Reuben. This is a surprise," I said.

"Yes. How are you?"

"I'm doing well, and you?"

"I've been covered up at work, but I guess that means job security, right? Listen, I don't mean to be brusque, but I have a reason for calling."

"What's up?" I asked.

"I was hoping to meet with you and explain it in person. Would this afternoon be convenient?" he asked.

"I don't think I'll be back in town anytime soon. Tomorrow morning would be better. What's this about?"

"Ah, I'd rather discuss it in person. Tomorrow morning will work. How about I swing by around nine?" he asked.

"Sure. I'll see you then," I said.

Each of us offered a few additional cordialities before ending the call. I glanced at the call duration as I pondered Reuben's reason behind him phoning me. There could have been multiple reasons; perhaps new information had arisen about the late Special Agent Enrique Hernandez. Or, it might have something to do with my loose association with the Baroques. They were an outlaw motorcycle club and prone to get involved in shady activities. The list could go on, but for some reason, I had a sneaking suspicion he wanted to meet in regards to the murder of Jason LeClaire Belew. One thing was for sure, it definitely was not going to be a social call.

I felt the need for a cigar. After all, I had not imbibed all day and found myself chewing my lip a couple of times. I had a travel humidor I religiously carried with me and it was stocked with an eclectic assortment. I parked on the shoulder of the interstate before reaching into the backseat for the humidor. Opening it, I picked a Nat Sherman Metropolitan. I happened to glance over to the right as I lit up. I was in Rutherford County now, which was in between Davidson and Coffee County. This part of the county was still rather rural, and there was an open field in the distance with an old rustic pole barn sitting in the middle. It was sagging precariously to one side and the main doors looked like they had fallen off of their hinges, but that's not what had my attention.

"No way in hell," I mumbled.

I fumbled for my kit and came out with a pair of binoculars. Confirming what I thought it was, I rushed down the interstate, took the next exit, and backtracked until I found what I thought was the driveway leading to the farm where the barn was located. The driveway was a muddle of gravel, leading several feet off of the road to a galvanized cattle gate which was closed and blocking access to the farm. I parked, got out, and checked it. There was no lock, but I knew farmers took a dim view of some stranger opening a gate and riding in uninvited.

I was going to leave a note in the mailbox, but before I could start writing, an old green Chevy truck pulled in behind me. A man who looked old enough to have been friends with Andrew Jackson was sitting behind the wheel and a large German Shepherd was sitting in the passenger seat. He motioned me toward him. I walked up to his open window, keeping close attention to the dog, who was in turn staring intently at me. There was a large caliber revolver sitting between the dog and himself.

"Good morning," I said.

"Open up the gate and get the hell out of the way," he gruffly replied.

I obliged, walked back to the gate and opened it, but instead of moving off to the side, I drove forward and didn't stop until I'd reached the house. I parked, got out, and waited.

The old man took his time getting out. The dog got out with him and stood by his side. He produced a pouch of Tennessee Chew out of the front pocket of his bib overalls and put a wad in his mouth the size of a midget's fist. He chewed on it a few seconds before speaking.

"Who the hell are you and what do you want?" he demanded.

"Sir, my name is Thomas Ironcutter. I have a fondness for old cars and I couldn't help but spot a car parked in your barn over there. I'd like to take a look at it, and if it's what I think it is, I'd like to try and buy it off of you."

He stared at me through squinted eyes for a long moment, and then spit before speaking.

"What kind of car do you think it is?" he asked.

"A Cadillac Coupe LaSalle, and if I had to guess, I'd say it's a thirty-seven or thirty-eight."

He spat again. "You saw all of that from the interstate, did you?"

"Yes, sir."

He squinted while he chewed. "Where're you from?" he asked.

"Nashville."

"Nashville? What the hell are you doing down here?"

"I had business in Manchester," I answered. "So, what do you say? Do you want to show me that raggedy old car?"

He stared for a moment longer, and finally grunted, which I guess meant he'd reached a decision.

"That barn's awfully dirty for a man wearing his Sunday best," he said, referring to my suit.

"I won't mind."

He grunted again and worked his jaw.

"I guess it can't hurt for you to have a look at it. Let's take the truck."

As soon as he opened his door, his dog jumped in and planted himself in the passenger seat. Rather than fight him for it, I climbed into the bed and sat on the edge. The barn was located fifty yards back behind his house and it appeared to be used only for storage these days. The car was exactly what I thought it was, a thirty-seven LaSalle Opera Coupe, and even though it was covered in a heavy layer of grime and bird shit, she was beautiful.

"What can you tell me about it?" I asked.

"It's a series seventy. They only made them for three years. That one has a V-8 in it, and I remember it being damn fast. My daddy bought it off of the showroom floor. The engine threw a rod back in the fifties and it's been sitting here ever since. I was going to fix it up, but I never got around to it."

"Would you mind if I gave it a closer inspection?" I asked.

"Help yourself," he said, but not before he spit out a voluminous gob of brown-colored liquid. His dog walked over, sniffed it, and snorted. He didn't seem interested in taking a bite out of me so I walked into the barn.

I looked it over from top to bottom. The tires were flat and rotten, as was everything else made of rubber. The seats were black leather, and they were dry and cracked. But everything was there. There was only minimal surface rust, and it did not appear it had ever been wrecked. I was careful not to ruin my clothes, so I refrained from crawling under the car. Even so, I knew the car was worthy of restoring. I turned to the old man.

"I have good news and bad news," I said, starting the haggling process. Unfortunately for me, the old fart had other ideas. He interrupted me by holding a hand up and spitting out another gob of tobacco juice.

"Son, I don't give a fart in a whirlwind what your bad news is. I'm ready to sell it, but only if the price is right. You either want to buy it or you don't. If you don't, just say so and stop wasting my danged time."

His dog gave a short yip, as if to put a punctuation mark on his master's proclamation. I thought for a minute or two as I looked over the car.

"Alright, let me ask you this; do you have the original title?"

He spit again. "Not only do I have the original title, I have the build order and the first license plate for the car. Now, do you want it or not?"

"I want it," I said. As far as I was concerned, this was a no-brainer.

CHAPTER 13

The old fart must have been a horse trader back in the day. He stated a price, stood fast, and rebutted all of my attempts to haggle him down. In the end, I finally gave up and agreed to pay the price he wanted. I gave my friend Bubba a call, gave him the address, and directed him to come pick it up and tow it to my house. Concluding the fleecing I endured at the hands of the old man, I got back to business and drove to a sprawling apartment complex located on Bell Road in south Nashville.

I recognized Charlie Thomas when he answered the door.

"Hi, Charlie," I said.

He stared in confusion. "Do I know you?"

"My name is Thomas Ironcutter. I'm investigating the death of your friend, Jason Belew."

His expression did not change and he stood there, mute.

"May I come inside, or do you want to talk right here?" I asked.

"Um, we already talked to some detective from Manchester," he said.

"Yes, you did. I'm hoping to get some additional information. I hope you don't mind."

"Um, yeah, sure. Come on in," he said. Another young man whom I assumed was Benny was sitting on the couch with a game controller in his hand. The TV had monsters killing each other. He paused it when I entered.

"This is a detective," Charlie said to him. Benny eyed me curiously.

"Guys, I'm actually a private investigator. I've been hired by Jason's brother to investigate his death. I won't take up too much of your time; I was only hoping to get your input about Jason's death."

Charlie sat on the couch with Benny and the two of them recounted the night down in Manchester.

"Did either of you notice if Jason had met someone or talked with anyone?"

Charlie glanced at Benny. "He went and talked with one of the fighters," he said.

"Which one?" I asked.

"The Wolf dude," he answered. "He followed him to the back room."

"What do you mean by back room?"

He shrugged. "The back room. You know, where they hang out and get ready for their fight."

I nodded in understanding. "Did either of you see him after that?"

The two young men glanced at each other again before shaking their heads.

Charlie seemed to have an epiphany of sorts. "I never thought of that. Do you think that's where he was killed?"

"That's a good question," I said. "Is that something Jason would've normally done? Wander off?"

"Um, no, not really," Charlie answered. "I have to be honest though, I wasn't really paying attention to him. I mean, I never worried about Jason, he could take care of himself."

Benny nodded in agreement. "We were hooked up with those two girls."

While we talked, I applied my skill craft and asked several behavior-provoking questions in an attempt to catch any deception, but I found none. The two young men seemed sincere and genuinely upset about the murder of Jason. I gave them my business card and ask for them to call me if they could think of anything. Once in my car, I jotted down some notes. After a few minutes, I tossed my notepad onto the passenger seat and sat there, contemplating what I'd learned, which wasn't much. A yawn involuntarily escaped and I rubbed my temples. It felt good, and after a minute, I picked my notepad back up and reread my notes.

"Who said this would be easy," I muttered to myself and was momentarily distracted by two young women parking a couple of spaces down and getting out of their car. From their attire and figures, I deduced they were fresh from the gym. One of them looked back as they walked toward their apartment. Satisfied that the old man was ogling them, she turned her head sharply, causing her ponytail to bounce in a dismissive gesture before they entered the breezeway and out of my sight.

Sighing, I tossed the notepad again. I was done for the day and decided to head home. My phone rang while I was at a stoplight.

"Ironcutter Investigations," I answered.

"Hi, Thomas, it's Al."

I did a mental stutter. "Hi," I answered. For some reason, I did not expect her to call me back. Well, what do you know?

"How are you?"

"I'm doing well," I said. "How're you?"

"It's been a little hectic. Raising two teenage boys by yourself is always hectic, it seems, but I wouldn't trade it for anything. What are you doing right now?" she asked.

"I've been down in Manchester most of the day on business, but I heading back to Nashville as we speak."

"Have you eaten dinner yet?" she asked.

"No, I haven't," I said. "Did you have something in mind?"

"I have my sons with me and we were thinking of pizza. Would you be interested in joining us?"

It was an interesting question. Sure, I was interested in her, but was I interested in meeting her sons? I thought it over for all of two seconds.

"You bet. When and where?"

She directed me to an all-you-can-eat pizza place off of Briley Parkway in south Nashville. On the way, I stopped off at a convenience store and cleaned up in the restroom. I bought one of those body sprays and did the best I could before heading to the restaurant.

They drove into the parking lot at the same time I did. When she exited her car, I must admit, I was impressed. She was wearing a collared orange and white shirt with the UT logo over her left breast and black yoga pants, which she filled out nicely.

"I like the suit," she said, giving me the once over.

"Thanks," I answered, wondering if the deodorant was working.

I told her about the car, and then she introduced her sons.

"This is Sterling and Steffen."

They were typical-looking teenage boys, lanky, a little bit of acne, shaggy brown hair, and the same bright blue eyes as their mother.

"Hi, guys," I said.

Both mumbled hi back at me. They didn't seem the type to shake hands, so I excused myself and headed to the restroom. I don't know why, but I didn't feel like I'd done an adequate job of cleaning myself up, so I washed up once again and checked myself in the mirror before joining them at the table.

"Wow, you guys must be starving," I said when I looked at the two plates sitting before the boys. They were stacked with slices. Al chuckled and motioned for me to follow her to the buffet line. She opted for only a couple of slices, as did I.

"I swear, they're bottomless pits. They would happily eat here every day if I allowed it. Don't get me wrong, I cook, but sometimes I need a break and this keeps them happy."

"I understand. Is their dad in the picture?"

She glanced over at me. "No. I'm a widow."

It took me by surprise. I guessed her in her late thirties, but there was no way she was older than forty. She saw my look and smiled.

"I'll tell you about it later, let's eat," she said and led the way back to our table.

"Mom said you used to be a cop," Sterling said before I'd even taken a bite of my first slice.

"That's right," I said. "Now, I'm a private investigator, like Mike Hammer."

"Who's that?" Steffen asked.

"Mike Hammer was a fictional character created by Mickey Spillane," Al said and then glanced at me. "He was notorious for getting into fights and carousing with loose women."

"Well, maybe that wasn't a good analogy," I quickly said. "Anyway, I'm a private investigator. It's sort of like being a police detective, but I have no police powers. It's mostly boring work."

"Mom said you were arrested for your wife's murder, but you were framed," Sterling said.

"Alright, that's enough," Al interjected.

"It's okay," I replied with a smile and looked at Sterling. "That's true. It's a little bit more complex than that, but in the end, the truth came out."

"Yeah, mom said you killed the man who really murdered your wife."

"Okay, that's enough. I mean it," Al chastised and then looked at me. "I'm sorry."

I gave her another smile. "It's okay. So, where do you guys go to school at?"

"MBA," Sterling said and then felt he needed to explain. "Montgomery Bell Academy."

"Wow, nice school," I replied.

"And expensive," Al said. "I use their father's pension to pay for it."

"What did he do?" I asked.

"He was in the Army; he was a war hero," Sterling said.

"Boy, I'd like to hear that story sometime," I said.

Sterling nodded somberly and resumed devouring his pizza. The conversation became somewhat muted as everyone ate. It wasn't until the boys left the table to go back for seconds that Al explained the fate of her late husband.

"He was a career soldier. He was in a Special Forces Unit and he thought he had the world by the tail. Unfortunately, he was killed during his second tour in Afghanistan."

"Oh, how long ago?"

"Going on three years now," she said. I saw a hint of sadness, but she covered it quickly. "The first year was tough, but we've adjusted."

"That's good." I had no idea what else to say, so instead, I ate another slice. The boys came back with two new plates stacked. My eyebrows arched.

"Oh, Lord, if I ate as much as you guys, I'd weigh four hundred pounds."

"They could eat all day and not gain a pound," Al said.

"You guys have to be physically active. Do you two play any sports?" I asked.

"Soccer and golf," both of them said in unison.

"Ah, I'm no good at soccer, but I enjoy golf. Maybe we can play a round sometime," I said.

"Sure, but you better be good or we'll kick your ass," Steffen said with the grin of a typical cocky teenager.

We talked some more while we ate, and afterward, I walked with them to their car, a pearl white Nissan Murano. The two boys got into the car without asking, giving their mother a slight amount of privacy with me.

"Did you have a good time?" she asked with a hopeful smile.

"I did," I answered. "We'll have to do it again."

"What did you have in mind?" she asked.

I was no dummy. She was ready for another date. A real date.

"How about something this Friday?"

She instantly shook her head. "I have to work Friday, what about Saturday?"

We agreed on Saturday and she told me to plan something nice. I had no idea what would be nice in her eyes. To me, a nice evening was a Nicaraguan blend cigar and a single malt, preferably one that was several years old. I'd have to get Anna to suggest something.

CHAPTER 14

Reuben Chandler's official title was Special Agent in Charge of the FBI's Nashville office. We'd met under nefarious circumstances when one of his agents had gone rogue, murdered my wife, murdered at least two other people, and later attempted to murder me.

He arrived promptly at nine and he had company with him. When my driveway sensor activated, I walked outside and waited on them. Three people exited his Ford Explorer, which looked a lot like mine, except his was black with dark-tinted windows. Mine was the platinum model and blue in color. Reuben walked over with an outstretched hand.

"Good morning," I said.

"Good morning, Thomas," he replied. He had not changed much since the first time I had met him. He was in his fifties, salt-and-pepper hair he kept short, and only a slight hint of a middle-aged paunch peeking out from under his starched white shirt.

He motioned at the other two people with him. "I believe you know Agent Meeks with the TBI, and this is Special Agent Juanita Stainback."

I shook hands with both of them. Special Agent Stainback was an attractive black woman in her early thirties, and even though she was wearing a conservative cut outfit, she had broad shoulders and her skirt revealed muscular calves. She gave an indecipherable, almost taunting smile as she gripped my hand tighter than most grown men were capable of. I got the impression she was an avid tennis player. I saw Reuben looking over at my Explorer.

"Is that new?" he asked.

"Yeah, I bought it recently."

He nodded toward his own Explorer. "It's a couple of years old now. I've put over a hundred thousand miles on it already, but it still runs great. You made a good purchase."

I already knew that, but I nodded in agreement. He was making small talk, delaying telling me the reason for the visit. But the presence of Agent Meeks told me exactly why they were here. It was all about Jason Belew. I gestured toward the door.

"If you all would like to come inside, I have a pot of coffee brewing."

They followed me to my kitchen table and sat. I played the dutiful host and poured them each a cup. The men took it black, but Special Agent Stainback liked hers with plenty of sugar and cream. Once everyone was taken care of, I sat and started it off.

"I can't help but notice Detective Brannigan is not with us," I observed.

"He does not need to be a part of this meeting," Special Agent Stainback said. Her tone was snippy and not altogether friendly. I think pugnacious would be a good word to describe her attitude.

I glanced over at Reuben. He met my stare but said nothing.

"I'm having a feeling of déjà vu," I said. Before he responded, I explained it to the other two.

"Not too long ago, back last summer, I was enjoying a cup of coffee, much like I am right now, when Reuben and three of his agents showed up with a search warrant. Little did he know, one of the agents with him was dirty, and had even committed a couple of murders."

They pivoted their heads in unison and stared at Reuben. He set his cup down and cleared his throat.

"That is unfortunately true." He then focused on me. "I'd like to think we've resolved our differences in that matter, Thomas."

I took a slow sip of coffee before responding. "I'd like to think so as well. So, what's on your mind, Reuben?"

"Candy is Agent Stainback's confidential informant," Reuben revealed.

"Interesting," I said.

"She and another agent have been working a case for several months now that is of a highly sensitive nature. In fact, it has international dimensions."

"International, huh?"

"Yes, and Candy's involvement is vital in the successful prosecution of the case," Stainback declared.

"What kind of case?" I asked.

"That's on a need-to-know basis," Stainback said.

"Interesting," I said again. "The inference is, you believe your case supersedes a murder, would that be correct?"

"You'd be correct," she replied. She kept the same tone when speaking to me. I'm not sure I liked that.

"We're here as a professional courtesy and I'm here as a friend," Reuben said. "Special Agent Stainback's case has reached a critical stage and her team is extremely close to obtaining the necessary evidence to allow her to obtain indictments. It is imperative the investigation not be compromised."

"And you believe a murder investigation would compromise said investigation," I stated.

"If you're referring to the young man found in the railroad boxcar, it has not yet been classified as a murder," Special Agent Stainback said.

"Incorrect," I retorted. "The cause of death was a crushed throat due to blunt force trauma. He was murdered."

"How do you know that?" she asked in surprise.

"That's on a need-to-know," I answered. In fact, all it took was a phone call to my friend, Doctor Holly Gross. She told me everything, but I wasn't going to tell them that.

The agent arched an eyebrow at me. Reuben looked sour. Agent Meeks looked uncomfortable. When he saw me staring at him, he shrugged his shoulders. He'd been ordered to ceded authority to the Feds, that's what he was tacitly telling me.

"I've already received my orders," he said, confirming what I was thinking.

Yep, submission. Kowtowing. Dropping your drawers and bending over. Any of those expressions would apply.

"The investigation of the murder of Jason Belew has been terminated, would that be correct?"

"It's temporarily on hold," Reuben said. "Once Agent Stainback's investigation reaches a point where there is enough evidence to secure indictments, the murder investigation can be reactivated."

I made pointed eye contact with each of them. It was obvious the decision had been made and my input was neither needed nor desired. I was being told to stand down. I finished my coffee and stood.

"I appreciate your meeting with me, Reuben. Detective Meeks. Special Agent Stainback, it was a pleasure to meet you, I guess."

I motioned them toward the door. I'm not sure they cared for me pushing them out, but they did not argue. Reuben waited until they were standing at their government car before speaking.

"So, do we have an agreement?" he asked.

"I didn't say that," I replied.

Special Agent Stainback glowered and started to say something. I think she was going to give me the standard, don't mess with the FBI threat, but Reuben cut her off with a look. She remained silent, but that did not stop her from giving me the stink-eye. I stared back pointedly.

"I've no doubt you have an important investigation going on, but to me, nothing usurps the investigation of a murder. Often times, we, or should I say law enforcement, are the only voice for a murder victim. You three should think long and hard about that."

I had more to say, but my phone pinged, soon followed by a rollback coming down the drive. It was Bubba, and he had the old Cadillac tied down on the back. He grinned as he drove up.

"Hoss, this is a good one!" he shouted over the noise of the wrecker's loud exhaust. He gave a grin and a thumbs-up and drove around my house to the shop in back.

"What was that, an old Cadillac?" Agent Meeks asked.

"Yeah, a Coup LaSalle," I answered.

"It looks like a piece of junk," Agent Stainback remarked.

I glanced at her. She was still giving me the stink-eye and I was getting tired of her attitude.

"Thomas restores old cars as a hobby," Reuben said. "He has a beautiful Cadillac and Ford Mustang parked in back."

I got the impression Reuben thought if he made a few compliments, I'd concede to their request. Yeah, fat chance.

"I would appreciate your professional courtesy on this one, Thomas," he said.

"You know, all of this reminds me of a time when I worked for Metro as a real detective. A man who worked on Music Row was shot to death as he was walking to his car one night. At first, we suspected it was a robbery attempt gone bad because this man had no enemies, no criminal record, didn't do or sell drugs, none of that stuff.

"It took a lot of investigative work, but we were able to determine it was a professional hit. You see, the victim was working with the FBI to expose payola in the record industry. In the ensuing investigation, we were able to identify a suspect." I glanced over at Meeks. "It goes without saying, we were working closely with the FBI on this case. After all, the victim was a confidential informant for them."

Meeks nodded in understanding. I kept going with it.

"One would think the Feds would go above and beyond in assisting with the case, but no. They offered nothing more than lip service. It took a little over a year before we found the suspect. He was working as a pit boss in a Vegas casino."

I waved a finger. "Now, here is where it got downright weird. The Fibs called for a sit-down and advised us the suspect was working as an informant and he was going to help them blow the lid off of a major organized crime outfit. To arrest him for a piddly murder would compromise the case and all they wanted was for us to delay the arrest until they gave the go-ahead. They were able to convince the chief of this nonsense and he agreed.

"Five years went by. By then, the primary detective had retired and the case was handed off to my buddy. He attempted to contact the FBI and get a status update, but he was stonewalled. So, he obtained an indictment and the Vegas cops had the suspect in custody within two hours. One of the Fibs called Percy a few days after the arrest to express his outrage."

I did not bother telling them Percy invited the agent to a private meeting whereupon they could settle it one way or another. The not-so-special agent hung up on Percy, never to be seen or heard from again. I gestured at Reuben.

"Tell me, what do you think my opinion is of professional courtesy when it concerns the FBI?"

Reuben gave a contrite nod and after a few more meaningless things were said, they bid their goodbyes and left.

After watching them disappear down the drive, I walked around to the back and watched Bubba unload the Cadi. We got it moved into the shop without much trouble and chitchatted about the car. Bubba expressed an interest in helping me restore it, but only if I supplied the beer.

"Hey, I know I said it before, but thanks again for the help with my nephew," he said.

"Is he doing okay?"

"Yep, them boys don't even look at him anymore," he said with a chuckle. "They first told everyone they'd gotten jumped by a gang, but when the other kids at the bus stop told the real story, they shut up and don't talk about it."

I nodded. "Good."

A month ago, Bubba told me about his nephew, a special needs kid. It was the same old story, a couple of boys did not like him because of his disability and started bullying him.

"Nobody wants to do anything," Bubba had said. "I talked to the principal and she said since it wasn't happening on school property, her hands were tied. The cops said without eyewitnesses, there wasn't much they could do. Yesterday, the two boys took turns kicking him in the nut sack. I'd take care of them myself, but I'm still on parole."

Bubba asked if there was anything I could do. I thought about it and then called my old friend who ran a boxing club off Jefferson Street. He hooked me up with a sixteen-year-old who had won the golden gloves in the 135-pound division. I dropped the kid off a block down from the bus stop where all of the bullying was happening and watched in awe as that skinny kid walked up and beat the hell out of the two bullies. He then told him Bubba's nephew was under his protection. The two punks got the message.

After Bubba left, I fired up a fresh cigar and gave Ronald a call. When he answered, I told him of the visit by Reuben Chandler and company and the ensuing discussion.

"It may be nothing but be sure to erase any digital footprint of your search of Candy-Man," I instructed. Ronald responded with a scoff.

"Already done," he said. "The only thing left is on your phone. I showed you the app to shred the data. Do you think they'll do something to you?"

"I'm not sure, but anything's possible," I said.

"Do you want me to do some snooping and see exactly what they're investigating?" he asked. "I can do that."

"Tempting, but too risky right now," I said.

"Okay. If you change your mind, let me know."

"What're you doing today?" I asked. "You want to come over and hang out? I just got that car I told you about. You can help me get started on it."

"Um, well, I got some things I'm doing on my computers and I need to keep a close eye on them."

"No worries, buddy. I'll talk to you later."

I smiled to myself. Getting Ronald out of the house was like trying to win an ass-kicking contest and you only had one leg. I changed into some grungy clothes and began working on the Coup LaSalle.

I started by putting it on jack stands and removing the tires. The rims had a little rust, but were still in good shape. I grabbed a notepad, jotted down the tire size, and then began a more thorough inspection, taking notes of everything that needed fixing. Eventually, I finished both my cigar and my notes. The car was old and needed a lot of work. I sat at my workbench and started figuring a rough estimation of how much it would cost. Not counting labor, it was going to be a little bit expensive. After all, finding parts for a car that was manufactured in the thirties were going to be hard to find and would not be cheap.

It was time to make a decision. Did I want to do a full restore or simply get it running and put it up for sale? I kept weighing the pros and cons, but could not reach a decision. My thoughts wandered to other projects I had in mind for the place. I was up watching TV late one night and there was a program where the main character had himself a Japanese Zen garden. It gave me the idea to build one behind my house where there were two big old shag bark hickory trees. I also wanted to remodel my shop and I'd also toyed with the idea of expanding the back of my house and creating a proper office.

I got a big glass of water and was slurping it down when my phone rang. It was Anna.

"What's happening, hot stuff?" I asked with a heavy accent.

"Um, let me think… Sixteen Candles, right?"

"Excellent," I said. It was a game we frequently played. I'd quote a line from a movie and she'd try to guess the movie's title.

"Guess what I'm doing?" she asked, which was the other game she liked to play. She'd never simply be direct and tell me what she was doing. Instead, she'd always phrase it in a guess.

"Let me think," I said, mimicking her. "Someone has convinced you that essential oils will cure everything, so you bought a lifetime supply."

She laughed. "Nope, but that's a good one. I've been at Ms. Braxton's. We've been working on her ancestor tree."

I started to ask her if she was logging down the billable hours, but Anna was funny about Ms. Braxton, so I let it go.

"She took me to Belle Meade Country Club for lunch."

"Oh, that's nice," I said.

"Yeah, and she introduced me to several people and told them what I did. She might have drummed up some business for us."

I nodded. Getting business from people who were members of the oldest, most prestigious country club in Nashville was a good thing.

"Do we have anything going on tomorrow?" she asked.

I told her about some people I wanted to question in regards to the Belew case and she wanted me to go with her to research some church records.

I refilled my glass of water and went back to work on the old LaSalle.

CHAPTER 15

Anna rode with me to a part of town known as Woodbine and turned onto a side street off of Nolensville Pike into a commercial area. The Juggernaut was nestled between a garden supply company and a cabinet shop.

"The Juggernaut?" Anna questioned. "Seems like an odd name for a gym."

"It's a martial arts dojo," I corrected. "The owner was known as The Juggernaut back when he fought professionally."

"Oh," Anna said. "I guess that makes sense. What does it mean?"

"A juggernaut is an overwhelming, unstoppable force. So, I'd say it's an appropriate moniker for the martial arts world."

There was no reception room or lobby, the entry doors leading directly into the workout area. There was a boxing ring, no octagon, but lots of mats, punching bags of various sizes, and a decent assortment of free weights and kettlebells on the far end. A man about my age watched me walk in. He was showing some younger students the basics of the mount and guard positions. When he saw us, he partnered them up and walked over to us.

"Hello, can I help you?" he asked.

He was wearing a simple blue Gi, but there was no mistaking the well-worn black belt with a couple of narrow, horizontal red stripes on the end. I introduced myself.

"I'm Dan Sousa, this is my dojo," he replied in an affable tone. "What can I do for you?"

"I'm hoping I could talk to you about Jason Belew."

He eyed me curiously. "I've already spoken to a detective about him," he said.

"That would be Detective Walter Brannigan with the sheriff's department down in Manchester," I surmised.

"Yes, that's right."

"I understand and you probably feel this is unnecessary, but allow me to explain. I'm a private investigator hired by Jason's brother. I guess you could say I am conducting an independent investigation, so I hope I can ask you a few questions, if you don't mind."

"Yeah, sure, no problem," he said. "What would you like to know?"

"What was your opinion of him?" I asked.

"He was a good kid. He'd been a student for four years. He worked here part-time and I think he was about to get a job delivering pizza."

"Were you two friends?"

"I was his sensei, but yeah, I'd say we were friends too. We spent a lot of hours here together and he was a frequent guest at my home. My wife thought he was a great kid."

"Was there anything he confided in you about? Did he have any kind of trouble with anyone?"

He glanced down at the floor a moment before giving me a plain stare. "What has his brother said to you?"

"He told me Jason recently came out and that he caught some flack about it from some of his friends who train here."

"Yes, that's true. I had a couple of knuckleheads who were making a few snide remarks, but I squared them away. Jason had no problems after that. Besides, Jason would have wiped the mat with either of them."

"Yeah, how was his skill level?"

"Are you familiar with Brazilian Jiu-Jitsu?" he asked.

"A little. When I was younger, I did some training, but honestly, I've not kept up with it. Any skills I might've had are definitely rusty."

I had a flashback to the night I was attacked by Officer Ben Smith. I'd put up a decent fight, but my rusty skills and drunkenness almost got me killed.

"He was a legitimate blue belt," Dan said. "A blue belt is the second rank, which basically means he was a novice, but more skilled than a beginner. In order to be awarded a blue belt in my school, you have to be able to have at least two strong escapes from the top mount, side mount, and back mount, and your technique in passing the guard must be strong. Jason was proficient in all of these." He paused and smiled slightly, as if recalling a pleasant memory of him.

"Jason was athletic and had a good head on his shoulders. If he had continued with his training, he would have advanced well ahead of the curve."

"Did he compete?" I asked.

"Only in some amateur stuff. His record was five and one. It would have been six wins but got disqualified for performing a heel hook. It was an illegal move in that particular tournament."

"Let me ask you, in your opinion, would any of his opponents held a grudge?"

"I wouldn't think so. Jason was honorable. All of his wins were by submissions. When his opponent tapped out, he would immediately release the hold. And he wasn't a trash talker either. Like I said, he was a good kid."

"Did you know about this so-called underground fight he went to back in February?"

"The one in Manchester, right?" he asked. I nodded. "Yeah, I'd heard about it, but I've never liked them."

"Why not?" I asked.

"They aren't sanctioned, which means no drug tests, refs that may or may not know what they're doing and prone to taking a bribe, no medical personnel on hand, cheating, the list goes on. You get the idea. I told Jason all of this, but he wanted to go see it. I guess it's the allure of something taboo that makes kids want to do it even more."

I nodded thoughtfully and after a moment, I came to a decision. "What I'm about to say isn't public knowledge and I'd like for you to keep it under your hat."

His focus, which was already sharp, became even more so. "Of course."

"The cause of his death was a crushed throat. It wasn't a compression injury, like a choke hold, but blunt force trauma. And, Jason did not have any other injuries which would have been consistent with a fight. No skinned knuckles, nothing like that. What are your thoughts of how someone could do that to him?"

Sensei Sousa crossed his arms and one of his hands found his chin. He rubbed it thoughtfully before responding.

"Alright, it could have been a sucker punch, but Jason had good reflexes and he didn't do any kind of drugs or alcohol. So, if it was a sucker punch, whoever did it had to be damn fast, and it had to be one hell of a punch. Or kick."

"That'd have to be a mighty fast kick, wouldn't it?" I asked.

Sensei Sousa gave a slight smile, looked around, and called out. "Shelly, come here a minute, would you?"

A teenage girl in pigtails and braces came bounding over and looked at Sensei Sousa expectantly.

"This is Shelly," he said and led the three of us over to some striking dummies.

"Show these two your best spinning back kick," he said and pointed to one of the dummies.

Shelly grinned, squared off, spun, and landed her heel squarely on the striking dummy's chin. It struck with a loud thud and the dummy was knocked backward several feet. For a little girl, she was damn fast.

"Wow," Anna said in amazement.

I agreed. Shelly grinned again and curtsied before skipping back to her workout buddies. Sensei Sousa had a smug grin of his own.

"She's my niece," he said and then gestured to the dummy. "In answer to your question, someone fast, like Shelly, could've surprised Jason and landed a strike like a spinning back kick and crushed his throat. If he was not suspecting it, that is. If Jason knew he was going to be attacked, he was good enough to prevent it from happening, unless his opponent was extremely skilled."

I nodded. "Something tells me you have that level of skill."

He acknowledged the compliment and pointed to the far side of the dojo where there was a wall adorned with fight pictures and awards. Even from where we were standing, I could see a lot of the pictures were of Sensei Sousa raising his arms in victory.

"Yeah, I was pretty good, back in the day, but that was before a motorcycle wreck busted up my legs. Now, I train other people and run a janitorial service to pay the bills."

"What about Benny Newton or Charlie Thomas? Are they members here?" I asked.

"They are, or they were. Both of them are behind on their dues, and I know what you're about to ask next. Neither one of them is skilled enough to take Jason in a fight. If one of them did it, it'd have to have been a lucky punch. A very lucky punch." He shook his head. "Nope, I don't see it happening, not with those two. Not even if they ganged up on him."

"That girl is good," Anna said after we'd left.

"Yes, she is," I agreed.

"Did Mister Sousa help you any?"

"I'm not sure," I said. "Jason's manner of death is an important clue. I'm fairly certain it eliminates several people who might otherwise be considered suspects."

"Like his two friends," Anna surmised.

"Yeah, but I'm still stuck. I still don't know if there are any eyewitnesses and there is virtually no physical evidence." I emitted a long sigh. "Okay, let's get on your case. Where to?"

"New Zion Baptist Church in Franklin. I've got the directions on my phone," she said. "Oh, and can I drive?" she asked sweetly.

I grunted. She had encouraged me to take the Mustang this morning and now I knew why. I handed her the keys and got in the passenger side. She put it in gear and took off. Soon, we were in Williamson County and whatever navigator app she had led us to a smaller, but pleasant-looking church on Mack Hatcher Parkway.

Reverend Cornelius Hollinsworth greeted us at the front of the apse like he was greeting new members of his congregation. He was a bald, heavyset man in his sixties with an amiable smile and wearing a white suit with padding in the shoulders to offset his abundant waistline.

"Welcome to the New Zion Baptist Church," he greeted.

We made our introductions, and much to my delight, he offered us fresh coffee.

"So, you're researching your ancestry," he said to Anna while making no attempt to be subtle at staring at her breasts. In all fairness to the good reverend, Anna was wearing a light blue V-neck shirt which was showing off her cleavage. It's not like she was well endowed, but they were definitely perky and often received a lot of attention.

"Not mine personally," she said, crossing her arms. "I've been hired to research a client's ancestors."

"Ah, I see. Well then, let's get started," Reverend Hollinsworth said with a broad smile. He led the two of us to the back of the church, down a set of stairs, and into a basement that looked more like a small library than the basement of a country church. The walls were neatly lined with shelves of ledgers and old books, and the far wall contained several file cabinets.

"The first white settlers moved into Williamson County about 1798 or so. The white folks had slaves, of course, so the community had its share of African Americans. Eventually, the black folks were allowed to worship the Lord. This is the oldest surviving African-American church around these parts." He waved a hand at all of the shelves.

"We have ledgers from other old churches that are now defunct. Baptismal records, family Bibles, you name it. So, where do we start, young lady?"

Anna retrieved an A4 pad out of her knapsack and turned to the appropriate page. "The Carmike family," she said. "Herman Carmike is supposed to be one of the first settlers in Franklin in 1800. The family eventually created a plantation on Columbia Pike."

Reverend Hollinsworth cupped his chin with a hand, deep in thought. He slowly moved his eyes from shelf to shelf before absently pointing.

"Could be, could be," he mumbled as he walked to the shelf and began scanning the books. After a moment, he tapped a ledger. Pulling it out, he walked over to the conference table and sat. Opening the ledger, he thumbed through several pages, and then motioned for us to sit with him.

"This is a ledger written by Reverend Hezekiah Smith," he stated. "He was the pastor of the Hebron Baptist Church for over fifty years, between 1812 until shortly after the war broke out. He was killed in 1862."

"Killed?" Anna asked

"Murdered," Reverend Hollinsworth said matter-of-factly. "I have a copy of the newspaper article around here somewhere. It speculates the reverend was killed because he was too friendly with the slave population and he was a Yankee sympathizer."

"Was anybody ever arrested?" I asked.

Reverend Hollinsworth gave a thoughtful frown. "Not that I am aware of. Anyway, Reverend Smith kept good records, and as you can see, his penmanship is eloquent. People just don't write that way anymore. He kept a yearly list of the members of his congregation, along with a record of all of the marriages and baptisms he performed."

The sound of a ringing doorbell interrupted him. "That's somebody upstairs," he said. "You folks help yourselves; I'll be back down in a few."

"I better get started," Anna said. She sat at the table with lithesome ease, arranged her notepad, and started reading from the ledger. I browsed the shelves of books. I spotted a ledger dated 1862 and saw it was a collection of old newspaper clippings. Curious, I pulled it out and sat across from Anna.

There were a few articles about local events, events in Nashville, and the state of the war. The local events gave a little bit of an insight of the community of that era, which was interesting. I read for several minutes before one particular article caught my eye.

"Hey, I found the article Hollinsworth was talking about," I said to Anna. She looked up.

"What, the one about that old preacher getting murdered?"

"Yep, Hezekiah Smith," I replied and began reading.

The article was dated October 13th, 1862. It described how the reverend was found the evening of the 12th, behind the pulpit of his church with his head stove-in by an unknown blunt object. The newspaper's journalist noted that although the reverend was colored, he was nevertheless beloved in the community. He speculated the murderer was an outsider, possibly an inebriated idler. It then went on to describe the reverend's life. He was one of thirteen children, all of whom had died off of childhood diseases. He was the slave of Joseph Smith, who owned a plantation in North Carolina. Upon the death of Joseph, the widow Smith granted all of her slaves their freedom. Somehow, Hezekiah made it to Franklin, Tennessee and became a preacher.

"The man overcame a lot of adversity during his life," I commented.

"Yes, he did, up until somebody bashed his head in," Reverend Hollinsworth said. He had come back downstairs and had quietly taken a seat at the table. "But that's okay, he was a good man and he's with Jesus now."

"Why do you think he was murdered?" I asked him.

"I'm glad you asked," he replied and stood. He walked over to the far end of the room and retrieved a plain cardboard box off of a shelf and walked it back to the table. Sitting, he opened the top and gingerly pulled out an old, well-worn leather book.

"What do you have there?" I asked.

Reverend Hollinsworth smiled broadly. "This is one of my most treasured possessions. It is my great-great grandmother's diary. Back when she was alive, the notion of an African-American woman being able to read, write, and work her numbers was unheard of. When she was a child, the mistress of the house where she was a slave took a liking to her and taught her. Later in life, she worked as a clerk for a businessman who was also her lover." He patted the book tenderly.

"Now, I'm reluctant to open it up because the pages are very brittle, but I've read it almost as many times as I've read my Bible. As you might assume, the colored community of Franklin was quite close and they knew everything about each other, and, they knew about the goings on of the affluent whites in the community. She wrote a passage about Reverend Smith's murder and said everyone knew he was killed because he married two white kids. And, even more important, the teenage white girl had a bastard child."

Anna's jaw dropped open. "You're kidding."

Reverend Hollinsworth continued smiling. "I kid you not. Apparently, the father of the child had gone off to war and came home to marry her. She wrote a couple of paragraphs about it."

I cleared my throat. "Reverend, would it be possible to take some photographs of those paragraphs?"

It took some cajoling, but he finally agreed. Unfortunately, the reverend was right; the paper and fading ink caused the writing to become almost illegible.

"I've got an idea," I said and hustled out to my car. Returning with my camera kit, I set up a tripod and then pulled out a couple of alternative light sources, along with the corresponding lens filters.

"What in the world are you doing?" Reverend Hollinsworth asked.

"With an old document like this, you have to manipulate the light source in order to bring out the writing. I'm going to start with infrared light and a contrasting color lens filter. That should do the trick, but if it doesn't, I've got an ultraviolet light as well."

"Interesting," Reverend Hollinsworth said. "Will the lighting damage the paper?"

"Short-term exposure will not," I said.

He watched attentively as I manipulated the f-stops and shutter speeds until I obtained some fairly clear photographs of the two pages in question. We took turns looking at my work on the camera's view screen.

"Man, that's good stuff," the reverend said and then I could see a gleam in his eye. "Would you mind doing this with the entire book? I could probably pay you, if you don't charge too much."

I thought about it for a moment. It would be a kind gesture, and I'd have a copy of the diary, which was a nice piece of history.

"I believe I can. I'm already set up and dialed in to get good pictures. If you help Anna with her research, I think I can get the entire diary photographed in a couple of hours. And, I wouldn't think of charging you."

The reverend's grin became a full-fledged beaming smile. "You've got a deal, Mister Ironcutter."

After leaving the church, we ate lunch at an overpriced bistro near downtown Franklin before heading over to the Williamson County Archives, which was located in a government brick building on West Main Street, which coincidentally was also Route 31, but closer into downtown Franklin.

Anna and I walked to the front counter and waited while an elderly lady engaged in a telephone conversation with someone who was decidedly a relative. We could not help but overhear her talking about a food recipe and an upcoming birthday party. The conversation lasted five agonizingly long minutes before she finally hung up. She pointedly looked at some papers on her desk, and only after a long ten seconds she looked up and acknowledged our presence with undisguised irritation.

"Yes?"

"Good morning," I said. "We are conducting some research and we'll need to review records from 1840 until 1865."

"All of them?" she asked with a frown.

"Great question, no. We'll be researching deeds and tax records only for the property on the eastern side of Columbia Highway, specifically between Henpeck Lane and Snowbird Hollow Road."

"They are not organized in that fashion," she said with a huff.

"Well then, we'll need to take a look at all of them. We'll also need to research wills and marriage licenses for the same time period."

She scowled at us over the top of her bifocals before turning her back on us and disappearing through a doorway. Anna looked at me.

"Where did she go? Did she leave?" she asked.

"I'm not sure. Let's wait and find out."

That's what we did. Wait. Anna was antsy but I reminded her that a good PI had patience. She rolled her eyes. At the ten-minute mark, a lady walked in the door, said hello, and looked around in puzzlement.

"Is Ms. Welchance here?" she asked.

"She stepped out," I said, assuming Ms. Welchance was the sourpuss who waited on us. "I'm not sure when she'll be back."

The lady was confused, but as soon as I said it, Ms. Welchance walked back in carrying several old ledger books. They looked cumbersome and heavy, and she made a point of loudly dropping them onto the Formica counter. Dust exploded from them like they were spewing out pollen.

"These are not to leave this office, nor are you to tear out any pages. If you do that, I'll have you arrested."

"You won't have to worry about that, ma'am," I said.

She eyed me over her bifocals a moment and then continued. "When you're finished with these, I'll get the rest of the ledgers. If you need copies, they will be a dollar a page. Checks are not accepted."

She did not wait for a response and turned her attention to the woman who had walked in. I shrugged at Anna and handed her one of the ledgers.

"Let's get started," I said.

It took us the rest of the day. When we found something, one of us would snap a picture with our phone and then make notes. It was tedious, but we found a stopping point shortly before closing time.

"We're all finished here," I said.

She looked up from her word search puzzle, stood, and walked over.

"Thank you for your help," I added.

She had not done much of anything, but it didn't hurt to be nice. After all, one or both of us might need to do some more research here one day.

She looked over the ledgers, and then looked at our notepads, possibly searching for ripped out ledger pages.

"Don't you need any copies?" she asked.

"No, ma'am, we took pictures of everything we need."

I didn't bother telling her there was an app that could convert a photograph into a portable document file. I doubt she would have understood. Instead, she silently grabbed a couple of the ledgers, and began walking them back to the file room, or wherever they were stored.

"Have a nice day," I said as we walked out. Anna snickered.

CHAPTER 16

The afternoon sun was pleasant. I pointed to a decorative wrought iron picnic table.

"Let's sit for a few and go over what we have," I suggested. Anna was agreeable and led the way. She opened up her notepad and started.

"Alright. Penelope Carmike was born in Williamson County in March of 1849. It appears she lived on the family homestead on Columbia Highway all of her life. She had three siblings, all brothers. All of them died during the Civil War. Only one of them was married, but none of them had children that survived into adulthood." She frowned. "Was that common back then?"

"I'm afraid so. Childhood diseases and other factors caused the mortality rate to be rather high back in those times," I said.

Anna frowned in thought a moment before continuing. "So, Ms. Braxton's family lineage comes directly from Penelope and Chester's child," she said.

I reached for her spiral notebook and turned a couple of pages. "So, the child's name was Claire Carmike. She grew up in Williamson County, married, and had a passel of children."

"Claire was Ms. Braxton's grandmother," I said. "I wonder why she was so fixated on Penelope in particular? It must be because of Chester Bond. There's some kind of connection there she wants us to find, but she's not telling us."

Anna ran a hand through her hair. "Yeah, and we don't have jack-shit on him. Our report is going to look weak if we don't find out more about Chester." She paused and sighed. "Let's get out of here."

We gathered up our stuff and walked to the parking lot. A couple of young men gave Anna the once over as we walked past; she pretended not to notice.

"I want to drive," she said once we got to the car.

I handed her the keys and soon we were peeling rubber out of the parking lot. I wondered if she did it to impress those two men.

"I love this car," she exclaimed.

"Yeah, well if you get pulled over by a local cop, it's on you."

She giggled like a schoolgirl as she sped down the road. As soon as she entered the on-ramp to the interstate, she gunned it. The throaty growl of the exhaust was almost like a dare and in no time she had it up to a hundred.

"The exit is up ahead, slow it down," I chided.

"This car is the shit," she exclaimed with a girlish grin as she cut across three lanes and exited the interstate. She finally decided to slow for the red light, and then she glanced over at me, noting the disapproving expression on my face.

"What?" she asked.

"Oh, nothing," I said.

"No, tell me," she insisted.

"I just think you should be more ladylike with your language, that's all."

"Oh, Thomas," she drawled and gunned it when the light turned green.

"You are who you are," I said. "But, if you're going to hang around Ms. Braxton and her highbrow cronies, you should work on your savior faire."

"Savior faire, acting appropriately in social situations. You've used that phrase on me before," she said.

"I have?"

"Yes."

I had no response, so sat in silence while she weaved through traffic and arrived at Mick's Place in record time. When Anna parked, she looked over at me.

"You wanted to come here, right?"

"Sure. Now let her idle a minute or two. You rode her pretty hard."

She gave a mischievous grin. "I bet all the women tell you that."

I gave her the eye but couldn't keep it in and laughed. I watched the temperature gauge as she fished a brush out of her purse and began straightening her hair. She'd let it grow long over the winter, but recently got about four inches chopped off and highlights added. Now, her sorrel brown hair had that sun-kissed look. She was a beautiful young woman.

"Say, where's William been lately?" I asked.

Her grin vanished and for a micro-second, I saw a flash of pain.

"Nowhere," she replied, jammed her brush back into her purse, and shut the car off.

It was obvious something was bothering her but I didn't push it. She'd tell me when she was ready. We walked in and the bar was crowded with the regulars. We said hello to everyone and bellied up to the bar.

"What are you two drinking this evening?" Mick asked.

"Nashville Lager for me," I said.

Mick nodded and looked at Anna. She seemed preoccupied about something and Mick had to ask her again.

"What? Oh, no. I'm not in the mood for beer. I'll be right back."

And with that, she bounced off of the stool and was peeling out of the parking lot a moment later.

"What'd you do, dumbass?" Mick asked as he set my beer in front of me, implying I'd committed some kind of egregious act. I answered with a shrug and wondered if I was going to be Ubering home later.

But, not to worry, she zoomed back into the parking lot ten minutes later. Exiting the Mustang, she breezed in the door with purposeful steps, carrying a bottle hidden in a brown paper bag and something else in a Delta Express plastic bag. She set them both on the bar in front of Mick. He looked in the bags and nodded thoughtfully. He then set them both under the bar out of eyesight of nosy people who might be inclined to snitch to the ABC.

"How do you want it?" he asked.

"How do you think?" she retorted.

Mick smirked, filled a glass with ice, and held it under the counter as he poured the unknown contents. After a moment, he emerged with what looked like a cosmopolitan; vodka and cranberry juice. Anna took it with a nod of thanks. She saw me looking and waved the glass at me.

"High in vitamin C. More nutritious than beer and less fattening. Plus, it's good for the bladder."

"Yeah, okay," I said, and made a mental note to temper my beer consumption because I had no doubt I was the one who would be driving home. Apparently, while I was thinking all of this, I had asked a question.

"And, in answer to your question, no. I am not going out with William tonight. We are officially broken up." She took a long drink before speaking again. "And since I don't know how to be ladylike, not only am I officially single, I am damned single!"

The last part was loud enough to be heard by the entire bar. Everyone turned toward her, especially Wally, who looked like someone had stuck a finger up his ass and pushed his magic button. I watched out of the corner of my eye as Wally stood and tried to discretely pull his britches out of his butt crack. Succeeding, sort of, he casually sauntered over. When Anna looked up, he gave a broad, lurid grin.

"How are you two doing this evening?" he asked.

"Not bad, Wally," I replied. "How about yourself?"

He barely acknowledged me and focused on Anna. "How are you, beautiful?"

Anna responded by rolling her eyes and taking a big swallow. "Wally, Wally, Wally. The last time we spoke, you told me you were going to play golf on the old fart's golf tour."

"The senior's tour," he corrected. "Yes, I was."

"And yet, you're here. What happened, did you get cut already?" she asked.

Mick howled in raucous laughter, as did several of the other patrons. Wally's face was a strained smile and his cheeks started to redden.

"I did not get cut," he rejoined, heavily emphasizing the two words, 'did not.'

Anna snorted. "If you say so." More laughter.

Wally looked around in annoyance. "If all of you must know, I was ambushed by an old college rival."

Anna took a swallow of her drink, finishing it off. "Oh, this I've got to hear," she said and pushed her glass toward Mick for a refill.

Wally's wolfish grin reappeared. It was a familiar expression. Mick gave me one of those looks. We knew he was about to launch into yet another fanciful yarn. Anna stared with mock expectation.

"Well now, we had a contract all worked out. It was going to be a sweet deal. Seven figures," he said with a wink. "But then, Callaway hired a new CFO, that's a chief of financial operations for you people who have no business savvy." He made pointed eye contact with a couple of patrons for emphasis.

"So, what happened?" Mick asked with feigned interest.

"This guy played golf for Michigan. Well, as you all know, I'm an Ohio State alumnus and the two universities are major rivals. Back during that time, I crushed him in every tournament the two of us competed in. He did not take it well and has apparently held a grudge, even after all of these years. When he heard of my pending contract, he squashed the whole deal and attempted to sign me for a considerably less sum. Purely out of spite, of course. I flatly refused and informed them I would not, could not perform under the revised terms."

"Couldn't perform? I bet all the women say that about you," Anna said.

The regulars broke out in laughter again. Even some customers whom I've never seen before joined in. Anna smiled sweetly and took another long drink. The redness in Wally's cheeks intensified, but he wasn't ready to give up yet.

"Well, for your information, I'm currently in negotiations with Titleist. Once the numbers are hashed out, I will be signing on with them and dropping Callaway like yesterday's news."

Anna took another drink before speaking. "Allow me to quote the living legend, Mick O'Hara: it smells like horseshit to me."

This elicited another chorus of laughter. Wally's smug smile was fixed in place, but his brain finally realized he was striking out. He turned and walked back to his barstool, his shoulders stooped and his tail between his legs. I shook my head. Why in the world Wally thought a beautiful twenty-something woman would be interested in his old, fat ass was beyond me.

"So, what have you two been up to?" Mick asked.

"Research," Anna replied.

She drained her glass and held it out for a refill. Mick dutifully obliged.

"What kind of research?" he asked as he slid the glass over, but then pointed at it. "And slow down on that second one or I'll cut you off."

Anna smirked and grabbed the glass. "I've been hired to trace the family history of a prominent Nashville family."

"Oh, yeah? Have you made any progress?" Mick asked.

"Some," she said. "But there are some issues."

"Like what?" Mick asked.

"Did you know there was a big battle in Franklin?" Anna asked.

"Back during the Civil War, sure," Mick answered. He then pointed. "In fact, a couple of days later, they had another battle right over there where the interstate is now. If we were sitting here back in 1864, we probably could've watched the whole thing."

Anna took a long drink. "Yeah, well, I didn't know about it. It just goes to show you how stupid I am."

Mick looked surprised and then glanced at me. "I don't think you're stupid," he said.

"Oh, but I am," she retorted. "I don't know anything about the French and I don't know anything about the Civil War."

Mick glanced at me again. I shrugged, not knowing what the hell she was talking about. Anna made a sarcastic face.

"I bet William's an expert," she said, mostly to herself.

I was now getting an inkling of her current displeasure with William. I wanted to ask her about it, but there were too many nosy people in here listening, Mick being one of them, and her personal issues were nobody's business.

"How many of you fuckers, I mean, how many of you gentlemen are war experts?" she asked loudly enough so the whole bar could hear.

I groaned inwardly when I heard a bar stool squeak and the occupant stood. He had a broad grin on his face as he began sauntering over in much the same way Wally had done five minutes previous.

"Here we go," I muttered under my breath.

"This'll be good," Mick added.

It was going to be something alright. Ebbie was yet another regular; an old fart who was full of himself and liked everyone to know it. In his seventies, he was stick thin, looking like slabs of old bologna had been glued onto his skeleton. When he was a younger man, he was over six feet tall with a head full of brown hair. Now, he was slightly stoop-shouldered and mostly bald, but he had enormously furry eyebrows and enough hair growing out of his ears to knit a baby's blanket.

"Good afternoon, young lady," Ebbie said with a haughty air. "I believe I heard you asking if anyone here knew about the war between the states."

Anna stared in drunken amusement. "Would that be you?"

Ebbie smiled. "As Thomas can attest, I am a world-renowned expert of American History. If you have a question on the topic, I will undoubtedly have the answer."

Anna stared a moment longer at him before fixing her gaze on me.

"Anna, this is Professor Ebenezer Farquhar, but everybody calls him Ebbie. Currently, he is professor emeritus at Belmont University. And, yes. He is probably one of the top-rated authorities of American History."

Anna focused back on Ebbie and burst out in laughter. "Ebenezer Farquhar? What kind of name is that? Did your parents hate you or something?"

The bar patrons once again roared in laughter. Ebbie blushed, but he managed to maintain his composure.

"I was named after my great grandfather, but please call me Ebbie." He offered a smaller, hopeful smile, to which Anna returned.

"Alright, Ebbie, I do have a history question. It has to do with the city of Franklin during the war."

"Ask away," Ebbie said, his smile growing.

"Alright, here goes. Who is Chester Bond?"

Ebbie's smile turned to confusion. "Excuse me?"

"Who is Chester Bond?" Anna repeated.

Ebbie's confusion deepened. He looked to me for some kind of help. I shrugged.

"Chester was a Confederate soldier who apparently came from Williamson County," I added.

"He fought for the south," Anna added needlessly. Her words were slurring now. "He was listed as being born in Williamson County and he enlisted in 1861. I need to know what happened to him."

Ebbie frowned and shrugged. His smile had disappeared. "I'm sure I wouldn't know."

Anna made a mock pouting expression. "Oh, Ebbie, you were so close to getting a blowjob, but you blew it, no pun intended." She then burst out in an uncontrollable giggle at her own joke.

Ebbie was flustered. His face had turned a nice shade of crimson, much like Wally's had. He then patted me on the shoulder, as if to say, she's all yours, and then slinked back to his seat. Anna smiled at me sweetly and polished off her drink.

We left at eight. Although it was still early, Anna was starting to slur her words and when she'd hopped off of her bar stool to visit the lady's room, she lost her balance and fell on her ass. I waited for her to go to the restroom before telling Mick to cut her off.

"Okay, I think it's time to go home," I said when she'd returned.

She looked at me in confusion. "Are you sure?"

"Yeah, I'm pretty tired."

"Are you okay to drive?" she asked.

"I'm fine," I answered. If she had been paying attention, she would have known I'd only had two beers. She acquiesced and allowed me to guide her to the passenger door where I gently assisted her in sitting.

"You're going to feel like hell tomorrow," I remarked once I'd gotten in and started the Mustang.

"Yeah, well, so what?" she retorted.

I couldn't decide what the best course of action was at this point but decided to be nosy. "So, what happened between you and William?"

She pulled her head back in the window and turned to face me. She looked like a hot mess; her eyes were bloodshot and her hair was all tangled.

"Let me tell you what that so-and-so did to me. So, we go to a party that some of his friends hosted, and it's all of his law school buddies and their stuck-up, snotty wives."

"Okay," I said.

"Yeah, and like they made a point of talking all about the prestigious colleges they went to, even though none of them work."

"Um-hmm," I said as I drove. She kept talking.

"So, they figured out I haven't been to college and it became something of a cruel little game to them. They acted all nice and started talking about stuff like Greek philosophy or French literature. You know, crap that doesn't matter in the real world, and then they'd ask my opinion about something like, what do you think of Voltaire's position on the Catholic Church?"

She reached into her purse and pulled out a pack of cigarettes. I thought she'd been trying to quit, but alcohol often ruins good judgment and self-discipline. She lighted up and blew out a lung full of smoke.

"And then they brought up my previous employment and that's when it got even nastier. Do you know what William was doing while this passive-aggressive crap was taking place? Nothing. Not a damn thing. All he did was stand there, looking embarrassed because his girlfriend is so stupid and used to be a stripper."

"I'm sorry to hear that. Have you talked to him about it?"

She gave a disgusted scoff; the way women do when a man screws up.

"I tried, but he thinks he didn't do anything wrong." She turned and stared out of the passenger window, as if something out there in the night held an answer for her.

"I'm sorry to hear that. At some point, I'm sure he'll understand why that upset you."

"No. I'm done with him," she said in a voice barely above a whisper.

I glanced over. She was still staring out and I couldn't see her face. She reached up and wiped her face, which made me wonder if she was crying. She made it as far as my driveway before puking. I gave silent thanks she didn't do it in my car.

CHAPTER 17

I was sitting at the table enjoying a couple of buttered biscuits with my coffee when Anna emerged from her bedroom. She was wearing an oversized bathrobe and moved noticeably slower than normal. I guess I must have been smirking or something because she stared at me threateningly with puffy eyes and held up a finger.

"Not a word."

"I was merely going to say there is fresh-squeezed lemonade in the fridge and some ibuprofen sitting on the counter for you."

She nodded with pained gratefulness and washed down the pills before sitting at the table with me.

"Try out a buttered biscuit; it'll settle your stomach."

She groaned. "I can't eat anything right now."

"A long hot shower then. We have an appointment at ten."

She looked at me in confusion. "What kind of appointment?"

"With Doctor Holly Gross at the medical examiner's office," I said.

"Why?"

"Because they are possibly in possession of the remains of the late Chester Bond."

Anna's eyes widened and she began stammering. "Wait, what? How?"

I opened my laptop and turned it so she could see the screen, which had an old news article featured. The headline read: Treasure Hunters Find Skeletal Remains.

"I kept thinking about the research we did and thought something sounded familiar," I said and pointed to the screen. "The location where those skeletal remains were found is the same location where Esther Braxton's great-great grandparents had their homestead."

She stared at the screen and tried to focus. "So, who is it?"

"Chester Bond," I said. It took a second before she understood what I said and her eyes widened. Now I had her full attention. "Doctor Gross will explain everything. Now go get that shower."

She kept asking questions, but I shushed her and pointed toward her shower. She didn't like it, but dutifully shuffled off, her slippers sliding along the floor as she walked.

We arrived at the medical examiner's office promptly at ten. I'd not seen Holly in a few months. Back then, she had some work-related issues that had been extremely stressful. To use a pun, she looked like death warmed over. She was waiting for us in the lobby and looked like a totally different person. She'd put on weight and her skin had a healthy color to it. She greeted me with a warm smile and a hug. I made introductions.

"This is my business partner, Anna Davies. Anna, this is Doctor Holly Gross."

The two women said hello to each other and then we followed Holly through the security door to her office. The décor was the same, but there seemed to be more stacks of files. She pointed to two chairs while she retrieved a cardboard file box and placed it on an empty corner of her desk. She opened it up and pulled out a CD.

"This one is a bit of a mystery," she said and glanced at Anna. "Thomas said you may be able to provide some important information."

Anna's eyes widened as she looked at me. I gave her a wink.

"Well, um, we've found some historical archives with a little information, but it's not much," she said. "We first found a ledger entry of a marriage between Chester Bond and Penelope Carmike in October of 1862 by a Reverend Hezekiah Smith. What was unusual about this is Reverend Smith was an African American and not the pastor of the church the Carmike family regularly attended."

"Okay, I'm not a southern girl, is that unusual around here?" Holly asked.

"Not so much anymore," I said. "But back then, slavery and segregation were in full force. Reverend Smith was a free black man, but an African-American preacher marrying two white kids was not only unusual, it more than likely would have created an uproar in the community."

"I imagine the reverend caught some flak over that," Holly surmised.

"Yeah, you can say that; he was murdered," Anna said.

Holly arched an eyebrow. "He was murdered for marrying two white kids?"

"That's what it looks like," Anna replied.

"Wow," she muttered. "What happened to the two of them?"

"We've located some records," I said. "Specifically, we found a baptismal record of a girl named Claire Bond, born in January of 1862, with Penelope listed as the mother and Chester listed as the father, but there was also a denotation that he was deceased."

"So, wait a minute. He did not marry her until October of that year, but his child was born in January?" Holly asked.

"Yes, she was already three months pregnant when they married," I said. "The rationale is Chester was the father, but the problem is he had already enlisted and the unit he was in was camped a great distance away when conception apparently occurred. It could've been another man's baby for all we know. Anyway, nothing more is ever mentioned of Chester Bond. We found a death notice for Penelope in 1928. She's listed as a widow."

Holly took a moment to take it all in. "It's definitely a mystery. Okay, I've already pulled the file up. I'll give you a summation while you two take a look at the photographs," she said and turned the monitor toward us. "A tract of land was sold to a developer for the purpose of building a subdivision of high-end houses. They had done some bulldozing and whatever they do to build houses, and a bunch of men came out one Sunday with their metal detectors." She clicked on a photograph of six men gathered around a pile of dirt and a hole in the ground. All of the men had been sweating profusely and grinning like Cheshire cats.

"That's their group photo. The hole in the ground is actually a cistern well." She clicked on another photo, which showed a pile of rusty iron balls.

"Those look like old cannon balls," I surmised.

"Good eye, Thomas," she said and clicked on another photograph. This one was overlooking the cistern well. There was a lot of dirt, but skeletal remains could clearly be seen down in the well. "Here's the victim in his final repose. He was at the bottom of the well. Dirt and loose rocks were dumped on top of him. The cannonballs were stacked on top as a final touch."

"That's certainly an interesting place to be buried," I remarked. "Whoever did it did not want him to be found."

Holly nodded as she clicked to another photo. This one was of the skeletal remains laid out on a stainless-steel table, which I assumed was back in the examining area. She clicked on another photo, which focused on the back of the skull. A hunk of rusty metal was wedged into the skull.

"What is that?" Anna asked. Holly clicked her mouse again. This one showed the rusty hunk of metal, no longer embedded in the skull, and lying by itself on a sheet and a scale.

"It's what is left of a hatchet," Holly answered, reached down, and pulled it out of the file box. It was an unremarkable hunk of steel, obviously hand-forged. "The wooden handle rotted away years ago."

"So, he was murdered," Anna surmised.

"That is my conclusion," Holly said in agreement. She pointed at the fracture lines radiating out from the hatchet impact. "The hatchet wound was definitely antemortem."

"So, Thomas never said how you identified the skeleton," Anna said.

She clicked to the next photo. It showed some old brass buttons and a gold coin. Off to one side was a silver pocket watch with a heavy patina on its surface.

"The buttons are Confederate army. The coin is an 1861 Liberty Head gold piece. It's my understanding it could probably be auctioned for ten thousand, or more. Those are good pieces of evidence, but this," she said, tapping the screen with a pen, "gives us a tentative identification of the remains."

"From the watch?" Anna asked.

Holly grinned like a mischievous girl and clicked to the next photo. The watch face was now open and there was a close-up of the engraving, which was intact and easily readable. It read: Chester Bond.

"Holy moly," Anna muttered.

"So, the big question is, how did Chester Bond end up at the bottom of a cistern well on property that once belonged to the Carmike family?" I said.

"It's a codumbdrum," Anna said. I started to tell her the correct word was conundrum, but felt it probably wouldn't be wise given her current hangover.

We discussed it for several minutes before Anna and I left. I started the car and glanced over at Anna. "How're you feeling?"

She made a face like she had ingested poison. "I could be better."

"Do you want to try to get something to eat?" I asked.

She grimaced again and thought a second. "If there's a Starbucks nearby, I could use a chai latte."

I had no idea what a chai latte was, but Siri directed me to the nearest Starbucks and ten minutes later, Anna was sipping a hot chai latte.

"We need to find out more about Chester Bond," Anna said after she'd taken a few refreshing sips.

"Yep, I believe we do," I said in agreement and glanced at my watch. "But that'll have to wait. Ronald is expecting us in fifteen minutes. You know how he gets when we're late."

CHAPTER 18

After leaving the medical examiner's office, Anna and I went to Ronald's and the three of us discussed hiring Marti for the Reavis case. Ronald was even more reluctant than I was, but Anna presented a compelling argument, which was impressive given her hungover state.

So, Anna called Marti, relayed the good news, and gave her directions to Ronald's house. She had to leave, so I agreed to wait with Ronald. Thirty minutes later, I met her at the door. She was wearing one of those pairs of jeans that'd been torn all to hell and a green pullover shirt with a low cut that showed plenty of cleavage.

"What happened to your pants?" I asked.

"Nothing, they came that way," she said.

"Yeah, okay, follow me."

I escorted her to the basement where Ronald waited in nervous anticipation.

"Ronald, this is Marti," I said.

"Hi, Ronald," Marti said with a warm smile. Ronald's eyes went immediately to her breasts. He was stupefied and could not stop staring.

"Ronald runs our technical operations," I said, trying to get his attention.

Marti was about to say something, paused, and then snapped her fingers in front of his face. "Eyes up here, slim."

Ronald flinched, briefly made eye contact with Marti, and then quickly looked away.

"Alright, so what exactly am I supposed to be doing?" she asked.

"Ronald, why don't you give Marti a layman's explanation," I suggested.

"Um, okay." He pointed to one of his monitors. "As you know, the client is suing a business named Quadrant Realism Health Care. A subpoena was served on them two weeks ago requesting their emails for a specific time period and we've been hired to review and analyze those emails. They honored the subpoena with a data dump of their entire business's emails. This computer system has the data dump." He glanced at me. "It's almost eighty terabytes of data. I had to buy some new equipment for this job."

I nodded. "Make copies of the receipts for me. I'll add it to the expense report."

"What's a terabyte?" Marti asked.

"A trillion bytes of data," Ronald replied.

"Is that a lot? It sounds like a lot," she said.

"Yes, it's a lot," Ronald said in a tone like he was speaking to a simpleton.

Marti's eyes widened. "Am I expected to read that much?"

Ronald glanced at me in annoyance. "No, you won't have to read all of it. You'd never be able too."

I jumped in and tried to explain. "The health care company is pulling some shenanigans. We served them with a subpoena to produce their emails. They responded by dumping every single email onto several hard drives and claimed they were merely complying with the subpoena. It would take ten people years to read that much and they know it."

"Then how am I supposed to read all of it?" Marti asked.

Ronald blew out an impatient sigh. "If you would pay attention, you'll understand."

Marti made a face. "Okay, fine."

Ronald pointed again at his computers. "I have installed software which is commonly known as a crawl and pull program. The program searches the entire database at a much faster speed than any human could and tag emails with particular names and certain phrases. Once they are tagged, they will be automatically sent to you via an internal email account I have created for you. Your workstation will be here," he said and pointed at a computer monitor located at the far end of his tabletop of multiple computers.

"Okay, then what?" she asked. I knew Ronald was growing impatient with her, so I jumped in.

"Those are the emails you will have to actually read. Your job is to analyze those specific emails for…" I held up a questioning finger and waited for her to answer. Not more than an hour ago, I'd explained what her job was and I wanted to see if she had paid attention.

"I'll analyze each email for context which would lead a reasonable person to conclude the party was cognizant of the terms of the contract," she finished.

"Excellent. That's exactly correct, right, Ronald?" I asked. I looked over to see him once again ogling. I swear, the boy was about to start drooling.

Marti saw it too, and before I knew it, she grabbed Ronald's head and forcibly pulled him into her breasts and vigorously wiggled while making motorboat sounds. Ronald's head bounced back and forth like an oversized cue ball several times before regaining his wits and pulling away. His eyeglasses were askew and he was breathing heavily.

"Stop that!" he huffed, his face turning beet red.

Marti began giggling uncontrollably.

"Okay, quit playing around," I admonished.

"He should learn not to ogle," Marti countered.

I made a mental note to tell her more about Ronald so she'd understand, but not in front of him. Later. Or maybe have Anna talk to her.

"So, you print off the relevant emails, highlight the relevant parts, and write a report of your analysis," I said.

"Got it," she said. "When do I start?"

"Right now," Ronald said, his glasses still askew. He stabbed a finger at a chair. "That's where you sit, and you're not allowed to touch my computers, or any other keyboard other than the one in front of you."

She eyed Ronald. "Why do I have to be stuck down in this basement? Can't I do this on my laptop while sitting on your back patio? I want to get some sun on my legs."

"Of course, you can," I said. "Ronald can set it all up, right, Ronald?"

Ronald was still out of sorts. Marti stepped closer to him again and reached out. Ronald flinched, but before he could step back, Marti straightened his glasses and then gently caressed his cheek. I knew Ronald did not like to be touched by strangers, but he didn't resist. I guess maybe a pretty girl was an exception to the rule.

"If you're out there on the patio by yourself, you'll think you can do whatever you want."

Marti gave Ronald a sweet stare with her big hazel eyes. "Not for a minute; you're the boss."

"Well, okay, I suppose I can connect your laptop to my network."

"You can do that?" she asked in mock wonder.

Ronald shrugged. "It's easy stuff, if you know what you're doing."

"Thanks, Ronald, you're awesome," she said with a smile of wonderment, and then gave me a wink when he wasn't looking.

"Oh, wait a minute." She looked back and forth between us. "How do you know the emails haven't been altered, or faked, or something like that?"

Ronald squared his shoulders and actually puffed his chest out. Well, I mean, Ronald was so skinny he didn't have much of a chest, but he tried.

"I have a separate software program which scans the log history." He pointed at another computer monitor. "That's where I'll be stationed." He then walked over to the table and picked up some papers.

"I went ahead and did an email, because I'm certain you don't have any idea what to do." He handed one of the papers to her. "That one is a printout of an email that discusses an upcoming meeting with our client. The author writes about some key talking points, which is quite interesting."

Marti glanced at the printout. "You call this interesting?" she asked.

Ronald exhaled again. "In the context of this case, yes, it's extremely interesting. As you can see, the relevant parts have been highlighted in yellow. That's part of your job, to highlight the important passages. Always use yellow. And use a ruler. No squiggly highlights. They must be straight and even."

Marti frowned as she looked at the printout. "Why yellow?"

"It's a requirement from the law firm," I said. I wasn't going to explain to her Ronald's Asperger's Syndrome and his obsession of doing things a certain way with no deviation. "It's some crazy rule, so just roll with it."

"Okay, yellow highlights only, got it," she said.

Ronald pointed to the second page. "This is how a proper report is to be written. I have created a template for you, so do not deviate from the format."

"Don't deviate, got it," she said.

Ronald stared a moment and then gave me a look of uncertainty. "I don't know about this, Thomas. She's...different."

Marti responded by rolling her eyes, much like Anna would have.

"Don't worry, it'll be fine. How's the software working?" I asked. The one thing I learned about Ronald, when he started getting anxious, all I had to do was guide him to talk about computer stuff. Computers were his comfort zone.

"It's working well. Currently, we've searched through eight hundred terabytes. We should be completely through the entire batch in a week."

"Excellent," I replied and focused on Marti. "Hey, why don't you go ahead and get started. I need to speak with Ronald about some private matters."

I gave Ronald a look, tacitly telling him to hold his thoughts, and led him upstairs. He started to speak but I held a finger up. "I know what you're thinking."

"This'll never work, Thomas. She's…different."

"Nah, she's okay, she was just messing with you."

"But, she's a convicted criminal," he rejoined.

Before hiring Marti, we did a background check. Percy found an arrest from a couple of years ago where she was charged with public intoxication and disorderly conduct. She'd gotten into a barroom fight, but the charges were ultimately dismissed. Her credit rating was abysmal though and it was obvious she could use some extra money.

He started to say more, but I shushed him. "Listen, we need extra help on this case. She's a hoot, no doubt, but she's intelligent. She can handle this. And besides, she's Anna's friend."

Ronald breathing was coming in quick pants. "Is she going to be alone with me?"

"As soon as Anna finishes her job with Ms. Braxton, she'll be here helping out."

"When will that be?" he asked.

"A couple of more days at the most."

"Maybe I should call Anna," he said. "Emphasize the importance of her being here."

I held back a frustrated sigh. "It'll be okay, Ronald. In fact, I'm betting you and Marti will be good friends in no time. Besides, I saw the look on your face. You liked it when she pushed your face into her boobs."

He tried to fight it, but a boyish grin crept across his face.

My phone rang as I turned into my driveway. At first, I was going to let it go to voicemail, but decided to answer. I'm glad I did.

"Hello, Thomas. It's Reverend Hollinsworth. I hope I did not catch you at an inconvenient time."

"Not at all, Reverend. What can I do for you?"

"It's more like what I can do for the two of you," he said. "With your photography skills, I was able to read the journal with greater ease, and last night, I decided to sit down with a tumbler of scotch and reread the sections where the ink was badly faded."

"Oh, you're a fellow scotch drinker, are you? I knew there was something I liked about you."

The reverend chuckled. "I like the single-malts with peat accents, what about you?"

"I'm mostly a Balvenie man," I replied.

"Ah, yes, an excellent brand. A few of us get together once in a while and have a tasting. We alternate between scotch and bourbon. Perhaps you'd like to join us one evening. Sometimes we engage in Bible study, sometimes we'll talk about women." He chuckled at his own joke.

"I'd love to," I replied.

"Excellent. Don't tell anyone, but we usually meet at the church. I'll text you when we have the next get together. In the meantime, let me ask you. Do you still have a copy of the journal?"

"Yes, I do. I was planning on converting it to a PDF and read it when I had the time."

"Perhaps you should read it as soon as possible," he said. "I would recommend going straight to page 351 and start reading from there."

The page number was easy to remember; it was the same cubic inches of the engine of my Ford Mustang.

"Alright, Reverend, I'll get right on it. Can you give me a hint?"

I heard the reverend make a tsking of his tongue. "Thomas, I cannot in good conscience allow those words of condemnation to cross my lips, even if it was written by my blood kin. It's best that you read them for yourself."

"It sounds serious," I said.

After the reverend's mysterious phone call, I proceeded directly inside and downloaded the images from my camera onto my computer. It was going to take a while to convert them all to a PDF format, so I went directly to the picture in question.

I read it twice, and then decided maybe now was a good time to read the entire journal. I'd been good about abstaining from adult beverages during the day, but I couldn't help myself. I poured a finger of scotch before sitting at my desk and started at the beginning.

Sassy Hollinsworth had a natural flair for writing. Her opinions of the local aristocracy were hidden in cleverly veiled sarcasm. It was a great read and lasted me throughout the night. Anna texted me at midnight.

You awake?

Yeah, what's up?

At a nightclub with Marti and we'll probably be here a while. I'm spending the night at her apartment instead of driving home.

I responded that I understood and admonished both of them to be careful.

Okay, dad!

She punctuated it with a bunch of silly emoticons. I continued reading the entire journal and finished at two in the morning. I couldn't wait to tell Anna what Sassy had to say about the Carmike family.

CHAPTER 19

My phone gave off the signal indicating I had a new email, and it was from Ronald. Curious, I opened it, but before I could read the attachment, Ronald called.

"He's got another fight going," he said breathlessly.

"Who?"

"Candy-Man. He posted it. Didn't you see the email I sent you?"

"Are you referring to the email you sent me ten seconds ago? Why no, I haven't had the chance."

Ronald sighed, like he was dealing with a slow-witted child. "Well, I thought you'd like to know."

"I appreciate it," I said.

"Are you going to go to it?"

"Yeah, I believe I will."

There was silence on the other end, and if I didn't know better, I believed Ronald was contemplating going with me.

"Okay," he finally said. "But he didn't post the exact address of where it's going to be."

"What do you mean?" I asked.

"The event is somewhere in Memphis, but the instructions direct you to a bar first. You order a Blue-Ribbon beer from a bartender named Grupp and then you ask for the address. Oh, and he said if Grupp doesn't like you, he won't tell you where it is."

"Ah, he's using a cut-out," I said.

"What's that?"

Ronald was a genius when it came to computers, but he was naïve to the ways of the world, so I gave him a brief explanation.

"The bartender is most likely a friend to Candy. His job is to vet people. He makes sure they're not cops or troublemakers before he gives them the location."

"Oh." Ronald then chuckled. "Then you're screwed. You look so much like a cop it oozes out of you."

He had a point. I was square-jawed, clean-cut, and maybe a little hard around the edges. And, my age would be a factor; Grupp was looking for the younger crowd. Yeah, it was going to be a problem.

"I guess I have to figure something out," I said.

"Yeah."

"Okay, I appreciate the info. How's things going with Marti?"

"Um, she's not so bad, I guess."

I chuckled. "I guess she grows on you. Alright, I think I have some phone calls to make."

"So, are you going?" he asked again.

"Yep."

"Be careful. And keep your phone on so I can keep track of you."

I assured him I would before disconnecting and read his email, which gave more detail about the event. I plugged the address in Google. It was a little over two hundred miles away. Taking traffic into consideration, the drive would take around four hours.

There was no doubt I was going. I'd not uncovered a single lead since finding Jason Belew's decomposing remains. Detective Brannigan had said the same, although I wasn't sure he'd tell me if he did. Either way, I had nothing.

So, yeah, I had to go. I had no idea if it would be productive, but as my old homicide sergeant used to say, you'll never sell that vacuum cleaner if you don't knock on the door. We used to tease him about being a door-to-door salesman back before he became a cop, but he'd laughingly deny it and instead claimed he was once a male stripper and had to quit because the women kept getting into fights over him.

Now it was time to figure out who I could use as backup. I instantly thought of Duke, but he was currently living in Colorado, as far as I knew. Thinking of Duke made me think of a biker brother of his, Flaky. One thing about Flaky, he'd never be mistaken for a cop. The twin brother of Charles Manson? Definitely, but not a cop. I scrolled through my contacts and pushed the dial icon.

"Hey, Thomas, what're you up to?" he greeted.

"I have a little job I'm going on tonight and I'd like someone low-key to watch my back. Are you interested?"

"Me and Bull have a little club business going on, but we'll be through in an hour or so. What've you got in mind?"

He listened as I explained.

"And it's in Memphis?" he asked.

"Yeah. I'll drive, and I'll make it worth your while."

I listened to him repeat everything to someone, who I assumed was Bull. Both Bull and Flaky were outlaw bikers. Technically, I met Bull first. He was the bouncer at a local gentlemen's club and I had served civil papers on him. He didn't like it, and made it clear I had offended him and he wanted to take a piece out of my hide, but we eventually worked our differences.

I met Flaky when I was in jail. I had been charged with murdering my wife and Flaky had been caught in a stolen car. I'd been put in isolation, for my own safety they said, and Flaky was a trustee. Our mutual friend, Duke, had put in a good word for me and we'd become decent friends during my short stint.

"Yeah, I'm in. Bull wants to come to, what about it?" Flaky asked.

I thought about it a second. Bull was a big man and a good guy to have on your side if things went sideways. The problem was, he had a quick temper and was hard to control.

"Yeah, okay. Tell him I'll even spring for the beer if he keeps his temper in check."

We settled on them coming to my house in an hour and we'd leave from here. I spent the time getting ready. I packed an overnight bag and then, out of habit, I checked the fluids and tire pressure of my Explorer, even though it was only a week old. It was a long-ingrained habit and I'd probably never change.

I chuckled to myself at the thought of thinking of Bull and Flaky as friends, but we were. Anna said I had a likeable personality and people naturally trusted me. I didn't know about that, but I always tried to be honest and straightforward. And even though I was once a cop and those two were hardcore bikers, we'd still developed a friendship.

I always believed I inherited my personality from Uncle Mike. He was a courageous and honorable man and I tried to emulate him. His only flaw I ever knew of was he fell in love with the wrong woman, which I had also done. My wife was beautiful, bubbly, even a little zany. We'd fallen in love and married quickly. But there was something missing, something flawed. Whatever it was, it led her into the arms of another man, and it ultimately led to her murder.

After her death, I lapsed into somewhat of a funk. I had heard one of those radio talk show therapists once call it functional depression, which seemed apt. In the months after her death, I learned more about my beloved wife and I realized I had married the wrong person. It wasn't until the death of her lover, the man who had murdered her, that I was able to find a sense of closure.

That led to me finding Simone. Simone was a wonderful woman. Beautiful, smart, down to earth, she had it all. She was the one for me. But then she and her daughter were murdered by her ex-husband. It damn near drove me over the edge.

So, did I have a character flaw? Did I find the wrong women to fall in love with or, worse yet, was I some kind of evil jinx?

Only God knew the answer.

Bull and Flaky were punctual and we were on the road in minutes. I explained to them about the cut-out man and how my clean-cut appearance probably would raise his suspicions. The two men assured me they'd have no problem getting the directions to the location. We spent the time on the road catching up and talking about Duke. Bull and Duke were at odds with each other when Duke decided to retire from the outlaw biker life, but Bull grudgingly admitted he respected the man.

"I'd like to be able to retire with a million bucks," Flaky remarked.

Bull gave me a look. "You know where he's living now, don't you?"

"I have an idea of the general part of the country, but that's it, and don't bother asking me where."

Bull glared at me and grunted, killed a beer, and changed the subject to a 1950 Indian Chief that recently came into his possession.

"Sure, as long as it isn't stolen," I said. He responded with another grunt.

Once arriving in Shelby County, my phone directed us off of the interstate and down a couple of side roads before reaching our first destination.

"Nice bar," Bull said when I'd parked.

He was being sarcastic. The bar was seedier than the garden section at Home Depot. It was a one-story affair of concrete blocks that was painted black and stuck in between a vacant lot of abandoned cars and a boarded-up barber shop. I gave them some beer money and the two of them went inside while I stayed in my SUV. A homeless panhandler managed to sweet talk a dollar out of me and ten minutes later, I saw Flaky and Bull walk out.

"We were the only white boys in the place," Flaky said.

"He charged us fifteen bucks for two beers," Bull added. "Fucking asshole."

"Did you get the address?" I asked.

Flaky handed me a cocktail napkin with some scribbling on it. I plugged the address into my phone and exited the parking lot.

The event was located a couple of blocks off of I-40 in the inner city of Memphis. It was an abandoned warehouse, a rectangle of steel and concrete blocks. Memphis loved concrete blocks. The building may have been painted white once. Now, it was a grimy gray mixture of soot and other pollutants. There were already several cars in the parking lot when we drove in and a line forming at the front door.

As usual, I scanned the area and the people, mentally performing a threat assessment. There were no security cameras that I could see and what little lighting there was only managed to cast off a dull alabaster hue. The demographics of the customers was one dimensional, to say the least.

"Are we going to be the only white people here?" Flaky asked. "All I see are black folks."

"I honestly have no idea," I said. "But that's what it looks like."

"I hope you're packing," Flaky said to me.

"I am," Bull replied.

I pointed at the door-men with their metal detecting wands. "We won't be able to go inside if we're armed."

"Shit," Bull muttered.

"Yeah, I agree. C'mon, we'll lock them up."

When I bought this shiny Explorer with all of the bells and whistles, I purchased an aftermarket gun storage safe which was specifically designed to fit into the center console. Yes, the glove box was big enough to hold two guns and had a lock, but I liked the hardened steel of the aftermarket safe. Bull grumbled in protest, but he surrendered his gun, a Charter Arms Bulldog, and I secured both of our firearms in the safe.

We got a few odd looks when we got in line, but in between Flaky looking like a crazier version of Charles Manson and Bull's enormous size, any smartass remarks were said in whispers. The interior of the warehouse was fairly plain looking. More peeling paint on the interior walls, and a few portable lights here and there. An old wrestling mat was in the middle of the building that people were lingering around.

I spotted Candy almost immediately. He was standing by a dry erase board, which had the odds listed for each fight. He was hustling and taking bets. There was a Slavic-looking guy standing nearby doing some hustling of his own. I watched as he made multiple hand-to-hand transactions and would deftly slide the money into his pocket. In the short time I watched, it looked like he'd pulled in a hundred bucks. Not bad.

There was more side action going on here and there, and I caught a couple of hard stares. Sometimes, young men would get their bravery up from their friends, booze, and drugs. This was not a place to give anyone a stare down. I had a polymer blade hidden in my belt. It wasn't metallic so the metal detecting wand did not catch it, but I preferred to avoid any type of confrontation. Besides, Bull's looks alone discouraged anyone from getting froggy.

I made an effort of appearing to be casually looking around, never resting my eyes on anyone for more than a second or two, but I was scanning, making mental assessments. Every time I gazed around, I'd center back on Candy and watch his action. He was taking bets and selling baggies of weed as fast as he could, all with a broad grin, showing a little bit of gold in his mouth. After several minutes, he turned it over to his assistant, a greasy-looking man wearing an outdated Adidas warm-up suit, and casually strolled to the wrestling mat, which had been laid out in the middle of the warehouse. He then produced a cordless microphone, turned it on, and tapped it with his finger.

"How's everyone doing tonight?" he yelled. There was a lackluster response, so he yelled even louder. "I said, how's everyone doing tonight!"

This time, he got some raucous cheers, which brought a smile to his face, revealing a couple of gold teeth, which he did not have when we went to his house.

"Alright, much better. Tonight's going to be a night you'll be talking about when you're old and sitting around in the nursing home. We've got some fantastic fighters, and after the fight's over, we're going to party until the sun comes up and all you playas have to either go to work or go back to your ole ladies!"

There were more cheering and catcalls, which made Candy grin even more. He jawed a little more before getting the first fight underway. A ref stepped up and got the first two fighters ready. They were so young they looked like they were still in high school. The ref called them together and gave a convoluted set of instructions, which led me to doubt he was a trained referee.

They touched gloves, backed up to their respective corners, and waited for the ref to make the call, which he did by shouting, "Hell yeah!"

They started slowly and were applying their technical skills, but it soon denigrated into a primal brawl of swinging for the fences. The ref stood there, grinning gleefully, which made me suspect he was high. Eventually, one of them connected with a roundhouse right. His opponent staggered. A couple of additional punches sent him into sleepy-land. Needless to say, the crowd went wild. The next three fights were more of the same.

"This is some decent shit," Bull said. I turned to look at him. He'd found a fifth of Jim Beam from somewhere, and he and Flaky were doing their best to kill it.

The fourth fight was a heavyweight match. Some god-awful rap music started blaring over the loudspeakers as a large black man started strutting out of a door from the far end of the warehouse.

"That boy's been doing some juice," Bull declared.

It wasn't often that I agreed with Bull, but he was right. The man was huge, with a torso the shape of an upside-down Christmas tree and not an ounce of fat on him. He bounced on his toes as he made his way to the mat.

"Now, entering the ring, our hometown boy, Chocolate Thunder!" Candy shouted.

The crowd now legitimately went nuts. His entourage of four crackhead-looking men, encouraged by the cheers, began breakdancing. Honestly, it looked like they were going into some kind of epileptic seizure. Candy presented Chocolate Thunder's opponent, a man who was almost my age, balding, and with considerably more girth. He didn't look like he stood a chance.

Still, I saw a hardness to his eyes and despite the fat, he was surprisingly light on his feet.

"Shit fire, I wonder if I can still put in a bet," Bull said and looked over at the dry erase board. There was a solitary figure standing there, the Slavic-looking man I saw selling drugs earlier.

"Who are you betting on?" I asked. He looked at me like I was on drugs.

"The big steroid head. He's going to wipe the floor with that fat ass. Why would you even ask?"

I shrugged. "If you ask me, this looks like a set-up. That old fat ass might have a little something-something going on, just saying."

Bull made some derisive remark before handing the bottle of Jim Beam to his friend and walking over to the makeshift betting booth. I caught Flaky staring at me.

"Do you really think that old fat ass is going to win?" he asked.

"He might be nothing more than cannon fodder, but my gut tells me something different," I said.

Flaky's only response was by taking a sip out of the bottle.

The fight started explosively with Mister Chocolate Thunder charging the old man and trying to land a haymaker right. The old man casually ducked, sidestepped, and landed a brutally hard right-left combination to the jaw. Before Thunder could retaliate, the old fat man deftly stepped back, creating a space where Thunder could not utilize his superior reach.

For the next minute, the two men sparred. Thunder was far superior in this respect; he was quicker and had a longer reach. The old man took several hard punches and his left eye started swelling shut.

It was looking bad for him and even though I had respect for him, I now believed it was only a matter of time now before he got knocked out or Thunder got one of those massive arms around his throat and choked him out.

Thunder landed with a massive right and the old man staggered backward. But then he did something amazing. When big bad Chocolate Thunder stepped in to finish the job, the old fat man grabbed Thunder by the right wrist and then executed a flawless flying armbar.

Mister Chocolate Thunder tried desperately to remain on his feet but could not. He fell to the mat and struggled to escape, but to no avail. He tapped within three seconds.

"Shit!" Bull shouted.

"How much did you lose?" I asked.

"A hundred."

I swapped a glance with Flaky who looked at me with knowing admiration.

The next fight was the one I was waiting for. It was the main event featuring the Wolf and some nobody. The nobody was introduced first. He was another African-American man and the local crowd favorite. He strutted out with his entourage, and I had to admit he appeared to be exceptionally fit. He was close to my height, and I guessed he weighed around a hundred and eighty pounds.

When Candy introduced Wolf, the crowd erupted in a cacophony of loud boos and jeering. As I watched, a group of four people emerged from the same door Chocolate Thunder had walked out of fifteen minutes earlier. Three were old men. Each was playing musical instruments; a tambourine, a weird-looking guitar, and an accordion. The fourth person in the entourage was a scantily clad woman dancing provocatively to the music. I recognized her immediately.

Lilith.

CHAPTER 20

Yeah, I stunned for a moment. She looked the same. Pale, raven-haired, a lean, taut figure, and let's not forget the elaborate tattoo covering her back. I'd not seen her since last fall. She'd looked like she'd lost a little weight, if that were possible, but otherwise, she was unchanged.

"Holy shit, is that who I think it is?" Bull asked.

Flaky glanced over at me, but I didn't answer. She led them to the mat as she danced to the lilting music, and I must admit, her moves were mesmerizing. I actually felt my pulse quickening and a stirring down below.

Wolf walked through the door a moment later. He was dressed in nothing more than black kick-boxing pants. He walked with seeming casual ease, like he hadn't a care in the world. He had the same swarthy appearance as Lilith, but with darker eyes the color of obsidian and devoid of emotion. As he got closer, I noticed something else. His torso had a thick sheen to it. Not like sweat, but more than likely Vaseline. It was an old trick to keep a skilled grappler from getting a tight hold on you. So, the man didn't like to grapple. Interesting.

"They look like gypsies," Flaky said.

I didn't comment, but Flaky was right. Especially the old men, they looked like they came straight out of the nineteenth century. I tore my eyes off of Lilith and focused intensely on the two old men. I wanted to be able to recognize either of them if I saw them on the street sometime in the future.

The oldest one was playing a short, fat-looking guitar that I think was called a lute. He was as tall as me and had deeply etched lines on his face, making him look like a block of weathered driftwood. His long hair was the color of fireplace ashes with the exception of a nasty-looking yellow streak starting to the right of his widow's peak and going all of the way back to where it disappeared somewhere in his ponytail.

The second one was playing an accordion. He was younger, my age, and a few inches shorter. He was built like an old beer keg, no neck, with wide hips and bulbous buttocks. Maybe he was fat, maybe he was once a power-lifter or wrestler. His jet-black hair was also tied back in a ponytail and he had a full, untrimmed beard of Gandalf proportions. It covered his entire mouth and extended several inches downward. If I looked closely, I bet I could see a remnant or two of past meals buried in those whiskers.

The Tambourine Man was a little guy and his face was pitted with scars, like he'd had chicken pox when he was a child. His nose and ears had multiple piercings.

So, Tambourine, Guitar, and Accordion. I gave them a final once over and focused back on Lilith. She either did not notice us, or worse, she pointedly ignored us. She gave Wolf a kiss on the cheek before he turned and faced his opponent. The stare down by the two fighters was menacing but uneventful. Gloves were touched and the fight started.

There were a couple of tentative punches and then Wolf launched a lightning-quick spinning back kick. It landed squarely on his opponent's chin and it was lights out. Before the ref could step in, Wolf quickly stepped forward, lifted a leg high in the air, and dropped an axe kick on his unconscious opponent's face, crushing his nose. Even from where I was standing, I could see blood squirt out. It was unnecessary and there were a few in the crowd who booed him, but the majority of the crowd erupted in bloodthirsty cheers.

"He's wicked good."

I turned to the voice. Candy-Man, AKA Raymondo Calendar, was standing beside me.

"Yes, he is," I said in agreement.

"Why are you here, Ironcutter?" he asked.

I gestured toward Wolf, who was disappearing through the doorway he'd come out of less than two minutes before.

"I want to talk to them about my murder victim," I said.

He frowned. "I thought you were done with all of that."

"I would be, if someone in the law enforcement community gave a damn about it," I said.

He frowned and scanned the crowd. "I shouldn't even be seen talking with you," he said. "There's some shit going on that you wouldn't believe, even if I were allowed to tell you."

"How'd you get involved in this? Are you working off a charge?" I asked.

He gave a pained smile. "Yeah, something like that."

"Are you going to tell Stainback I was here?"

"All I'm going to say is, if you're going to mess with Wolf, be careful he don't bite you." He glanced around. "He generally doesn't hang around after he's fought. He and his crew are in a brand-new RV parked out back. They'll be gone as soon as I pay him."

He turned and made his way toward the door where Wolf and his entourage went through. I assume he was going to pay Wolf, who in turn was going to leave soon after. I turned to my buds.

"Let's go wait on them outside," I said.

Bull looked at me like he didn't want to leave, but Flaky made a head nod, agreeing with me.

The RV was parked in back by the loading docks, exactly like Candy said they'd be. It was a newer model Coachman, one of the higher-end ones. I glanced around to make sure nobody was watching, then I hurriedly snapped a few photos of the tag and VIN. I also pointed my phone through the front window and took several photos in case there was something inside of interest.

The five of them walked out a couple of minutes later. Wolf and Lilith both had changed into jeans and T-shirts. When they saw us, they all stopped in their tracks. I gave a friendly wave. Lilith leaned close to Wolf and whispered something. He looked at her sharply for a moment and then walked toward us. The rest of the entourage followed.

"Hello, Wolf. I watched your fight earlier. You have some amazing skills," I said.

He acknowledged my compliment with a small nod.

"What do you want?" one of the older men asked in heavily accented English.

"Oh, forgive my manners. My name is Thomas Ironcutter and these are my two friends, Bull and Flaky."

I waited to see if Lilith would say something, acknowledging she knew us, anything, but she simply stared.

"What kind of business are you in, Thomas Ironcutter?" Wolf asked. He had a distinct eastern European accent.

"I'm a private investigator," I said.

"A private investigator," he said. "You investigate people. You pry into their secrets."

"Tonight, I'm here to ask you about a young man you encountered back a few months ago," I said. "His name was Jason Belew. He attended the fights in Manchester back in February. I was hoping to talk to you about him."

Instead of responding, he stared at me, and even though the only lighting was from the cracks around the dock doors, those armor-piercing black eyes of his shone brightly.

"A couple of his friends said he spoke to you after your fight. I have a picture of him; maybe it'll jog your memory."

His only response was to continue to stare, so I fished my phone back out of my pocket and scrolled through the photos until I found one of Jason. I turned it toward him and waited. He was still staring at me, ignoring my phone.

"What do you do when you learn the secrets of others, Thomas Ironcutter?" he asked.

I shrugged noncommittally and glanced at Lilith. She was staring back intently, but broke eye contact immediately when I looked over.

Wolf gave what I assume was a smile, but it was more like he stretched his lips into a tight line. He took turns staring at each of us, slowly appraising me before doing the same to Bull and Flaky.

He reminded me of a time back when I was in high school. A friend had a pet, Wolf. There were four or five of us hanging out in his den one afternoon when he brought the boa out. We watched in fascination as he held a mouse by the tail and Wolf went into action. The mouse tried to run for it but could not go anywhere. Billy's Wolf slithered closer and then struck. However, once he'd squeezed the mouse to death, he stared at each of us with its reptilian eyes.

Billy explained Wolf was vulnerable when it was feeding and it was its way of making a threat assessment before deciding whether or not it should swallow the mouse. Sure enough, that Wolf's reptilian brain determined there were too many strangers in the room, and slithered off, leaving the dead mouse lying there, uneaten.

Wolf apparently made the same threat assessment with us and did not like what he saw. He turned to Lilith and the rest of his entourage.

"*Vom merge!*" he barked.

I had no idea what he actually said, but the meaning was clear. The men then walked past me and got into the RV. Lilith lingered for a moment and stared. I thought she was going to say something, but then she followed the men into the RV and closed the door behind her. A moment later, the engine started, the headlights came on, and they drove out of the parking lot.

"I'd wondered what had happened to her," Bull said. "And here she is. The bitch acted like she didn't even know us."

It was true. I don't know why, but she acted as if we were strangers. A few possibilities ran through my mind, but I suspected she did not want the men to know she knew us.

Bull scoffed and spit. "Well, they were decent enough fights, I guess. Are we going to stay for the party?"

"Like you said, we're the only white people here," I said. "Why would you want to stay?"

Bull shrugged. "I haven't gotten my black wings yet. I figure one of those sisters might be willing."

Flaky burst out in laughter. Eventually, the two men agreed it was time to go home and we were soon on the road. I offered to buy them a twelve-pack but they insisted instead on a bottle of Jim Beam. I found a liquor store on the way back to I-40 and the two men accepted the bottle with eager grins. After they took substantial swallows, Flaky offered the bottle to me.

"I better not, I'm driving."

They talked about the fights and the women as I drove, and they even bandied the idea of their biker club organizing something similar. I threw in an occasional "yeah," or "uh-huh," but my mind was elsewhere.

Their conversation became background noise and my thoughts drifted to Wolf, but I had to admit I was thinking more about Lilith. It didn't take a detective to deduce she and Wolf had some type of connection. Were they lovers or were they merely related? I had no idea which. For that matter, they could have been both.

Aside from discovering Lilith, I learned absolutely nothing from this endeavor. It was a waste of time and gas, and I was damned if I knew how to proceed with the investigation. My gut told me Wolf was involved in Jason's murder, but I had no proof. For that matter, I could not even offer a motive. Was it because Jason had made a pass at him and it triggered him somehow? Had Jason seen something? Again, I had no clue.

I was about to ask for a taste, but my thoughts were interrupted by a vehicle approaching from behind at a high rate of speed and got right behind me. Within a second, my mirror lit up with flashing blue lights complimented with the blip of a siren.

CHAPTER 21

"Heads up, guys," I said in warning. The two men twisted their necks in unison and stared behind us.

"What the hell?" Bull asked.

"Toss that bottle," I directed.

He didn't need to be told twice. He lowered his window and flung the bottle as far as he could. If the officer had sharp vision, it's possible he saw the bottle being tossed, but I had a feeling an open container violation had nothing to do with the reason there was a cop car behind us with his lights flashing.

"What's going on, man?" Bull asked.

"Good question, just be cool," I answered.

I had slowed and moved to the right shoulder of the interstate, but I didn't stop yet, trying to get as much distance from the whiskey bottle as I could. A couple of blips of the siren told me the officer was growing impatient. Thankfully, our handguns were still locked in my console safe. I stopped and put my vehicle in park, my thoughts similar to Bull's; why were we being stopped?

It was not a simple traffic stop. As soon as I stopped, we were joined by two additional police cars. Orders were barked out over the loudspeaker telling us to exit the vehicle one at a time and to lie face down on the asphalt, or else. It was a textbook felony takedown. Six Memphis police officers cuffed us, searched us, and then unceremoniously stuffed us in the back of the patrol cars. The one in charge of me was a no-nonsense-looking guy about my age.

"What's the charge, officer?" I asked.

"Not for me to say," he replied before shutting the car door.

The backseats of modern-day patrol cars are simply not large enough for a six-foot, three-inch man. Especially a handcuffed man. My back and knees were already stiffening up. I could only imagine how Bull was faring.

While I was pondering why exactly I was sitting here in handcuffs, it all became crystal clear. Two people, a man and a woman, emerged from back behind the patrol cars. Both were wearing identical dark blue windbreakers. I didn't see the backs of the jackets, but I didn't need to. I had no doubt there were three large letters embossed on the back. Probably in gold letters, because gold letters always made people feel special. The back door opened and Special Agent Juanita Stainback stuck her face in.

"You were told to cease and desist," she said. "This is your own doing."

Her face was fixed in a smug smirk. It was not an attractive look.

"What are we being charged with?" I asked.

"*You* will be charged with obstructing an FBI investigation. We're undecided what to do with your two white trash friends, but I'm sure we'll think of something. One of the officers said something was tossed when they turned their blues on. Is there anything you want to tell me?"

"It may not be what you want to hear," I replied.

"Try me."

"Alright, it goes like this. You are conducting an illegal arrest. If you don't want to face civil and possibly even criminal repercussions, you should, hmm, what's the phrase I'm looking for?" I feigned confusion for a moment. "Ah yes. You should cease and desist."

The smirk turned to a withering stare before she straightened and slammed the car door. I figured any chance I had of sweet talking myself out of this situation wasn't going to happen, so I accepted my predicament in stride and tried in vain to wiggle myself into a comfortable position.

We left the scene minutes after I witnessed my brand-new and freshly waxed Ford Explorer being towed away. The officer returned to his car and a caravan formed. We exited I-40 and soon drove into the parking lot of the FBI headquarters located on North Humphreys Boulevard. The building looked surprisingly similar to the Nashville office, lots of glass accentuated with red brick trim.

Flaky and I were escorted by one officer each. The rest of them had Bull surrounded and a couple of them even had their hands on their tasers. If I had to guess, Bull probably made a few threats of what he'd do if he got hold of any of them. They dumped us into individual interview rooms. The older officer who was in charge of me silently pointed at a chair.

"Can you at least tell me where my vehicle was towed?" I asked.

"Memphis PD impound lot," he answered and then walked out, closing the door behind him.

My cuffs were tight and I was starting to ache both in my wrists and shoulders. Back in the day, I had a suspect manage to slip his cuffs from the back to his front. Of course, he was a skinny crackhead. I tried to do the same, but there was no way.

So, I sat there, pondering the situation and looked around. It was a typical interview room; dull green walls, which psychologists claimed was the best color to subtly soothe a hostile person, three folding chairs, and a solitary government-issued table. I spotted the hidden camera immediately. It was hidden in the smoke alarm, which instead of being mounted on the ceiling, like most smoke detectors, it was mounted on the wall.

Cop mentality always amazed me; they thought they were smarter than everyone and every criminal they encountered was stupid. I'm sure whoever mounted the camera thought the same way. But it also surprised me. The FBI's protocol is to not record interviews. Instead, one agent would conduct the interview while another agent took notes. It went without saying those notes were always slanted to make the Fibbies look good.

It took an hour before the other FBI agent stuck his head in the door. He was an unremarkable looking sort, about my age, under six feet, male-pattern baldness, and probably weighed a buck eighty. Like I said, a plain-looking guy who would never stand out in a crowd.

"If you don't want us to destroy that lockbox in your console, you're going to need to give us the code."

"I'd like to take a look at that search warrant first," I said. "For that matter, how about the arrest warrant? Why don't you let me take a look at that too?"

"Are you sure that's how you want to play it?" he asked with a pointed stare.

"You never have identified yourself."

He gave a slight, unfriendly smile. "Mister Ironcutter, my name is Special Agent Avery Pollard, and I'm going to see to it that you spend a long time in prison."

"Oh, dear," I replied.

He stared at me a moment longer before leaving me with an ominous threat. "I'll be back."

"You said it wrong. You don't sound anything like a Terminator."

I was once again alone. Don't think it escaped my attention that Agent Pollard did not bother removing my cuffs. I guess he thought my discomfort would increase my stress, keep me off balance. It was true, at the moment I was in a pickle. Oh, I'd eventually get out of all of it; they'd committed too many errors to make a case, even if they had a case. But, in the meantime, they weren't going to make things easy for me.

Special Agent Pollard made good on his threat and returned thirty minutes later. Agent Stainback was with him. I breathed a feigned sigh of relief.

"Oh, thank God, I thought you'd never come back," I said.

They didn't laugh and sat in the two seats on the opposite side of the table. Agent Stainback had a manila folder stuffed with papers. She opened it and slid a few of the papers to me.

"Here is your copy of the search warrant," she said.

I looked down at the front page, which had the FBI emblem as a watermark.

"Nice cover page. Are you going to uncuff me so I can read the rest?"

"We've delivered your copy of the search warrant, we're under no obligation to read it to you, and no, you will not be uncuffed," Pollard said.

They were both giving me the hard-ass police look, which was amusing, in spite of the discomfort of the cuffs.

"So, since I'm unable to read this nonsense, let's move on to the charges. What are they?" I asked.

"The three of you will be charged with obstructing an FBI investigation," he said.

"I've never heard of that law, are you sure it exists?" I asked.

"I can assure you it exists, Ironcutter," Pollard said.

"Well then, what are we doing here? Carry us down to the federal magistrate and charge us. I don't have all night."

The two of them exchanged a glance. I happened to know federal magistrates kept banker's hours; feds don't normally arrest people in the middle of the night. I wondered if they were aware that I knew this little factoid.

"Alright, Ironcutter, we will do so, but first let's have a little chat," Pollard said.

"I haven't been able to feel my hands for the past hour. Why should I chat with you?"

There was another exchange of glances before he stood and fished a key out of his pocket. Agent Stainback stood to one side as Agent Pollard opened the cuffs and placed my hands in front before reattaching them. I waited for the two of them to sit before speaking.

"So, what kind of chat are we about to have?" I asked as I rubbed my wrists. "Wait, let me guess. You two want to know what I spoke to those gypsies about, correct?"

"We can start with that, if you like," Agent Pollard said.

"Hmm, I don't think I want to start with that," I said.

"Alright, smartass, what are we going to start with?" Agent Stainback asked.

I leaned forward and started reading the search warrant. After a moment, I looked up suspiciously.

"Your affidavit is filled with vague innuendo. There's no credible PC here whatsoever. How in the hell did you get a judge to sign it? Oh wait, let me guess, it's one of those judges who will sign anything a Fibbie sticks in front of him, am I right?"

Stainback could not keep from allowing a smirk to cross her face, like I had walked right into their trap. "Well then, let's talk about our probable cause, shall we?"

I shrugged. "If you want. I'll have to tell you though; a good cup of coffee makes me loquacious."

Her eyes narrowed. "A what?"

"Chatty, talkative, an affable raconteur."

"You like to use big words, don't you, Ironcutter." She said it like it was an insult.

"I feel like I need to do my best," I said. "After all, the mental perspicacity of the FBI is legendary, wouldn't you agree?"

She gave a somber nod of agreement. I doubted she knew the definition of the word and my sarcasm attached to it.

"It's good you're aware of this, so any attempt to lie to us will only have negative consequences for you and your friends."

"I'll state for the record right now, my friends have done nothing wrong and as far as they knew, we only came down here to watch the fights."

"Why did *you* come down here, Mister Ironcutter?" Agent Pollard asked.

"To watch the fights," I replied.

Pollard stared daggers at me and slowly leaned forward. "Do you think this is a game, Ironcutter?"

I leaned forward as well until we were inches apart and locked eyes with him. "On the contrary, I'm taking this extremely seriously. You conducted an illegal traffic stop, you obtained a search warrant under nefarious circumstances, and you have charged not only me but my friends as well on absolute bullshit. And now, the two of you are attempting to interrogate me without benefit of obtaining a waiver of my constitutional right to an attorney. Yes, Special Agent Pollard, I am taking this extremely seriously. The question you two should be asking yourselves is how is this going to stand up under the scrutiny of a jury?"

Agent Pollard broke eye contact and leaned back. After a couple of seconds, he regained his composure, fixed me with a glare, and smirked.

"You can be certain of one thing, Ironcutter: you will be spending a long time in federal prison. Cops don't do well in prison, but you already know that, don't you?" He thought he was scoring points and the smirk intensified. "I couldn't help but notice you sitting a little funny. The boys had a good time with you that time you were locked up recently, didn't they?"

I gave him a withering stare. "You're an idiot, Pollard. Do you think your insults are accomplishing anything?" I then turned to Agent Stainback. "Oh, wait. This is the bad cop, good cop routine. Am I right? Juanita, are you supposed to be the good cop?"

She responded with her own withering stare, but then she remembered her role and tried for a worried and concerned demeanor.

"Ironcutter, you just don't get it, do you? You are in serious trouble here. Your only chance is to get in front of this immediately. If you cooperate, I'll do what I can for you, but if you keep playing these games, there will be no chance for you." She then leaned forward, putting more concern in her expression. "I can tell you this: one of your friends is already talking. I won't snitch out which one it is, but they have a lot to say."

I kept myself from laughing. Neither Bull nor Flaky knew the details of my investigation. The only thing they knew was we were going to watch some fights and I was hoping to talk to one of the fighters. The two agents stared expectantly.

"That really hurts," I said. "You just wait and see if I give either of them a ride home. That'll show them."

The expectant stares turned angry. The tension was broken by an abrupt knock on the door. The two agents glared a few seconds longer, reluctant to break eye contact. Whoever it was on the other side of the door knocked again.

"Whatever you do, don't open that door," I warned. My sarcasm was on fire tonight.

Pollard gave yet another withering stare, stood, and walked the three steps to the door. When he opened it, a civilian security guard in need of a shave was standing there. He motioned for Pollard to join him in the hall. Agent Pollard shut the door and there was a brief, muffled conversation before he walked back in.

"Who is your attorney?" he asked.

"I have the Goldman Law Firm on retainer. It's a prestigious firm in Nashville with several attorneys on staff. Why do you ask?"

Pollard said nothing. Instead, he motioned for Agent Stainback to join him in the hall and shut the door behind them. I tried to listen but the door was too thick or they were whispering. After a couple of minutes, they came back in the room.

"There's a young man here who looks like he's a snot-nosed teenager, but he claims to be your attorney," Pollard said.

My first thought was William Goldman was here, but I was a little confused. William was a handsome man who was in his late twenties and a little on the slender side. I suppose one might say he looked younger than he actually was, but I didn't think a reasonable person would ever think of him as a teenager. Plus, I had no idea how he knew I was sitting here in handcuffs. I hid my confusion and went on the offensive.

"Well, are you going to allow me access to my attorney or is that yet another one of my constitutional rights you're going to trample on?"

They exchanged another glance before shutting the door. This time only a few seconds elapsed before the door once again opened and Ronald walked in.

CHAPTER 22

To say I was surprised was an understatement, but I kept the best poker face the world had ever seen as the two FBI agents appraised the young man standing in the doorway. My little buddy Ronald Hardison, all five feet six inches, one hundred and thirty pounds of him, strode in with his shoulders squared and his pale face fixed in a harsh, somber expression, like a man with a sense of purpose.

He was wearing the same suit he wore during my murder hearing, the tie slightly crooked, and his horn-rimmed glasses perhaps a little too large for his face. Nevertheless, he stopped across the table from me, stared a moment, and then braced the two agents.

"What is my client being charged with?" he asked.

"Thomas Ironcutter is your client?" Agent Stainback asked.

"Why else would I be here this early on a Sunday morning," Ronald said. "Should I repeat my question?"

"Obstructing an FBI investigation," Stainback replied. "How were you notified of his arrest?"

That's something I wanted to know as well, but Ronald ignored the question. Instead, he nodded somberly, pushed his glasses back up on his nose, and gave Stainback an appraising stare.

"You are Special Agent Stainback, correct?" he asked.

"I don't recall throwing out my name," Agent Stainback retorted.

Ronald appeared unfazed and faced Pollard, giving him an appraising stare.

"And Special Agent Pollard, I presume. I have already received a briefing about the two of you."

"From whom?" Agent Pollard asked.

"From an individual with the DOJ whose pay grade is much higher than yours. The two of you intend to charge Thomas Ironcutter with Title Eighteen of the United States Code, section fifteen-zero-five, am I correct?"

"You would be correct," Agent Pollard said and looked at the business card. "Mister Hardison, is it?"

"Yes, I am. Sherman Goldman, the founder of the Goldman law firm, is the personal attorney for Mister Ironcutter. Under any other circumstances, he'd be present, but unfortunately, he is out of town at a funeral. So, I will be acting in his stead. Now, let's proceed, shall we? Have you taken Mister Ironcutter and his associates before the federal magistrate?"

"We were about to, before you interrupted," Agent Stainback replied.

Ronald nodded, as if he already knew the answer. "Yes, very good. I got here just in time."

"Just in time for what?" she asked. The two agents were now on the defense. I marveled at Ronald's bravado.

"Just in time to save the two of you an enormous amount of embarrassment," he said. He then opened his briefcase and pulled out a stack of papers held together by one of those springy binder clips. He made a show of holding it out in his hand.

"Agent Stainback, I have been advised you are the more impetuous, but you are also more intelligent than Agent Pollard. Therefore, I urge you to look over this document before you proceed any further."

Agent Pollard grabbed it out of Ronald's hand and eyed it with undisguised suspicion. "What kind of lawyer nonsense do you think you're pulling?" he demanded.

"I assure you it is not nonsense, Agent Pollard," Ronald replied. "The pages you are holding are a printout of an appellate case out of the western district of Kentucky heretofore known as United States versus Higgins."

"And why would I waste my time looking at this?" Agent Pollard asked. He was staring at Ronald with undisguised disdain, but I also caught a small hint of uncertainty.

I saw Ronald gulp and his pale color turned a little more ashen. I thought he was going to lose it, so I spoke up.

"I'd listen to him, if I were you, Pollard. He may not look like much, but the Goldman Law Firm only has the best and brightest on their staff."

Agent Pollard cast a baleful frown at me a moment before focusing back on Ronald.

"Why don't you give us a summation of this case you feel is so important, counselor?"

"Please, call, me Ronald," he said and managed to flash a polite, yet nervous smile.

I'll have to admit, he had not yet actually claimed to be an attorney, which was a crime, but he was walking a tight rope and he knew it.

"Alright, *Ronald,* explain."

"I'd be glad to," Ronald said. "It's a rather old case, I'm sure they teach it at the academy." Ronald paused to look at them, but neither of them responded.

"Yes, well, in the early eighties a Kentucky police chief allegedly alerted certain nefarious individuals about an undercover FBI investigation in which they were the targets of said investigation. He was charged under 1505, but the indictment was dismissed by the appellate court. In the ensuing opinion, the court defined the threshold that must be breached before an individual can be charged with this offense. The Supreme Court of the United States declined to hear the case so the precedent set in the appellate court has stood to this day. I have highlighted, in yellow, the pertinent information."

Ronald paused and let it sink in a moment. Agent Stainback was about to speak, but Ronald cut her off. "From what I have been advised, neither Thomas Ironcutter nor his two friends have interfered in any way with your ongoing investigation, which is, how to put it delicately, about a group of so-called gypsies and their possible involvement human trafficking?"

Special Agent Juanita Stainback would be well advised to never play poker. When Ronald divulged that information, she inhaled sharply. Her co-worker gave her a sharp look. I have no idea how my diminutive friend discovered that information. For that matter, I had no idea how he determined I was in trouble.

I'd ask him about it later. Right now, I was rolling with it. Ronald continued his ploy.

"Agents, I have no doubt the two of you and the bureau are doing good work, but I'll not allow the rights of these three men be trampled upon any further. I am prepared to file an emergency writ of habeas corpus, if need be. And, if I do that, I will be holding a press conference in which I will expose not only the violation of my clients' civil rights, I will also make public your investigation, and perhaps even divulge certain tidbits of information that you would probably want to remain secret. Agents, if I have to do that, it's going to get rather unpleasant."

I sat back and watched the reactions of the agents. Stainback was so livid I thought she was going reach out and throttle Ronald. Pollard looked downright confused. Well, let me clarify, Ronald had confused the hell out of both of them, and yeah, add me to the list. Pollard slowly stood.

"Excuse us a moment," he said and nodded to Stainback. The two agents gruffly left the room, Pollard tightly clutching the papers Ronald had handed to him.

Ronald started to speak, but I gave him a subtle shake of the head. Yet another thirty minutes passed before Special Agent Stainback reentered the interview room.

"All of you are free to go, but if I was you, I'd be expecting an indictment to be lodged against you any day now."

The handcuffs were removed and we were led to the front entrance. Stainback used her security card to activate the lock and let us out.

"The other two will be joining you shortly," she said, did not wait for a response, and pulled the glass door closed. As an afterthought, she opened the door again and tossed my cellphone out. It clattered to the sidewalk. I glared at her, but she did not even acknowledge the act. I picked up my phone and inspected it. The screen now had multiple cracks.

"That bitch," I muttered.

A couple of minutes later, she returned with Bull and Flaky, performed the same ritual, and let them out.

Bull looked around and spotted Ronald. His eyes narrowed. "Who the hell are you?" he bellowed.

Ronald winced and started trembling.

"Lay off him, he's the one who got us out of this jam," I said and briefly explained.

"You did all that? That's righteous, brother," Flaky said and patted him on the back. "I'm Flaky and the big one here is Bull. What's your name, brother?"

Ronald briefly glanced at Flaky before running to the end of the sidewalk and puking.

CHAPTER 23

We crammed into Ronald's car, which wasn't easy. He had a two-door Kia, and four grown men made for a tight fit, even if one of them was only half-grown.

"Where to?" Ronald asked.

"The impound lot," I replied.

The Memphis Police impound lot was a large area of asphalt surrounded by fencing and concertina wire. It was full of vehicles of all types and ranged from brand new to totally FUBAR'ed. The front office was an atypical prefab metal building. The officer behind the bulletproof glass was a rather snarky old fart and refused to release my Explorer unless I paid the four-hundred-dollar tow and impound fee. I made it clear I thought the exorbitant fee was a scam and he retaliated by claiming the credit card machine was down and insisted on cash only. Lucky for me, I had it on me. I slapped down some hundreds and fed it through the slot. A minute later, he slid my keys through the slot and gave me vague directions to the parking lot where my Explorer was located.

They'd done a job on it. The panels and seats had all been disassembled and were now lying in disarray. The gun safe I had mounted in my console had also been cut open and our two handguns were missing. Looking around, my detective's kit was missing too. I'd kept my anger in check up until now, but the sight of the desecration of my new vehicle went beyond the pall. I pulled out my phone and tried it, but either the battery was dead or it too was FUBAR'ed.

"Let me see your phone," I demanded of Ronald. I knew Reuben Chandler's cell number by memory. I called and it went to voicemail. I took a few photos of my Explorer, sent them, and then called back.

"Alright, you little cocksucker, you want to play dirty? I'm going to ruin you. It's bad enough you people illegally arrest my friends and me, but you couldn't stop there. You had to have your people tear up both my phone and my SUV. Based on what you assholes did to me in the past, do you think you're going to come out of this smelling like a rose? This is going to court, my friend, and the FBI legal staff may delay it for a few years, but I'll win in the end. And, it may not do any good, but I'm also going to file a civil rights complaint with the Department of Justice against you, Stainback, and Pollard. And, if none of that does any good, I'm just going to hunt you down and beat the ever-loving hell out of you."

I hit the end button and handed it back to Ronald, who tentatively took it from my grasp and eyed me worriedly.

"Are you okay, Thomas?" he asked.

I took a deep breath. "No, but I will be. How in the world did you end up down here anyway?"

"Um, well, you know I monitor you because, well, sometimes you get yourself into trouble."

"No shit," Flaky said and chuckled. I ignored him and kept staring at Ronald.

"Alright, so you saw on the phone's GPS that I was at the FBI headquarters. How did you know we were in a fix?" I asked.

"Um, well, I put an app on your phone where I can monitor any conversations within a few feet of your phone."

I continued staring at him, wondering how long that app had been on my phone and how many confidential conversations he'd listened to.

"I had a feeling something was wrong, so I turned on the app and started listening. The first thing I heard was them telling you that they were sending you to prison. I knew then I needed to help you. I tried calling William, but he didn't answer, and your phone eventually died, so I came up with a plan."

"You pretended to be an attorney," I accused.

"Yeah, sort of. I kind of thought it up on the way down."

"And you drove all the way down here?" I asked.

He nodded. I don't remember Ronald ever traveling more than a few miles from his home unaccompanied. For him to do so was a major breakthrough, regardless of the circumstances. I set that thought aside for the moment.

"Is that phone app how you knew about their investigation?" I asked.

Ronald nodded again. "One of them had taken it but kept it with them almost the whole time. I activated it at about two o'clock this morning and listened to them talking. They didn't say a whole lot, but they mentioned Wolf and something about abductions. Apparently, they think Wolf and his people are involved in some kind of human trafficking ring and they were worried you'd messed up their case. They said some pretty harsh things about you."

"You are certainly a sneaky little shit," I finally said.

"Are you mad?" he asked.

"Of course not," I replied. "You did good, didn't he, guys?" I asked Bull and Flaky.

"Wait a minute, you told the FBI you're an attorney but you really ain't?" Bull asked.

When Ronald timidly nodded his head, Bull roared in laughter and draped one of his enormous arms around him. "You got some balls on you, little man, I like that."

I thought Ronald was going to puke again.

All I had in the way of tools was a Leatherman and a crescent wrench that had been left in the glove compartment. And, it seemed like we were missing a few nuts and bolts. While we tried to get the seats bolted back down, the old fart from the impound office drove up in a golf cart and demanded to know what was taking so long. When I explained and showed him what the FBI agents did, he grunted like it was our fault, but relented and brought us some tools. He pointed at a wrecked Explorer the next row over.

"You can probably find some replacement bolts off of that, but don't get greedy. Also, those tools ain't gifts, bring them back when you're finished," he instructed before driving off.

It took us an hour, but we got the seats secure enough to ride in. After a stop at a gas station, we headed back to Nashville. Bull opted to ride with Ronald. He gave me an anxious look but I assured him it'd be okay. As soon as Bull got in, he reclined the seat. I had no doubt he'd be asleep within minutes.

"He's an odd little guy, but I like him," Flaky commented.

"He came through for us," I replied. "If not for him, we'd be sitting in jail right now."

"Yeah, he's alright." With that, he made himself comfortable and closed his eyes. He was soon breathing deeply.

I fumed in silence as I drove. My car was a mess, my phone did not work, my handgun was gone, and I had no doubt those two Fibbies were going to try their hardest to make good on their threat.

Since it was a Sunday morning, traffic was light and we made good time and arrived back in Nashville by three in the afternoon. We parked our cars, got out, and stretched. I looked around, wondering where Anna was, but her car was absent.

"So, what's next?" Flaky asked.

I was looking at the exterior of my new car and spotted a couple of dings and scratches, causing me to sigh heavily.

"I'm not sure yet, my friend. I have to think this over."

"Are those Feds going to charge us?" Bull asked.

"I seriously doubt they'll charge you two, but if they do, I'll have legal representation for you."

"What about you?" Flaky asked. "Are they going to charge you?"

I started to let out another sigh, but caught myself. "I honestly don't know. I'm going to fix myself a drink. Do you two want one?"

Flaky shook his head. "Nah, man, we need to get going."

"I understand. I appreciate you two, I really do," I said.

"One thing's for sure, you never know what's going to happen when you're around," Flaky said.

Bull laughed in agreement. He then walked over to Ronald and grabbed his shoulder. "Alright, little man, you got yourself a couple of new friends, and we take care of our friends, ain't that right, Flaky?"

"Damn right," Flaky agreed.

CHAPTER 24

Ronald and I shook their hands and watched them exit my driveway. After they'd left, I motioned for Ronald to follow me inside.

"I'm going to fix myself a drink, do you want anything?" I asked.

"I'll take a Coke, if you have one," he said. "Lots of ice."

Refreshments in hand, I motioned for him to sit with me at the kitchen table.

"So, tell me how you came up with this scheme?"

He took a sip of coke and shrugged. "I don't know. I mean, I keep tabs on you. You want me to, right?"

"Yeah, but I didn't know about this spy app you put on my phone," I rejoined.

Ronald shrugged. "Anyway, I kind of monitored your trip down to Memphis and saw where you had parked and figured that was where the fights were taking place."

"Keep going."

"So, I had it on one of my computers and just kind of watched some while I played one of my online games."

"When did you activate the spy app?" I asked.

"Um, sometime after you left the fight. I was kind of curious what kind of guys Bull and Flaky were, so I turned on the app and was listening to you guys talk."

He hastened a glance at me to try and gauge how I felt about him spying on us.

"Go on," I directed.

"At one point, I heard you guys get real tense and then I heard the sirens and the police on their loudspeakers and I realized you guys were in trouble. It took me a while to figure out when that woman FBI agent took your phone, but I was able to hear everything she said, and she doesn't like you at all."

"And you came up with the wild idea of posing as my attorney," I said.

Ronald gave a deprecating shrug. "I tried calling William, and then Sherman. When they didn't answer, it was the only thing I could come up with."

"You didn't call Anna or Percy?" I asked.

Ronald now looked decidedly uncomfortable but didn't answer.

"When did you start recording?" I asked.

"They left your phone somewhere while they were interrogating Bull and Flaky. Maybe somebody's office, but then they'd come back and talk about the interrogations." He looked somberly at me now. "The man suggested to the woman that if you didn't confess anything, they could, in his words, create some kind of incriminating evidence."

My blood ran cold. These two were already playing fast and loose with their authority as government agents, but if they were willing to fabricate evidence, this put a whole new perspective on the matter.

"Alright, and then what?" I asked.

Ronald finished his coke and sucked on an ice cube. "I was on the road by then. At first, I was just going to tell them I was your business partner, but when they started talking about setting you up, I knew I had to do something drastic."

"Set me up?" I asked.

"Yeah. They were talking about planting evidence in your car, but it was like two stupid people talking. First, they couldn't decide what to plant. So, they finally decided on drugs, but then realized they didn't have any drugs on hand to use. It was funny listening to them. If not for the fact that they were, you know, trying to screw you."

"You had a business card with the Goldman Law Firm embossed on it," I reminded him.

Ronald blushed. "Yeah, I made those to impress Barbie."

Barbie, the crack whore who had bamboozled him. I finished my scotch and started to pat him on the arm but remembered he did not like to be touched. He was still rubbing his shoulder where Bull had grabbed him.

"Like Bull said, it was ballsy, and I have to admit, I'm proud of you, but I'm not happy with you eavesdropping on my conversations. You probably put the same app on Anna's phone too, didn't you?"

Ronald turned a deeper shade of red and reluctantly nodded.

"She'd be furious with you if she finds out. We're going to get it deleted immediately, copy?"

"Yessir," he answered.

"And, even though you saved our asses, it was risky. Too risky. If they figured out who you really are, they could have arrested you, and we can't have that. Unless you want your current lifestyle to make a drastic change, we have to keep you under the radar."

Ronald nodded and slurped on another ice cube before his face lit up.

"Oh, by the way, the doctor's office called. I don't have any STDs."

He started grinning like a Cheshire cat. In spite of things, I couldn't help but laugh. I held up my tumbler of scotch in salute.

"Congrats."

Ronald downloaded the snippets of conversation he had recorded onto my laptop before leaving. Some of it was garbled, but the part where they discussed setting me up was crystal clear. Like Ronald said, those two agents actually talked about planting evidence in my vehicle. It would seal the deal on a lawsuit.

I looked at my cellphone; it was trashed. Yet another thing those idiots were going to answer for. Perhaps it was the lack of sleep coupled with my downing of the scotch quicker than I normally did, but I decided to pen an eloquent email to Special Agent-in-Charge Reuben Chandler. True, I'd already left him a profanity-laced voicemail, but in my opinion, that wasn't enough.

My verbiage was slightly more civil this time, but I made it clear I was not pleased. I included a photograph of my SUV and phone, and emphasized I was holding him personally responsible and had every intention of filing a lawsuit. I clicked the send button with a slight amount of satisfaction and went to bed.

The aroma of coffee roused me the next morning. Anna was sitting at the kitchen table doing something with my laptop when I walked in. I poured myself a cup and sat across from her.

"Where've you been?" I asked.

"I tried calling you last night," she replied. I pointed to my broken phone sitting on the table and explained. She listened in incredulity as I talked.

"Can they do that?" she asked. "I mean, can they tear up people's property like that and arrest them?"

"Not legally. I'm going to call William in a little bit and get the ball rolling on a cause of action."

Her expression tightened and she gave me a cool stare. It wasn't difficult to know what she was thinking.

"Listen, I love Sherman, he's a good man and the best lawyer I've ever known, but he's getting old and winding down his career. So, my second choice is William. You know he's a damn good attorney."

"What about Hal?" she asked. "You've always said he's good."

"Yeah, he'd be a good one for this as well, but he has too much on his plate at the moment. Besides, William came through like a champ when I sued Nashville."

I know she did not like it, but after a moment she gave a slight, reluctant nod.

"You two still aren't talking?" I asked.

"No, it's over." She got up and carried my coffee cup over to the pot.

"I'm sorry to hear that," I said.

She acknowledged my conciliation with a slight, sad smile and sat back down with my cup refilled. She then changed the subject.

"Do you want some breakfast?" she asked and then stood again. "I'll fix some eggs and bacon."

"No, that's alright," I said. "I need to head to the phone store and get this fixed. I can stop at a restaurant on the way."

She nodded and sat back down. She fidgeted some more, but now focused on me. "I need to tell you something."

"Okay, what's on your mind?" I asked.

"You may have noticed I didn't come home last night. I called to let you know, but obviously your phone wasn't working."

"Yeah, no worries," I said, and meant it, but when I made eye contact with her, she immediately looked down at the table.

"Alright, I'm not the guy to stick my nose in your business, but I'm getting the impression there's something you think I should know but you're reluctant to tell me."

"I spent the night with Percy," she blurted. "I mean, we didn't sleep together, but I stayed over." She looked at me anxiously and waited for my reaction. I nodded slowly and sipped my coffee.

"Say something," she implored.

"Um, I'm not sure what to say." I was telling the truth. I was at a loss for words, but I now understood why Ronald had looked so uncomfortable earlier. Thanks to his spy app, he knew she was with Percy.

"You don't approve," she said.

"I didn't say that. I'm not sure what to say. How long has this been going on?"

"Last night was our official first date. He took me out for my birthday," she said.

"Oh, shit, I totally forgot. I'm so sorry."

"It's okay," she said. "So, let's hear it, what do you think about Percy and me?"

"Um, well, that's not an easy question to answer. Percy's a good man, a complicated man, you might even say he's a troubled man, but a good man. He's also a few years older than you." In fact, he was forty-two, only two years younger than me, and Anna was twenty-two. Correction, twenty-three.

"You don't like our age difference."

I struggled to find the right words. "I mean, it's not an issue for me, but it could prove problematic for you two in certain social situations."

"Like what?" she pressed.

"People like to think of themselves as enlightened, but the truth is they're still prejudicial hypocrites. There will be many who will disapprove of your age difference."

"I don't care about that, and I don't think anyone will criticize Percy to his face and get away with it."

She was right. Most of the time, Percy's stare alone would prevent someone from running their mouth. I sipped my coffee, thinking of the appropriate piece of advice. Anna was a beautiful young lady, but emotionally, she still had a lot of kid in her.

"I just want to you to be happy," I finally said.

I finished my coffee and stood. She stood as well. I reached out and gave her a hug, which seemed like the right thing to do. In the brief time we'd known each other, she'd come to look at me as a father figure and frequently sought my approval. I patted her on the back and gently broke contact.

"Alright, we can talk more about Percy later. Right now, I have a surprise for you."

I refused to tell her what it was, and instead coaxed her to my Mustang.

"Where are we going?" she asked.

"Not far," I answered, and soon we were turning into my neighbor Buford's driveway. He had his garage door open and was tinkering with something on his workbench. Two dogs were in the driveway playing tug-of-war with a length of rope. One of the dogs was a German Shepherd puppy mix. As soon as we got out of the car, she forgot all about the rope and bounded over to Anna. Anna crouched down and she was quickly assaulted with licks to the face, which caused her to giggle uncontrollably.

"Happy birthday," I said.

She looked up in surprise. "What do you mean?"

"Buford found her in a ditch on the side of the road. She's a sweet girl and in good health. We talked about it and thought she'd be a good birthday present for you."

Buford had stopped whatever he was doing and walked up.

"You were supposed to give it to her yesterday," he remarked.

"Yeah, I messed up."

"She's beautiful," Anna said.

"The vet said she's about ten to twelve weeks old and in good health," Buford said. "As you can see, she's full of energy, but she ain't housebroken and she needs her second round of Parvo shots."

"What's her name?" Anna asked.

"Well, Thomas and I were going to let you name her, but I've been calling her Gracie," he said. "She's young enough where you can change her name though. It won't mess her up any."

Anna held her at arm's length. "Gracie is a beautiful name," she said and then hugged the dog tightly. The dog responded by trying to eat her hair.

Special Agent-in-Charge Reuben Chandler and a sizeable black man were standing in my drive when the three of us arrived back at my house. Gracie yipped at the sight of the two of them. Whether she sensed she was guarding her new home from strangers or she saw them as playmates was debatable. I gave it fifty-fifty.

"I would have brought my wife to protect me, but she had to work," Reuben said. "So, I brought a co-worker. Thomas, Anna, this is Special Agent Dresden Carpenter."

"Good morning, sir, ma'am," he said in a deep baritone voice. He was dark skinned and even though he was wearing a suit, it looked like he had the physique of a linebacker. I had no doubt he could handle himself.

"Why are you here?" I asked.

"You wouldn't answer your phone," Reuben replied.

"That's because one of your minions destroyed it," Anna huffed and gave Reuben a brief withering stare before turning and carrying her yipping present into the house.

I pulled my phone out of my pocket and handed it to Reuben. "Thanks to Un-Special Agent Stainback, it no longer works."

He looked it over thoughtfully before handing it to Agent Carpenter. Agent Carpenter tried to turn it on. He didn't seem surprised when it didn't work.

"Now that wasn't very nice," he remarked, and to my surprise. he pulled his own phone out of his jacket pocket and took a few photos of my damaged phone before handing it back to me.

"Would you like to take a look at what they did to my Explorer?" I asked.

I led them around to the back of the house and watched as the two men inspected my SUV. Agent Carpenter did not hesitate and began taking more photos.

"Agent Carpenter is with OPR, the Office of Professional Responsibility," Reuben said. "He is conducting a formal investigation of Agents Stainback and Pollard."

Reuben caught my look and offered a small, friendly smile. "Contrary to what you may think, I did not authorize Stainback and Pollard's actions." He gestured toward Agent Carpenter. "Special Agent Carpenter is one of our best and he expects nothing but professionalism from our agents."

"Mister Ironcutter, we would like for you to come to the office where we can conduct a formal interview," Agent Carpenter requested. "Your cooperation would be greatly appreciated."

I shook my head slowly. "I believe I'm done being ordered around by Fibs. If you want to question me, we can do it here."

They reluctantly agreed and we relocated to my kitchen table. I poured myself a large glass of ice water and reluctantly offered them coffee. Agent Carpenter produced a notepad that seemed to look a little different than a normal notepad. Dresden saw my interest.

"It's one of those smart notepads," he said, showing it to me. "I write my notes on it, take a picture with a special app on my phone, and it automatically converts my notes to a PDF and emails it to a cloud account."

I looked at it a moment longer before handing it back to him. "Why don't you simply record me with your smartphone?" I asked.

"That is against FBI protocol. As a rule, we only record an interview under special or extraordinary circumstances."

"That's dumb," I muttered. "You should record all interviews."

Dresden offhandedly nodded. "Shall we begin?"

Reuben remained quiet and let Agent Carpenter conduct the interview. The questions and answers lasted no less than two hours. I started with the fight in Memphis.

"It is my understanding you were advised to stand down from your investigation," Agent Carpenter asked.

"Yes. Reuben and Stainback paid me a visit a few days ago. I chose to continue my investigation into the murder of Jason Belew, but let's be clear: my investigation in no way interfered with any FBI investigation. To infer differently would require proof, which there is none. Have you read the affidavits on the search warrant?"

Dresden pursed his lips. "I admit, the probable cause is weak."

I scoffed. "Yeah, that's one way of putting it."

Agent Carpenter jotted a few notes before looking up. "Please continue."

I continued with minimal interruptions and went slowly so Agent Carpenter could keep up with his notes. I had to admit, the man was both professional and thorough. He asked about my attorney. I replied my attorney of record was Sherman Goldman, but the entire staff of the Goldman Law Firm was at my disposal. He did not question me about Ronald's presence in Memphis. That could prove problematic if anyone found out who Ronald was, but I'd deal with it if it happened.

Which led to another dilemma. If I played the recording of the two agents conspiring to set me up, I would have to give them the details about how the recording was obtained. I decided to keep that information to myself as well—for now.

Once Agent Carpenter was finished, he tucked away his notepad and offered a placating smile.

"I'm sure you know these things take time, but I can promise you there will be a resolution to the matter," Reuben said.

I peered closely at the two men.

"I'm sensing there is more going on here than two agents trampling on my rights."

"Indeed," Agent Carpenter replied.

"Care to clue me in?" I asked.

I watched Reuben give a subtle nod to Agent Carpenter.

"Agents Pollard and Stainback are under investigation not only for their actions regarding you and your friends, but for the entire case investigation."

"What kind of case is it?" I asked.

Reuben finished his coffee and deliberately set the cup down on the kitchen table. "Why don't we go outside and take another look at the damage to your vehicle." Without waiting for an answer, he stood, which caused Agent Carpenter and me to stand as well. I followed them outside and the three of us stopped in front of my Explorer.

"I bought it off of the showroom floor, did I mention that?" I asked rather sarcastically.

"Twice now," Agent Carpenter replied.

"I don't believe I've mentioned the Nashville office has a fleet of Ford Explorers," Reuben remarked. "All of them have been modified, of course, but we have a contract with a local Ford dealership to service and repair the vehicles."

"How nice," I said.

"I know you are an avid mechanic, but if you would be willing, we can have your Explorer towed to the dealership and they can make the necessary repairs," he said. "I'll have them make it a priority and it should be repaired in a couple of days. Would that be acceptable, Thomas?"

"Will the FBI be paying the bill?" I asked.

"Of course," he replied.

"What about my two stolen handguns and other property?"

"It is currently in Memphis. I am in the process of having it shipped to the Nashville office."

"I have a better idea: ship it directly to me, or else arrest Agent Stainback for theft," I said.

Reuben smiled patiently. "One of us has to deliver it to you personally. It should be here within a couple of days. I'm sure you have one or two backup weapons to tide you over in the meantime."

That was an understatement. I had several weapons stored in my gun safe I could choose from.

"What is your decision, Thomas?" Reuben asked.

I thought it over. They would probably take the opportunity to install a GPS device in it, but I'd be able to find it and disable it. "Alright."

He nodded. "Good."

I pulled my key fob out and handed it to him. "Now, are you two going to clue me in on what this super-secret investigation is all about?"

Reuben answered in a manner of a man accustomed to deflecting and avoiding a direct response. "A formal investigation of Agents Stainback and Pollard is underway."

"I see." He answered my question vaguely enough to not tell me jack-shit. Typical FBI. "You know, that doesn't tell me much. I guess you don't trust me with the information."

Reuben's expression tightened and he glanced at Agent Carpenter, who shrugged.

"It's your call, sir."

Reuben's frown intensified somewhat before he cleared his throat.

"Over the course of the past five years, there have been thirty-seven abductions of young women in which those groups of gypsies are the primary suspects," he said.

CHAPTER 25

My mouth went dry. "Did I hear you correctly?"

Reuben gave a terse nod. "You did. This is a joint investigation with Interpol. The first known abduction occurred in Romania five years ago. The majority of them are in eastern European countries, but there have been three in the United States. Three that we know of. The last one occurred on February twenty-first in McMinnville. That is the last one we know of. There may be others."

Enlightenment dawned on me and hit me like a sledgehammer. "Telisha Thompkins," I said.

"Yes. Interpol believes this is the work of a white slavery ring. It wasn't until the last month that we got a major break when Raymondo Calendar contacted his cousin and wanted to make a deal."

Reuben gave what you'd call a pregnant pause, waiting to see if I made the connection. I thought about it a moment before figuring it out.

"His cousin is Special Agent Juanita Stainback," I said.

"Yes. Second cousin, I believe. He was arrested by the DEA and was facing the possibility of several years' imprisonment."

"Did he have good information?" I asked.

"He did. I'm going to decline to get into specifics, I'm sure you can understand, but we're close to breaking this case," he said.

I digested the information and worked it over in my mind.

"What are you thinking, Thomas?" Agent Carpenter asked.

"I'm trying to figure out how Jason Belew's murder figures into all of this," I said.

"You seem certain the suspect in his murder is one of the gypsies," he said.

"I am. Jason had no problems with anyone at that event and he was last seen talking with Wolf. The only injury he had was a crushed throat and someone made the effort to hide his body. It was a rush job; they only intended it to stay hidden long enough to allow them some time to get away. They did not know it would stay hidden for as long as it did."

"Perhaps he saw the abduction of Telisha Thompkins," Agent Carpenter surmised.

"Yeah, perhaps."

I thought about it a moment. "I'm sure you guys know Telisha also went to the event."

"Yes," Agent Carpenter said. "The TBI has located some video of her in the audience, but we do not have much more than that. Agent Meeks has begun the process of interviewing people who were at the event. Unfortunately, people have not been very forthcoming."

I nodded. "She had been interacting with someone on social media."

"Another dead end. By the time that was investigated, the information had been deleted from the internet."

"Alright, see if you agree to the following: Telisha meets someone online who promises her the moon and stars. Let's say that person is Wolf. He lures her to the fight and promises to take her away with him. She agrees. Maybe Jason sees the two of them together. Wolf and his crew decide he is a potential eyewitness and therefore a liability. So, Wolf gets him alone and kills him."

"It is certainly a viable scenario," Agent Carpenter said. "So, indulge me, please. What do you think happens next?"

"They get Telisha in their RV somehow, either by ruse or force. Maybe Jason sees this. Wolf kills Jason, but he realizes he has to do something with the body. He spots the abandoned train cars. For a physically fit man, it would not be difficult for him to throw Jason's lifeless body over his shoulders and carry him.

"Or, even better, he lured Jason to the train cars with the promise of sex or something. Once they were out of eyesight to any potential witnesses, he then kills him."

Both men gave slight nods. "And then what?" Reuben asked.

"Simple, they carry Telisha to their transfer location. My guess is Chicago. After all, Chicago has an international airport and shipping ports. If I were to guess, I'd say they use the shipping ports, simply because security is not as strict and it'd be easier to get into and out of."

This time Reuben frowned. "But why Chicago?"

Surprisingly, they were unaware of the Chicago link.

"They have connections to Chicago."

I gave a somewhat brief explanation without fully explaining Lilith. Dresden took out his phone and began tapping on it. I assumed he was texting someone, or perhaps accessing an FBI database. They didn't tell me much—it was more like a one-way street on information exchange—but that was okay. I gleaned bits and pieces from the nature of the questions they asked me.

As soon as they left, Anna walked outside and put Gracie in the yard. She promptly started sniffing around and pounced on a bug.

"She's already peed on the floor," she said. "Don't worry, I've cleaned it up."

"You're responsible for training her," I admonished. "And cleaning up after her."

"I know, don't worry. What are you doing today?" she asked.

"I'm going to a phone store and get this thing fixed. What about you?"

"Ms. Braxton is paying Marti and me to help her with a charity function she's hosting."

"What are you going to do about Gracie?" I asked.

She bit her lip when she realized she was going to be leaving Gracie alone on her first night in her new home.

"She'll be alright inside, won't she?" she asked.

"Nope. She's still a puppy. She will need frequent potty trips outside and if she doesn't get attention, she'll find stuff to chew up."

We talked about it and decided to set up a bed for her in the garage. The weather was decent enough and anything in there that she could tear up would not be that much of an issue.

"You shouldn't be gone all night though. She's like a little kid; she needs lots of attention."

"The function is over at six, so I should be home an hour later. I promise," she said.

"Good. I might grab a bite to eat somewhere and hang out at Mick's a little while."

"Why don't you ask Debbie out?" she said with a teasing smile.

"I'm not up for it right now. Maybe in a day or two," I replied.

I hopped in my Mustang and went to a meat-and-three restaurant on Charlotte Pike. The bubbly waitress informed me the day's special was country fried steak. I got sides of potatoes, green beans, coleslaw, and a large glass of sweet tea, of course.

The place was full of strangers who had no idea who I was, so I was left to my own thoughts as I ate. I wondered about the abductions, and if my phone worked, I would have got on the internet and see what I could find. The thought of what Stainback and Pollard did to me continued to irk me, but Reuben and his agent had at least temporarily placated me. I made a note to, at the minimum, give Sherman a call and at least talk to him about it, even though I knew I wasn't going to sue.

Finishing my meal, I left a decent tip and headed to the phone store. The kid who waited on me looked at my ruined phone and snorted.

"What happened, did your wife get mad at you?" he asked with a gleeful grin.

"Something like that," I answered. "What are my options?"

He stared at the phone, making a face the whole time. "Dude, this one is toast. And it's an older model. You should get the latest model. Upgrade, that's the way to go."

"Yeah, alright," I said.

He typed up my name on his computer and happily informed me I had not purchased the optional insurance plan. I guessed he worked off of commission.

"No problem, though. We can put you on a payment plan and even upgrade you to the latest model," he said. "Plus, you really ought to get the insurance."

"Can you download the data I have on this one to the new phone?" I asked, pointing at my broken phone.

"Oh, sure. It'll only take a few minutes."

Ten minutes later and the young man had me set up. I signed the new contract, which included insurance. I activated it before stuffing it in my pocket and walking out the door. My phone jingled within a minute, but it was an unfamiliar ringtone. Not realizing all of the ringtones had been reset, I ignored it and looked at my watch.

"Plenty of time," I mumbled and headed over to Mick's.

When I patronized Mick's, I usually measured the passage of time by the number of beers and/or cigars I consumed. On this occasion, I'd had exactly one beer and one cigar while playing with my new phone. Most of the new features were nothing I needed but they were still fun to play with. I got another beer and started browsing the internet on the abductions.

The most informational item was a long article written by a woman. I searched her name and learned she was an award-winning investigative journalist from France named Hannah Barron. She wrote a series of articles featuring the victims from Romania. Each woman was young, between sixteen to twenty-four, and all of them were from low socioeconomic backgrounds. The first abduction was a nineteen-year-old who the journalist described as a troubled girl battling a drug addiction and had started working at an escort service prior to her disappearance.

Ms. Barron went on to describe the apparent ineptitude of the local law enforcement agencies and their reluctance to admit the disappearances were related. It was not until a young woman barely escaped with her life that the detectives were able to develop the common denominator.

The victim told a story of how she had met a man through an online dating service. They had met at a bar for a few drinks and to get to know each other. She described him as a ruggedly handsome man in his thirties, and although she felt he was rather crass, she liked him enough to accept his invitation to accompany him to a popular discotheque. Looking back, she felt like she was drugged while still at the bar. She stated she barely remembered leaving the bar and getting into a waiting car. She thought someone other than her blind date was driving, but she was not certain.

When she regained her senses, she was tightly bound and inside the boot of the car. She managed to kick the lid open and roll out, landing heavily on the road. She was badly injured, but fortunately, she picked a spot where several people were outside and witnessed her escape. Whoever was driving the vehicle slowed, but then sped away. Police later found the car. It had been reported stolen two day's previous. The article finished with a composite drawing of her abductor. It bore a likeness to Wolf, but it could have been a match for a thousand other Romanian men.

I clicked off of the internet and ordered another beer. Debbie sent me a flirtatious text and I responded in kind. We went back and forth a couple of times and I found myself wondering what she'd be like between the sheets. Someone slapped down a manila file folder on the bar top beside me. I looked to see Puffessor Ebenezer Farquhar standing over me, giving me a toothy grin.

"How are you, Ebbie?" I said. He pulled out the bar stool beside me and sat.

"I've been looking for you," he proclaimed.

"Oh, yeah?"

He waited until he'd lit a cigar before responding. "Yes indeed." He then gestured at the file folder with his butane lighter. "I've been doing some extensive research since my last conversation with that little split-tail roommate of yours."

"Don't call her that," I warned.

He held a hand up in mock regret. "My apologies," he said.

He was quiet now, only holding up a finger for Kim to bring him a beer. Kim took a moment to chat with me. I noticed this agitated Ebbie, so I continued chatting with her about random things until Ebbie could not stand it any longer. He slammed his beer down and vigorously tapped a stubby finger on the folder.

"Aren't you going to read this? I spent a lot of work on it."

"Okay, I suppose I'll give it a look," I said and subtly winked at Kim.

I casually set my beer down and opened the folder. After a couple of minutes of reading, I looked at Ebbie.

"This is good stuff, Ebbie. I'm impressed."

He grinned smugly. "I believe a certain somebody owes me a blowjob."

Ebbie and I talked about his research for a while before he finished his cigar and left. I had almost forgotten about the voicemails, started to ignore them, but then clicked on the icon. A couple of them were old messages from Anna. The rest were either spam or potential customers.

When the fifth message began playing, my pleasant disposition disappeared and the cigar fell out of my mouth.

CHAPTER 26

"Thomas, I need you. Please call me back."

The tone of her voice held a hint of concern, perhaps urgency. By her fourth message, she sounded frantic and was practically begging for help. I called back immediately, but it went straight to a voice mailbox that had not been set up to receive messages.

I puffed frantically on my cigar as I repeatedly called her, but each time it went directly to the nonfunctioning voicemail. I called Ronald and gave him the number provided by my caller ID. Several tense minutes elapsed before he called back and informed me the number was a burner and it had pinged a phone tower in north Nashville several hours ago. He gave me the location of the tower and I took off. It was located in the Bordeaux area, near Whites Creek Pike and Briley Parkway.

My next instinct was to call Percy, but that would've been problematic. After all, she was the primary suspect in an open murder case he was investigating. If I got him involved, and we found her, he would have no choice but to revert to detective mode and take her in.

I drove around the area of the cell tower all night, up and down every street, some more than once. At times, I parked and walked. I looked everywhere. If I drove by a ditch that wasn't illuminated by street lights, I'd get out and walk the ditch, up and down, exploring with my flashlight. A rational person would have reasoned it was a futile effort; she could have been anywhere. But it was the only lead I had.

It wasn't until the sun was coming up, that I realized two things; I'd forgotten all about the puppy and I'd been driving in aimless circles for the last two hours. I'd driven by the sign identifying the entrance to the Whites Creek quarry so many times I barely gave it any thought, but this time I happened to notice the gate was standing open, and it occurred to me as I drove by that the gate had been closed during the night.

I hung a U-turn and drove through the entrance. The road was a dusty gravel drive that led to a prefab metal building and the quarry. I could see a car and a man in a security guard's uniform standing a dozen feet away from a clump on the side of the drive. As I drove closer, I could see the clump was actually a body.

She was lying on her stomach, motionless, like a piece of discarded trash. Her head was turned to the side and facing me. Her face was the color of old alabaster and she was staring with vacant eyes, like she'd been patiently waiting for me. Or perhaps it was an accusing stare, wondering why I had forsaken her. All men were pigs, right, Lilith?

I absently put my car in park and stepped out, all the while never taking my eyes off of her. A wave of emotions washed over me as I slowly walked toward her, feeling lightheaded, almost like vertigo. I'd not felt this way since I was a rookie cop and walked into a small apartment where the sole occupant had died several months previously. The thick, rancid smell of decomposition had made me nauseous and lightheaded then. Lilith did not smell, but I felt the same. I dropped down to one knee to steady myself.

"Excuse me, but you can't be here."

I looked up to see the security guard. He'd moved away from the protection of his car and walked toward me but came no closer than twenty feet from the two of us. I ignored him and focused back on Lilith. She was dressed casually; jeans, a long-sleeve white shirt with a logo of a Daytona Beach bar on the front, braless, Chuck Taylor sneakers that were dirty from where she had been dragged. There were no overt signs of injury, but the misalignment of her neck told me everything.

"Sir, you can't be here," the security guard implored. "The cops are on their way and they aren't going to be happy with you in their crime scene."

I stood and pointed at his phone. "Are you still on the line with 911?"

"Yeah, I am," he replied, sounding a little bolder now.

"Tell them they need to dispatch Detective Percy to this location. The victim's name is Lilith Gray and she is a person of interest in one of his murder investigations."

My statement seemed to befuddle him. He looked at me like I was speaking in tongues. I snapped my fingers.

"Do it!" I barked.

To his credit, he cleared his throat and repeated verbatim what I'd said. He listened to the response and his confused expression intensified.

"The 911 lady wants to know who you are."

I ignored him, got in my Mustang, and sped off.

I had not slept in over twenty-four hours, but the blood was coursing through my veins like a feral mixture of adrenalin and anger. The Mustang roared with fury, matching my mood. I negotiated the morning traffic like I was a fleeing bank robber and arrived at Candy's condo within thirty minutes.

Candy opened the door as I bounded up the steps. The scowl on his face made it obvious he was not happy to see me.

"Man, you can't be here," he declared. "Now, get the hell going, or else…"

Before he could finish his ultimatum, I gave him a chest slap, much like professional wrestlers do to each other. Unfortunately for Candy, he was no professional wrestler. The slap knocked the wind out of him and he stumbled back. I followed him in, slammed the door behind me, and grabbed him by the shirt before he fell to the floor.

"Enough of this bullshit," I growled. "You are going to tell me what you know, or else."

"Daddy?"

I jerked my head toward the voice to see a cute little girl standing in the den, staring in fright at me with big brown eyes and hugging a doll with both arms. It was Candy's daughter and she'd witnessed me assaulting her father. I had no doubt I was frightening her.

"Jesus," I muttered under my breath and immediately helped steady Candy. "We were just playing around, sweetie," I said.

Candy had regained his balance but was still gasping for breath and scowled at me in indignation. I gave him a brief stare of my own before letting go of him and walking back outside. To my surprise, Candy followed and confronted me before I made it to my car.

"What the hell, man? Do you think you can just come to my crib and jump on me in front of my daughter? I'm going to get you charged, man. This is bullshit."

"Lilith is dead," I said. "She was murdered."

Candy's expression turned from anger to puzzlement. "Who the hell is Lilith?"

"You probably don't know her by her real name. She was the woman with Wolf," I said.

"You mean Midnight?" he asked.

"Yeah."

He gawked in a mixture of bewilderment and suspicion. I guess he was trying to decide if I was lying or not.

"Daddy?"

His daughter was now standing in the open doorway, confused by the strange, angry white man with her father. I was not going to be able to talk to Candy as long as she was around, but it wasn't like I could do anything about it. Thankfully, Candy's curiosity was piqued.

"I'll only be a minute, boo. Go watch your TV show," he said. "Go on now." He waited until she had shut the door. "What happened?"

"I don't know everything, but she was found this morning up in north Nashville. It looked like her neck was broken."

"You saw her?" he asked.

"Yeah."

His eyes narrowed. "So, how do I know you didn't kill her?"

I took a long deep breath before answering. "Midnight used to live in Nashville. She and I were friends. Good friends. I had no reason or inclination to kill her. You and I both know who really did it."

He continued staring. "Look, Ironcutter, you're getting in over your head. Hell, I'm in over my head. That Wolf dude is mean, and those old men look harmless, but they are just as dangerous."

"How did you get involved in this? Are you working off a charge?"

He scoffed. "One charge? Man, the DEA's hemmed me up for over a dozen charges. The way the indictment reads, you'd think I was Pablo Escobar."

"You're looking at a few years in federal prison, I take it," I said.

"Yeah. My baby's momma has her in one of those fancy pre-schools, and let me tell you, that ain't cheap. I'm a high school dropout, man. I'll never have a high-paying white-collar job. All I know how to do is hustle."

"You looked like you made quite a bit down in Memphis," I remarked.

Candy shrugged and rubbed his chest under his T-shirt. "Man, that shit hurt, you didn't have to do that."

"You said he generally does not stay long after a fight. Did he leave immediately after his fight in Manchester?"

Candy stared in silence before slowly shaking his head.

"Tell me what you know," I repeated. "Look, your cousin is convinced I'm out to sabotage her investigation. That's not true. I started out with the sole intention of finding out who murdered Jason Belew, nothing else. Now, I'm going to find out who killed Lilith." I stopped and held up a finger. "Let me correct that statement, I know who killed both of them, I want to be able to prove it. I'd like your help."

He started shaking his head as he continued rubbing his chest. "Juanita's already told me about you. She said the FBI has a dossier on you and that one of the things it said was you're a loose cannon." He rubbed his chest some more. "She's right."

"Yeah, well, I apologize for that. How do you contact Wolf?" I asked.

"It's all through the internet, man. They don't even have permanent cell phones." He looked at his condo and back at me. "That TBI agent said you were the one who found me. How'd you do that?"

"A little internet research, a little luck. Would you give me Wolf's internet particulars?"

Candy frowned. "Particulars? Oh, yeah, sure. I can do that. I need to get online, but I don't want you to come back inside, you'll upset my daughter."

"Fair enough," I said.

After the way I acted, it was the best I could hope for from him. He could have easily locked the door and called the cops, but he was true to his word and forwarded the information to my email. I sent it directly to Ronald and gave him a phone call.

"I don't know what you can do with it, but I think they're in Nashville somewhere," I said.

"If they post pics and talk about where they eat dinner and things, I might be able to do something," Ronald said. "It just depends on how much info they put out there."

"Do what you can, buddy. Oh, by the way, I know about Anna and Percy."

"You do? How?" he asked.

"Because Anna told me. You know, you could have told me."

"I didn't want to start any trouble," he said.

"You wouldn't have, but I understand."

"Are you mad at them?" he asked.

"No, I'm not mad at them. Maybe they can make each other happy."

"I'd like someone I could be happy with," Ronald lamented. "But I don't think that's ever going to happen."

His statement took me by surprise. His Asperger's made him socially awkward to the point of a slight case of anthropophobia, and with the exception of that damned crack whore, he'd never been intimate with a woman.

"You should consider getting out and socializing more often," I suggested. "That's a great way to meet people. There are all kinds of activity groups out there. I think they all have Facebook pages, or whatever you call it."

"Yeah," he replied.

That was his way of ending a conversation that made him uncomfortable. If I kept going, all I'd get were more yeahs and okays. I yawned, realizing how fatigued I was.

"Alright, I'm heading home. If you learn of anything, please call me immediately."

"Okay," he said and disconnected the call.

Immediately after ending the call with Ronald, Percy called.

"I'm on the way to the scene. Is it Lilith Gray?" he asked.

"Yes." I looked at my watch. "They took their sweet time contacting you."

"You could have called me," he rejoined.

He was right. I could have called him, but I didn't and I didn't know why I didn't. It could've been due to stress and fatigue, or it could have been something else. Maybe I was subconsciously avoiding talking to him, I didn't know.

"How did you find her?" he asked.

I told him of the frantic phone messages, followed by me driving around north Nashville all night. He listened in silence and waited until I have finished before speaking.

"I have to ask, are you holding anything back?"

"Not that I can think of at the moment, but if it changes, I'll call you." I ended the call. Option B was probably the correct answer to my earlier question; I didn't want to talk to him. I didn't want to talk to anyone.

The adrenalin had worn off and I found myself nodding off, so I exited I-24 and parked at a truck stop. I debated on getting a cup of coffee before going home, but the truth of it was, I didn't want to go home. I didn't want to sleep in the bed that Lilith and I had slept in. I would have to eventually, but at the moment, all I wanted was to take a nap.

A 1973 Ford Mustang did not have reclining seats, which made it hard for a taller man to sleep in. Even so, I cracked open the windows and got as comfortable as I could. I did not remember falling asleep.

When I awoke, the sun was going down. My body was stiff and my mouth was crusty, reminding me the smart thing would've been to drive home after all. I'd turned my phone off before going to sleep. I had no doubt there were one or two messages awaiting me, but they could wait. A lot lizard sauntered by and gave me a hopeful smile, revealing discolored teeth. I waved her off and lit a cigar before driving home in silence.

CHAPTER 27

My home rested on five acres in the western part of Davidson County. It was still a fairly rural area, quiet with lots of trees. It had an agreeable rustic ambiance. It wasn't going to last much longer; Davidson and the surrounding counties were growing by leaps and bounds, and new subdivisions were being developed all around me, but I enjoyed it while I could.

In spite of the nap, I was still exhausted by the time I got home. I showered and made a sandwich, but I had no appetite. I tried watching TV, but it only irritated me, so turned it off and went to bed. But it was one of those nights. I was too stressed out. I got about five hours of sleep which consisted of a lot of tossing and turning before I gave up and threw the blankets off.

I splashed cold water on my face and dressed. I then filled a travel mug with coffee and took Gracie for a predawn walk around the property. She had a good time attempting to catch one of the numerous squirrels, but she was still a clumsy pup with oversized paws. The squirrels had nothing to fear.

My phone pinged and showed Percy's unmarked car coming in. He and Anna were sitting on the porch by the time we made it back. Tommy Boy was sitting on Anna's lap, and the look on his face made it clear he did not want Gracie anywhere near his girl. Gracie had been on the receiving end of more than one swipe of his claws, so she opted to scamper over to Percy and chew on his shoes.

"What time did you finally turn in last night?" I asked Percy. It was one of the few things I did not miss as a homicide detective; when there was a fresh murder afoot, it was a guarantee of working long hours with little sleep until the case was closed.

"I called it off at midnight," Percy said and then realized what he had said. "No offense, I wasn't being a smartass there."

"None taken. It looked like a dump job, would I be correct?" I asked.

"Yes, it was. As of yet, we've not located the assault scene and the primary scene yielded absolutely no physical evidence."

"Wait, isn't the primary scene where she was killed?" Anna asked.

I started to answer, but Percy beat me to it.

"The location where the body is found is always referred to as the primary scene. She was killed at location-A and dumped at location-B. Therefore, location-B is the primary scene and location-A will be the secondary scene. Whatever was used to transport her to the primary scene is also referred to as a secondary scene. Sometimes it will be called the tertiary scene, but that's splitting hairs. Hollywood directors and mystery writers frequently get it wrong, but that's how it is."

"Oh." She soaked in that information a moment. "Well, what about the autopsy?" she asked.

"The postmortem was done yesterday afternoon. The toxicology tests will take a week or two, but the preliminary ruling is a catastrophic, spiral fracture of three of the cervical vertebrae in the neck."

"What does that mean?" Anna asked.

Percy waited, but I gestured for him to go ahead and answer.

"In simplistic terms, someone twisted her head around until not one but three of her vertebrae fractured, which severed the spinal cord. It takes skill and a lot of strength to inflict that amount of damage intentionally."

There was a lull in conversation, the only noise coming from the morning birds and Gracie attacking one of Percy's polished wingtips.

"Alright, don't hold back, was she sexually assaulted?" I asked.

"She'd had sex," Percy answered. "There was no trauma indicative of an assault, other than her fractured neck, and there was no semen recovered from her."

I nodded as I thought over what he said. He most likely had sex with her, using a condom, and then snapped her neck. Either he did it while having sex or shortly after.

"She had a cell phone," I said.

"No cell phone has been recovered. We've already executed an emergency subpoena on the number you provided us. It's a burner, the last call was to you, and it pinged on a tower on Lickton Pike, but that's it. There has been no activity since."

"Nothing on the canvass?" I asked.

Percy shook his head. "The UPS hub has a lot of employees. We convinced their HR to put out a blanket email to their employees, but so far, nothing." He shook his head. "These are union people. They generally don't cooperate with management, but I've put in a call to the union president. If he feels me worthy enough to call me back, I'll to try to talk him into sending out a similar email through the union. If somebody saw something, maybe that'll convince them to talk to us.

"In the meantime, I've tasked a rookie detective with pulling all surveillance videos up and down Whites Creek Pike, including UPS, which has cameras everywhere. Maybe we'll get lucky."

Anna stood and went inside. She came back a moment later with a pot of coffee for Percy and myself, and some kind of rubber play toy I learned was called a Kong. When Anna tossed it along the porch, Gracie barked in excitement and chased after it.

"What can I do to help" I quietly asked.

"Locating those gypsies will help," Percy said. "Perhaps establishing a timeline for Lilith would help as well. Anything you can think of?"

"Yeah, there's one thing. The Fibs are going to be paying you a visit soon," I answered and explained.

As I spoke, a scowl appeared on Percy's face, but he did not openly offer any commentary. He finished his coffee and stood.

"I better get going. I've got a ton of paperwork to do and the media is expecting a follow-up press conference."

I stood as well. The two of us shook hands. Anna lingered. I got the hint and walked inside, giving them some privacy. I turned the TV on and booted up my computer. Anna walked in a few minutes later.

"Do you want me to make a fresh pot of coffee?" she asked.

"No thanks, I'm good."

I heard her put the kettle on the stove eye before coming into the den and joining me.

"Are you okay?" she asked.

I shrugged. "As well as can be expected. What are your plans for today?"

"I can hang out with you, if you want."

I knew what she was thinking. I was hurting and needed company. I gave her a smile. "I appreciate it, but I think I'm going to take a break for the day and hang out here. Maybe work on that old Cadi for a while."

She paused for a moment. "Ms. Braxton called last night and left a message. She wanted an update. I don't have much."

I jumped to my feet. "Damn it, I'm glad you said something." I hustled outside and retrieved the file folder out of the backseat. Bringing it back inside, I handed it to Anna.

"What's this?" she asked.

"The esteemed Professor Farquhar did some research on Chester Bond. I have to admit, it's impressive stuff. He even cited all of his sources. Chicago style, of course. As he once told me, only a socialist would use MLA style on history research."

Anna thumbed through the pages. "This is a lot. What does it say?"

"It is the military record of Chester Bond. He enlisted for the Confederacy on April 26th, 1861 with the Williamson Grays. They were first sent to Camp Cheatham for training. Camp Cheatham was close to Springfield."

"Wow, this is good," Anna said.

"It gets better. The unit's first battle was at Perryville, Kentucky, which was also known as the Battle of Chaplin Hills. That was in October 8th, 1862. It was a loss for the Confederates and they retreated from the field of battle." I fumbled through one of the pages and found what I was looking for. "At first, Chester was listed as MIA, and then KIA, but somehow they determined he went AWOL."

"He went back to Franklin to marry Penelope," Anna surmised. "They were married on the twelfth of October."

"Yeah, that seems to fit. If I had to guess, his moment on the battlefield put the fear of God into him and he wanted to do the right thing with his family. Anyway, he was never heard from again. At some point, his AWOL status was changed back to being KIA at the battle of Perryville."

Anna eyed the papers before looking up. "Somebody committed the perfect murder."

"Yeah, I'd say you're right. Well, that's a mystery we're not being paid to solve," I said. "We're only being paid to complete the old gal's family tree. I think you've got the missing piece right here and we can wrap this one."

I looked over the report and corresponding family tree Anna had completed. Included were the photocopies of all of the tax records, censuses, birth records, and death records from 1850 until 1950. "You've done some good leg work here."

"You helped," Anna added.

She began taking the pages Ebbie had supplied and began the task of scanning each page. After each page was scanned, she put them into sheet protectors and added them to one of the three-ring notebooks for this case. There were two of them and each was carefully organized. Anna had done it all. It reminded me she was becoming a pretty good PI, but I wanted more for her than this kind of life.

My thoughts drifted away from the Braxton case. I was perplexed about Lilith's murder. Why were they in Nashville and why was she killed? It didn't seem to make any sense. She was Wolf's lover, that much was obvious. They'd had sex at some point before she was murdered. Did they get into a lover's quarrel? But why were they in Nashville? I pondered it for a minute or two before a possible explanation came to me. I sent a text to Percy.

I have an idea why Lilith was in Nashville. Were there any abductions or attempted abductions reported in the past few days?

Thirty minutes went by before Percy responded. He called instead of texting.

"How did you know?" he asked.

"The gypsies Lilith was with are suspected of some abductions. They're believed to be a part of an international human trafficking ring. That seems to be the only possible reason why they were here. Tell me what you have."

"It was an attempt. A woman approached a teenage girl at Opry Mills shopping mall. The victim liked the Goth look and she said this woman was dressed the same. They struck up a conversation and at one point, the woman invited her to go back to her apartment and get high. The victim was going to go, but when they got to the parking lot, the woman's demeanor changed suddenly. She grabbed the girl by the shoulders and told her that her life was in danger and to run.

"The kid was confused at first, but the woman slapped her. That was all it took. The detective assigned to that case is going to show the victim a photo lineup with Lilith's picture included."

"Yeah, I think we already know it was Lilith," I said. "That might be why they killed her, but still, it seems harsh."

"Perhaps she told them she was leaving them," Percy surmised.

"Could be."

"Alright, if you think of anything else, give me a call," he said.

I disconnected the call and pondered the new information. So, they decided to try an abduction in Nashville, and in broad daylight. Had they failed to meet their quota or something? But why Nashville? Why not some other city? I sighed in exasperation knowing I'd probably never learn the answers.

CHAPTER 28

I was drinking my first cup of coffee and watching the morning news when Special Agent-in-Charge Reuben Chandler called. He didn't bother saying hello or any other formalities.

"Have you heard?" he asked.

He was referring to the current story plastered on the news.

"Yeah, I'm watching it now."

"Yeah," he mimed.

"How is she?" I asked.

"Not good; she's in a coma," he replied. He sounded fatigued, like he had not seen his bed for over twenty-four hours. I knew why he was calling me, but I played along.

"I'm sorry to hear that. Have you guys got any solid leads?"

"We're working on it. By the way, your Explorer is ready. I have it parked here at the office." He paused a moment. "Since you have an involvement in this matter, I would like for you to come in for a formal interview, if possible."

"Will I need a lawyer?" I asked.

"It's up to you," he answered. "You know how it goes."

Yeah, I knew how it went. I was intimately familiar with how it went. We discussed it a few minutes and I ultimately agreed, which I think surprised him. After ending the call, I immediately called Ronald.

"Have you seen the news?" I asked.

"No. What's up?"

I quickly filled him in. "So, the Feds have his cellphone and most likely his laptop too. Can you delete that spyware?"

"Sure, but they won't be able to trace it back to us," he said.

"Yeah, but I don't even want them to know somebody was spying on him. The Feds are funny about things like that."

"Alright, consider it done. Oh, I don't know if you're aware of it, but his cell was synced up to his laptop. I'll look over what data we have and see if there's anything of value."

I was about to tell him that was a good idea, but he hung up before I could speak.

I continued watching the news as I finished my coffee. The talking heads proceeded to tell the viewing audience an FBI agent was pursuing an investigation with an undercover operative when both of them were attacked and viciously beaten. They were found by a truck driver at an untended rest area on I-65 near Cornersville, Tennessee. Both of them were rushed to the local hospital whereupon one was declared deceased and the other life-flighted to Vanderbilt Hospital. The names had not yet been released to the media, but I instantly knew who it was.

I showered and shaved, but opted for casual attire; jeans and a Tiger Woods signature golf shirt, which cost as much as most dress shirts but was worth it. I got an Uber ride to the FBI's Nashville office on Elm Hill Pike and arrived promptly at nine. Reuben was waiting for me in the lobby. The fatigue on his face was easy to see. He greeted me in a somber voice.

"Thank you for coming," he said and without any further preamble led me through the security doors.

The place was a bustle of activity, which under the circumstances was not surprising. The two of us walked in silence down the hallway and stopped in front of an unmarked door. A man and woman were waiting.

"Thomas, this is Special Agents Carter Pike and Hope Delmonico. Since I consider you a friend, I am going to exclude myself from this interview in order to avoid the perception of bias."

"I suppose I understand," I said.

Reuben gave a small nod. "Thanks. If you'll excuse me, I am needed elsewhere." He left quietly, walking down the hall to an unknown destination, leaving me with the two agents. I turned to them and gestured to the door, which I assumed was an interview room.

"Shall we go in?" I suggested.

I briefly scanned the room before sitting. The room was exactly like the one in Memphis. "Is this interview going to be recorded?" I asked.

"Yes," Agent Pike answered. I peered at him closely. It wasn't normal for a Fibbie to give an honest answer and I wondered if he was medicated or something.

The two of them sat across from me at a table with a gray-patterned Formica top. Agent Pike was close to my age, Delmonico a little younger. Both were clean-cut and professional in appearance. In other words, typical FBI agents.

But what was more important, Special Agent Delmonico was a looker, with cinnamon-colored hair pulled up in a bun, variegated hazel eyes, high cheekbones, and a pert nose. Her makeup consisted of a light application of base and a touch of lipstick. I must admit, I hastened a quick look at a particular area a few inches below her neck. I couldn't help myself, those babies were threatening to bust a button or two on her blouse. I felt her eyes on me and hastily looked down at her notepad. When I looked up, she had me fixed with an undefinable stare. Some women, like Debbie, liked it when a man ogled; others did not. It was hard to say which category Agent Delmonico fit in. I broke eye contact and focused on Agent Pike.

"Let me start by saying you are not under arrest and are free to go at any time of your choosing," Agent Pike said, breaking my thoughts.

I gazed at him for a moment before responding. "Let me respond by saving us a lot of time and effort. I already know everything you are going to ask and how you're going to ask it. You are not going to be able to apply any type of behavioral pattern analysis to detect deception. Every answer I give will be the truth or I simply won't answer you. Now then, the purpose of this interview is to determine whether or not I was involved in the assault of Special Agent Stainback and undercover operative Raymondo Calendar, correct?"

Agent Pike seemed taken aback. "We have not released Raymondo's name to the media. How do you know he was the second victim?"

"Simple deductive logic," I replied. "Now, although you've not yet asked, I'll go ahead and answer. I did not perpetrate the assault on either of them, I was not involved in any way, nor do I have any firsthand knowledge of the incident."

Agent Delmonico jotted down some notes. Agent Pike nodded slightly, as if agreeing, but he seemed unsatisfied. "I could not help but notice you declined to assert you do not know *who* was involved in the assault of Special Agent Stainback."

"True enough. That's because I am reasonably certain I know exactly who did it, given the nature of the assault and the circumstances. Both of them were physically beaten, no known weapons were used, correct?"

"That'd be correct," Agent Delmonico answered.

Her partner gave her a brief, rebuking look, which she ignored. She set her pen down and placed her elbows on the table, making a steeple with her fingers and straining her blouse even further.

"The evidence indicates Agent Stainback put up a fight," she said.

"Would it be possible for you to be more specific?" I asked. The two agents glanced at each other. Pike whispered into Delmonico's ear and she whispered back.

"Look you two, stop dancing around and let's get down to it. Otherwise, let's end this interview and I'll get my car and get the hell out of here." The two of them glanced at each other again before Agent Pike gave his partner a subtle nod.

"Alright," Agent Delmonico said. "Agent Stainback and I were in the academy together. I happen to know she is in excellent shape and is an avid kickboxer. When she was found, she had heavy abrasions to her knuckles. We are certain she put up a hell of a fight."

"What about her duty weapon?" I asked. Delmonico slowly shook her head.

"It has not been recovered," she said.

I nodded slowly. "Okay, so, the current speculation is she somehow lost control of her duty weapon, but she fought back against her assailant, or assailants."

"That is the theory," Agent Pike said.

"And you believe her attacker may have sustained injuries," I surmised. The two of them did not answer, merely stared.

I gestured toward my face. "Alright, I don't know what you two see, but when I shaved this morning, I didn't notice any injuries to this handsome mug."

"Point taken," she said. "But perhaps you have injuries that are covered by your clothing. You would not object to us having a look, would you?"

She had a hint of a tantalizing smirk. I glanced over at Pike, who stared back stoically. I thought it over. I'd always kept in shape, and after that near-death experience with the overgrown rogue cop, I'd been working out on a regular basis. So, I had a decent physique for my age, if I do say so myself, and it was no cause for embarrassment. I stood, pulled off my shirt, and then dropped my pants.

I stood before the two of them bare-chested and my pants at my ankles. Thankfully, I had put on a clean pair of boxer briefs this morning.

"No injuries," I proclaimed and held my hands out at shoulder level. I might've even sucked my gut in and flexed a little.

The two of them sat there in silence a moment before Agent Delmonico stood and walked around the table. She stopped when she was within inches of me and slowly looked me over. Before I knew it, she reached behind me, grabbed the elastic waistband of my underwear, and pulled it out. She then proceeded to give my ass a rather close inspection. After a moment, she let go, causing the elastic band to pop against my skin.

"There's not a mark on him," she said to her partner. She then leaned in close and whispered in my ear, "Not bad, but you've got a hairy ass."

I shrugged. She was right, I did in fact have a hairy ass. Blame it on my Italian heritage. I wasn't embarrassed, never have been. The only thing I was currently worried about was the little soldier. I doubt she was aware, but her up close and personal inspection had awakened him. I hurriedly pulled my pants up before either of them noticed. Once I was clothed again, I tried to put on a nonchalant air as I sat back down and scooted my chair close to the table.

"Well, thank you for your transparency," Agent Pike said. "My only other question would be to ask you for an alibi for the hours of ten last night until four in the morning."

"I was home. I went to bed at approximately eleven. I have a roommate who was home as well. She can vouch for me, if you feel it is necessary."

"Female roommate?" Agent Delmonico asked with an arched eyebrow.

"Roommates only," I said. "She has her own bedroom." I turned back to Agent Pike. "Her name is Anna Davies. If you want her number, I'll have to look it up on my phone."

He nodded and waited while I pulled out my phone and scrolled down to Anna's contact information. I once again made a mental note to memorize her number in case something like Memphis happened again.

While Agent Pike jotted down the information, I glanced over at Delmonico. She was staring at me plainly, but there was a hint of something in her eyes, or maybe I was imagining things. Agent Pike got my attention by clearing his throat.

"If you two will excuse me a moment, I'll go make the call." He stood and left the room. I turned back to Agent Delmonico.

"Alone at last," I said. "What shall we do to pass the time?"

She gazed in amusement. "I think you should know, we are convinced you know more about these people than you've told us."

I gave a slow, agreeable nod.

"Would you care to be more forthcoming, in light of the current situation?" she asked, and then leaned forward. "We are desperate to catch these people, Thomas. Juanita is in critical condition and there is a strong possibility she won't make it. If that happens, we'll have a murdered FBI agent and nothing to show for it. Please help us."

"Alright, let's see. It began one night when I was looking for a friend who'd gone off the radar. I went to a strip club he owned and met a stripper who went by the alias, Midnight. Her real name was Lilith Gray."

I gave a brief synopsis of my relationship with Lilith and went on to tell her she was suspected of murdering a man in Nashville.

"She fled the city. Nobody knew her true name at that time, but I was able to find her family in Chicago."

"How did you do that?" she asked.

She stared in curious interest as I described the internet search of Lilith's unique tattoo and how it led to the tattoo shop in Chicago.

"You must have been up close and personal with that tattoo to remember all of the details," Agent Delmonico remarked.

"I have a good eye," I replied and winked.

She offered another, small smile. "I have no doubt. What was the name of the tattoo parlor?"

"The Gypsy Dragon. I have the address, if you want it." She nodded and I pulled up the info on my phone. I don't know why, but I had never deleted it.

She wrote the information down and then looked up. "You said was, as in past tense."

"I've heard it has since shut down, but the Chicago police had it under surveillance at one time. They may have good intel on the players involved."

She nodded thoughtfully. "Were you able to make contact with Lilith?" she asked.

"No, I haven't. That leads to my next item that you guys don't seem to be aware of. Lilith is dead."

Agent Delmonico stared at me blankly for a long five seconds before speaking. "Would you please elaborate?" she asked.

"I found her dead yesterday morning. She'd been murdered. Broken neck. The investigation is ongoing, but it appears she was involved in an attempted abduction of a teenage girl, but backed out at the last moment. Somebody here ought to contact the investigating detective with Metro and see if he has any other useful information."

She picked up her pen and began writing furiously. After a moment, she paused and looked up. "Something tells me you know the name of the investigating detective and you possibly even have their phone number."

"It just so happens he is one of my closest friends, Percy Trotter. He may have some additional information. I should caution you though, he's not a big fan of the FBI."

"You don't seem to be either," she said.

"True enough, but I kind of like you." I motioned for her notepad and wrote down Percy's info. While I was writing, Agent Pike returned. He walked over to Agent Delmonico and showed her something on his notepad. She read it and then looked up.

"Would you excuse us a moment, Thomas?" she asked. "We need to go speak with the boss."

"There is a restroom and water fountain down the hallway," Agent Pike said.

I took the hint and stood. They wanted to talk about me behind my back. I understood. Besides, the coffee was having an effect. I found the restrooms without problem. They were clearly marked with signs that were written in English, Spanish, and Braille. They were also spotlessly clean, unlike the restrooms at the old police headquarters. Those restrooms could have been used for hazmat training. Once in the restroom, I sent a text message to Ronald.

Have you seen the news about the FBI agent being attacked?
Yeah. Did you know her?
Yeah, it was the same agent from Memphis.
Oh, man. Who was with her? Her partner?
No. Candy.
Oh wow.

I sent him a couple of additional texts before someone walked into the restroom. He looked like a typical agent, dark suit, starched white shirt, muted tie, black wingtips, clean shaven. He gave me a look, I guess wondering who the hell I was. I ignored him and walked out.

Special Agent Delmonico found me at the water fountain, which was also spotlessly clean.

"I'm not sure I have my clothing on properly. You want to come to the men's room and check me out again?"

She responded with an amused smile. "Maybe later. In the meantime, we have work to do."

When the two of us returned to the interview room, Special Agent Dresden Carpenter was now present. He offered a pleasant smile.

"So, am I still considered a suspect?" I asked after I sat.

"Not at all, Thomas," Agent Carpenter said. "The preceding interview was merely a formality. Now that we have established your innocence in this matter, we can now proceed to the next step."

"Which is what?" I asked.

Agent Carpenter's smile broadened. "Are you aware each regional office has the authority to hire people on a temporary basis as independent contractors?"

I stared. "Are you suggesting hiring me as an independent contractor? Doing what, cleaning the restrooms?"

Carpenter smiled patiently. "In your case, you will be an investigator," he said.

"Wait, you're offering me a job?"

"Temporarily, yes. Your sole mission will be to assist in locating these gypsies and pass the information along to us."

Well, this was surprising. When I came here this morning, I knew I was going to be interrogated. I understood the logic behind it, considering the recent conflict between myself and Stainback. But, to formally include me in the investigation was something I had not considered. Agent Carpenter continued.

"Let me be specific, Thomas. As a temporary contractor with the FBI, this will be your only mission," he said. "I'm sure you can understand, at no time should you identify yourself as an FBI agent, circumvent any laws, or deviate from your mission."

I nodded thoughtfully.

"Do you have any questions?" he asked.

"Do I get paid?"

I caught a smile on Agent Delmonico's face before she hastily resumed a professional demeanor.

"Yes, there will be a stipend," Agent Carpenter said. "Also, I would add, you are to have absolutely no contact or communication with the media for the duration of your contract."

I scoffed. "You won't have to worry about that."

"You'll also be expected to be a team player," he said.

I made a subtle glance over at Delmonico. She declined to make eye contact this time. "Yeah, well, I'm more of a maverick these days."

Agent Carpenter leaned forward, putting his large hands on the table palms down. I noticed his cuticles had a fresh manicure. "I've read the dossier on you, Thomas. I'm impressed, I must say, but there have been times where you have played a little fast and loose with the letter of the law."

"I prefer the descriptor, unconventional."

Delmonico snickered. Carpenter again exercised his patient smile. "I'm not judging, but in this case, we must do everything by the book."

I nodded again and mulled over what he said. The three of them waited a minute before Carpenter spoke.

"Well, Thomas, what is your decision?" he asked.

"I must admit, I am intrigued, but I have concerns," I said.

"What kind of concerns?" Agent Pike asked. I eyed him.

"Agent Pike, with a few small exceptions, I have had nothing but shitty interactions with your esteemed bureau." I made air quotes with my fingers when I said bureau. "Back when I was a cop, there were more than a few occasions when bureau agents hindered, interfered, and sometimes even sabotaged our investigations. And, that does not even include my episode with the late Special Agent Enrique Hernandez. In case you guys didn't know it, I killed him. So, short answer, I can't find it in my soul to trust any of you guys."

"Point taken," Agent Carpenter said. "Which is why you will be working directly under my authority."

"Why you?"

He smiled again. "I have taken over the original case. Once you get to know me—for that matter, once you get to know the three of us—I am certain your view of the bureau will change dramatically. We are going to become very good friends, Thomas."

Or mortal enemies, I thought. It was true, I had no warm and fuzzy feelings for the Feds, but if I rejected this offer, I'd get a handshake and then shown the door. I'd be out of the loop.

The truth was, this was a hell of an opportunity. I'd be able to get an inside glimpse of how the Feds worked and perhaps, with their resources, I'd be able to find Wolf and his crew. But, one thing was certain: If I had the opportunity, Wolf was a dead man. I could not tell them that though.

"Alright, I'm in," I said.

Agent Carpenter smiled broadly. "Excellent." He then proffered a manila folder and opened it. "Now then, let's get the paperwork out of the way and get to work, shall we?"

The paperwork was the usual stuff, and it was no surprise there was a confidentiality agreement included in the contract. He gave a brief explanation of each form and I signed them without comment.

After all of the signatures were completed, we exited the interview room and proceeded down the hall to a large room similar in design to an auditorium capable of seating a hundred or more people. Currently, it was a beehive of activity. There were multiple flat-screen monitors lining the front wall and a few dry-erase boards were on the dais below them. One screen currently displayed a Google Earth view of I-65 in southern Tennessee.

A large dry erase board had, "Stainback Incident Command" written on the top in big bold letters. The various job positions were identified in a neat block diagram. As I watched, one of the monitors updated. It had a clock in the upper right corner which did not have the current time. Instead, it was like a timer, counting off the hours, minutes, even seconds of the time that had elapsed since the two victims were found. Below it, a message scrolled across announcing there would be a section-level briefing in five minutes.

"Are you familiar with the incident command system?" Agent Carpenter asked.

"Yes, I am," I said and pointed at one of the dry erase boards. "It appears your job is the intelligence section chief."

"In name only," Agent Carpenter said. He pointed around. "Everyone has a job. My question for you is, where can I best use your talents?"

"That's a good question," I answered. "I have one or two ideas, but if you don't mind, I'd like to sit in on this staff briefing before I answer."

"Certainly," he said. He started to say more, but an agent walked up to him with a clipboard in hand and began showing him something. I took up a position at the back of the room and watched the activity. The briefing began exactly five minutes later when Reuben stepped up to the podium. He turned the microphone on and spoke into it.

"May I have everyone's attention, please?" The volume of chatter dropped, but there were always those three or four people who felt they were exempt from such orders and continued chitchatting about fantasy baseball or something equally important. When they noticed the harsh glares, they reluctantly closed their pie-holes and feigned an attentive demeanor.

"Excellent. Everyone here knows me, but we currently are on a conference call with both Chicago and the DOJ, so I am going to be slightly redundant in this briefing. Please indulge me. I am Special Agent-in-Charge Reuben Chandler and for the moment, I am the Incident Commander for this operation.

"At approximately zero-three-eleven hours, the Marshall County Emergency Services received a 911 call from a truck driver. He was parked at a turnout lane on Interstate 65 in Marshall County at the 25-mile-marker. He reported finding two victims, unconscious and badly beaten. A Marshall County Deputy responded to the scene and immediately called for an ambulance. The two victims, identified as Special Agent Juanita Stainback and Raymondo Calendar, were transported to a local hospital. Mister Calendar was pronounced deceased at that time."

I already knew he was dead, but hearing it like this made me inwardly grimace. Raymondo was a drug dealer and a hustler, but even so, I found myself liking him and I got the impression he was a great father to his kid. I listened as Reuben continued.

"As a result of the investigation thus far, we have been able to put together the following." Reuben made a head nod toward a woman who was sitting in front of a computer. One of the monitors changed. The title identified it as a timeline. Reuben explained.

"At approximately 2120 hours, Special Agent Stainback received a telephone call from her operative, Raymondo Calendar. The conversation lasted thirteen minutes. She then attempted to call her partner, Special Agent Avery Pollard. That call was placed at 2136 hours. Agent Pollard's phone was apparently turned off at that time. Agent Stainback tried calling again once more and left a voicemail." He paused, and a moment later, the sound of Stainback's voice could be heard over the speakers.

"Hey Ave, you need to stop turning your damn phone off. You ain't going to believe what's happened. Wolf called Candy. He wanted to know if Candy knew anyone who was interested in buying a white baby. Can you believe this shit? This is big, Ave. If we can catch them with an abducted baby it'll bring this case down. The man wants to meet at a gay bar on Church Street. I told you that boy was on the down low, but you didn't believe me. If you get this message anytime soon, call me on the burner."

"As deduced by the conversation, Agent Stainback did not take her government-issued cell phone with her and opted to carry a burner phone. She also did not use her personal vehicle. It is assumed they were in Raymondo's vehicle, which is a 2015 Chevy Corvette, red in color. We have obtained surveillance video from the business known as The Nations, which is the location where they met."

The screen flashed again to some screenshots of the bar. The video was not bad quality, but the cameras were mounted on the ceiling. The high angle did not help, but I had no difficulty recognizing Stainback, Candy, and the person sitting at the table with them.

Agent Carpenter stepped close and whispered in my ear, "Just to confirm, would you agree that man is Wolf?"

I nodded. As I watched, Wolf pulled out a phone and showed it to Stainback. It appeared he was scrolling as Candy and Stainback stared intently at the screen. If I had to guess, I'd say Wolf was showing them pictures of this child they allegedly had. The screenshot then segued into a video. It started at normal speed and showed the three of them conversing. It then sped up before freezing as the three of them exited the bar. Without realizing it, I leaned forward slightly. Agent Carpenter noticed.

"You see something?" he asked in a hushed voice.

"I'm not sure yet," I said. Agent Carpenter peered at me curiously a moment before focusing back on Reuben.

"We have located a surveillance camera of another business at their entry door which faces Church Street." Again, on cue, the monitor changed to another image. It was a black and white video at a much lower resolution, but Candy's Corvette was easy to recognize as it exited a parking lot across the street and turned east onto Church Street. It appeared to be following an unknown type of dark compact car. A grimy-looking dually truck exited a few seconds later. Due to the street lights reflecting off of the windshields, it was impossible to see who was in any of the vehicles. The timestamp read 12:44 am.

"For those of you who are not familiar with Nashville, they are traveling toward downtown, but they are also traveling toward an onramp to Interstate 40. Again, for those of you who are unfamiliar with Nashville, there are three interstates that run through this city; I-40, I-24, and I-65. It is a simple matter of entering I-40 East and traveling approximately a mile before one can merge onto I-65 South."

The image changed again to a Google Earth photo. Someone had overlaid a route in yellow. "It only takes an hour at average speed to travel from the bar in question to the location where the two victims were found." The lady zoomed in on a section of the interstate. "This is a turnout lane, located near the 25-mile-marker. This is where the victims were found. As I mentioned, driving at a normal speed, it will take approximately an hour to reach this location."

The screenshot changed to an outdoor scene with Candy's Corvette parked on the side of the road. Reuben described the scene.

"This is Raymondo Calendar's Corvette, the vehicle he and Special Agent Stainback were apparently in when they went to the bar on Church Street." The picture changed to some dried blood in the gravel. "This is the location where Special Agent Stainback was found. It is approximately thirty feet from the Corvette. Mister Calendar was located approximately ten feet from her."

He went through a series of crime scene photographs. There were a few close-ups of tire tracks, but there was no way of knowing if the tracks belonged to the suspect's vehicle or some random traveler who stopped to take a leak.

"As I mentioned a minute ago, the 911 call came in at 0311 hours. A Marshall County Deputy arrived on the scene less than three minutes later. Special Agent Stainback was life-flighted to Vanderbilt Hospital. She is in critical condition and has not yet regained consciousness."

He paused for effect as a picture of Juanita flashed onto the screen. It looked like a picture of her from graduating from the FBI academy. She appeared slightly younger and thinner, and was grinning smugly for the camera. The room was ominously quiet now. One of their own had been violated.

Reuben waited a few more seconds before continuing. The lady running the computer needed no prompting. The screen was filled with a still photo of Wolf. He was sweaty and bare-chested, indicating the picture was taken at one of his fights. The next picture was a candid shot of the gypsies, including Lilith.

"The first photograph is of the subject known only as Wolf. His full name is currently unknown, as are the names of the other two individuals. This man," he used a laser light to point at accordion player, "has an Illinois driver's license identifying him as Pekoe Gray."

Peko Gray, interesting. Lilith's last name was Gray. I wondered if that was his real name. The screen changed images. It was a Google Earth photograph of an intersection.

"This is exit 22 of I-65. Three miles from the turnout. As one can see, there are several businesses around this intersection. Detectives with the local law enforcement have graciously volunteered to go to each of these businesses and obtain copies of any and all CCTV surveillance videos." He gestured at an older woman wearing a police uniform and bearing the insignia of captain. "Please thank your chief and your people for all of their efforts."

She grinned like a schoolgirl at the praise. Reuben continued.

"We are confident there will be video found, which will strengthen the case against them."

The screen reverted back to the default of the incident command information. "I will now take a limited amount of questions," he said. Hands immediately shot up and some did not even wait to be called upon.

"Do we have photographs of the female who is with them?" somebody asked.

"The woman who was with them has been tentatively identified as Lilith Gray. She was recently murdered in north Nashville. Therefore, there is no reason to have access to her photograph, unless you intend to leak it to the media."

The man who asked the question—I saw a TBI badge clipped to his lapel—scowled as if he'd been caught, and then quickly fixated on his notepad. Another hand raised.

"What is the strategy for apprehension?" The question came from the state trooper with brass on his collar.

"Our current focus is to saturate the I-65 corridor, from its beginning in Indiana to its termination in southern Alabama."

Reuben talked for another five minutes, and spent another ten minutes answering questions before ending the briefing. When it was over, I casually walked toward the woman who was controlling the visual presentation.

"Excuse me," I said, getting her attention. "If you don't mind, I'd like to look over those surveillance videos again."

She narrowed her eyes and began stammering a reply. Agent Carpenter interrupted.

"It's alright, I'd like to see them as well," he said.

"Of course, sir," she said and clicked open the video of the interior of the bar. I watched it on the large monitor as it ran through.

"Okay, could you run it again and when I say so, could you pause it?"

"Certainly," she said. She reset it and hit play again. When it had run for almost a minute, I held up a hand.

"Freeze it," I directed. She complied. I stared at it for several seconds. "Jog it forward slowly, please."

She did so, and at my direction, did it two additional times.

"Alright, Thomas, what do you see?" Agent Carpenter asked.

I pointed at the screen. "See the man sitting at the bar wearing the fedora? That's Pekoe."

Agent Carpenter frowned. "Are you sure? It doesn't look like him, and Juanita did not recognize him."

"It's him, the accordion player. He's cut off his beard and either he's cut his hair too or he has it tucked up under that hat. Also, look at his position at the bar. He intentionally sat at the far end where there are people in between him and your agent. Plus, he's got that hat pulled down low and he's watching them with the mirror behind the bar. That's him, no doubt. I don't see the other ones though. Let's say the other two are acting as lookouts or they are already in Cornersville waiting."

Carpenter needed no further convincing. He motioned Reuben over and explained. Reuben watched the video a couple of times before agreeing.

"Good eye, Thomas," he said and turned to the computer woman. "See if any of the cameras picked up what vehicle that man left in."

"I'll save you some time," I said to her. "He's in that redneck truck that exited the parking lot behind Candy's Corvette."

"How do you know?" she asked.

I shrugged. "Call it a gut feeling."

She frowned but made no comment, at least not to me, and turned to Carpenter. "I can print these off, but we already have still pics from the case file of all actors."

Agent Carpenter nodded. "Add it to the investigative timeline and see if you can get anything off of that truck."

"You're the boss," she said under her breath.

He was about to say something, perhaps an admonishment, but another agent came bustling up with a handful of papers in one hand and a phone in the other. He had it set to speaker mode and somebody on the other end was chattering about something. While he was busy, I walked around and looked everything over, hoping to glean as much as I could. The command center was impressive, no doubt about it. They had the latest in computers and electronic gadgetry and everyone seemed to be working hard.

After ten minutes, I learned little of consequence. It was time for me to make an Irish exit. Having a fancy command center was nice, but crimes were not solved while sitting in an office. Nope, it doesn't happen, no matter what they showed on those stupid TV shows. The way to investigate a case is get off your butt and follow the evidence. Once in the hallway, I oriented myself and headed toward the employee parking lot in the back of the building.

CHAPTER 29

Reuben had returned my key fob while we were still in the lobby. Once I found the exit leading to the parking lot, a touch to the panic button was all I needed. The horn on my Explorer began honking, allowing me to find it with ease in the crowded lot. I hit the panic button again, silencing the horn, and hurriedly walked across the lot. I gave the exterior a quick inspection. There was a fresh coat of wax and the two scratches on the driver's side door were gone. So far, so good.

The interior looked as good as it did when I drove it off of the car dealer's lot. They'd also installed a new gun safe in the console. It was not the same brand I previously had, but it would do. I started it up and found the gas gauge registering on empty.

"Typical," I muttered.

I stopped at the nearest station and filled up before speeding home and picking up an assortment of weapons and my newly refurbished bag of PI gear. My phone rang as I merged onto I-65. I normally ignored it when I was driving because I did not have a Bluetooth, or whatever they were called. Mentally noting for the fiftieth time to get one, I managed to get safely onto the interstate and answered.

"Hello, Thomas. Where are you?"

"Special Agent Carpenter, how nice of you to call," I replied, even though it wasn't.

"Actually, my correct title is Senior Special Agent, but please call me Dresden," he said.

"What can I do for you, Dresden?" I asked.

"I was hoping to speak with you before you left. We need to get with the operations section chief and integrate you within the command structure," he said.

"Yeah, these days I don't take directions so well. I'm more of an individualist."

"Yes, you described yourself as a maverick. You should try to be a team player," he admonished.

"I'm sure you're correct, Dresden."

I heard him emit a long sigh. "Would you please tell me where you are at, Thomas?"

I paused for a moment before answering. "I'm heading to Cornersville."

"Okay, I'll bite. Why are you going to Cornersville? The scene has already been processed."

"Yeah, I got that, but I thought I'd look around anyway," I said.

"Thomas, I appreciate your initiative, but the scene has been processed and even now the area is saturated with local cops and state troopers. It would be better if you were here at the command center."

I was growing irritated, but kept my temper in check. "Dresden, do you have any kind of solid lead for me to follow-up on?"

He paused. "Well, not at the moment, but our SOP dictates agents that are not assigned a task are to stage in the command center."

"Dresden, cases are not solved by sitting around in the office with your thumb up your ass," I said, growing more irritated by the minute.

"Point taken," he conceded. "Even so, any leads that may be uncovered in Cornersville can be handled by the personnel who are already there. Whereas, if something comes up in the Nashville area, your area, your response time will be at least an hour."

"I would normally agree, but I saw at least a dozen agents standing around that conference room acting like they were busy, but they weren't doing anything. If anything comes up, I'm sure they'll jump right on it."

Dresden gave a slight sigh. "Yes, Thomas, that is true, but the main reason you were hired is due to your expertise in Nashville."

"Yeah, but you guys also had some commentary about my investigative style, right? Look, I know I'm probably wasting my time, but I'd just be in the way up there. Let me satisfy this urge I have. If anything comes up, give me a call and I'll be sure to do the same." I disconnected before he could reply and waited for a Dodge Charger to blow by me in the HOV lane. I fell in a safe distance behind him and matched his speed. If a State Trooper was out running radar, he'd hit the Charger first. While I drove, I thought of the matter at hand.

Something serious must have happened for those gypsies to take such drastic measures. I was convinced they somehow figured out what Candy was doing and lured him into a trap. And Stainback got caught up in it. They must have been desperate to attack an FBI agent. I suddenly thought of something.

"We're assuming they knew she was FBI," I muttered to myself. I started to call Dresden and talk to him about it, but then thought better of it. They'd probably already come to the same conclusion and he'd probably use it as an opportunity to tell me to come back and discuss it in a meeting or something.

The rest area where they were dumped was on the southbound side of I-65 near the town of Cornersville, Tennessee. Normal travel time was an hour; I got there in fifty minutes. There was a State Trooper parked on the side when I arrived, probably keeping the rubberneckers away. He exited his car as I parked and put on his Smoky Bear hat.

"Good morning," I said as he walked up. He was a few years younger than me, almost as tall, muscled, and his uniform was heavily starched.

"Good morning," he replied. "Almost lunchtime."

"Yes, it is," I replied.

"You don't look like a Fed," he said. I guess it was due to the fact I was not wearing a conservative suit, instead wearing casual khakis and a polo shirt.

"That's a good thing, right?"

He chuckled at my response. I introduced myself and told him why I was there.

"Not much left here. The forensics guys towed the Corvette and left about an hour ago. My job right now is mostly to maintain a police presence and discourage the lookie-loos."

I nodded in understanding and looked around the area. My first thought was how quiet and unassuming the location was. There wasn't much to it; nothing more than a side road maybe a quarter of a mile long off of the interstate. The side of the road consisted of grass and weeds. Fifty yards west was a wood line of several trees, separating the interstate from what looked like farmland.

"I take it this is your zone?" I asked.

"Yeah, this county and the one north of here."

I nodded thoughtfully. One trooper was responsible for two counties. That was a lot of roads to cover. Troopers usually stuck to the interstates, but they had jurisdiction over all roads in Tennessee.

"Is there anything you can tell me about this rest area?" I asked.

He pursed his lips slightly. "It's not used much. There are no restrooms here. Most truckers go down to exit 22, three miles south of here. It has all kinds of businesses, a truck stop, and a couple of hotels."

"Can you show me the spot where the Corvette was parked?" I asked.

"Sure."

He walked with square shoulders but with a distinctive walk which I called a trooper's swagger. I followed along, sans swagger. More of an amble. We stopped at a spot on the side of the road where the grass and weeds were all trampled.

"Right here," he said. "It's my understanding the two victims were lying a few feet away from the car. When I came on duty this morning, there must have been forty or fifty people walking around. There's no telling what kind of physical evidence they destroyed."

"Sounds familiar," I grumbled. His statement brought back old memories of other crime scenes contaminated by the so-called good guys. "I understand a truck driver found him."

"Yeah, that's what I was told. He wanted a few hours of quiet sleep away from other truckers and lot lizards." He pointed west. "There's a house over there on the other side of the fence and trees. Some FBI agents interviewed the people who live there. It's my understanding they didn't see or hear anything."

I nodded to myself. This was the spot where they set them up. The question was, how did they lure the two of them here? I mean, Stainback was a trained FBI agent and Candy had street smarts. It didn't seem to make sense. I felt like there was a lot of information we were unaware of. We talked a few minutes longer before the trooper decided he was done with me and walked back to his car. I walked around and scanned the area. I even walked the fence line, but the trooper was right. If there was any physical evidence left behind by the suspects, it was gone now.

It only took five minutes to flip-flop on the interstate and exit onto Lynnville Highway. The entrance to the campground was less than a quarter of a mile from the interstate. A sign proclaimed, "Welcome to the Shady Haven Campground!"

There were a couple of bullet holes in the center of the O. I had to admit, I liked the grouping. One MOA, definitely. I paused a moment to take a photo before I drove in and parked in front of the office. It was a two-story affair with wraparound porches on both levels. It looked more like a farmhouse than an office.

The interior was rather drab, full of cheesy knickknacks, dust, and other assorted clutter. An old, self-standing oscillating fan creaked from a far corner. It was in a perpetual battle against the stale air and losing badly. An older man with an enormous potbelly and indefinable smile greeted me from a rocking chair.

"Well, I declare, it looks like another lawman coming to visit," the man said.

"Yes, sir. My name is Thomas Ironcutter."

"I'm Ernest Humphreys, I run this place. What can you do for me?" he asked. He thought he was funny.

"I'm doing some follow-up work on the case. I hope you don't mind."

He drained the remains of tea out of a Mason jar and gestured at it. "It'll cost you," he said. "Why don't you pour me a refill. There's a pitcher over there in the fridge. Help yourself to a glass, ifn' you're thirsty."

"Sure." I took the jar from his hand with a pleasant smile. The kitchen surprised me. It was full sized with modern high-end appliances. A large crockpot on the counter was on and emitting mouthwatering aromas. I found a similar Mason jar in the cupboard and helped myself to some tea before walking back into the main room.

"Appreciate that," he said when I handed his tea back to him. He took a sip before eyeing me. "You ain't wearing a badge."

I took my own sip and found his tea delicious. "Well, sir, I'm currently working as an independent contractor with the FBI."

"Sounds ominous," he replied with that same indefinable smile. "Are you something like an undercover CIA agent or something?"

"No, nothing like that. I'm simply helping out with this case. Most days, I'm a private investigator."

"I see. Well, Mister Private Investigator, what brings you here?"

"The suspects were last known to have been in an RV…" He interrupted me before I could say more.

"I already know that, son. Those G-men and G-women came in here and they've already got my surveillance videos downloaded."

I grunted to myself. Reuben had talked about the campground during the briefing, but left this part out. I wondered what else they were keeping confidential. I pulled my phone out and located the pictures I took of the RV and of the gypsies. He put on his bifocals and looked them over.

"Yep. That's them and that's the RV they were in. They were gone when I woke up this morning."

"What time was that?" I asked.

"Five. I'm up at five every morning. I don't even need an alarm clock. Put me in a dark room with no windows and I can still tell you when it's five am."

"I believe you," I said.

"Yep. They were gone, but they were paid up until the end of the week, so I wasn't too concerned. I got two outdoor surveillance cameras. One of them is pointed at the entrance. It showed them leaving at three o'clock, more or less."

"Would you mind terribly if I watch that video?" I asked hopefully.

He grunted before hoisting himself out of his chair and motioned for me to follow him. He led me to a side door which entered into an office. A teenage boy was sitting at a desk. It looked like a spreadsheet program was on the monitor and the boy was rapidly entering numbers.

"Cason, this here is a fancy private detective working for the FBI," Ernest said. "He's come all the way from Nashville just to talk to us."

The boy looked up and hurriedly clicked off the program. I guessed him to be sixteen or seventeen, average height, and a little on the slender side. Ernest gestured at him with his Mason jar. "This is Cason, my grandson. He's so smart I let him handle the business."

"Nice to meet you, Cason. I'm Thomas," I said with an outstretched hand.

"Cason, show him those surveillance videos. I've got something to take care of. I'll be back shortly," he said and walked out, closing the door behind him.

"He has to go poop," Cason said as soon as Ernest shut the door. "He always says he'll be right back, but he'll be gone for at least thirty minutes. I think he takes a nap while he's sitting there."

I chuckled. "Could be, I guess."

"Are you wanting to see the RV leaving?" he asked. "There's not much to it."

"If it's not too much trouble," I said.

Cason scoffed, much like Ronald would have if he were sitting there. Within a few seconds, he had the video online. I watched it carefully. The streetlight by the entrance illuminated the front passenger compartment, but all you could see was a person behind the driver's wheel.

"Yeah, you're right, not much to see." I had him rewind and play it a couple of times and was about to thank him for his time when a thought came to me.

"Did you ever talk to them?" I asked.

"Just Wolf and Pekoe," he said. "Wolf could do one-handed pushups. He's a professional fighter."

"Yeah, that he is. Describe Pekoe to me."

"He's older, but I couldn't tell you how old. He has one of those faces where he could've been fifty or ninety, you know what I mean?"

"Yeah, is he the one with a long beard?"

"Yeah, but I saw him yesterday and he'd shaved it off. In fact, he had Lorilee shave him and cut his hair. He sure looked different. Did you know that old man could do one-handed pushups too? I wouldn't have believed it if I didn't see it myself."

"Really? Impressive. Does anyone around here drive a beat-up four-wheel drive truck?" I asked.

Cason chortled. "You just described half the population of Marshall County."

"The one I'm thinking of is a dually."

His expression turned perplexed. "Um, yeah. One woman who's living here has a dually."

"Oh yeah?"

"Yeah. She's been living here a while and works here part-time."

"Do you know if she's around at the moment?"

"I don't know. I can try calling her if you want me to."

"Yeah, give her a try," I said.

Cason tried calling and after several seconds, he hung up. "No answer."

"Do you know her well?" I asked.

Cason shrugged and looked slightly uncomfortable. "We talk sometimes. She isn't the sharpest knife in the drawer, but she's okay. My grandfather is a retired judge and he knew her family. He lets her live here rent-free in exchange for housecleaning and keeping the laundromat serviced."

"What else can you tell me about her?" I asked.

"Um, well, she has a kid. A little girl who's about eight months old now. Her baby's daddy is currently serving time in the workhouse for stealing a car. He's a big thief. Our change machine was broken into a year ago, back before he got locked up, and I'm positive he did it."

"Let's go talk to her," I urged.

Cason agreed and stood. He suggested a refill of tea first, which I readily accepted. The aromas from the crockpot had won out over the stale air and made my stomach grumble. I heard a toilet flush from behind a closed door. Cason and I made eye contact. He gave me a knowing smirk.

"Her camper is parked in lot six," he said as we walked outside. There were two additional buildings behind the main office. Cason pointed them out.

"That's the laundromat. The other one is restroom and shower facilities. That's included in the price, if you ever want to come camping down here."

"Thanks, I'll remember that. Where was the gypsy's RV parked?"

"In lot eight. There's nobody in seven." He gave a running commentary as we walked. "That's the Chastain couple over there in lot one. They've lived here a little over a year and they're both crazier than outhouse rats. We've called the police on them a couple of times now."

"Why do you let them continue to live here?" I asked.

"I know this sounds silly, but they always pay their rent on time, so, Pop-Pop lets them stay."

"Makes sense, I suppose. What about Lorilee?"

"No problems at all. She does her job and takes care of her baby."

"Does she ever have any visitors?" I asked.

"There's a woman that comes and visits sometimes," he said. "Lorilee said it's her aunt, but I've never actually met her."

As lot six came into view, Cason stopped and I heard him inhale sharply. I looked over.

"What's wrong?" I asked.

"Her truck's gone," he said. "That's odd."

We continued walking and approached Lorilee's trailer. It'd definitely seen better days and I seriously doubted it could be driven on the street.

"Give it a knock," I suggested. He did so.

"Hey, Lorilee, you there?" he asked in a low voice and then turned back to me. "I gotta be careful not to wake the baby."

Cason knocked a couple of additional times before giving me another questioning look.

"I think it's time to knock harder," I suggested. Cason did so and pounded on the door. Again, there was still no response.

"She might be gone shopping or something?" he guessed.

"I take it you didn't see her leave?" I asked. Cason shook his head. "Give your Pop-Pop a call and ask him if he saw her leave."

"Yeah," he muttered and pulled his phone out. After talking for a minute, he hung up and stared. I could see worry on his face.

"He didn't see her either I take it?" I asked. He shook his head.

"Your hearing is probably better than mine. Try giving her a call again and see if you hear it," I suggested.

His eyes lit up. "Yeah." He did so. Within a couple of seconds, he got an odd expression on his face. "I hear it," he whispered and pointed toward the camper. I listened close and detected a faint chime. It was definitely coming from inside the camper. He gestured with his phone.

"It went to voicemail."

I kept a neutral expression, but this was not a good sign. I pulled out a handkerchief and used it to try the doorknob. It was unlocked. The door swung open on creaky hinges. The interior was dark, but as I peered in, I saw something on the doorjamb.

Some people might have questioned what it was, but I knew instantly. It was a drop of blood. It was only a small, singular drop. Most people might have missed it, or wrote it off as someone who cut their finger. Not me. I grabbed Cason by the shoulder.

"Step back," I hissed as I pulled him back toward me.

Getting Cason safely behind me, I lifted the tail of my shirt with one hand and pulled out my handgun with the other.

I stood to the side of the door. It was a sunny day, which hampered me from seeing inside the dark interior. "Yo, Lorilee, you in there?"

Still there was no answer. I used the flashlight on my phone to peer inside, but I could only see a couple of feet. Part of my brain said, this is a crime scene, don't fuck with it. But, another part of my brain wondered if Lorilee and her child were inside and in need of help. My inclination was to go inside and check, but I also didn't want to eat a bullet, or get kicked in the throat. I could have backed off and called the cops, but it didn't seem feasible for some stupid reason. Summoning up my courage, I went inside.

CHAPTER 30

The camper was small, as one can imagine, and Lorilee was not a good housekeeper. There were clothes and baby things everywhere, and the place smelled like home-grown marijuana and baby poop. In spite of the clutter, it only took a few seconds to determine there were no dead bodies. Holstering my handgun, I walked back outside. The bright sunlight caused me to squint my eyes.

"Is anybody in there?" Cason asked.

I started to answer, but was surprised to see Agents Pike and Delmonico walking toward us.

"I'm glad you're here," I said, realizing I was talking to Delmonico only. Agent Pike was nonplussed.

"Dresden sent us," he replied. "He's worried you'd find something and not pass it along."

"Fair enough," I said and pointed back at Lorilee's camper. "You have a possible crime scene in there, and a possible abduction of Lorilee…" I paused and stared at Cason.

"Pushnell," he said. "Lorilee Pushnell. Do you want her kid's name?" I nodded. "Amber. I think she has her dad's last name, so that would be Sowell."

"Okay, Lorilee Pushnell and baby Amber Sowell," I said.

The two agents stared at me, swapped a glance at each other, and then stared at me again. Finally, Agent Pike spoke.

"How certain are you that she has been abducted?" he asked.

"Call it a gut instinct," I said, and then gestured toward the camper. "Her camper's still here, but she and her kid are gone, along with her truck. Oh, and her truck is a beat up dually, much like the truck that was caught on camera leaving the same parking lot on Church Street."

"Have you determined she simply isn't out running errands?" Agent Delmonico asked.

"Cason and his grandfather have been here all day. And, I happen to know the old man was up at five this morning." I saw Cason smirk. "Neither of them observed Lorilee leave, which means she left before five. Cason here says she never leaves that early, right, Cason?"

"That's right," he replied, nodding vigorously. "And she's wasn't planning on visiting her baby's daddy today either."

"Could she have gone anywhere else?" Agent Pike asked.

Cason responded with an unknowing shrug. "She went out sometimes. You know, like getting groceries or going to visit her baby's daddy. But I've never known her to go out in the middle of the night. She's not that kind of person." His tone was slightly defensive, as if we were accusing Lorilee of nefarious activity.

The two Feds looked pointedly at each other. "I think we should call Dresden and recommend an Amber Alert be issued," Delmonico said.

Agent Pike nodded in agreement. "An Amber alert on Amber. Yep. I'll go over the facts and then emphasize it would be better to err on the side of caution. I'll also contact the locals and have a BOLO broadcast." He faced Cason. "Young man, do you happen to know what kind of truck Miss Pushnell has?"

Cason nodded eagerly. "It's a red Dodge crew cab. I think it's a 2000 model and it has a Cummins diesel, which has a distinctive exhaust sound." He paused a moment and his head swiveled as he glanced at the three of us. "I have a couple of pictures of Lorilee, if that'll help. They're kind of, um, risqué though."

"Anything you have, kid," Pike said with a touch of anxiousness in his voice.

"Yeah, sure," he said and looked at our phones. "Okay, you two have the latest iPhones, turn on your AirDrop."

Now it was time for Agent Delmonico and me to exchange a glance.

"What is AirDrop, Cason?" I asked.

He shook his head in exasperation and held his hand out. I handed him my phone and watched as he gave instructions about the app and set up my phone to receive the photos. Agent Delmonico had been paying attention and set her phone up too. Cason then dropped several photos onto our respective phones.

He had several photos of Lorilee. Some were G-rated. Some were of her and her child. But there were several that were definitely R-rated. Lorilee was a little on the chubby side, and she had huge breasts, which she apparently loved to show off. She was in various suggestive poses and one picture showed her squeezing them to the point of milk dripping out. When I looked at Cason, he grinned like a little kid. Agent Delmonico was not amused.

"We'll use the ones with her kid," she said, "and you ought to be careful with women like her. Before you know it, she'll be pregnant with your child."

Cason was duly chastened—at least, he acted like he was—and walked back to the office to tell his grandfather what was going on. Agent Pike then declared Lorilee's camper on lockdown until the TBI forensics team arrived. A detective from the Marshall County Sheriff's Department soon arrived and added his expertise.

I had nothing much to contribute, so I walked around the campground. If someone were to ask, I'd tell them I was looking for clues, but there was nothing here. I eventually made my way back to lot six. By now, there were several people milling around. Agent Delmonico saw me and walked over.

"How's it going?" I asked.

"Both mother and daughter are in the system now. An Amber Alert was issued a couple of minutes ago and is being broadcasted nationwide. The forensics teams should be here any minute now."

"What now?"

"Now, we wait," she said.

"Okay, we wait. Changing the subject, I'm curious about something."

"What's that?"

"What's the status on Agent Pollard?" My question drew a somber stare.

"Can I trust you?" she asked.

"I like to think I'm a trustworthy kind of guy, but I suppose that's something you'll have to determine for yourself," I answered.

"Alright. As of this morning, Pollard is on administrative leave. Both he and Stainback are currently under investigation," she said and bit her lip momentarily, which had a sexy look. "I don't know everything, but apparently there are several issues pertaining to their conduct over the past year, and it might even lead to both of them losing their jobs."

"Including what they did to me in Memphis, I hope," I said.

"I believe your case is at the top of the list, courtesy of the boss."

I nodded and had to admit to myself I was somewhat surprised.

"So, Pollard is off the case," I said.

"Most definitely. They assigned it to Dresden this morning," she said. "Carter and I as well, but Dresden is in charge."

"I'm tired of calling you Agent Delmonico. Remind me of your first name again."

She looked at me and gave a slightly mischievous smile. "It's Hope."

"Let me guess, you have two sisters named Faith and Charity."

"No, smartass, and don't think you're the first man who has used that line."

"Ah, but I bet I'm the only man who knows the reference," I said. She ignored me at first, but she decided to test me.

"Alright, let's hear it."

"Faith, Hope, and Charity were three sisters who became Christian martyrs in the second century."

"Not bad. Let me guess, you're Catholic?"

"A fallen Catholic, but yeah. Are you single?" I asked.

"Divorced," she answered. "Three months since it was official, but we were done long before that. He found a nineteen-year-old college co-ed who is dumber than a box of rocks but has big tits and a desire for older authority figures."

"I hate it when that happens. Is he still stationed in Nashville?"

"Nope. I transferred here after the divorce. He and his little girlfriend went to Cheyenne, Wyoming."

"I went there, once. Everyone was wearing cowboy boots, even the women."

She laughed. "Sounds about right."

"No kids?" I asked.

Her features darkened for a microsecond. "No kids."

I realized I may have hit a nerve. Thankfully, she changed the subject.

"Your dossier is an interesting read," she said and punctuated it with a slight smirk.

I acted surprised. "Wait, you've read my dossier and you're still speaking to me?"

She laughed. I liked the sound of it. "Yep. It's an interesting read, no doubt about it."

"Yeah, kind of like a Shakespearean tragedy."

She laughed again. "I like your sense of humor, but yeah, there were some rather unpleasant factoids."

"If you are referring to the murders of two women I loved, yeah, I guess you could call them unpleasant factoids."

She was silent for a moment. "I'm being insensitive. I'm sorry."

"It's alright, but it's a topic for another day. Or night. I'm thinking drinks and a candlelight dinner would be good."

She smiled again. I was scoring points. "It's possible."

"Excellent. Alright, back to work. Have there been any hits on their RV?"

"None yet. The tag we had was bogus, so, all we have is the description."

I frowned. "You people have the VIN, correct?"

"No, why?" Her eyes widened and she stared, as if I was playing a cruel joke. "Do you have the VIN? Oh, fuck me. Have you been keeping that to yourself the whole time?"

"Um, the answer is yes, I have the VIN and no, I haven't been keeping it to myself. I just assumed you high-speed, low-drag Feds would've already had it."

"Well, we don't," she huffed. "Are you going to share?"

I activated my phone and logged onto my cloud account. Finding the pics of the RV and the VIN, I handed it over to Hope.

"Where did you get this?" she asked.

"Back in Memphis during the fight," I answered. "Which begs the question, why didn't Stainback and Pollard have this in the case file?"

"I don't have an answer for you. Between you and me, there are a lot of issues with the investigation of this case, but if you repeat that, I'll deny I ever said it. Could you forward this to us?"

"Certainly," I replied. She provided me with her email address. I attached the photos and sent them promptly. She looked them over in satisfaction.

"I'm going to cc them to Carter, Reuben, and Dresden," she said. Agent Pike was still over at Lorilee's camper. Hope waved him over and then began working her fingers across the screen of her phone. It only took a minute before she had the task completed.

"Thanks, buddy," she said.

"What's up?" Agent Pike asked. Hope quickly updated him.

"I'm calling the boss," she informed him. His phone vibrated while she spoke. He looked it over.

"Okay, got 'em."

Hope nodded and put the phone on speaker mode. Reuben answered on the first ring.

"Sir, I just learned Thomas has a copy of the RV's VIN."

"He does?" Reuben asked.

"Yes, sir. You should be receiving an email with the attached photos any minute now."

"Please don't tell me Thomas was intentionally withholding that information," he said.

Hope looked at me. She'd forgotten to tell her boss he was on speaker and I could hear the conversation.

"No, sir, he did not. He assumed we already had it, and he's right, we should've already had it in the case file."

There was a pause. "Yes, I suppose he's correct. There are a lot of things that should've been in that case file. Alright, we'll get this entered into NCIC on this end. Keep me updated." He hung up without further comment.

After the end of the phone call, Hope took a moment to take another look at the pictures of Lorilee.

"The poor kid has it bad for her. He probably lost his virginity to this girl," she said.

"Yeah, probably," I agreed. "I hope he doesn't get her pregnant."

"This is one screwed-up case," she grumbled. I agreed again. "Before I transferred to Nashville, I was in New Orleans investigating public corruption. So, I guess I have some experience in screwed-up cases."

"No doubt," I said.

"Do you think they're still in their RV?" she asked me.

"Hard to say," I said. "Now that you guys have the VIN, if any small-town cop runs it, they'll get a hit, so maybe we'll get lucky."

"Do you think they went north or south?" Hope asked.

"They left a trail of crumbs pointing south, but I think they're going back to Chicago." I glanced at my watch. "They've had a good head start, so they're probably already there."

"Any ideas?" she asked.

"Not really, but I can't stand around here doing nothing. I'm going to get on the road and check out any out of the way exits or side roads."

"Would you mind if I joined you?" she asked. "Two sets of eyes are better than one, right?"

I looked over at her partner. Agent Pike in turn focused on Hope.

"Your car is back at headquarters," he said.

"I can drop her off when we go through Nashville," I said.

Pike shrugged. "Your call," he said to Hope. "I'm going to finish up here and head back to Nashville. If anything comes up, give me a call."

I was hoping Pike would go along with her desire. Although I had no intention of messing around, I definitely found myself wanting to spend a little time with Hope and getting to know her.

"Alright, it's settled," I said. "Let's get going."

Once we got into my SUV, Hope made a suggestion. "Hey, why don't we stop off in Nashville and run by HQ? You can park your car and we'll take my government-issued car. It'll save you some mileage on your car."

"Oh, hell no," I replied. "I just got it back and I'm not leaving it."

She laughed. "Okay, I understand."

CHAPTER 31

We were back on the interstate within minutes. Hope was the eyes while I drove. She occasionally used my miniature binoculars and scanned the side roads and exits. I drove below the speed limit, giving her ample time. It was a slow and tedious process. It took well over an hour to get to Nashville. After we passed the Old Hickory Boulevard exit, she set the binoculars in her lap and emitted a long sigh.

"It's like looking for a needle in a haystack," she said.

I agreed. "I think you can take a break for a few until we're through Nashville."

Hope set the binoculars in her lap and rubbed her eyes. "So, let's talk."

"Sure. What would you like to talk about?" I asked.

"I want to ask all about you, Thomas, but I don't want to open up any old wounds."

"Well, let's see if I can summarize. There was a time when I thought my wife and I had a decent relationship. It was rocky at times, but that's normal stuff, right?"

"Yep, I suppose," Hope said in agreement.

"Anyway, I was oblivious to her affair. So, she got herself pregnant and she was killed. I was framed for it, but eventually, her real killer was identified. But you know all of that, right?"

"Yes," she said. "And then a woman you were dating was murdered by her ex-husband."

"Yeah, her and her daughter."

"Did you have feelings for her?" she asked.

"Yes, I did," I said quietly. In fact, I was heading down the road of being hopelessly in love with Simone. In my eyes, she was perfect.

"Are you over her?"

I glanced over at Hope. Her expression seemed sincere.

"That was back last summer, almost a year ago. What do you think?"

She nodded slightly. "The shrinks think it takes somewhere around eighteen months to go through all of the stages of grieving."

"What's the last stage of grieving?" I asked, although I believed I already knew the answer.

"The Kübler-Ross model theorizes there are five stages, the last stage being acceptance." She saw me glance at her. "I had a double-major of psychology and sociology at LSU." She saw me looking at her. "What can I say, I suck at math and I wanted an outstanding GPA for when I applied with the bureau. So, I chose majors that might have a scintilla of practical application."

I chuckled. "To answer your question, I suppose I'm right in the middle of stage five. So, I suppose I'm ahead of the curve." I was about to say more, but she changed the topic.

"Hey, check that out." She pointed.

Up ahead, ten or so car-lengths in front of us, was a red dually truck. I sped up and was soon following behind them. Hope got on her cell phone and called in the tag. After a moment, she hung up.

"Properly registered. Let's pass it and take a look inside, just in case."

I did so. There were two elderly black men in it.

"Well, they certainly don't look like gypsies to me," I declared.

Hope gave me a look. "Your sarcasm is duly noted."

"We'll no doubt see more than one Dodge dually pickup in these parts."

"Yeah. So, where were we?" she asked.

"Stage five," I said.

"Oh yeah. You said you were in the middle of stage five. What exactly do you mean by that?"

I gave a noncommittal shrug. "Once I learned the truth about my wife, it sped up the grieving process, but in the short time Simone and I were together, I knew she was the one for me. When you know that about a person and they're taken from you, do you ever really get over it?"

"I suppose it's possible to fall in love again. I thought Dan and I would be together for the rest of our lives. It took a while for me to realize it wasn't going to happen, but I'm over it now."

"Do you want to fall in love and get married again someday?" I asked.

Hope thought a moment. "Yes, I do. Do you?"

"I did with Simone, but since her death, I'm not so sure anymore," I said.

"That's understandable. You're definitely not through grieving yet, but let me ask, isn't it possible you'll meet someone one day and you'll feel that chemistry again? Wouldn't you like for that to happen?"

"I don't know. Yeah, I guess so, but honestly, I wonder if it's possible with me," I said.

"How does that make you feel?" she asked. I glanced over at her.

"You should've pursued a career in therapy; you're a natural."

She laughed. "That was my back-up plan if I couldn't get into the bureau."

After a moment, I cleared my throat. "I like talking to you though," I said.

"You like my breasts too," she retorted. "I've seen you staring."

"Is it that obvious?"

"Oh, please. You ogle like a horny teenager."

I instantly thought of Ronald and how he couldn't stop ogling Marti. I undoubtedly looked the same. Definitely not a good character trait.

"Note to self, stop staring at women's breasts."

She laughed again and stared off at a side street. "At what point does this become a fruitless endeavor?" she asked. "Are we going all the way to Chicago?"

I read the digital clock on the dash. "Yeah, it's getting late. If we turn around now, we'll be back in Nashville by seven. I can drop you off and we can start again in the morning."

"Okay, next exit, turn around," she said.

I'd been in the right lane driving under the speed limit the whole time. Now, I accelerated and began passing cars. Suddenly, Hope inhaled sharply and pointed.

"Pull over!" she shouted.

"What do you see?" I asked as I looked intensely in the rearview mirror. Traffic was heavy, and I was in the left lane. If I tried to stop, I'd probably cause an accident.

"I saw skid marks and a damaged guardrail running off of the side of the interstate, and I could swear the tracks looked like it came from a vehicle with dual wheels."

"Alright, bear with me."

There was no way I could stop and back up without causing a major accident. Instead, I sped up. Five car lengths ahead of me was an opening to merge into the right lane. I took exit 177 and flip-flopped back south. I then backtracked to the previous exit before once again turning back around and heading north. This time, I stayed in the right lane and soon the Red River was before us. I veered onto the shoulder and parked fifty yards back from the bridge. I now saw the marks in the road she was referring to.

"Dual tracks alright, but it could be from a bobtail semi," I said. "Let's check it out anyway."

We got out and began walking toward the bridge. When we were within twenty feet, I could clearly see the skid marks leading to the damaged guardrail and the ensuing trail down the embankment. I pointed at the damaged bushes.

"It looks fresh," I surmised. Hope agreed. "Alright, we need to walk down there and check it out."

"Shouldn't we call it in first?" she asked.

"It might be some unrelated accident," I said. "Let's make sure of what we have before raising a fuss. By the way, where are you from?"

"A small town called Walker, Louisiana."

"Ah, Louisiana. I've visited there. The summers are killers."

"Yes, they are," she agreed.

"So, being a Louisiana girl, you're familiar with copperheads and water moccasins. There might be a few hanging around down by the water, so watch your step."

"Got it," she said and smirked. "You can lead the way."

I was about to make a smart-assed remark about equality, but decided to stow it and led off. The embankment was sharply angled and the undergrowth was thick; myriad bushes and briars. It was difficult, and it took us several minutes to reach the bottom. Even though the vehicle had knocked a lot of it down or compressed it, the going was slow, and visibility was limited. When we emerged from the undergrowth at the edge of the riverbank, both of us were stunned.

The back end of a Dodge dually was sticking out of the river.

CHAPTER 32

"Oh, God," Hope exclaimed. "Is that it?"

"I'd say so. It's got Marshall County tags on it," I said while pointing at the license plate. "Alright, go ahead and call it in. I'm going to check it out."

As quickly as I could do it without turning an ankle or busting my ass, I worked my way to the backside of the truck.

"Is anyone in there?" she asked.

"I'm not sure yet."

The truck was a crew cab. The entire front passenger compartment was underwater, but the back portion was sticking out. I grabbed the bumper and hoisted myself into the bed of the truck. Making a quick decision, I kicked in the back window. When I did so, I heard a soft whimper from inside. Peering in, I could see the shape of a person crumpled down behind the driver's seat. It had to be her.

"Lorilee, can you hear me?" I implored. She whimpered again but did not answer. I turned to Hope and shouted.

"She's in here and she's alive! We'll need rescue personnel!"

Hope gestured at her phone. "I can't get a signal! I'll need to go back to the interstate!"

I waved her on and focused back on the truck. It was facing downward at a thirty-degree angle, making it awkward to maintain a balance. I stuck my head back in the broken window. It was dark, so I used the flashlight on my phone.

I could see Lorilee now. She was in the floorboard behind the driver's seat. Only her head and shoulders were above water.

"Lorilee?" I asked. She did not respond.

Working my way further in, I reached out and checked her carotid pulse. It was barely there and she was ice cold. I pinched her right shoulder muscle and she flinched slightly. So, she wasn't totally out of it. At least, not yet.

"Lorilee, I think you can hear me. My name is Thomas and you've been in an accident. We've got an ambulance and rescue people on the way, so you hang on, okay?"

She did not respond, but I could see her breathing. The rescue crew would no doubt have to cut the truck open to get her out and I did not want to risk exacerbating any injuries by trying to move her, so I took the opportunity to feel around in the murky water. There was nobody else in the back, so I worked my way forward until I could see into the front seats. There was another body slumped behind the wheel. When I reached out to check for a pulse, the head of Tambourine Man turned toward me.

I'd seen a number of dead people over the years. Even so, I have to admit it startled me. So much so, my phone slipped out of my hand and dropped into the water.

"Dang it," I muttered and felt around until I found it. As I suspected, the water killed it, so now I was in the dark with an injured woman and a dead gypsy.

I started to settle back and wait, but I knew I needed to search for little Amber. If she was under water, she was most certainly dead. Even so, her body needed to be recovered. I had no desire to do what I was about to do. The only way I was going to be able to search the floor area of the front was to work myself into an uncomfortable and distasteful position. I did not see any other way.

So, working myself in between the two front seats, I stuck my upper torso under the water and began searching with my hands. It took more than a few minutes and I had to come up for air several times before I was satisfied little Amber was not inside the truck. It did not take long before I was frigid. I worked my way back to Lorilee.

"Don't worry, help is on the way. They'll be here any minute." When I said it, I was mentally wondering where they were. I could not even hear the approach of any sirens. I didn't know if she could hear me, but I kept talking anyway.

Suddenly, the truck shifted and sank further down into the river, jolting me and causing Lorilee to moan again. I pulled a Bic lighter out of my pocket, and sure enough, I got a flame on the second strike. Damn good lighters, those Bics. The water was now up to her chin. I shouted her name again, and when there was no reaction, I tried for a moderate slap to the face. Even that didn't work. Within seconds, the water was caressing her lips. I tried holding her head up, but I knew I had to get her out of there or else she was going to drown. I put my mouth close to her ear.

"Lorilee, I'm going to have to pull you out. It might be a little uncomfortable, but it has to be done."

As soon as I said it, I felt the truck move again. I gave a quick, silent prayer. She was wedged in tight. I was trying to be gentle, but the rising water increased my sense of urgency. Gentleness changed to brute muscle. I pulled on her with all my strength. She cried out in pain, but there was nothing I could do.

"I'm sorry, sweetie."

There was no way to do it easy. I got her in a bear hug, chastised myself for thinking of her big breasts, and hefted her up. Once I had her worked loose, the water actually helped me with buoyancy. The lessened weight allowed me to push her through the broken rear window. Her arm scraped against the little shards of broken glass still stuck in the rubber edging around the window frame. It caused another whimper, which caused me to apologize again. The bed of the truck was now mostly full of muddy river water and when I pushed Lorilee through the window, her head went under. I cursed myself as I quickly reached through and pulled her up.

The truck shifted again and the strong current began pushing the truck down river. I fought my way out of the window and found my footing. The truck broke free of the embankment and began sinking to the bottom. I did not know how deep the Red River was around these parts, but I knew I had to get both of us to the safety of the bank or we were both going to drown.

Lorilee was dead weight, and she wasn't a small girl. Kicking my shoes off, I began desperately trying to flutter kick to keep both of our heads above water. Even so, the weight of Lorilee and my clothing bogged me down. I went under once, and then a second time. I wasn't going to make it unless I let go of her, but for some crazy reason, my brain was telling me that was not an option.

I went under again and I simply did not have the strength to fight back to the surface. My lungs were burning and my vision was nothing but blinking stars. Suddenly, I bumped against something. Something hard. I instinctively reached out. I couldn't see shit, but it felt like a fallen tree. I grabbed blindly and latched onto something, a stub of a branch maybe. I grabbed it as tightly as I could and pulled while getting my feet against it. It seemed like an eternity, but I suddenly broke the surface and found air. I gasped and coughed, fighting for breath. Lorilee, who I was holding tightly with my left arm, began coughing too. It was a good sign.

"Thank you, Lord," I croaked between gasps.

I forced myself to calm down, take deep breaths, and look around. It was indeed a fallen tree I was hanging onto. The current of the water was strong, but it was pushing us against the tree rather than pulling us away from it. That was the good news. The bad news was, I was so cold my teeth were chattering and I was too fatigued to work my way over to the riverbank. Lorilee was worse. I tried shouting to her, but she was still incoherent.

I desperately looked around for help. I saw nothing but trees and undergrowth along the bank. I tried shouting for Hope, but there was no response. Lorilee's head lolled onto my shoulder. For all I knew she was dead by now, but there was no way I was going to let go of her.

I knew I had to get both of us out of the frigid water. Summoning what little strength I had, I began working my way along the fallen tree toward the embankment.

It seemed to take forever, but I finally got us mostly out of the water. I was scraped up and utterly exhausted, but I never let go of Lorilee. She was as limp as a ragdoll and I knew if there was any hope for her at all, I needed to get her up to the interstate, but I was so exhausted I did not have it in me to even stand up and yell for help.

"Thomas!"

I heard my name several times before I realized someone was yelling at me. Looking up, I saw a woman standing up on the side of the hill.

"Simone?" I mumbled through chattering teeth. Only it wasn't Simone. It was Hope, and it looked like she had a dozen fire and police personnel with her.

CHAPTER 33

I sat on the guardrail and watched Lorilee being placed into an ambulance. The sun had gone down sometime during all of this, and there were so many flashing lights it looked like a rave party. One of the firemen had not bothered to argue with me when I refused to go to the hospital. Instead, he graciously offered one of those silvery space blankets and a cup of coffee he poured from his thermos. I was shaking so bad at first, I spilled more down my chin than I got in my mouth, but eventually, I began warming up.

"You really should go to the ER and get checked out," Hope suggested.

I shook my head. "I'm okay, just a few scrapes. Any idea what kind of injuries she has?"

"Hypothermia, probably a concussion and a broken leg. They'll know more when they get her to the ER."

I nodded in understanding. "She's alive though, that's good."

"Yes, it is. I'm going to ride in the ambulance with her. Carter is on his way up here," she said. "I'm going to stay with her."

"Yeah, that's a good idea." I gestured with a thumb over my shoulder. "We can only speculate what caused the wreck. I wonder if the rest of them know about it."

"Do you think they're still heading to Chicago?" she asked.

"I'd say they're already there," I replied.

"Yeah. What are you going to do?"

"I'm going to wait until they haul the truck up and make sure her little girl isn't in there, then I suppose I'm going to head home, get cleaned up, get some sleep." I suddenly remembered my phone and pulled it out of my pocket. As I suspected, it was kaput.

"Let me give you my roommate's phone number. If anything comes up, give her a call; she'll know how to get in touch with me."

The blip of the ambulance's siren ended our conversation. There was a moment when I thought she was going to kiss me, and maybe she was, but then she caught herself. Instead, she stuck her finger out and tapped my nose instead.

"You're something else, Thomas. Get yourself rested. They'll want a formal statement in the morning."

"You get some rest as well," I said.

She made a face. "Fat chance of that, but I'll try."

I watched as she hustled over to the ambulance and climbed in. She was a pretty woman, and dedicated to her job. I liked that, and I liked her. I think she liked me too. In spite of my fatigue, I smiled, and in spite of how cold I was, the little soldier let me know he approved as well.

The ride back was quiet, too quiet, and I was out of cigars. I was still soggy, muddy, tired, and hungry, but that didn't matter. I was concerned about Lorilee. We had no idea what she'd gone through and most importantly, nobody knew the fate of her child, Amber.

I parked in my driveway a little before ten. Anna and Marti were sitting in the den watching TV. Both had a cocktail glass in hand. Gracie immediately jumped off the couch and scampered over whereupon she began sniffing my soggy pants. I'm sure I smelled interesting to her.

"My phone's been blowing up with people calling for you," Anna said. "What kind of shitstorm have you started?" Then she seemed to notice my physical state. "Damn, you're dirty. And where are your shoes?"

"It's good to see you too. What are you drinking?"

"I'll fix you something," Marti said, jumping up from the couch and going into the kitchen.

"Make it a tumbler of scotch, neat. I don't want anything cold."

"You got it," she said.

I was too dirty to sit anywhere, so I stood at the back door where I had a floor mat and gave them a rundown of the day's events. Anna got up and went into my bedroom. When she emerged, she handed me a bath towel.

"So, who's been calling?" I asked.

"Reuben called twice. Two men who said they were special agents, and a woman named Hope. She said to forget everyone else and call her first."

"Okay, got it. I guess I better call." I held my hand out and took her phone.

"What's up, Buttercup?" I asked when Hope answered.

"Lorilee is conscious," she said. "I know what you're about to ask. She confirmed it was the gypsies who kidnapped her. Apparently, Wolf had lured her out on the pretense of a dinner date. He had drugged and beaten her and tied her up. She was trundled up in the back of the truck for several hours, but at some point, she was able to get loose. The one we're calling the Tambourine Man was driving. She tried to escape and the two of them began fighting, which caused him to lose control of the truck and wreck."

"I don't suppose he had any identification on him?" I asked.

"He had a driver's license, but it was fake. No hits on his fingerprints either. They're putting a priority on his DNA analysis. Hopefully, it'll give us something to work with."

"Well, I'm glad she's going to be okay. I'm assuming her child hasn't been located."

"No, she hasn't. The locals have search and rescue team on the river and the Highway Patrol are searching with helicopters. Even so, this is a major break for us."

"Yes, it is," I agreed.

"Dresden probably has one or two messages on your roommate's phone. He wanted you to report in for debriefing. When I told him of your heroics, he relented and directed me to tell you to come in tomorrow, but no later than ten."

"Okay, I appreciate that," I said. What I did not tell her is I fully intended on getting a good night's sleep and was going to report in when it suited me, not at the direction of someone else.

"I have something I need to tell you," Hope said.

"Oh? What's that?"

She hesitated a moment before speaking. "The upcoming press release is giving me all of the credit for rescuing Lorilee." She pushed on before I could reply. "I'm sorry, Thomas. If not for you, Lorilee would have been swept away and drowned. I plan on having a talk with Reuben in just a few minutes and straighten everything out."

"You'll do no such thing," I said.

"No, Thomas, it's the right thing to do."

"No, it's not," I rejoined. "Let me explain."

"Okay," she drawled.

"Reuben is no dummy. He knows how it all went down. And, he knows I don't care about getting credit for anything. He's taking care of you. You're the new girl in the office and he's sticking a feather in your cap. Go with it."

She thought about it a moment. "I guess you make a good point, but it's not fair to you, Thomas."

I scoffed. "Hope, things like that aren't important to me and Reuben knows that. You're worrying over nothing."

She paused before answering. "Alright, I hope you're not being disingenuous."

"Oooh, that's a mighty big word you're using on me. Remember, I'm just a dumb, has-been city cop." I could sense her smiling.

"That's not at all how I think of you and you know it," she said.

"Fair enough, but don't worry about me. Besides, this is a good way for me to have a friend in the FBI who owes me a favor."

That got a laugh out of her. "Now that I believe."

We spoke some more before ending the call. The two girls looked at me expectantly.

"I'm going in tomorrow to do some paperwork," I said.

"Do you really work for the FBI now?" Marti asked.

"Temporarily, yes."

She grinned. "That is so cool."

I grunted. "It's something. Alright, I've had a heck of a day. I'm showering and heading to bed. Keep the noise down, please."

"Yes, Dad," Anna teased.

I smiled to myself as I headed toward my bedroom and shut the door.

I slept like a rock and woke up the next morning to find Tommy Boy lying on the pillow inches from my face. He was staring at me the way cats stared, and when he realized I was awake, stuck a paw out and swatted my nose. I was certain he wasn't in my bedroom when I turned in last night, so someone had come in and checked on me.

I took another hot shower and dressed before heading into the kitchen. Anna, bless her heart, had a pot of coffee fixed for me. She was nowhere around, but there was a notepad resting on the kitchen table listing a couple of phone messages and telling me she was spending the day serving subpoenas for a ball-busting attorney by the name of Rochelle Anderson. I was probably only one of three men Rochelle liked, and she only tolerated me, but she loved Anna and hired her whenever she needed subpoenas served. The last note was in capital letters. She insisted I get a landline if I was going to keep screwing up my cell phone.

I fixed a couple of egg sandwiches to go with my coffee before heading out. The driver's seat and floorboard of my Explorer was filthy, so I took the Mustang and soon arrived at the FBI headquarters. The security guard manning the front lobby was dubious of my employment status until Dresden came out and got me.

"You need to issue me a security card," I suggested.

"All in due time, Thomas," he said as we walked.

"Yeah, right. Any developments?" I asked.

"If you are asking if anyone is in custody, the answer is no," he replied. "Miss Pushnell's medical condition has been upgraded. In addition to many bumps and scrapes, she has a concussion, a broken left femur, and a broken left wrist, but she is expected to make a full recovery."

"Has Hope been able to interview her?" I asked.

"Yes, Agent Delmonico has developed an excellent rapport with her."

"That's good. Nothing on her kid though, right?"

He shook his head again. "Agent Delmonico relayed to me you did not believe the child was in the truck, would that be correct?"

"Correct. I never saw a child. I looked around, but it could be possible she was ejected during the wreck."

"Yeah, the locals have rescue teams performing a diligent search," he said. "But we are also keeping in mind they still have the child and are going to attempt to leave the country with her." We reached the doors leading into the conference room and he held one open for me.

"You have a temporary account. Your full name is your login and your date of birth is your password. Find an unoccupied desk and use the approved report template for your report. When you are finished, email it to the following." He pointed at the dry erase board. It had a group email address, which I assumed went to everyone who mattered.

"Consider it done," I said.

"Please be professional in your verbiage, Thomas," Dresden admonished before leaving.

I followed instructions, typed up a two-page report, and attached it to the group email address provided and I also cc'd my business email address. After sending it, I looked around to see if anyone was watching me. They were not. Curious, I browsed the computer to see what I had access to. Other than some boilerplate templates and interdepartmental email, I had access to nothing. I wasn't surprised, but it didn't hurt to try it.

Logging off, I stood and looked around. The incident command timer was prominently displayed on the center screen. It was a glaring reminder of how long it had been since one of their fellow agents had been assaulted and left for dead. I walked around to the various makeshift work stations and either eavesdropped on conversations or looked over a shoulder or three at what was being typed into the computer. It looked like a concerted effort was being conducted at every airport, shipping port, and border crossing.

I spotted the same female captain from the Marshall County Sheriff's Department sitting with an agent in front of a computer. I wandered over and said hello.

"We found them," she said with a grin. The agent looked up.

"She means we found surveillance video of them," he corrected and pointed at the monitor.

It was a decent quality video. The camera was mounted up high, as usual, but the video was in color and had a high-pixel count. It clearly showed Lorilee's truck driving up to a set of gas pumps. Tambourine Man got out and walked inside. The camera switched to him at the counter paying in cash.

"No credit card transaction," the agent commented.

I understood what he meant. If Tambourine Man had used a credit card, they could find the account number and track wherever it was used. I watched as he paid and walked out. The agent pointed at the timestamp in the bottom right corner. It showed a time of 0158 hours.

"Has the timestamp been verified?" I asked the captain.

"I believe so," she answered.

It wasn't much of an answer. I had to assume the deputy who obtained this video verified the accuracy of the time.

"This is from the truck stop," she added. "They said their cameras are monitored by corporate, so I would assume they make sure the time is accurate."

I nodded. She made a good point.

"Alright, assuming that's the correct time, this is after they've left Nashville. They go to the turnout while Tambourine Man continues down to exit 22 and gasses up. They were definitely planning on leaving immediately after the interaction with Stainback and Candy."

"Why do you call him Tambourine Man?" the captain asked.

"He played a tambourine," I said. "As far as I know, he has not yet been identified, so that's what I call him."

"Oh," she said and pointed. "Well, he kept looking outside toward the truck the whole time he was waiting in line."

"Probably watching to make sure a cop doesn't drive through and spots the truck," the agent said.

"Yeah, and Lorilee is probably hogtied and stuffed in the backseat at this point," I added. The two of them nodded in agreement. We watched in silence as Tambourine Man got in the truck and drove away.

"We don't have anything else," the agent said. "What do you think? You seeing anything here?"

I watched it over and over, but I didn't see anything new. I shook my head.

"Alright, thanks for showing it to me," I said. The agent gave me a dutiful nod and then focused on something else.

After leaving the FBI office, I headed to the phone store. The same kid was working. When I dropped my phone on the counter, he frowned.

"What'd you do, drop it in the toilet?" he asked.

"Something like that. Is it repairable?"

He reached under the counter and pulled out a box of nitrile gloves. Putting on a pair, he grimaced as he daintily picked up my phone and inspected it with a magnifying glass. After only a few seconds, he frowned and shook his head.

"No, dude, it's toast."

"Well, it's a good thing I bought that insurance, right?" I said cheerily. "Oh, and I want one of those Bluetooth things for when I drive."

With a new phone in hand, I texted Hope and told her I had a functioning phone again and asked if there was anything new. She responded after a couple of minutes and advised there was nothing. Lorilee was under guard and asleep, so she was going to stop by the office before going home and catch a few hours of sleep.

I then called Dresden. The call went to voicemail, which told me he was too busy to talk, or perhaps he was catching some shuteye. I left a message, repeating that my phone was working again and I was available if he needed me for something.

I stopped by the auto parts store before heading home. I ate a sandwich for lunch before changing into some grungy clothes and lit a cigar before starting in on the old Cadillac. As I started working on rebuilding the brakes, I thought about how far I wanted to go with this car. It was actually in decent shape. Not much rust at all. But the car was old and parts were hard to come by. And, I had not even gotten into the engine yet. If I had plenty of free time, I could get it rebuilt and painted in a few months, but at the rate I was currently going, it was looking like a two-year project. I thought about simply cleaning it up and selling it, but for now, it was a hobby.

I thought about the Ironcutter Investigations caseload while I worked. The Reavis case was done. Ronald and Marti had culled twenty-one email chains that were so significant, I'd be surprised if the lawsuit went any further. And, even Ronald admitted Marti did a good job, so hiring her, at least on a part-time basis, was going to be doable. I decided to text Anna and say as much.

I was attempting to scrub my arms in the laundry sink when my phone pinged. Glancing at my phone, I saw a familiar car coming down my driveway. I grabbed a towel and walked outside. Al parked, saw me, and exited. It was only then that I remembered we were supposed to go out the night before.

"Dang it," I muttered to myself. "This won't be pleasant."

CHAPTER 34

Watching her get out of the car, I had to admit, she looked good. Her blonde hair was freshly brushed and flowing freely across her shoulders. She had on a pair of jeans and a navy-blue Nike Polo shirt that seemed to accentuate her blue eyes.

"If you're wondering how I know where you live, I Googled you, remember?" she said.

Her voice was even, but even so, she was staring daggers at me. She was not the first person to find out where I lived by doing a simple computer search. I wasn't sorry she was interested in me, but I was a little concerned that she had no qualms about showing up uninvited. I mean, what if I had company?

That was a conversation for another day though. At the moment, I did not want this to be unpleasant. The best thing to do here was apologize for my shitty behavior toward her.

"I won't even attempt to make an excuse, I totally forgot we had plans and I am terribly sorry," I said.

"I tried calling you."

"I jumped in a river with my phone in my pocket. It drowned."

She did not seem fazed. "Did you get my text messages?"

"No, I'm afraid not," I said.

"I sent you a few after I'd had a couple of drinks. They were pretty, hmm, I think scathing would be the appropriate word. That's why I'm here; I was going to apologize in person."

"No apology is necessary," I said. "I never got them anyway. And besides, I'm the one who was in the wrong. I totally forgot. One would think that sometime during the day I would have remembered and called, but I didn't. I've had a lot going on. I hope you can forgive me."

She stood there a moment, frowning. "The last time I was stood up was back in high school. He was supposed to take me out after a basketball game, but they scored a victory in overtime and the team had their own little impromptu party afterward. I got payback though."

"What'd you do?" I asked.

"I married him," she answered.

"I bet he learned his lesson," I quipped, and then realized that may not have been an appropriate response. "I mean, you know."

She tried to glare, but ended up cracking a smile. "Okay, I admit, that's funny."

"I hope you'll let me make it up to you," I suggested.

She folded her arms. "What do you have in mind?"

"I don't know if you've eaten yet, but I just put a pasta casserole in the oven. It should be ready in about thirty minutes. I don't have any salad or sides though. Even so, would that interest you?"

"I like wine with pasta," she replied.

"Well then, you're in luck. I have an eclectic variety of wines in my cellar. Actually, it's the kitchen closet, but that doesn't sound quite as impressive."

She smiled again, which was a positive sign. "Alright, you've sold me, but only if you get cleaned up first."

I thanked her, got her seated on the couch with a fresh glass of tea, and hurried into the restroom. I consciously spent a few extra minutes scrubbing myself down from head to toe. Exiting the shower, I opted for some cologne, put on a fresh pair of jeans and a Polo shirt similar to Al's, and hurried out of the bedroom. Al had set the table and poured us glasses of chardonnay. When I walked in, she gave me an appraising stare.

"You clean up pretty good," she said.

The oven's timer went off as I walked into the kitchen. Donning a pair of mitts, I removed the casserole and put it on the stovetop. Al helped me put portions into our plates. Seated, I held up my glass.

"I have a toast. Here's to second chances."

She clicked my glass without comment. After taking a drink, she tried a small forkful of the casserole.

"Oh, this is delicious. It might need a touch more salt, but I'm not complaining."

"Thanks," I said and slid the salt shaker over to her. "I'll never be a gourmet chef, but I can cook pasta."

"Did your mother teach you to cook?" she asked.

I shook my head. "My Uncle Mike did. He was a great cook." I wasn't ready to discuss Uncle Mike with someone I hardly knew, so I changed the subject. "So, how angry did you get?"

"Pretty mad. I alternated between thoughts of something must have happened to you to thoughts of you found someone else to spend the evening with. So, tell me what happened that was so important that you forgot all about me," she said.

I told her the entire story as we ate and finished up with the river rescue.

"Wait, I saw that on the news. You were involved in that?" she asked.

"Yeah, that's how I ruined my phone. My wallet and clothes aren't in much better shape."

She frowned. "The noon news didn't mention you. They said a woman FBI agent found and rescued her."

I shrugged. "Yeah, she was there."

She glanced at the clock on the microwave. "It's five o'clock. Turn the news on."

I'm not sure if she was trying to verify my story, but I didn't care. I found the remote stuffed in the couch cushions and turned on my TV.

The live press conference was held at noon, so this was merely a replay. I offhandedly listened to Reuben give his speech as I fixed myself a second helping.

"Is that your partner?" Al asked while pointing at the TV. Hope was standing in the background. She was wearing a conservative business suit, and although it hid her figure, she still looked nice. She also looked fatigued. I wondered how much sleep she'd gotten last night.

"That's Special Agent Delmonico. She was there at the river, but I wouldn't call us partners."

"That older man said she's the one who found and rescued the girl. He didn't say anything about you."

When she said it, she was eyeing me with a little bit of suspicion. The news report changed to some video footage at the side of the interstate. Suddenly, Al gasped and pointed.

"There you are."

She was right. The cameraman had panned over to me where I was sitting on the guardrail. There was a three-second shot where a fireman draped that survival blanket over my shoulders. I was muddy and looked exhausted.

"I've looked better," I said and poured us some more wine. "Be honest though, you were doubting me."

She offered a tight smile. "Maybe."

I wasn't mad, or even a little irked. I know it sounded like a tall tale conceived by one of the blowhards that hung out at Mick's, but in my case, it was true. We chatted as we ate.

"You look like you work out a lot," I mentioned.

"Yes, I do. I've always been health conscious. You wouldn't believe the types of people we get called out on. They get winded and fall down when they walk to the mailbox. I swore I'd never let myself be like that. Hank was Special Forces, so he was in phenomenal shape. We'd work out together. You're no slouch, from what I can see."

"When I was younger, I stayed in shape. I got a little lazy there for a while, but I've been doing better."

"I bet I have better stamina," she said with a flirtatious smile and a gleam in her eye.

I smiled back. I'd like to think I was making headway. "I have no doubt about that. Hank was the love of your life, I take it."

"He was," she agreed. "His death hit me hard. He wasn't perfect, far from it, but he was the father of my kids. The boys are a spitting image of him."

"Has there been anybody since?" I asked.

"I didn't even consider dating the first year after he died. Then I started seeing a co-worker named Vincent. I thought it was good until I walked in on him with another woman."

"Oh, damn," I said. "He didn't do the old, this isn't what it looks like spiel, did he?"

Al choked on her wine and wiped her mouth. "That's exactly what he said," she said with a rueful laugh. "Not very original, is it?"

"No, I guess not."

"Did you ever cheat?" she asked.

"Not on my wife. And not on Simone, but after she died, I had a casual fling with a woman. Even though Simone was long gone, I still felt guilty. I don't know how to explain it, but I kind of felt like I was cheating."

"So, whatever happened with this other woman?"

"Oh, it's over and she's long gone," I said. Telling her about Lilith's death was a story for another time.

"What about Debbie?" she asked.

I smiled. "You already asked me about her."

"Did you sleep with her?"

"Nope."

"Are you sure? I heard she's very friendly."

"That sounds like your friend talking. What was his name, Eddie?"

"Yeah, Eddie Barker. His father had a popcorn business. Made millions. Eddie lives off of the trust fund."

"It must be nice."

She scoffed. "Hardly. He's been married four times and cheated on all of them. The only thing that saved his ass was the prenuptial agreements. But he's always been nice to me and we're good friends. Do you like what you do?"

"For the most part, yes, I do," I said. "What about you?"

"Absolutely. It can be a stressful job, but I don't think I'd ever consider doing anything else."

We chatted while we ate, and the first bottle of wine was empty before I knew it. After dinner, we agreed to open another and moved to the couch. She made the first move by thanking me for dinner and then kissing me. It was a wonderful kiss and I responded in kind. It wasn't long before we were getting hot and heavy, but my pinging phone quickly brought us to a halt.

"What's that, a text message?" Al asked.

"No, if it were a text message, I'd ignore it. It's an alert. Someone's coming down the driveway." I went to the kitchen table where my phone was lying and looked at the screen.

"Who is it?" she asked.

"My roommate, Anna. She has lousy timing," I grumbled.

We had ourselves straightened and reasonably normal looking when Anna walked in.

Anna was slightly surprised at the sight of Al, but recovered quickly and smiled.

"Hi, I'm Anna."

The two women chatted amicably for a few minutes before Al stretched and announced she needed to go home. I walked her to her car and was going to try for a kiss, but I sensed a coolness in her demeanor. When we reached her car, she stopped and turned to me.

"I'm really glad you didn't give up on me," I said and stepped a smidgeon closer.

"How old is Anna?" she asked.

"Um, twenty-three," I said, wondering why she asked.

"So, you have a drop-dead gorgeous twenty-something sex kitten living with you and there is no blood relation? Thomas, the more I get to know you, the more I sense you're a good guy, but come on, really? The guys I work with would be stumbling over themselves trying to get in bed with her and you expect me to believe the two of you are platonic?"

"Yes, I do," I said, growing a little irritated. "During the short time we've known each other, we've become close friends, but that's it. She looks at me like a father-figure. And, for the record, she's currently seeing a friend of mine."

Al paused and looked down at my feet. "I'm sorry," she said in a quiet voice. "I have trust issues. After Hank's funeral, a young woman walked up to me and said she was Hank's lover and she wanted to offer her condolences and perhaps we could get together sometime and share our good memories of Hank."

"Ouch. How did you respond?" I asked.

"His friends had to pull me off of her," she said.

I laughed before I could help myself.

"Yeah, and when I'm finally ready to date again, I had that incident with Vincent. By the way, the woman he was cheating with was about the same age as Anna."

I slowly nodded. "I guess I can certainly understand your apprehensions with me. Personally, I don't see why a man who was with you would find it necessary to be unfaithful."

"Why do you say that?"

"Look at you, you're beautiful. You have a beautiful face, sexy eyes, and I'm betting underneath that shirt you have six-pack abs."

She almost smiled. "I do, but apparently, that's not enough," she lamented.

"I wasn't finished. Your two sons are living proof you're a good mom, and I've seen you in action at work. You're a hell of a paramedic."

She smiled now. "Actually, I'm still an EMT. I still have a ton of training before I'm eligible to become a paramedic."

"Are you going to do it?" I asked.

She shrugged. "Something is always getting in the way, but I'd like to. It'll be a long four years." She then reached out and grabbed my hands. "I admit, I'm attracted to you, Thomas. Very attracted. You're a handsome, interesting man."

"I sense a but in there somewhere," I said.

"My kids and my career take up a lot of my time. I'm not necessarily looking for a husband, but I'd like to keep that option open and I'm wondering if you'll ever even consider getting married again."

Wait, did I just hear her saying those dreaded H and M words? We had not even been on a single real date yet and she was already talking about husbands and marriages.

She reached up and kissed me lightly. "Thank you for the dinner and wine, Thomas."

I watched her drive away and walked back inside.

"She's new," Anna said when I'd sat down.

"Yeah, I'm not so sure about that one."

"Too bad. She seems like she likes you," Anna said.

I scoffed and resumed my seat on the couch. "Don't think I don't notice you're drinking the rest of the wine," I observed.

She gestured at the two glasses on the coffee table. "I refilled yours."

"How did you know which glass is mine?" I asked.

"Because I don't think you wear lipstick, but I could be wrong," she said with a grin. "So, you said her name was Al."

"Short for Alison," I said. "She's the paramedic I told you about. I mean, EMT."

"Is she a natural blonde?" she asked with a sly grin.

"I have no idea and I don't think I'm going to get the opportunity to find out."

"Pity," Anna said. "I could see you two together, even though she's a little young for you."

I scowled. "Too young? Maybe I should start hanging out in senior citizen centers to pick up women." I was going for sarcasm, but I think she actually thought I was being serious. Then she giggled.

"Make sure she's drawing Social Security and she's a VIP member with AARP." She giggled harder this time.

I shook my head in exasperation and finished my wine. My phone buzzed. It was a text message from Hope.

Why don't you come by the hospital tomorrow? Lorilee would like to meet and thank you.

I did not hesitate in responding.

Absolutely. Will you be there?

Absolutely.

I texted back that I'd see her in the morning and put a smiley face on the end.

"What are you smiling at?" Anna asked. "Is new chick sexting you?"

"Could be," I said and gave her a wink.

CHAPTER 35

Hope texted me the room number, but as soon as I stepped off of the elevator, I was stopped by hospital security. I flashed him my temporary FBI credentials. He seemed satisfied and signed me in. When I walked into the room, Hope was sitting beside the bed with Lorilee.

"Good morning, you two," I said.

"Well, speak of the devil. Your ears must be burning," Hope said. "Lorilee, this is Thomas."

"The man who saved me," she said. She was looking at me like a puppy dog looks at someone who is holding a handful of kibbles. Well, with one eye. The other eye was badly bruised and swollen shut. She looked like hell.

I gave a friendly smile. "How are you, Lorilee?"

"I hurt everywhere, but at least I didn't get raped."

I wasn't sure the proper response to that statement, so I gave an agreeable nod.

"Agent Delmonico said there's no way they would have killed Amber. Do you believe that too?"

I glanced at Hope. "I do. I don't know how much you've been told, but we're certain they'll keep her alive, which is good because it increases our chances of rescuing her."

Lorilee did not respond. Instead, a single tear fell down her cheek. She quickly rubbed it away with her good hand. I looked at Hope, who made a head gesture toward the door. She then gently rubbed Lorilee's good hand. "Get some rest, honey. We'll talk more later."

She waited until we were down the hall before speaking. "She's relatively calm now, but that's because she's medicated."

"She's worried about her child," I surmised.

"Yes, she is," Hope agreed.

"Can you give me a brief summary of how it happened?" I asked.

"The gypsies had befriended her from the start, and she became infatuated with Wolf. He came over that night with a bottle of wine. Somehow, he had drugged her, because the next thing she knew, she was tied up and in the back seat of her truck going down the interstate."

"That's when she attacked Tambourine Man," I surmised.

Hope nodded. "She managed to work the ropes loose and jumped on him. That's what caused the wreck. Oh, I forgot to mention, she said her baby was not in the truck when she regained consciousness."

"The rescue squad people will want to know that," I said.

"Already taken care of."

"Good. Has she remembered anything else?" I asked.

Hope shook her head. "Little things, like Wolf was wearing New Balance running shoes and black socks. Things that have no significance. Oh, she did confirm Peko had shaved his beard and hair. In fact, she was the one who did it. He paid her twenty dollars."

"Does she know the name of Guitar Man?" I asked.

Hope shook her head. "They mostly spoke in their own language around her."

I nodded in understanding. It would've been foolish of them to freely talk about themselves around her.

"You know, in some respects, they're actions are professional, but in others, they're on the amateurish side," Hope said. "They're making mistakes. It's almost like they're getting desperate for women."

"Like they have to meet a quota or something," I said in agreement. "After the failed attempt in Nashville at the shopping mall, one would think they would have ghosted."

"Lorilee and her child were almost an afterthought," Hope said.

"Why do you say that?" I asked.

"Lorilee is as homely as a pig in mud," she said. "The little teenage goth girl, on the other hand, has model quality looks. I'm speculating on this, but I think they kidnap based on orders for a particular type of girl." She gestured toward the room. "Lorilee, for example, big behind and big breasts. The girl in Nashville, pale, slender, young."

"That begs the question, orders from whom?"

Hope avoided eye contact for a moment before fixing me with a hard stare. "You do not repeat what I say, alright?"

I gave a slight nod.

"Certain sheikhs in a certain Mideast oil-producing country," she said. "At first, we thought it was Russia, but prostitutes are a dime a dozen there. They don't need to outsource. The aristocracy in the Mideast have so much money from oil, they make cars out of solid gold, can you believe that? They're the ones who buy these girls. We've only heard rumors about what they do to them, Thomas, and it's horrible. Have you heard of hurt-core pornography?"

"I've read a little bit about it, but I can't say I have a good working knowledge."

"Hurt-core is a subculture of real sick people. It involves rape and other acts of degradation. The actor not only gratifies himself through the sexual aspect, but to also destroy the psyche of the victim. If they are rescued, they never recover. Suicide is common among the survivors."

"Sickos like that actually exist?" I asked and shook my head in disgust. "Never mind, it was a rhetorical question."

"We need them alive, Thomas. We need them to talk and tell us specifically who is buying these girls, where are they going, and how we can rescue these girls and dismantle the whole network."

"That sounds good, but in my humble opinion, they're beyond your reach."

A look of irritation crossed her face, but then she emitted a long sigh. "Yeah, you're probably right, but the command staff still want the names of those involved and as much evidence against them as we can obtain."

She was right, but I didn't admit it.

So, as I stood in the elevator a little closer to Hope than was necessary, I made the plunge.

"I know you've been working nonstop, but, if you're not too tired, do you think you'd be interested in going somewhere for dinner later?"

Hope turned in surprise. "I'd love to. I mean, I have no idea what time I'll be through for the day, but I'd love to."

"Good," I said, and then on impulse I leaned forward and kissed her. She kissed me back.

"I'll text you and let you know when I can get away."

I nodded. And then the elevator door opened and suddenly it seemed a little awkward.

"Alright, I'll see you later," I said. I got a grin from her before I walked off, which was nice.

I texted Dresden when I got to my car.

I'm going back to the river and have a look around.

I expected him to call me and implore upon me the importance of reporting in to the incident command to await further instructions, but surprisingly, he texted me back a minute later.

Copy that. Keep me posted.

Traffic was light and I arrived back at the Red River forty minutes later. There were a few rescue squad vehicles parked on the shoulder. I parked fifty yards away and sat there, wondering what the hell I was going to do next. Lighting a fresh cigar, I got out and approached a man who was sitting on an undamaged portion of the guardrail. He squinted up at me like I was some tourist inquiring about canoe rentals.

"Can I help you?" he asked.

"How are you? I'm Thomas Ironcutter with the FBI. I'm just checking to see if there are any new developments."

He eyed me a moment before standing. "What kind of cigar are you smoking?"

I held it out at eye level. "This, sir, is a Padron 1964, an extremely succulent blend. Goes great with coffee."

He eyed me a moment longer before reaching down into the side pocket of his cargo pants and pulling out a cigar tube.

"I agree," he said as he pulled a Padron out of the tube. "But I forgot my lighter."

"Not a problem," I said and retrieved my butane lighter. "It's got a punch on it."

He accepted it gratefully, punched the end with the little attachment, and lit up. "I've been jonesing all morning. Say you're with the FBI?"

"I'm a private contractor with them at the moment," I said.

He nodded like he understood. "Well, the short answer is, we haven't found a thing."

I looked at him questioningly. He saw it.

"What's the matter?" he asked.

"You guys received the word that the little kid is no longer believed to have been in the truck when it wrecked," I tell him.

He stared at me a moment. "Are you sure?"

I pulled my phone out and called Dresden. After speaking to him a moment, I hung up.

"Yep, I'm sure."

"When was that decision made?" he asked.

"An hour or two ago."

He muttered a string of invectives under his breath before getting on his portable radio and telling everyone the information.

"I guess there was a miscommunication," I offered.

He grunted, but after a moment of angrily smoking on his cigar, he seemed to settle down.

"We were going to call it off after today anyway. Most of us are volunteers and have real jobs we need to get back to."

"I understand," I said. We talked for several more minutes. His name was Jeb and he was a farmer by trade. He told me they had all of their boats in the water and even the State Troopers had their helicopter up in the air, although he understood now why he had not seen the helicopter in a while.

"Do you have anything else you need to tell us?" he asked.

I couldn't tell if he was being sincere or sarcastic. I told him I did not, thanked him for his time, and went back to my SUV. I had the notion that I was going to walk around the riverbank and see if I could discover anything, but it was clear to me now it would be a waste of time. As much as I wanted to think otherwise, there was nothing I could do here.

As I sat there wondering what to do next, it hit me. Maybe I missed it, but I was paying close attention during the briefing, so I did not think so. I called Dresden and got his voicemail. I hung up without leaving a message and tried Hope's partner, Special Agent Carter Pike.

"Hello, Thomas, what's up with you?" he asked.

"Listen, I'm up here at the Red River watching the rescue squad people do their thing and I'd like to ask a favor."

"What's that?" he asked.

"Is it possible I can take a look at the property and evidence reports from the rest area where Stainback and Candy were found?"

There was a long pause before he answered. "I don't see how that'd be a problem. What are you looking for?"

I hesitated for a second. I wasn't sure I wanted to tell him. Part of it was I did not want to appear silly, but part of it was I did not want to give away a lead. I decided for honesty. "During the briefing, nothing was said about Stainback's burner phone. I was curious as to whether or not it was recovered."

"Interesting question," he said. "I can already tell you that neither have been recovered." He paused, then explained. "I was the one who was tasked with trying to locate them. I obtained court orders on the call history for both phones. Candy made a few calls to a number during the time frame, but it's a burner phone that was bought at a store on Nolensville Pike. The prepaid hours have not been used, but there has been no activity on it since last Thursday."

"Has anyone gone to the phone store?" I asked.

"Yeah, a couple of our agents did. They described it as a shady little operation. No video system and they preferred cash transactions. The store manager remembered the person who bought it though. He described Wolf to a tee. Said he bought four phones. Paid cash for all of them. He did not have the paperwork that gave us the numbers of the other three burner phones. Like I said, it's a shady operation."

"Okay, Carter, thanks for your time," I said.

"If you come up with any other ideas, feel free to call," he said before hanging up.

I was out of ideas and out of cigars. Unlike what they show on TV, a detective's work was filled with dead ends. Even so, it still frustrated the hell out of me. I glanced at my watch. I mentally ticked off at least a dozen things I needed to do before my dinner date. With no other ideas to pursue, I started up and headed home.

CHAPTER 36

I checked myself in the rearview mirror after I had parked. I was overdue for a haircut, but I was freshly shaven and felt I still looked respectable. I'd changed into a pair of slacks and a pressed button-down shirt for dinner. I'd made arrangements for her to meet me at an upscale restaurant located on West End Avenue. Hope was waiting for me in the lobby.

"I have a bad habit of showing up early," she said with a smile. I smiled back in appreciation. I hated it when people were not punctual.

"I would have been here earlier, but there was a wreck on the interstate. Nashville traffic is like Atlanta these days." I checked my watch. "I made reservations for seven. Let's check in with the hostess."

We were seated immediately at a corner table looking out at West End. I looked out and absently frowned slightly.

"What's wrong?" Hope asked.

"Oh, nothing. I just remember Nashville back in the day when there wasn't continuous bumper-to-bumper traffic."

"The price of progress, right? Oh, I forgot to tell you, they found the RV."

My eyes lit up. "Really? Where?"

"In Chicago. In fact, it was in the parking lot of the former Gypsy Dragon Tattoo Parlor. Unfortunately, it had been set on fire."

"Did the Chicago cops have anything interesting on the people who owned the tattoo parlor?"

"Yes, a little. The entire family is named Gray, which they believe is an alias. They all emigrated from Romania and were suspected of running a heroin smuggling network out of the tattoo parlor. They had an undercover operative who made some controlled buys, but he disappeared a couple of months ago. The tattoo business shut down the same time he went missing and everyone disappeared except for the old woman. They said they interrogated her for hours, but she didn't tell them anything."

"Was the operative a cop?" I asked. She shook her head.

"Not here. He was a Romanian national who used to be a cop. He immigrated to America and got caught running his own little drug business. He had agreed to turn state's evidence and work for them to build a case. The only good thing that came out of it is they recovered nearly eight kilos of heroin the day before he disappeared."

"Did they have any intel at all on Wolf and his merry band?" I asked.

She paused with a forkful of food and peered at me. "Apparently, Lilith Gray was charged with murdering her stepfather when she was a young girl. Did you know about that?"

"I learned about it eventually," I answered evenly. "Due to the mitigating circumstances, she spent some time in a mental institution rather than prison."

"What mitigating circumstances?" she asked.

"He was molesting her."

She looked surprised. "Oh. Wow, they weren't aware of that. The record had been sealed because of her age."

"Yeah. She had a rough childhood," I said. "The things that happened to her when she was a child affected her the rest of her life."

"It happens. How was your childhood?" she asked.

"Oh, it wasn't all that good, but it could have been worse, I suppose. How about you?"

Hope took a sip of her drink. "I had great parents. My father died of a heart attack when he was still relatively young, but my mother remarried a good man. He treated us like we were his kids and he adored mom."

She then finished her drink and dabbed at her mouth with a napkin.

"I have something to tell you," she said. "I'm leaving for Chicago in the morning."

"You are? Is this related to the case?" I asked.

"Yes. We have agents from across the country going. We're going to saturate the airports and the shipping docks."

"So, the command staff believes my theory," I said.

"Yes, they do. Reuben had a lot to do with that, and after the past two days, you've picked up a few supporters."

"I hope you're one of them," I said.

"Oh, absolutely," she said and patted me on the arm. "In spite of the circumstances, I'm glad we've met."

"How long will you be gone?" I asked.

She shrugged and her features darkened slightly. "I'm uncertain. Probably until they are apprehended, but the Chicago office also has a couple of significant public corruption cases brewing. I've already been invited to transfer up there and take part in the investigations. Either of them has the potential of becoming really big."

"A career maker," I said. She nodded. "Have you ever been to Chicago?" I asked.

"I have not. Have you?"

"Enough to know it's different from Walker, Louisiana," I said.

She laughed lightly. "I'm sure it is, but I can handle it. Hell, I'm excited, Thomas. The entire reason I joined the FBI was to fight public corruption."

"Hmm, sounds like there's a story behind that passion."

Her smile faltered. "To make a long story short, my father got royally shafted by some local politicians when I was a teenager. I went to school with their kids and it was not a pleasant time. I'm convinced that's why he had a heart attack. When I was at his funeral crying my eyes out with the rest of my family, I had an epiphany and decided putting corrupt politicians in prison was going to be my life's work."

"I can understand that, but I think you should stay in Nashville," I said.

"Why is that?" she asked.

"Because I'm selfish," I answered. "I like being around you."

She laughed. "I like being around you as well."

Hope stifled a couple of yawns during after dinner drinks. She mentioned she was expected back at the office no later than seven and the flight to Chicago was at noon, so I insisted she go home and get some sleep, even though it was not yet eight o'clock. She didn't argue. I walked her to her car. I got a kiss. Not a deep, passionate kiss, but at least it was on the lips and not a handshake.

"I had a wonderful time, Thomas," she said.

"I did as well," I replied. "Maybe when you get back, we'll do this again."

"Or maybe you can come up to Chicago sometime," she said with a slight smile. I want to say it was flirtatious with a hint of wistfulness in it, but I've often been told I have an overactive imagination.

I watched her drive away. I wasn't tired, and ended up at Mick's. There were only a few people there, including a younger millennial-hipster type I had not seen in there before. He was talking loudly and telling some tall tale about how he sued someone and won a gazillion dollars. Normally, I would've ignored him and sat in my usual spot, but he was sitting in the next stool. Sighing, I went down to the end of the bar and sat by Puffessor Ebenezer Farquhar.

"How are you, Ebbie?" I said as I sat. Ebbie leaned close.

"We got us a know-it-all down there at the other end," he whispered.

"Sounds like it," I said. Ebbie continued.

"Yeah, self-proclaimed business expert, political expert, you name it. An all-around blowhard."

"Well, he fits right in around here," I muttered. That earned me a rebuking scoff from Ebbie.

CHAPTER 37

I walked in the back door of my home a little before ten. Anna and Marti were sitting on the couch with Gracie, who was snuggled up between them and sound asleep. Tommy Boy was on the back of the couch, curled up and asleep as well.

"How'd your date go?" Anna asked.

"I think she enjoyed herself," I replied.

"That's nice. What about you?"

"Yeah, I did too," I said. "But it's not going to go anywhere. She's going to transfer to Chicago."

"Chicago? Why?" Anna asked.

"It's a temporary assignment on the gypsy case, but her specialty is investigating public corruption and she's being considered for a position there. She's more than likely going to transfer there permanently."

"Did you give her a going away present?" Marti asked with a mischievous grin.

"Nope. Nothing but a friendly kiss," I said. I went to the kitchen and started to grab a beer, but opted for some scotch. Returning to the den, I sat at my desk and turned on my laptop.

"What are you girls up to?" I asked while I waited for the computer to boot up.

"Watching Netflix," Anna said, gesturing at the TV. It looked like some sort of romantic comedy. I suppressed a disgusted grimace and got online.

"What are you doing?" Marti asked. She had walked up behind me and was now peering over my shoulder.

"I haven't checked my emails lately. I thought I'd catch up."

"We're not taking any new jobs right now, are we?" Anna asked. "I mean, there's no telling how long you're going to be working for the Feds, right?"

"What do you mean?" Marti asked.

I grunted. "I signed a contract that says as long as I am on the Fed's payroll, I cannot take on any new jobs." I thought for a moment. "But it didn't say anything about Ironcutter Investigations, or its employees."

Anna bit her lip for a second and then understood. "So, Ronald and I can still take on jobs."

"And me," Marti added gleefully.

I chuckled. "I must admit, you did a good job with those emails. Even Ronald was complimentary."

"Is it over yet?" she asked.

"Our part is over. The lawsuit itself will probably take another year or two," I said.

She frowned. "When do I get paid then?"

"The end of the month," I said and briefly glanced at Anna before focusing back on her. "Is this type of work something you'd like to do on a regular basis?"

Her eyes lit up. "I think I would. I mean, I don't know if I'd make a career out of it, but I think it's interesting work."

"We could use another person on a case by case basis. The PI business can be sporadic. Sometimes you're turning customers away, sometimes you can go a whole month without a case. So, until we get enough business for you to be full time, I'd suggest finding an alternative job to help pay the bills."

Anna sat up. "We totally forgot to tell you. Mick is hiring Marti as a bartender."

Marti was grinning sweetly. "It won't pay as much as stripping, but I'm never going back to that line of work."

"That's great. Is it part-time or full-time?"

"Weekends, starting off. Kim said she wants to see how it goes before giving me more hours."

I chuckled. "I'm sure the regulars are going to be thrilled."

Her grin continued. "I hope you'll be my best customer."

"It's highly possible," I said. "Alright, at some point, you'll need to get your PI license. Anna can help you with that, right?"

"Right," Anna said.

"PI license, check," Marti said. She was still grinning.

I chuckled and sipped my scotch. I had to admit, Marti working as the bartender at my one and only hangout was a pleasant thought.

"Do we have any new cases waiting?" Marti asked.

"Hmm, that's a good question," I answered. "Let's check."

I stood, walked over to my desk, and logged onto my laptop. I drained my scotch and was considering a refill, but before I could stand, Marti hurried into the kitchen and came back with two finger's worth in the tumbler. I caught a glimpse of Anna rolling her eyes. Once handing me the tumbler, she stood behind me and pressed close.

"So, what do we have, boss?" she teased and then inhaled. "Wow, I like that cologne you have on."

I heard Anna guffaw, ignored her, and opened the first email. Marti looked over my shoulder and read it.

"That one looks interesting," she said.

"Nah, we don't do infidelity cases," I said.

"Why not?"

"Those types of cases are problematic. If they don't like what you've discovered, they'll try to skip out on paying you, and if it ever gets to the point of a divorce hearing, we'll be subpoenaed to testify and we won't be paid for it."

"Really?"

"Nope," I said. "Once you are subpoenaed, the client is under no obligation to pay you for your time."

"Don't forget to tell her about the Knoxville case," Anna said. Marti gave us a questioning look.

"A couple of years ago, a PI in Knoxville was hired by the husband to prove his wife was unfaithful. She was. The husband used the information provided by the PI to track down and kill his wife's lover. Then he killed her before killing himself."

"Oh, man, that's messed up," Marti said.

"Yes, it was. Even worse, he got sued by the relatives of the wife's lover. We don't want to get involved in anything like that. Let's move on."

I sent a perfunctory one-sentence reply, deleted the email, and moved on to the next one. As I read, Marti read along with me and soon chortled.

"She wants you to set up her fiancé to see if he will stay faithful to her," she said.

"Yeah, it's called a honey-trap."

"A what?"

I explained. "Let's say the mark is a regular at a bar. We'd use someone like you to go into the bar, flirt with him, and then make some kind of sexual overture. You tell him something like you're only in town for the night and you're looking for some hot, no-strings-attached sex. You then ask him if he'd be willing to meet you back at your hotel. You're wired during this and recording the whole interaction, including his response."

"And you give the recording to the wife," Anna added.

Marti was wary now. "But do you have to have sex with him?"

"Nope. You're not really staying at the hotel. You tell him to meet you in an hour and break contact. If it all works correctly, you never see him again."

"Wow, that's sneaky," Marti said.

"Yeah, and with someone like you, it would take a man with an extremely strong will to turn you down."

Marti nodded. "I get it. That's easy. We could make bank doing that," she said. She saw me frowning. "What?"

"Nah, we don't do that kind of work. It's sleazy."

She didn't respond, but I could see the wheels turning in her head. I typed the rejection response, sent it, and deleted the email. The next two were more of the same.

"You're turning down some easy jobs," she remarked.

"Trust me, they're not worth the trouble."

I sipped my scotch and when I read the seventh email, I sat up in my chair. "Here's an interesting one."

"What is it?" Anna asked.

"It's an email from a law firm soliciting a bid to investigate a local insurance agency for possible fraud," I said. I did not mention that the author of the email said I was referred to him by William. Anna might demand I delete it out of spite.

"Oh, that sounds promising," Anna said. "Any specifics?"

"Not a lot, but it sounds like a research job," I said.

"Do you guys do a lot of research jobs?" Marti asked. "Don't get me wrong, I just thought a private investigator's work involved a lot more action. You know, a lot more time on the streets."

I chuckled. "That's only in TV shows. Most detective work is dull and tedious."

"So, what kind of work do you guys actually do?"

"We offer a wide variety of investigative skills. Criminal defense consultation, background investigation, surveillance, missing persons investigations, death investigations, and last but not least, fraud investigations."

"Is fraud what you investigate the most?" she asked.

"Not always, but lately we've had a few more than normal," I said.

"Thomas has a good reputation for handling the more complex cases," Anna said.

Marti gave a slow thoughtful nod. "I see. That's what allows you to pick and choose which cases you guys take on."

"Yeah, mostly. Sometimes work is slow and you have to take whatever is offered. But right now, we have some good offers." I gestured at the email on the computer. "Like this case. It's low risk, very little field work is involved, and cases with law firms have a higher guarantee of being paid."

Marti gazed at me. "I'm beginning to see how you think. Very smart."

I saw Anna in my peripheral vision rolling her eyes again. I waved her over. "Alright, let's perform some due diligence on this potential client."

"Like what?" Anna asked.

"We want to make sure there are no red flags with this law firm. What do you think we should do first?"

"Um, we should probably check to see if they've had any complaints or disciplinary actions," Anna said.

"Yes, exactly. Fortunately for us, the board of professional responsibility has a website and they post all disciplinary actions." I opened two tabs, went to the law firm's website, and clicked on the attorney's profiles. There were four of them. I then went to the second tab, opened the board's website, and proceeded to run each name.

"They look clean," I declared. "What's next?"

"Um, should we check their credit?" Anna asked.

"Yes, we should. Send Ronald a text with the info. He can run a credit check quicker than we can."

Anna grabbed her phone and I watched in bemusement as she typed it all out in seconds using only her thumbs. While she waited, I searched each of the attorneys through social media and anything else I could think of. After an hour, I found nothing concerning. Ronald had texted Anna back and gave the credit scores of each attorney, each of whom had an excellent rating.

"I like what I see. What about you two?" I asked. It was rhetorical—I'd already decided to contact the people at the law firm—but I wanted to see if they had any misgivings. Both of them agreed. "Alright. Anna, email them a response and arrange a meeting. I'll secure us the case and then you two can work it."

Anna's eyes widened. "Really?"

"Yep. I'll help if needed, but I think you two will have no problem with it."

The women grinned and gave each other a high-five with some sort of finger wiggle at the end.

"This calls for another drink," Marti said. She grabbed our glasses and hustled into the kitchen while I gave up my seat for Anna to use the laptop.

"Has there been any developments?" she asked. I shook my head. "Before you came home, Marti and I searched a bunch of news websites, but there's nothing."

"Yeah, the Feds are keeping a tight lid on it," I replied.

"So, how does the pay work now that I'm a PI?" Marti asked when she brought fresh drinks into the den.

"It will depend on the job," I said. "As a general rule, we charge a flat rate fee of one thousand a week, plus expenses, but some jobs are negotiated on an hourly rate. The email job, for instance, was charged on an hourly rate."

"Can we work on more than one case at a time?" she asked.

"Of course," I answered. I could see the dollar signs in her eyes as she smiled. "Don't go counting your money before it's in the bank. There have been times when I've gone a couple of weeks without a case."

"If that happens, we'll just have to do some honey-traps," she said, her grin broadening.

I laughed and thought about it. There were some people in this world who I wouldn't mind screwing over, but this method still seemed unethical to me for some reason. After all, if I were going through some marital troubles and I was on a business trip, nobody knew me, and I was a little drunk, would I be able to resist Marti hitting on me? I shook those thoughts off and took a generous sip of scotch. I looked down and saw two metal cubes in my glass.

"What are those?" I asked.

"They're called whiskey cubes," Marti said. "I had some at home that I never used, so I brought them over."

I took another small sip. My scotch was chilled and made for a pleasant taste. "Nice, thanks." Marti responded with a wink.

CHAPTER 38

I don't know if Marti had spent the night, but she was gone when I walked into the den the next morning. Anna was still asleep, so I fed the critters, walked Gracie, and had my breakfast on the front porch while Gracie played in the yard.

The first thing I did was text Hope, asked if she had a good time last night and if there had any new developments. She texted back quickly.

Nothing new on the case. I had a great time last night. Currently sitting at the airport waiting to board. Maybe the stars will align for us one day.

I thought it over. This was a time for a poignant and heartfelt response. I composed my thoughts and typed –

One day.

What can I say? I'm not much of a romantic.

I refilled my cup and played with Gracie while I thought about Hope. I liked her. She was attractive, smart, professional, and she had my kind of humor. I thought we clicked together. However, she made it clear she'd jump at the opportunity if they offered her a position in the Chicago office, so any kind of relationship we'd have would be long distance, which rarely worked.

I then thought about Al. She was a pretty woman and had a hell of a body on her. Plus, she exuded the sexual energy of a horny sorority sister on prom night. Did we click? Yes, we did. But there was something about her. I sensed a hard edge. She'd been hurt before. Deeply. I wondered if she'd ever fully recovered. Hell, for that matter, I wondered if I've fully recovered from learning the truth about my wife.

And don't think I was oblivious of Marti's flirtations. Maybe she was only playing to ensure I would hire her, maybe there was something more. When I was a younger man, I thought about women constantly. Then, after my wife, and definitely after Simone, I spent more time working cases and thinking about old cars. But now it seemed like I was a horny teenager again, although I honestly wondered if I had it in me to ever fall in love and perhaps get married again. I was a little too old to have children, so if I ever became interested in raising a kid or two, I would either have to adopt or find a woman with her own kids. It instantly made me think of Al. Her two sons seemed like good kids and I believed I could see myself hanging out with them on occasion, but try as I might, I did not picture myself as a stepfather. I was too much of a loner.

My phone rang and I saw it was Al calling. Smiling, I answered.

"Hey, Al. Believe it or not, I was just thinking about you."

"Oh, really? Like what?" she replied.

"Um, well, I'm not sure I can properly explain it over the phone. Maybe we should get together and talk about it in person. What do you think?"

"Do you mean like a real date?" she asked with more than a little bit of sarcasm in her voice.

I laughed. "Yeah."

It was time to start focusing on business. I dressed in a pair of pressed khaki slacks, a white shirt, a pair of John Lobb brown leather shoes with a matching belt, both of which cost far too much, and finished it off with a custom-tailored sport coat.

The shoes and belt were a Christmas gift from the Goldman family; I never would have spent that much on a pair of shoes. The rest I bought for myself. Checking myself one last time in the mirror, I headed out.

The Beaumont Law Firm was not located downtown, like most other law offices. Instead, they had an office located off of Murphy Avenue, west of downtown. It was still a pricey rent district, but traffic wasn't as bad and they even had a free parking lot.

They had no receptionist and I was buzzed in as I approached the door. Chad Beaumont and Cassandra Beaumont-Price met me in the lobby and introduced themselves. I liked them immediately, probably because they had a fresh pot of coffee ready. They were a brother and sister team, both in their forties, a little on the heavyset side, probably from too much time sitting behind a desk; nevertheless, they were pleasant people.

"It's a one-man law firm," Chad said. "And we believe he's a scammer. We have two clients who have slip-and-fall lawsuits against and we have had one other similar case a couple of years ago."

"In addition, he has sued numerous retail businesses for so-called ADA violations. Each time it is the same client, an African-American man who is confined to a wheelchair."

"Our clients are willing to take a stand," Cassandra said. "And, we want you to find enough evidence for us to file a complaint with the Board of Professional Responsibility so we can get this shyster disbarred."

We discussed the case at length and they had already compiled a thick dossier on this particular attorney. I told them I believed my partners and I could bring the case to a successful conclusion in a month or less. We worked out an agreement of a flat fee based on that and worked out a contract. Cassandra did not like my boilerplate template contracts and generously offered to "fix them up" for me. I readily agreed.

As soon as I got to the car, I called Anna. "Okay, we've got the case."

"Is Marti going to be involved?" she asked. When I said yes, I heard a gleeful shout in the background, which I assumed was Marti.

"When do we start?" Anna asked.

"Next week," I answered. "We'll sit down and go over everything soon and lay out a game plan. So, you need to put in some work hours on Esther's case and finish it up."

"You got it, boss. Are you going to help out?"

"Only if I am released by the FBI. Otherwise, I can only help in the background."

We spoke a couple of more minutes before ending the call. I had to smile; the two of them were excited to work a case together.

It wasn't even noon yet. I had the rest of the day free but that did not mean I could do whatever I wanted. If I went to Mick's, I'd smell like cigar smoke. If I tried to work on the Belew case, I may get tied up the rest of the day and into the night. If I worked on my new car, I'd get all dirty and grimy and may not be able to wash up to be respectable. Nope, I wasn't going to do anything that would possibly jeopardize the big date with Al. I'd already messed up one date; I wasn't going to mess this one up.

I did the safe thing and went home, whereupon I spent the rest of the day reading.

CHAPTER 39

When Al answered the door, I think my jaw may have dropped open. She was wearing a black dress that clung to her figure like saran wrap. Her legs were tanned, lean, and muscular. Hell, her quadriceps were better developed than most men.

"Wow," I exclaimed. She responded with a triumphant smile.

"Like what you see?"

"Yes, absolutely. You look incredible."

"Better than Debbie?" she asked with an arched eyebrow.

"Oh yeah, most definitely," I answered.

She smiled at that. A triumphant smile. She kissed me on the cheek and grabbed my arm.

"Let's go. I'm famished."

We went to an upscale restaurant in an area known as the Gulch.

"Their specialty is sushi and Asian fusion," Al had told me. It was pricey, but that was okay. Since my lawsuit settlement, I'd pampered myself a little more than usual. No more taking a date to Burger King.

We ordered drinks and appetizers of shitake dumplings and sushi for our entrees.

"I could never take my boys here," Al said. "Look at the price of the dumplings. I'd spend a week's salary feeding them here."

I laughed. "Yeah, it's pricey. I suppose you're worth it though."

She smirked. "You better believe I'm worth it." She gestured with her drink. "I'd rather have another drink, but if you want wine or sake, I'm good with that."

I looked at my cocktail, a kamikaze with a singular round ice cube. It was not my usual flavor, but I liked it. "I believe I'll have another one of these," I said. We reordered and continued chatting.

"How long have you been working out of an ambulance?" I asked.

"I started when I was eighteen. I was a young EMT when I met Hank. He was the medical officer on his special forces team and we had a class together. We hit it off immediately and he asked me to marry him on our first date." She smiled at the memory.

"I was pregnant with Steffen when we got married, and then a year later, Sterling came along. So, I was a stay-at-home soccer mom until Hank's death. By then, the boys were old enough where I could go back to work. That's been almost three years now. What about you and your wife?"

I shook my head slightly. "She was a few years younger than me and had a little bit of a wild, zany streak."

"That turned you on, didn't it," Al surmised.

"Oh, heck yeah. Looking back, I could see the red flags, but love is blind, I guess."

"What about your girlfriend? The one that was killed by her ex-husband?"

"Simone."

"Yeah, how did you two meet?"

"I have a good friend who has a law firm. She was his paralegal and personal assistant. And, I guess I was a little bit like Hank was when he first met you. I was smitten from the get-go."

"Tell me about her. Smart and beautiful?" She said it with a playful smile.

"Yes, she was. She had a daughter that was Steffen's age. She was a sweet kid and the two of them were like two peas in a pod."

"That was a shame what happened to them," she said.

"Yes, it was. She'd been divorced from her husband for several years. She wasn't hitting him up for alimony or child support, so it didn't make any sense."

"He was probably still in love with her," she surmised.

I nodded in agreement. "Yeah, probably."

"I must confess, I still miss Hank. I mean, when that little whore showed up at the funeral, it made me start thinking about certain occasions where, looking back, he was probably with her or somebody else, but I still miss him."

"Perfectly understandable," I said and thought back to my wife, Marcia. After her death, I had romanticized her and our relationship, purposely overlooking her faults. It wasn't until I learned of her affair that my adoration of her memory came crashing down.

Al raised her drink. "Alright, the best thing we can do is move on, right? Here's to new relationships."

"Here, here," I said and clinked her glass with mine.

My phone rang and I let it go to voicemail. It immediately rang again. Curious, I looked at the caller ID. It simply read 'unknown caller.'

"Is it someone important?" Al asked.

"I have no idea. No matter. They can leave a message."

When the phone rang a third time, Al insisted I answer it.

"Ironcutter Investigations, this better be damned important," I said in annoyance. There was a long pause before the person on the other end of the line spoke. The man had a distinct accent.

"Ah, I recognize the name and the voice. Thomas Ironcutter. The man who pries into the secrets of others."

When I recognized the voice, my mouth went dry.

CHAPTER 40

"Well, if it isn't Wolf turd," I exclaimed. Al stopped in mid-bite and stared in puzzlement. There was another long pause before I heard a condescending chuckle.

"I have been thinking of you, Thomas Ironcutter," he said.

"I've been thinking of you as well, Wolf. Why haven't you and your gay buddies killed yourselves yet?"

There was another slight chuckle. "Did you know I was her man?"

"Yeah, about that, aren't you gay?"

"I am not a homosexual!" Wolf suddenly shouted. I continued pressing him.

"And Lilith is your first cousin, isn't she? Is that what gay gypsies do, bang their cousin in between boyfriends?

I could hear him breathing heavily through the phone and guessed he was angry.

"You are the reason she is dead. She told me all about you," he said.

"Why did you kill her, Wolf?"

"She betrayed me. She betrayed her family." There was a pause. "We will meet again one day, Thomas Ironcutter."

"Where are you?" I asked. "I'll gladly come to you."

Another chuckle. "I am closer than you may think," he said.

"If I get a chance, I'm going to rip you apart," I growled. There was silence now and after a moment, the line disconnected. I looked at my phone a moment before putting it away.

"What in the world was that about?" Al asked.

"Nothing."

"You threatened to dismember someone, that's nothing?" she asked with a slight, questioning grin.

"Let's finish our dinner," I said.

By the look in her eye, my tone probably made it sound like an order, but I wasn't concerned. I needed to get her back to her house, drop her off, and talk to Ronald. And then my dumbass remembered the wonderful technology of texting. I picked up my phone off of the table and began texting Ronald as fast as my fingers would allow.

"Thomas, what is going on?"

I looked up in irritation. Her expression was also one of irritation. We were both irritated, go figure.

"Look, I'm sorry about this, but that phone conversation I just had was from a murder and kidnapping suspect. He called to taunt me."

"How does he know your phone number?" she asked.

I arched an eyebrow. "Well, I've been told all you have to do is plug my name in Google and all sorts of stuff comes up. Besides, my phone number is listed on my PI business, so maybe that's how."

"So, why is he calling you in particular?" she pressed.

I hesitated before responding. Why indeed? Was it because he knew about Lilith and me? How much did he know? My phone buzzed before I could offer an answer.

"What's up, Ronald?" I asked.

"It looks like a burner phone, so all I can tell you right now is the nearest tower it pinged."

"Okay, which tower?"

"It looks like it's located on State Route 52 near I-65. I'm looking at Google Earth now. There are a couple of businesses right off of the interstate, but mostly it's rural."

When Ronald had given the rough location where the tower was, the hair on the back of my neck stood up. The sonofabitch was at the Red River where his buddy had wrecked. I was sure of it. Ronald was still talking, but I was no longer listening and ended the call.

I got the waiter's attention with a slight but urgent wave. He brought the ticket to me immediately. I tossed cash onto the table. It was a generous tip.

"C'mon, we have to go," I said and made a head motion toward the door.

Al did not move. "I'm not going anywhere until you tell me what the hell is going on."

"Well then, I apologize for all of this, but I have to go." I stood and walked toward the exit.

I made it to my car when I heard the clicking of her shoes on the asphalt. I clicked my key fob and the door to my Explorer unlocked as Al reached me. She grabbed me by the shoulder and spun me around. I was absently surprised at how strong she was.

"Are you really going to leave me?" she demanded.

"I'm sorry, but yes. I've got to go."

"And what the hell should I do?" she asked in the same indignant tone.

"Do you need money for a taxi or for Uber?" I asked. I pulled my arm out of her grasp and started to reach for my wallet, but she quickly grabbed my hand with both of hers and held on tightly.

"Thomas, stop. I did nothing to deserve being treated this way," she said. There was a mixture of anger and pain in her expression. I immediately felt guilty and absently let out a frustrated sigh.

"You're right. I'm being an ass and I apologize, but I really have to leave. It's an emergency."

She stepped in between me and the door. "Tell me. Tell me what is so important that you have to treat me like shit."

I let out a sigh. "I told you, he's a murder suspect."

"Then call the cops," she rejoined.

"If only it was that simple. There's much more to it," I countered.

"Tell me. I deserve to know," she pressed.

I hesitated a moment, but then decided to tell her.

"Alright. For the past month, I've been helping with an investigation of a group of men who have been abducting women for the purpose of trafficking them. They have murdered at least two people that we know of and have abducted over thirty women." I tapped my phone. "The person I spoke with goes by the nom de guerre of Wolf. He's the ringleader. He just called me from a burner phone which pinged a tower near Portland. I think I know where he may be and I'm going to him."

"Why?" Al asked. "I mean, why don't you call the police, or the FBI?"

"Because, if I have the chance, I'm going to find out where those missing women are and then I'm going to kill him."

Al reached out and gently took my hands in hers. She waited until I made eye contact before speaking.

"Do you even know where you're going and what you're going to do when you get there?" she asked.

I took a deep breath. Maybe two.

"I have an idea or two, still working on it."

She arched an eyebrow and stared at me with those blue eyes. "You don't strike me as the impulsive type. What are you going to do, just jump in your car and start driving?"

"Do you remember when I stood you up and I explained about the river rescue?" I asked. She nodded. "Alright, that's where he is. I don't know what he's doing there, but that's where his phone pinged at."

"So, that's where you're going?" she asked. "Has it crossed your mind that he may be trying to taunt you and lure you up there to set you up?"

"It's entirely possible," I admitted after a few seconds. "But I have to go anyway."

"He's suspected of two murders and you're going after him alone," she remarked. "An old west showdown, right?"

"Well, it's a little more than that. Wolf is a martial arts expert and he has two other men with him."

She stared, wondering if I was making up a tall tale. She then frowned. "You remind me of my husband. His balls were the size of melons too and it got him killed." She then walked around to the passenger side.

"Unlock the door, Thomas. I'm not going to let you do this by yourself."

I briefly debated on simply driving off without her, but instead hit the unlock button on the fob and the two of us got in. Shutting my door, I turned to her. "Listen, I can't let you get involved in my escapade. Like you said, it's probably not the best idea in the world."

"Which is why you need me with you. Do you have a backup gun?"

"Um, yes, I do. Why?" I asked. She stuck her hand out. I reached down and pulled my Glock 43 out of my ankle holster.

"It's probably too late to ask, but do you know how to use one?"

She responded by taking it, checking the magazine, and then performing a press check, all while keeping the barrel pointed in a safe direction. "Yep. If you ever want to go to the range together, maybe we can make a friendly wager." She pointed toward the road. "What are we waiting on?"

I made a halfhearted effort to talk her out of it, but she was stubborn, far more stubborn than me.

Once I got clear of Nashville traffic, I stepped on it and arrived in a little over forty minutes. While I was driving, I brought Al up to speed.

"I want you to know what you're getting into, but I have to tell you, all of this is confidential information."

"Even the part involving you and Lilith?" she asked.

"I only told them we had a brief friendship," I said.

"It sounds like it was a little more than that," she replied.

I frowned. "I don't know about that. It was definitely brief and there were no commitments."

"A friend with benefits then," she surmised.

"Yeah, I guess so."

"Is that how you prefer your relationships with women?"

I shrugged in the dark. "For this particular situation, it worked for both of us. Both of us had our own personal issues we were dealing with and found comfort with each other. There was nothing more to it."

"I see," she said. I could see her staring at me out of the corner of my eye. "How do you view us, Thomas?"

I weighed my response carefully before speaking. "You're a beautiful woman. You're smart, you have a great career job, and I happened to know from firsthand experience you're very good at it. I don't know your sons all that well, but they seem like good kids, which means you're a good mom. And, I must admit, the first night I met you, I had an attraction toward you."

"Do you see us as friends with benefits?" she asked.

I glanced over at her. She was smiling now.

"I think that's one of those what you call a bait question," I said with a laugh.

We talked at length and soon we were approaching our destination. I pointed through the windshield. "The Red River is up ahead."

"Explain to me what happened again with the wreck."

"They kidnapped a young woman and her baby down in Cornersville. She was tied up in the backseat of her own truck. She got loose and attacked the guy who was driving, which caused the wreck."

"What about the baby?" she asked.

"Still missing," I said. "There's an Amber Alert and a nationwide manhunt going on, but nothing yet."

"So, what in the world are they doing here at the crash site?"

"That's a good question," I said. "We'll soon find out."

I went into condition yellow as I slowed and parked on the right shoulder. Shutting the SUV off, I adjusted the dimmer switch so the dome light would remain off when we opened the doors.

"You should stay in the car," I suggested.

Al shook her head. "If you're walking into a trap, you'll need backup."

"Those shoes you're wearing are nice, but the terrain is a little rough, walking in those heels will be difficult."

"Let me worry about that," she retorted.

I shrugged. On the one hand, I admired her grit, but on the other hand, I did not want to be the one leading her into possible danger. If she got hurt because of me, I'd be hard-pressed to explain myself.

The two of us exited the SUV together. I walked around to the passenger side and pointed with my flashlight. "We're going that way."

"Alright, hold on a sec," she said, then she took each shoe and broke the two-inch-long heels off.

"Lead off," she whispered. "I'm going to follow a couple of feet behind."

A car drove past and in the illumination of the headlights, I caught a look of determination on her face. I gave her a curt nod.

We carefully made our way down the embankment. I only used the flashlight intermittently and held my 45 at the ready. I glanced back at Al a couple of times, and to my satisfaction, she was keeping the Glock at a low ready position.

It looked like someone had run a bulldozer down the embankment. All of the undergrowth had been knocked down and now it was a trail of trampled dirt clods. Still, it was not easy walking down the embankment in the dark and watching out for a possible ambush. As we proceeded, I saw something. I stopped and put a hand against Al. After a moment, my eyes adjusted and I saw a faint glow. Al stepped close beside me and whispered in my ear, "What is that?"

"I'm not sure," I whispered back. "It might be bait for their trap."

She grunted slightly and then nudged me forward. We slowly, carefully, made our way closer until we finally reached the bank of the river. A blanket was spread on the ground, and the faint glow was of a candle sitting in the middle of the blanket. The flickering of the candle showed various items on the blanket. I could make out the largest item as a tambourine. It had been broken in two. I held my flashlight away from me and did a slow circle around us.

"It looks like we're alone," I said.

Al pointed at the array. "What is all this?" she asked.

"I'm guessing here, but it looks like some sort of memorial for their dead comrade," I said.

"Yeah, maybe," she murmured.

We inspected the articles. There was an old book written in a foreign language, a few coins, and the broken tambourine. Looking around again to make sure we were indeed alone and not about to be jumped, I pulled out my phone and took several photographs.

"They were definitely here, but presumably they're long gone by now," I said.

"Are you sure?" she asked.

I nodded. "There's no way anybody is hiding out in the bushes. The undergrowth is too thick to be traipsing through it in the dark. And besides, where is their car? Nope, they're gone."

"Good," she said, dropped the Glock onto the blanket, and then grabbed me, kissing me hungrily, aggressively.

"I am so fucking wet," she whispered huskily into my ear and then bit it.

I hesitated only for a second before reaching down and grabbing a handful of her dress. I pulled it up with one hand and plunged my other hand down her panties. She was soaking wet and my probing caused her to emit a moan from deep in her throat. We continued kissing while she began massaging me through my pants. I brought her down to the blanket and swiped everything aside. She pulled her dress up over her head while I eagerly undid my pants. She grabbed me again and pulled me down on top of her. I pushed her bra up and massaged her breasts. They were firm and tan, and they felt as wonderful as they looked.

"Pinch my nipples," she demanded. When I did, she emitted another animalistic moan and begged me to pinch them harder.

When she guided me into her, we both gasped in ecstasy. It took every ounce of self-discipline on my part to not immediately explode. Thankfully, I didn't and we went at it like rabid bunnies.

When we finally expended ourselves, I rolled off of her and the two of us lay there in the darkness, staring up at the inky sky. It was pitch dark, with the exception of the lone candle and the slight glow from the headlights of passing vehicles.

"Jesus, I needed that," Al exclaimed. I simply nodded because I was still trying to catch my breath.

"How many women have you been with since your wife died?" she asked.

I could not decide if her questions were bait questions, overly intrusive, or innocent. I opted for innocent, for now.

"Three," I answered. "After her death, I was seeing a fellow cop, but she kind of went haywire on me. Then there was Simone, and then Lilith." There was a one-night stand in there also, but I did not mention that. "How about you?"

"After Hank died, I was devastated. Not only because he was gone, but that crazy whore who had to show up at the funeral and make things worse. I eventually got back in the dating scene, had a couple of lovers, but only one person who I had a serious relationship with."

"The guy you work with," I said.

"Yeah, the asshole I work with who I caught cheating."

We talked some more before deciding to dress and go back to my SUV. Once inside, Al pulled off her shoes and inspected them.

"Ruined," she stated, rolled down the window, and tossed them.

"I'll make it up to you and take you shopping on our next date," I said with a grin.

She responded by turning in her seat, throwing a leg over, and straddling me. "Make it up to me right now."

CHAPTER 41

I sat at an open table at the FBI command center and carefully read all of the reports for the third time. It didn't get me anywhere. I stood and stretched before walking over to a table where there was a coffee urn and an assortment of donuts. I chuckled inwardly. Feds always thought of themselves at a higher echelon than city cops, yet they still ate donuts. I helped myself to one as well.

I took a bite and walked over to some bulletin boards. There were various printouts and photographs. Standing out was the picture of Special Agent Stainback. My eyes spotted and lingered on the set of photographs of the RV that was recovered in Chicago. As I stood there staring, I felt a presence beside me. I turned to see Dresden. He had his own coffee cup and donut.

"Good morning, Thomas."

"Back at you," I greeted. "You look tired."

He responded with a slight nod. "The director himself has been demanding regular updates, and he has begun voicing his opinion with great alacrity at our perceived lack of progress. So, no, I'm not getting much sleep."

"I understand." I gestured at the RV with my donut. "Did the techs recover anything?"

"Nothing. The RV was fully engulfed in flames before the fire personnel arrived on the scene."

"What about the location where it was abandoned?" I asked.

"The tattoo parlor has been closed for a few months, as you know. We obtained a search warrant for it, but found nothing of consequence."

"I've been there and there were several more businesses and buildings in the area. What about them?"

"A canvass was performed by agents, with the assistance of members of the Chicago Police. Same results," he said. His phone buzzed. "Excuse me." He answered his phone as he walked off to a quiet spot at the far end of the room.

I continued staring at the photographs for a long time. It was only when I took a sip of cold coffee that I realized I'd been fixated on the panorama photograph of the parking lot where the RV was found. Looking around, I found an open computer and sat down in front of it. A minute later, I had Google Earth online. I plugged in the address for the tattoo shop and watched as the monitor zoomed in on the location. I then manually zoomed it back out far enough so that I could see the surrounding area.

There were commercial areas and neighborhoods near the location, but try as I might, I was getting no epiphany. My phone rang and I saw it was Ronald.

"Can you talk?" he asked in a low whisper. "I know where you are, can you talk?"

"Of course, I can," I said in a normal voice.

"Oh, okay."

"What are you doing?" I asked.

"Well, since the Reavis case is over, I have a little extra time on my hands. So, I've been going over some of the stuff I captured on you-know-who's laptop."

"Uh-huh."

"And, like I told you, his phone was synced up to it," he said.

"Okay, you found something interesting, I'm guessing?"

"Well, um, I don't know if you'd call it interesting, but it is unusual," he said.

I kept my irritation in check. Sometimes Ronald took a while to get to the point.

"Tell me what you found," I urged.

"A day before Candy was killed, he made a couple of phone calls to a number with an Illinois area code. I did a reverse number search and it comes back to an auto body shop in Arlington Heights."

I sat up in my chair. Arlington Heights was only a short distance from the location where the tattoo studio was once located. "Give me the information," I directed. I jotted it down on a napkin as he read it off.

"Alright," I said once he had finished. "I think I might have to go up there and check it out."

"You're not going to make me go with you, are you?" he asked.

"Not at all," I replied. "I'll handle this one on my own."

"I can monitor you, if you want me to," he said. "But I won't do it if you don't want me to."

"Actually, I think that might be a good idea this time," I said.

I hurried home, packed, and hit the road. Once on the interstate, I made some phone calls. The first was to Anna. I only told her I was going to Chicago to follow-up on a lead and for her to finish up the Braxton case. After all, I'd committed us to starting on the insurance fraud case.

After hanging up with her, I called William Goldman. He had left me a message asking that I serve some subpoenas for him. I told him I would not be able to get to them for a few days. He then asked about Anna, but I did not give him any information, which did not sit well with him.

My final call was to a person I was not looking forward to talking to.

"Hey," I greeted when she answered.

"Hi, handsome," Al replied. "What are you doing?"

"Heading to Chicago."

"Why?" she asked. There was an edge to her voice.

"It is believed the suspects are hiding out somewhere there. I'm going to help search for them."

There was a long pause. "So, you're standing me up on our date, again. Is that what you're telling me?"

"Um, I was hoping that we could merely postpone it for a day or two."

"Thomas, I have a rotating work schedule and two teenage sons to care for. I had to make special arrangements just so I could be with you."

"Al, I'm really sorry, but this is important."

"So, I'm not important?" she retorted.

Before I could reply, she hung up on me. I could not blame her. This was the second time after all. I pulled over to the side of the interstate and parked. I then prepped and lit a cigar before sending a text.

Please forgive me.

I added a lot of stuff, but ultimately deleted everything except for the one line. I'd screwed up and I knew it.

It took a little over nine hours due to traffic before I reached Chicago. Nashville and Chicago are both on central time, so it was a little after five. After exiting the interstate, I stopped off at a fast food restaurant only to use the restroom and then got a to-go order.

CHAPTER 42

Arlington Heights was a section of Chicago that was mostly older homes and commercial businesses. I opted to first visit the location where the Gypsy Dragon used to be located, which was in a strip mall located on a side street off of Northwest Highway. I could still see the blackened scorch marks in the parking lot's asphalt where the RV had been set on fire. That was a clever move; between the fire and the shit ton of water sprayed on it, it guaranteed no DNA evidence could be recovered.

I had already read reports from the Chicago office agents. They'd canvassed the area and wrote up a perfunctory report, which also said they found zilch. In my mind, I was critical of their work ethic. It seemed to me they could have pushed the canvass a little harder, but it was always easy to Monday morning quarterback.

I activated my phone and spoke the address of the body shop. It spit out directions along with a map.

"Interesting," I said to myself as I looked at the map. The body shop was only a couple of miles down Northwest Highway.

Upon arriving, I parked at the front door and looked it over. This was one of those body shops that I'd never take one of my vehicles too. There was clutter lying everywhere and the place was grimy. It had no curb appeal whatsoever.

There were two men working on a Camaro. They ignored me as I walked inside the lobby and up to the counter. A third, older man in his late fifties was sitting in his office talking on the phone and smoking a cigarette. He was swarthy and stocky, like he might have once played sports in grade school, but he'd gone to seed years ago. His hair was black, like he dyed it, and he was in bad need of a decent haircut.

He saw me through the dirty window separating his office from the lobby and held up a finger. After a minute he hung up, lit a fresh cigarette, and walked out. He was wearing a black Adidas brand warm-up suit with matching shoes. For some crazy reason, Adidas was wildly popular in Russia and eastern Europe.

"Can I help you?" he asked in a heavy accent.

His accent was similar to Wolf's. So much so, they could have been brothers. It was like I was playing the slots and scored on the first spin. This man was not from here. Was this the connection I'd driven all the way up here to find? I suppose I could have simply asked him if he knew Wolf and Pekoe, but we know how that'd go.

"Yeah, I drive by here every day and I saw your shop. I don't live too far from here and I've got an old MG that has some front-end damage. Not many places will work on an old foreign car. What about you guys?"

"We work on all cars. You bring it in. I take a look at it. Yes?" he suggested.

"Okay great, I'll do that. See you in a day or two," I said and gave him a head nod before walking out.

I don't know if any of them watched me leave, so I drove down the road and out of sight before turning around. I found a place to park where I could keep an eye on the place and ate a granola bar for a late afternoon snack. Now the waiting began. Whether or not it would pay off was debatable. The odds of winning the lottery were probably better. I texted Ronald and told him what I was doing. He responded with a thumb's up emoticon.

For anyone who has never actually participated in a stakeout, it goes something like this—for the first hour, you're getting settled in, but you're diligent. You're paying attention and keeping your eye on the target. You also look around the surrounding areas, and remembering your training, you orient north, memorize other businesses and their addresses, the names of the side streets, identify potential blind spots, escape routes, kill zones, you name it.

Starting sometime around hour two, your attention begins to wander. You start watching the pretty women driving by. You start playing on your cell phone. First, all you're doing is sending a couple of texts, but before you know it, you're looking up your stocks online, playing online poker, and God forbid, if you have any social media accounts you'll be dabbling on all of them.

In the ensuing five hours, you've played on your phone so much you have to recharge it. You've walked over to the nearby fast food restaurant to use the head and refresh your coffee so many times there's a good chance you've blown your cover, and, oh yeah, you've occasionally monitored the target.

I must admit, I've been guilty of exactly that behavior in the past. Now, being a little older and wiser, I tried to avoid those pitfalls. I avoided caffeine, which is a diuretic, and only sipped water if I was parched. If I had to go, I had a gallon-sized plastic jug I peed in.

Oh, a word to the wise—at the end of the shift, absolutely, positively, throw that jug away immediately. Don't leave it sitting in your backseat. Find a dumpster or a gas station with trash cans sitting outside. Never, ever, toss it in your kitchen trashcan. Bad things always seem to happen when you leave a jug of stale urine lying around. Or so I've heard.

At around the three-hour mark, the fatigue took over and I dozed off. I only woke up because somebody laid on their horn at a nearby intersection for some reason. I looked at the time on my phone and panicked. Had I come all this way, chasing a hunch, only to fall asleep while the gypsies came in and got a paint job or something? Thankfully, I had a dash cam and it was actively recording. I played it back and watched the last hour. There was nothing. I don't know if that was good or bad.

"What a waste of time," I muttered to myself. I refrained from lighting a cigar. Instead, I sipped some water and texted Anna.

How'd the meeting go?

Awesome. It's all research. They want to pay a flat rate. I told them 2g for 40 hours. They are going to call back with an answer tomorrow. Marti wants in.

We exchanged a few more texts about the job. She asked when I was coming back home. I originally thought I'd spend a couple of days in the Windy City, snooping around and such, but the more I thought about it, the dumber it seemed. I was wasting my time.

I texted back and said I'd be home no later than tomorrow afternoon. I looked at my watch and saw it was a little before seven. They were due to close any minute now. In fact, I could see the two body men actively cleaning up.

At promptly seven o'clock, the bay doors were lowered and the front door was locked. They would be leaving any minute now. The plan was to follow the owner to his residence and sit on it a while, if I could. At some point, I was going to need to get a few hours of sleep, maybe get a hotel room.

The two body men left and the manager went around turning off most of the lights, with the exception of his office. I saw him sit behind his desk. He produced a can of beer from somewhere and alternated between messing with his computer and talking on the phone.

As I watched, he drank three beers within thirty minutes. Soon, he got up and went to the restroom. When he walked out, he looked like he was going to close up for the night, but then a car drove into the parking lot. I watched curiously as the man walked to the front door, unlocked it, and waited for the vehicle's occupants to get out.

When the two occupants exited the car, I said a silent prayer of thanks to the big man above for pushing me to Chicago. I was also thankful I still had my dash camera recording.

CHAPTER 43

It was dark out now, but the street lights were bright enough so I could see he still had a black eye. I was too far away to see any other injuries, and although I did not like Stainback, I was glad to see she got in some damage before she went down. The manager hurried to the door and unlocked it. Wolf pushed past him as he walked in. Pekoe paused at the doorway a moment and glanced back, as if looking for anyone who might be watching. It made me appreciate the blackout tints they'd put on my Explorer. Even though the front windshield was not tinted, the interior was dark enough to make it difficult for anyone to see me.

I watched as the three men talked in the front lobby. I could clearly see worry etched on the manager's face. He didn't like what Wolf was telling him. After a couple of minutes, they walked back into the shop area. As I watched, one of the bay doors was raised and a plain white full-sized van backed out. The manager watched the van stop at the intersection and then turn east onto Northwest Highway before closing the bay door. I waited a heartbeat and then started my Explorer.

The van was easy to spot in traffic, which allowed me to stay several car lengths behind. He continued into the Mount Prospect community, turned on a side street that passed by the Mount Prospect police department, and after he turned onto another side street, I had no option but to continue going straight. When following someone, if you take the same turns twice, and they notice, they'll become suspicious. Three times and they'll know they're being followed.

I sped up, turned onto a parallel street and tried to see if I could spot the van. I didn't.

"Damn," I muttered. I was worried I'd lost him. He was either performing counter-surveillance or he had parked somewhere. I didn't know which. I drove up and down several neighborhood streets with no luck. Stopping at a four-way intersection, I looked around, wondering where to go next. When I glanced to my left, I saw a white van parked in a drive several houses down. There was somebody standing beside it, but my vision was partially obscured by the growing darkness a bushy scrub tree.

Here is where the blackout tints were at a disadvantage. If I did a slow drive-by and whoever was outside happened to give me a hard look, or even a casual glance, the dark tints might make them suspect I was an undercover cop and spook them. I could not take that risk.

Or could I?

Technically, it was called extrajudicial punishment, which was a fancy way of saying vigilante justice. When I'd learned about Wolf and his boys, I told myself if I got a chance, I was going to kill them all. This was my opportunity. I could simply drive up, get out of my car, knock on the door, and open fire. It might be questionable, as the Feds would definitely be the investigating authority, but I was fairly certain I could get away with it. It would certainly save the taxpayers a lot of money.

Or I'd go to prison for the rest of my life. Decisions, decisions.

I sat there contemplating it until somebody behind me honked their horn. Instead of turning left, I went straight and found a place to park. Picking up my phone, I made a call.

"Hi, it's your old buddy, Thomas Ironcutter," I said when Hope answered.

"Hi, Thomas. What are you doing?"

She actually sounded happy I called, which made me warm and fuzzy all over.

"I'm a little tired, but nobody gives a shit about that. Guess where I am?" I prodded.

"If you say you're in Chicago, I'm going to go weak in the knees," she said and laughed.

"I'm in Chicago," I said.

She was quiet a moment. "Are you really? I mean, I'm working right now, but I should be able to get away in an hour or so."

"Don't clock out just yet," I said. "I just spotted Wolf and Pekoe going into a house in Mount Prospect."

I heard her gasp. She then got the attention of somebody. "I'm putting this on speakerphone. Tell me what you've got."

They listened attentively while I explained everything. When I was finished, a man's voice came over the phone.

"Hold your position, sir. I am going to send some undercover units to that street and evaluate what you may have. What is your current location?"

I told him, even though I had no idea who he was. But he was with Hope and that was good enough for me. Ten minutes later, a dark blue van drove into the parking lot. Hope and another man emerged from the back. She smiled when I got out of my car, but her body language told me there would be no warm embrace. I hoped it was simply because the man was her supervisor and she wanted to maintain her professionalism.

"Hello, everyone," I said.

The man, his persona screamed he was a man who was used to giving orders and having them obeyed. He wasted no time on pleasantries.

"Let me see the dash cam video you told us about," he ordered.

"Certainly. Come sit on the passenger side. Hope, why don't you take a look at it as well."

She nodded gratefully and got into the back seat. I sat back in the driver's seat and manipulated my dash cam. In a minute, I had the recording playing. After the first viewing, the man turned back to Hope.

"Is that them?" he asked.

"It appears to be, but Thomas has been up close with both men. If he says that's Wolf and Pekoe, it's Wolf and Pekoe."

Only then did he refocus on me and fix me with an appraising stare. After a couple of seconds, he extended his hand. "I'm William Lighthorse. I'm in charge of the Chicago office. We're going to need a sworn statement from you in order to obtain a search warrant for that house."

He could tell from the expression on my face I did not like it. He gestured at Hope. "Agent Delmonico can ride with you back to the office and expedite the matter."

He was interrupted by his portable radio barking. Whoever was tasked with doing a drive-by of the residence just informed him the van was still parked in front of the house. The voice was calm, at first, but then he became excited.

"Break-break! Three men are exiting the house. I'm slow rolling down the street so they aren't alarmed, but it looks like they're loading up. Two of them are carrying suitcases and one of them is cradling something in a blanket. It's hard to tell. Andy, drive down the street and see what you can."

"10-4," another man said. Hope and I exchanged a glance. The same man spoke again.

"They're on the move," he said. "Three males. One is a confirmed suspect and it looked like it was a child wrapped up in a blanket, Pete. They're taking a right and heading toward Evergreen."

Special Agent-in-Charge Lighthorse made a sweeping gesture with his hand at Hope. "Let's go." He then focused on me. "Wait here."

I didn't like it. I wanted to be in on the takedown. I caught a somber, pleading gaze from Hope. She did not want me to make any waves. I understood and gave her a subtle nod. She responded with her own grateful nod before running to the van.

So, there I was, sitting in my SUV in a parking lot on the side of the Northwest Highway. I didn't even have a radio to listen in on the activity.

"Damn," I muttered again.

I decided to at least make myself somewhat helpful. I went into the menu of my dash cam and created a dedicated file for the video I currently had. I'd no sooner accomplished this, when I heard the sirens. I could not yet see them, but I could hear them, and they were getting closer. I hurriedly hit the record button and started my car.

I sat in the parking lot, listening to the sirens getting closer. As luck would have it, they sped right past me. It was not a high-speed chase by any means, maybe sixty or seventy miles-per-hour, but it was reckless nonetheless and the suspects sideswiped at least one car when they blasted through an intersection.

I followed, but kept several car lengths between us. Within a matter of seconds, four marked police cars joined in. Whoever was driving the white van really tried to outrun the cops, but the engine was not finely tuned. Whenever they hit the accelerator, a thick black cloud burst out of the exhaust pipe. They did not stand a chance outrunning the patrol cars. I had no idea where they were trying to go; escape was all but impossible.

The van and the caravan of police cars sped down the road at maybe sixty or seventy. I followed along; hell, it was easy to keep up. After a minute, I saw a bunch of flashing lights several blocks ahead. I knew at least one set of spike strips awaited the fleeing gypsies. I closed the distance at about the same time the driver of the van tried to swerve and avoid the spike strips. He was unsuccessful. The tires blew with a puff of dirty air emanating from them. The van started swerving in spectacular fashion and hit an oncoming car before coming to rest. The cops and the Feds immediately surrounded the van with guns drawn. One of the Chicago cops, a woman, wisely stayed in her car and began barking orders over her PA system.

"Driver, this is the police, turn your vehicle off and slowly step out with your hands up!"

I turned into a parking lot and stopped well over a hundred yards away and positioned my SUV so the dash cam could capture the takedown. All other traffic had come to a standstill. Some people actually got out of their cars and were filming with their phones, oblivious to the possible danger they were putting themselves in.

The back doors of the van abruptly exploded open. From my point of view, I couldn't see what was going on in the interior of the van, but suddenly I saw spouting flames instantaneously followed by the sounds of automatic weapons fire. The closest cop car was riddled with bullets.

I instinctively scrunched down in my seat, even though the focus of gunfire was directed onto the cops and cop cars on the street. I could discern two different calibers of gunfire coming out of the van, one of which was a heavier caliber machine gun. The cops returned fire, but the amount of lead being sprayed in their direction severely hampered their accuracy. As I watched, two cops fell and one of the cars caught on fire. It's not like the movies—that car was not going to explode immediately—but it *was* going to explode.

A cop tried to run into the line of fire and rescue one of his compadres. He was instantly cut down. I don't know how much ammo the gypsies had, but they'd already shot off well over a hundred rounds. It looked like one of the Feds had been shot through the window of his undercover car. The van Hope was in was riddled with bullets and I was fearful she'd been hit as well.

The firefight continued and gunfire from the van continued in sporadic bursts. They had so much ammo, it was almost like they expected this. The burning cop car started with flames peeking out from under the hood, but now it was fully engulfed. A couple of tires exploded and there was a lull in gunfire. Pekoe suddenly stuck his head out. He had a revolver now and began firing again. I guess they finally ran out of ammo for their machine guns. Somebody, I'd guessed it was one of the street cops, put a round in his forehead. Pekoe dropped immediately. Scratch one bad guy.

Suddenly, the patrol car's gas tank exploded. Wolf took advantage of the distraction by jumping out of the driver's door and taking off at a sprint. The man could run fast, I had to give him that. One of the undercover Feds took off after him. Wolf fired a handgun over his shoulder. He quickly emptied the revolver, but scored a hit on the Fed, who went down in a heap. Wolf dropped the weapon and headed down a side street, which was, coincidentally, where I was parked.

He ran past, within ten feet of me. He was much too fast for me to try to run him down, but I had never left my SUV and it had been unscathed by the gunfire. He ran past a big blue water tower and toward a white multistory building. The entire street was blocked with cars and people who'd been shot all to hell. I hopped a curb and drove down a sidewalk in pursuit.

Wolf looked back and saw me. I mean, he did not actually see me, but he saw a blue Ford Explorer speeding toward him. He probably assumed I was a

Fed. He darted left, toward the building. I assumed he was still armed, perhaps with a backup, so I stopped behind a truck parked by the curb. He yanked on the door to the business, but it was locked. That did not stop Wolf. He launched a powerful kick and shattered the tempered glass. Barreling through it with his shoulder, he disappeared into the building.

I parked, got out, and ducked momentarily behind the truck. Looking back toward Northwest Highway, all I could see was carnage and destruction. A couple of car alarms were going off and in addition to the police car, there was at least one other car on fire. I heard multiple sirens in the distance. Additional help was coming but I had no idea how long it'd be before they got here.

Chicago had strict gun laws, which caused me to keep my Springfield XD secured in my lockbox, but I wasn't going to chase Wolf unarmed. As quickly as I could, I unlocked it, performed press check, and made my way to the broken glass door.

The sign on the building identified it as a bank, which, hopefully meant all of the employees were gone for the evening. The door Wolf went in was a back entrance, beside the drive-thru lanes. As soon as I made my way to the door, I saw Wolf running out the back, toward a parking lot.

Damn. He'd succeeded in getting me out of my vehicle. He had a good lead on me, at least fifty yards. If I ran back to my SUV, there was a good chance I'd lose him, so I gave chase. He continued across the street into another lot which provided parking for a strip mall of commercial businesses. As he reached the end of the lot and rounded the corner, he looked back. When he recognized me, he slowed and stared. And then, that reptilian smile spread across his lips.

I had to admit, it made the hair on the back of my neck stand up, but I wasn't dissuaded. After all, I had semi-jacketed hollow points loaded into my Springfield. They were proven manstoppers. More than enough to take him down.

Maybe.

I slowed from a sprint to a cautious jog as I went through the parking lot and around the building he disappeared behind. He was nowhere in sight. I stopped and looked around. There was a woman looking down on me from a second-story window and she had a phone in her hand. I had no doubt she was calling 911 and telling them a man with a gun was chasing another man. For that matter, if a local cop drove up and saw me, they were likely to shoot first and ask questions later.

I did not have a holster on me, so I did like they do in the movies and stuck my gun into the waistband at the small of my back. I pulled my shirttail over it and looked back up at the woman. Two other women had joined her. One was staring at me, the other two were peering at the area of the parking lot to my left. I started working my way through the cars, looking between and under them as I walked.

As I rounded a Range Rover, Wolf suddenly appeared from the other side of it and hit me in the face with a roundhouse kick. I had managed to get my hands up and take a step back before his foot made contact. It landed against my hand and side of my head. The impact jolted me. I stepped back quickly and tried to shake the numbness out of my hand. Wolf pursued and attempted to kick me again. I managed to sidestep this time and the only thing he kicked was the air. He continued trying a series of kicks and punches. I was doing a good job of avoiding any of them landing with full strength, and I even managed to get in a punch or two. He shook them off and continued pressing me so aggressively I did not have the opportunity to grab my gun. I finally tried a different tact

"You hear those sirens? They're almost here for you."

He stopped a moment and gave me a baleful stare. "Not soon enough to save you, eh?"

Before I could respond, he lunged forward and attempted a side kick. I already had about fifteen feet between us, but even so, he almost got me. I backed up quickly and began reaching for my gun when I crashed against the side of a parked car.

He smirked with those lizard lips as he charged in and hit me with a spinning wheel kick. This kick caught me on the side of the head, right above the left ear. It hurt, no doubt about it. It hurt like hell and I saw a few stars. I'd had a grip on my gun and was pulling it out of my waistband, but his kick rattled me so hard I lost my grip. My gun dropped to the pavement with a sickening thud.

He glanced down at it. It was all I needed. I caught him with a left hook that was hard enough to knock out most men. Unfortunately, his knees did not even buckle. So, I did the only other thing I could think of: I grabbed him in a bear hug.

When I was a young kid, my Uncle Mike took me to a pro wrestling match at the fairgrounds located off of Nolensville Pike. A bear of a man with long greasy hair and a walrus mustache and wearing nothing but a Speedo swimsuit stood in the middle of the ring, taunting the audience. He loudly proclaimed he was unbeatable and issued a challenge. Anyone who could escape one of his infamous bear hugs would win a hundred bucks. A young man in his twenties accepted the challenge and climbed in the ring. He was no small fry himself, almost as big as the wrestler. The wrestler shook his hand and then immediately grabbed him. The young man struggled feverishly, but the big man was like a human vise. After a minute or so, the challenger went limp and passed out. The wrestler dropped him on the mat and smirked at the crowd. There were no other challengers.

I was no pro wrestler, but I outweighed Wolf and I liked to think a lot of it was muscle. Besides, he wasn't greased up like he was when I watched him fight in Memphis. I began squeezing and pivoted so that he was sandwiched between me and the car. He had one arm free, and he tried in vain to elbow me and gouge my eyes. I tucked my chin in and pressed my forehead against the back of his neck. He tried foot stomps and at one point hit me in the groin with the back of his heel, but I knew if I let go, I was a dead man.

So, I squeezed with all of my might. The muscles in my arms and chest cried out in agony, but I refused to let go. My balls had been kicked up into my guts and I felt like puking, but still I didn't let go. He growled like a cornered animal and cursed me in his native language. But I held on for dear life.

Two minutes seemed to take forever, but I finally felt his body relax. I willed myself to continue squeezing him, although it felt like I was going to collapse at any moment. I heard the sirens, they were loud, but I kept my eyes scrunched shut, lest I get a finger or thumb shoved in one of them.

"Sir, you need to let go of him." It was a woman's voice. Authoritarian, but I wasn't sure who she was.

"He's a murder suspect!" I yelled. "Call the cops."

"I am a cop," she rejoined.

I opened my eyes. It was a woman about my age, stern expression, wearing a uniform and currently pointing her duty weapon in my direction. Her badge read Mount Prospect Police Department. She was not a small gal and she wouldn't ever win a beauty pageant, but at the moment, I thought she looked wonderful. I dropped Wolf and stepped back. He fell to the asphalt like a sack of potatoes.

I reached a hand out. "Cover me and I'll cuff him," I said. She responded with a suspicious stare. "I'm Thomas Ironcutter with the FBI," I added.

That seemed to do the trick. She dropped a hand to her duty belt, produced a pair of handcuffs, and slid them across the asphalt to me, never taking her gun off of either of us the entire time. At least her finger was not on the trigger.

Wolf was lying prone on his stomach. I grabbed one of his arms and was about to snap the cuff to his wrist when he suddenly rolled over and kicked me squarely in the chest. The air exploded out of me as I fell backward. He performed a move known as a kick-up and was quickly on his feet. In spite of the circumstances, I was impressed at how quickly he recovered.

"Sir, get on the ground, now!" the officer shouted.

Wolf held his hands out placatingly. "He attacked me! Please help me!"

Both Wolf and I could see the confusion on the officer's face. Wolf took two small shuffling steps toward her.

I tried to warn the officer, but I was having a hell of a time catching my breath. I struggled to get to my feet and tackled him from behind. He slithered out of my grasp, hit me in the chest with the heel of his hand, and then launched himself at the officer.

Police are required to follow what is known as the use-of-force continuum. It's like a scale which dictates the appropriate level of force to use against a suspect who is not behaving themselves. If the Mount Prospect officer followed the continuum, she was supposed to attempt some type of non-lethal use-of-force to subdue Wolf. Something like a taser or pepper spray. After all, he was unarmed.

She shot Wolf three times center-mass.

CHAPTER 44

The impact of the bullets caused Wolf to stumble. He did not fall immediately. Instead, he stopped, looked down at his chest and grabbed at the bullet holes. Blood squirted out from between his fingers. He stared at the officer in a combination of puzzlement and anger. He took a step toward her before falling to the asphalt.

"Officer, I'm going to check on him!" I shouted it as loud as I could in case the gunfire messed with her hearing. She was distraught, no doubt about it. Even so, she glanced at me and gave a curt nod.

I approached Wolf warily. Keeping to one side so the officer still had a clear line of fire, I carefully rolled Wolf over to his side. He grimaced in pain and coughed up blood.

"Anything you want to tell me?" I asked. "Now's your chance."

He stared, not with malevolence, but more like he was looking at a long-lost friend.

"Lilith told me of this day," he said and then coughed again. A foamy spray erupted from his mouth. I wanted to ask him about that conversation, but there were more important things to get out of him.

"Talk to me, Wolf. Is there anyone you want me to call for you? Do you want to confess your sins before you die?"

He reached out and grabbed my hand like we were buds and mouthed something, but it was futile. He was dead within seconds. I'd hoped to be able to get some kind of confession out of him, but no luck.

I stood and gazed at the officer. She had a questioning expression and I shook my head slightly. She took a deep breath and let out a shuddering sigh.

"You did good," I said. "Holster up and take some slow deep breaths."

She looked at me with a slight amount of uncertainty, but holstered her duty weapon and seemed to relax a little. I looked around and found my Springfield under a car. I had to get into the prone position in order to reach it. I stuck it back in the back of my waist before getting back to my feet. When I stood, I saw the officer watching me.

"It's my duty weapon," I explained.

She nodded slowly, as if she understood, but honestly, I had no idea if she was simply waiting for her compadres to arrive before arresting me for having a weapon. Within what seemed like seconds, we were surrounded by police cars.

I must admit, she was handling it well. She told me it was her first shooting. I talked to her gently as the parking lot filled with emergency response vehicles. It was utter chaos at first, but these were professional cops. While a couple of officers provided cover, another officer checked Wolf's vitals. He looked at his partners and made a slashing motion across his throat. I could've told him Wolf was dead, but he needed to confirm it for his own satisfaction. One officer radioed the information with his portable while another went over to the lady officer and checked her out.

"Who the hell are you?"

I turned to the voice. It was a gruff-looking uniform about my age. The lady officer answered for me.

"It's alright. He's with the FBI."

He was giving me a suspicious once over while I identified myself and gave him a three-sentence synopsis of why I was there.

"Alright, but stick around. I'm sure they're going to want to interview you."

I responded with a nod and walked over to the lady officer. "That was some good shooting."

The adrenalin was wearing off and now she looked both confused and frightened. Her hands began shaking.

"He was unarmed," she said.

"He was an extremely dangerous man, a martial arts expert. I can assure you if you tried anything else, he would have hurt you, maybe killed you. He's killed at least two people I know of with his bare hands."

She looked at me like I was asking her to solve Fermat's last theorem.

"Why don't we walk over to you patrol car where you can sit down and relax," I suggested. "Don't worry," I said once I got her seated. "They're going to grill you, of that you can be certain, but I witnessed everything and you're going to be alright."

She looked up at me. "Are you sure?"

"Absolutely," I assured her. I saw a bottle of water sitting in the console's cup holder and directed her to take a drink from it.

A crime scene perimeter was erected around several blocks and a mobile command RV was brought to the scene. It had all kinds of bells and whistles, including a small soundproof room that could be used for sleeping or interrogating a subject. I always suspected the Feds lied when they said they do not record interviews, but the two agents who were tasked with interviewing me had no objection when I used my phone to record their questions and my answers.

I was not worried. Even if Wolf was unarmed, he'd just been in a deadly shootout using automatic weapons and there was no way of knowing at that point in time if he was armed or not. This was going to be ruled a good shoot, I had no doubt, but they still needed to go through the formalities of the investigative process.

And then, I thought about Hope and immediately called her. It went straight to voicemail. I tried several more times and sent a text.

The officer and I were directed back to the original scene, where there was now a mobile command center parked and operational. The first thing I did was walked directly to a SWAT officer who had brass on his collar.

"I'm looking for Special Agent Hope Delmonico. She was on the original takedown team."

He looked me over. "There was a female FBI agent who I saw getting loaded up in an ambulance. I do not know her status."

"Which hospital?" I asked.

He looked a little perturbed at me. "I do not know, sir. I have my hands full here."

I left him alone and started to leave, but realized I had no idea which hospital to go to. So, I lingered around, somebody decided I needed to be interviewed, and directed me into the mobile command center. It took almost an hour and I finally had to stop them and tell them I was through for the night. They reluctantly released me with the directive to report to FBI headquarters first thing in the morning.

I made my way to my SUV and decided to drive back to the house that Wolf had driven to. It was surrounded by cops. A man I did not know identified himself as an FBI agent and asked who I was. When I identified myself, he gave me a brief summary of what they had.

"There was an old lady in there who claims not to speak English. She had an infant child with her who we believe is Amber Sowell."

"Let me talk to her," I said. My suggestion was met with an immediate shake of the head.

"There is no way. Sorry, but this has gotten way bigger than you can imagine. We have agents from Interpol flying directly in from New York as we speak."

"Alright, you know Hope Delmonico, the new agent who recently transferred in?" I asked.

"I know of her. Haven't met her yet," he said.

"She's been transported to a hospital, but I don't know which one. Could you find out?"

He looked put out, but started to take his phone out. Before he could do anything, my phone buzzed. There was an incoming text from Hope.

Are you alive?

I frantically texted back.

Yes where r u?

Hospital. Northwest.

I tapped my new pal on the shoulder. "Hey, buddy, where is Northwest Hospital at?"

CHAPTER 45

Hope was in one of the ER's rooms with the curtains pulled around, offering her some privacy. Security was not going to allow me to see her at first, but I sent her a text and a few minutes later, she sent a nurse out to get me.

"I've been waiting for you," she said. Her words were slightly slurred. "I knew you'd come eventually."

"How are you?" I asked.

"Sore as hell, but thank God I had the trauma plate in my vest." She pointed at it, casually lying in a nearby chair. "I caught one center mass. It literally knocked the wind out of me and I could not move for several seconds. My sternum has a hairline fracture, but the doctors said I was extremely lucky."

"Yes, you were."

She scoffed. "Yeah, well, I hurt like hell. I've only had one valium, but it's not doing too much. They told me Pekoe is dead and Wolf escaped."

"He is. So is Wolf. A local officer shot him. Baby Amber was found back at the house. An old woman was also there and she's been taken into custody."

Her eyes were closed, but then she opened them slowly and looked at me. "Were there any girls in the house?"

"Not that I'm aware of," I said. "They didn't tell me much."

I withheld any further comment. I was angry at them for shutting me out after all I had done, but I wasn't going to vent to her; she'd been through enough.

"Have you heard anything?" I asked.

Hope shook her head, causing her to wince in anguish. She then bit her lower lip. "You heard about Agent Lighthorse, I'm guessing."

I nodded. He, along with three uniformed cops, had been shot down and killed during the first minutes of the gunfight. Hope fought back the tears with an angry swipe of the back of her hand, which caused her to wince in pain again.

"It hurts every time I move," she said.

"You need more pain medication. I'll get the nurse for you," I said.

She responded with a slight nod. The tears were falling freely now. I stepped out into the main area and got a nurse's attention.

"I need to tell you something before the nurse sticks me," she said.

"What's that?" I asked.

"I don't know how you found them, but color me impressed. Just because it ended up the way it did, I don't want you blaming yourself."

"Thanks, beautiful," I replied. "That means a lot."

When they injected her, Hope's eyelids fluttered for a second and then she was out.

I walked back out into the waiting room and saw a multitude of lights and cameras out in the parking lot. A security guard was kind enough to escort me out a side door and I made it to my SUV without even a curious glance from the news people.

I was tired, so fricking tired. I wanted to go back to the scene and see what they had learned, if anything, but instead, I found the nearest hotel and paid for a room. My phone had been blowing up for the last hour. I sat on the bed and massaged my temples for several minutes before checking the numerous texts and voicemails. I opted only to call Ronald. Even if he was asleep, he'd answer if I called. I filled him in, asked him to call Anna, and then turned my phone off.

I don't remember falling asleep, only that I awakened while still wearing my clothes. I had not even bothered to take my shoes off. The clock on the nightstand read a few minutes before six in the morning. I wanted to strip and crawl under the covers, but I had a long day ahead of me at the FBI's Chicago office. Although I had been debriefed at the mobile command center the night before, they insisted on a formal interview the following morning and admonished me to be on time. After showering, I found a restaurant serving breakfast and overindulged in hot coffee before heading to their headquarters which was located on Roosevelt Road. Traffic was heavy and it seemed to take forever before finally arriving.

Apparently, my tardiness was going to be punished by making me sit in the lobby for over an hour. I wasn't even offered a fresh cup of coffee while I waited. I took the time to catch up on the texts and voicemails, but after ninety minutes, I'd had enough. I stood and walked over to the security guard who was sitting in the booth playing online poker.

"Would you mind calling whoever you need to and find out how much longer this is going to take?"

He gave me an indifferent stare before answering. "They're very busy, pal. Have a seat and they'll get to you when they get to you."

I fixed him with a stare for a moment before responding. "Thank you for your profound wisdom."

I received no response—I didn't expect to—and walked out. Leaving the esteemed FBI headquarters, I found a gas station where I gassed up and paid too much for some terrible coffee before getting on the interstate. It goes without saying they called about thirty minutes after I had left, wondering where I was and demanding I return to Chicago.

"Yeah, I sat in the lobby for over ninety minutes. I couldn't take it anymore, that security guard kept bugging me and showing me nudes of himself on his phone. He had pictures of him doing odd things with a couple of goats. It made me very uncomfortable."

The woman on the other end was stunned for only a moment. "We insist you come back," she demanded.

"As long as you got that security guard working there, I don't feel comfortable stepping inside that building. I'll report in to the Nashville office when I get back."

I disconnected the call before she could respond and tucked my phone into the console. The rest of the ride back to Nashville was uneventful. I listened to a radio talk show host for the first hour. He had a lot to say about the shootout, but he soon segued into some crazy conspiracy theory about the FBI. Remembering I'd subscribed to a satellite radio service when I bought the SUV, I found a station that played golden oldies and listened to some damn fine music the rest of the way home.

CHAPTER 46

Anna and I sat on the last row of chairs in the back. The only other person with us was Agent Carter Pike. Apparently, he did not care for dog and pony shows either.

The rest of the FBI staff and guests filled most of the seats and watched the press conference being held in Chicago via a huge projection screen. At the moment, Special Agent-in-Charge Reuben Chandler was outlining the details of the case and how it led up to the assault of Special Agent Stainback and her CI, Raymondo Calendar. Carter nudged me.

"See the gray-haired man with the red tie standing off to his left? That's the deputy director, the number two man. Standing off to the side are a couple of Interpol agents. There's already a brouhaha about Reuben getting to run the press conference and not someone from the Chicago office."

"Typical," I murmured.

Anna leaned over and whispered, "They're not even mentioning you."

Carter heard it and gave a small smile. I whispered back, "Yeah, just the way I like it."

"He would have if he had his way, but the unwritten code with the FBI is not to give credit to independent contractors when you can brag about FBI personnel instead."

No sooner had Carter spoke when Reuben began praising Senior Agent Dresden Carpenter and his crack team of agents.

"The boss man knows Thomas is not after publicity, so he's putting a letter of commendation in his personnel jacket instead," Carter whispered.

I wasn't sure that was such a good thing, but made no comment on the matter. Reuben gave a shout-out to Officer Leigh-Ann Hopper, the Prospect Hills cop. It was now Dresden's turn to speak. It was more of the same, lots of praises for his team and the personnel in Chicago before opening the floor to the media for their silly questions. I nudged Anna and stood. Carter stood with us and the three of us quietly exited.

"After this is over, they're going to have a little get together. Hors d'oeuvre and light refreshments. The deputy director will be there," Carter said.

I glanced at my watch. "Normally, I'd say yes, but we have another appointment in thirty minutes."

Carter gave a nod of understanding. "I'll send them your regrets."

We shook hands and said our goodbyes. Anna once again insisted on driving and soon we were speeding along in my Mustang to our next destination.

"Do you know what was odd about that press conference?" Anna said.

"What's that."

"They danced around who was behind all of this."

"It's all very hush-hush," I said.

"They're covering it up," she retorted. "That's bullshit."

She was right. They did not say who was placing the orders for women and children, and when asked about the women who were still missing and unaccounted for, they simply said it's still under investigation. I explained it all to Anna. She listened intently.

"So, what you're saying is the monarchy of an oil-rich country is behind all of this, but because they are so powerful, nothing is going to happen to them?" she asked.

"That's probably the gist of it," I answered. "I imagine the politicians will try to use it as some kind of leverage at some point."

"How is that justice for these missing women?" she asked. "I mean, what kind of hell is Telisha Thompkins going through right now? Nobody seems to care about her."

I nodded in agreement, but I had no answer.

"At least the fucker who killed Jason is dead," she remarked.

I nodded again. I went to Joseph's apartment late last night and told him about Wolf. I had no idea if Wolf and Jason had a consensual encounter or if Jason had witnessed Telisha with the gypsies and they decided he needed to be killed. It was one of those mysteries that died with Wolf, Pekoe, and the rest of them.

I told him everything except the Mideast connection. He listened quietly, cried a little, thanked me for my help, and then hugged me tightly. His girlfriend walked me to the door and then whispered to me, "So that's it? Jason doesn't get justice?"

"Well, Wolf and his buddies are all dead," I replied. She did not seem pleased with the answer, but it was the only form of closure I could give them.

Anna had sat in on the meeting and remained quiet. She did not speak until we got to the car.

"It went better than I expected."

"Yeah. Let's hope it goes that well for Ms. Braxton."

Esther Braxton, wife of Theopolis Braxton III, lived in an oversized estate nestled in the heart of Belle Meade. A maid escorted us to the sitting room where Esther was waiting. She was on a couch, drinking tea in a fancy China cup, dressed casually but still managing to look like old money. A big fluffy cat was sitting on her lap, purring contentedly.

"Hi, Mrs. Braxton," I greeted. Anna did the same.

"Hello, Thomas. Hello, Anna," she said without standing. She then turned to the maid. "Ginseng tea for Anna, extra sugar, and coffee for Thomas, strong and black if I remember correctly."

I nodded gratefully and looked at the coffee table in front of the couch. It was an elegant antique of dark walnut, as was most of the furniture. It had a couple of knickknacks on it. I pointed at it.

"We have quite a bit of paperwork. If you like, we can lay everything out right here."

"That would be satisfactory," she said.

I moved things around and then Anna laid out the paperwork. When she had it sorted and we spent the obligatory amount of time sipping our beverages and chatting, Anna started by pointing at a printout of a family tree. It was impressive, going all the way back to the 1300s.

"Obviously, you already know all of this information, so, per your request, I focused on the Carmike family lineage in the mid to late 1800s, and Penelope Carmike in particular," she said.

Ms. Braxton did not respond and instead took a sip of her tea.

"Penelope was born March 19th, 1849 in the family home, which was located on the Columbia Pike in Williamson County, Tennessee. Here is the corresponding notation found in the family Bible. As you can see, she had three older brothers, Michael, Mark, and Paul."

"Yes, yes, I already know this," Ms. Braxton said with a hint of impatience. "I'm the one who provided you with the family Bible, remember?"

"Yes, ma'am," Anna said, duly chastened.

"And, as you already know, she gave birth to a baby girl whom she named Claire, in January of 1862. At that time, Penelope was not quite thirteen." Anna paused, waiting to see if Ms. Braxton had any comment. She did not, so Anna continued. "Apparently, the family lore is the father of baby Claire was a man by the name of Chester Bond."

"Yes, Chester and Penelope married before he went off to war. He was killed in the battle of Chaplin Hills," Ms. Braxton said. Anna glanced at me. We'd already discussed how we were going to present this case to Ms. Braxton. It was at this point where I was going to take over.

"That's the lore, but it isn't factually correct," I said. My phrasing was a fancy way of saying the family lore was bullshit.

Ms. Braxton seemed nonplussed. "What do you mean?"

Anna reached for a pile of papers. "Anna is handing you a biography of Chester Bond. You can read it over at your leisure, but in the meantime, I'll summarize. Chester grew up in Williamson County. His family lived near the Carmike plantation. He was six years older than Penelope. We're not sure how they met, doesn't really matter. What does matter is they had a relationship and it was in all probability a sexual relationship."

Ms. Braxton stared with a sarcastic arch of an eyebrow. "The birth of a child would seem to agree with your astute deduction, Thomas."

"Yes, well, you have me there, or so it would seem. Here is what we've learned that you may not be aware of. Chester Bond did indeed fight in the battle of Chaplin Hills, but he was not killed in battle."

"Are you certain?" she asked. "The war records list him as KIA."

"But his body was never recovered, correct?" I asked.

Ms. Braxton nodded slightly. "He was probably buried as an unknown soldier, much like thousands of other soldiers have been."

Anna produced the photocopy of the journal notation and handed it to me. "This is a page from a journal written by Reverend Hezekiah Smith. He was an African-American preacher who married Chester and Penelope October 12th of 1862. What is important to note is the battle of Chaplin Hills took place on October 8th. The battle continued until dark, at which time the Confederates withdrew. The two of them were married three days after the battle, so one can speculate Chester went AWOL at some point during or immediately after the battle and made his way back to Williamson County."

Now, Ms. Braxton frowned. "Are you sure?"

"Yes, ma'am," I said, and then made eye contact with Anna. Anna picked up another group of papers. "Anna is handing you a report and official death certificate from the medical examiner. The remains of Chester Bond were found in the bottom of a cistern well recently in Williamson County. The land where the cistern well is located, coincidentally, is part of the original Carmike homestead. Before you ask if I am sure, a gentleman by the name of Robert Bond contacted the medical examiner's office and provided family lineage back to Chester Bond." I paused a moment. "I believe this is the same Robert Bond who recently announced his candidacy for mayor."

"He is indeed," Ms. Braxton replied. She said it with a slight tone of distaste. I got the impression she had a poor opinion of Chester Bond. "Tell me, was a DNA test performed to verify Chester Bond and Robert Bond are related by blood?"

Anna glanced over at me. "I don't believe so, ma'am. We can follow up with Doctor Gross, if you'd like."

"Not necessary," she said quickly. "Please continue."

"Based on our research, it appears Chester Bond walked away from his military unit during or after the battle of Chaplin Hills and made his way back to Williamson County. He married Penelope and soon thereafter was murdered and buried in a cistern well on your family's plantation."

"I see," she said after a long moment of silence. She then moved the cat off of her lap and stood. "You've done excellent work. I have my checkbook in the office. If you'll excuse me, I'll get it."

"There's more," I said.

Ms. Braxton stared a moment before slowly sitting back down. This time, I reached out and picked up the last stack of papers.

"During our research, we came across a diary written by an African-American woman who lived during the same time period. If she were alive today, she would have been an excellent gossip columnist."

"By your comment, am I to assume she repeated gossip about my family?" Ms. Braxton asked.

"She did indeed," I said, and handed her the sheets of paper. "These are photocopies made from her diary. She described the Carmikes as a seemingly prominent, church-going family who had some dark secrets going on behind closed doors." I paused, searching for a diplomatic way to phrase what I was going to say next. Ms. Braxton sensed my thoughts.

"Go on, just say it," she said.

"Very well. Paul, the second oldest brother, was sleeping with Penelope. Baby Claire was the product of that relationship. It was only after she became pregnant that she seduced Chester Bond and led him to believe he was the father of her child."

I waited for some kind of reaction from Ms. Braxton. There was none. She remained stoic and kept staring, so I continued.

"Chester was young and naïve, or perhaps he was aware of everything, but it did not matter because he was so much in love with Penelope. He decided to go AWOL during the fog of battle. We can only speculate why. Perhaps Penelope had sent him a letter and convinced him to come back. Or maybe he had gotten word that she was being treated badly because she was an unwed mother. What we know for a certainty is he did in fact come back and the young couple sought out Reverend Smith. Two white kids being married by an African-American man of the cloth was virtually unheard of in the south back in those days."

"So, why would they do that?" she asked. She seemed slightly upset now, but the old gal still had a lot of starch in her; she was maintaining a stiff upper lip as the Brits used to say.

"Perhaps their preacher, the Carmike family, and the Bond family went to the same church. Perhaps that preacher did not approve and refused to marry them. Like I said, we can only speculate about that aspect. Anyway, Reverend Smith was murdered shortly after performing the wedding. Chester Bond was also murdered, presumably during the same time period and by the same person. Interestingly, the lady who wrote the journal said the murderer of both men was Paul Carmike, the older brother of Penelope Carmike and the father of her daughter, Claire Carmike." I waited for that bombshell to sink in before continuing.

"Penelope never remarried. She referred to herself as a war widow and lived in the family home the rest of her life. Interestingly enough, so did Paul Carmike."

Ms. Braxton sat as still as a statue. Her cat rubbed up against her several times, seeking attention, but was ignored. I sat back and finished my coffee before standing. Anna hastily followed.

"I'm sure this is a lot of information to digest. Take your time and read it all over. If you have any questions, or if you desire any follow-up investigation to be performed, we're at your disposal. In the meantime, let's get that payment squared away and we'll get out of your hair."

"You were a little gruff with her," Anna said after we'd left.

"She's a big girl, she can take it," I replied. "Besides, we need to get you home, you have a date with Percy tonight."

"How did you know that?" she asked.

"I called him up this morning at about five and we had a long conversation. I told him everything I'd been holding back about Lilith."

"Like what?" she asked.

"I had a phone call from her a while back. She admitted to killing that old man. She claimed it was self-defense, but you know how that goes. Anyway, I'm going to give a formal statement next week so he can officially clear the case. I'm sure he'll tell you all about it later."

"They said in the press conference that the FBI woman is conscious and is expected to recover."

"Yes, they did," I replied. "Did you hear what Carter said about her?"

"That she had no recollection of that night," Anna said.

I nodded. She'd also stopped talking to her comrades and lawyered up. Strange behavior for a person who claims to have amnesia.

"What do you think will happen to her?" Anna asked.

I scoffed. "I'd bet a dollar she'll take a medical pension, avoid any possible charges, and probably hire a publicist to write a book about her."

Anna snickered. "They'll probably make a movie out of it and she'll make millions."

"Yeah, probably."

CHAPTER 47

I wanted to spend the rest of the day by myself, but after dropping Anna off, I found myself at Mick's Place, sitting on my favorite barstool. A couple of reprobates sat at the far end in their own respective stools. Each gave me a nod.

"You don't look right, Dago," Mick remarked. "Do you need some Irish therapy? I'm an expert you know."

I couldn't help but smile at the man. "Nah, I'm good."

"What are you up to? You got a client to meet or something?" he asked.

"Not today. I have a clear schedule."

"Good, then you'll be needing a fine cigar and a delicious beer to go with it," he said and soon had a glass of Nashville Lager draft sitting in front of me. Marti came in a few minutes later. She was wearing Daisy Dukes and a bright pink tank top that hugged her puppies tightly. The regulars were drooling all over themselves. She gave them all a friendly hello before focusing on me.

"I'm working the rest of the night. Are you going to hang out a while?" she asked.

I looked outside the plate glass windows. A front had moved in. The temperature had dropped several degrees and Nashville was currently being soaked by one of those famous April showers. It was a dreary afternoon. A good afternoon to sit somewhere dry with an adult beverage and a fine cigar.

"I believe I will."

She stepped close, pressing her breasts against my shoulder. "I'd love your company, and you don't have anything to worry about. If you drink too much, I'll drive you home." She then kissed me on the cheek and walked around behind the bar.

I chuckled to myself. She sure was friendly with me. I had no idea if she had ulterior motives, but at the moment didn't care.

I sipped my beer and absently watched some golf on one of the big screens while I thought about Esther Braxton. When we'd told her that her family lineage had a line of incest, she seemed unfazed. For some reason, that seemed peculiar.

My thoughts jumped to Lilith. She was sleeping with her cousin, Wolf. It wasn't like they were hillbillies living deep in the mountains, separated from the rest of society. I thought I knew Lilith well enough to say she would have never done something like that. I suppose incest is not something that is casually talked about. Things like that are kept under the covers, no pun intended.

That led to my next thought. Little Penelope Carmike was only twelve when she and her brother began having sexual relations. I thought about different scenarios and plausible explanations for Paul to rationalize molesting his little sister, but could only come to the conclusion that he was a sicko.

So many unanswered questions.

It wasn't until I'd finished my second beer that I had a eureka moment. "She already knew," I said to myself and gave a sardonic chuckle.

"What's that, handsome?" Marti asked.

I glanced at Marti on the other side of the bar and smiled. "Did you ever have one of those moments where you realize you've been hoodwinked?"

"Um, yeah, I guess so. Why, did someone hoodwink you?"

"Yeah, you could say that."

She gazed at me and waited for an explanation. I gave none.

"Alright, I guess your lips are sealed. You want a fresh beer?" she asked.

I looked down and realized I'd drank my second beer quicker than I realized. "I believe I will," I said.

Marti set a freshly filled glass down in front of me. "So, who hoodwinked you?"

"An old gal who I'll never play poker with."

She grinned. "You must mean Ms. Braxton. When I first met her, I could tell right away she's a shrewd woman."

"That she is," I said.

I took a swallow of beer and wondered what Ms. Braxton was up to. She was scheming, and I bet it had something to do with Robert Bond running for mayor. Needless to say, my level of respect for her went up a notch or two and I wondered if I would ever learn of her true intentions.

My phone rang. I glanced at the caller ID before answering, but I didn't recognize the number.

"Thomas?"

"Yes, who is this?" I said.

"This is Kalina, do you remember me?" she asked. I set my beer down.

"Yes, of course. Lilith's cousin," I said. "How are you?"

I'd met Kalina several months ago in Chicago at The Gypsy Dragon, back when it was still open. Her attitude toward me at first was aloof, but I think she had eventually warmed up to me.

"I'm calling to warn you," she said. Or, maybe not.

"What's the problem?" I asked.

"My family believes you have brought ruin upon them. You are *bibaxt*, bad luck. Because of this, an *amria* has been put on you."

I frowned, wondering what the word meant. "Is that like some kind of gypsy curse?"

"Yes."

I waited for her to start laughing. She didn't.

"Are you joking?"

"I'm dead serious, Thomas," she said.

"That seems rather drastic, Kalina. After all, I didn't kill any member of your family."

"It is believed you are the cause of their deaths," she said. "The elders believe this."

"Well, somebody needs to sit them down and give them the facts. Wolf killed Lilith. He and Pekoe were killed by the cops, and that goofy-looking old man who ran around with them banging on a tambourine was killed in a car wreck while in the act of abducting a woman. So, why am I the one getting a curse put on me?"

"You are not a gypsy, you are *gadjo*. You would not understand."

"No, I don't guess I do," I said. "But you need to tell your people to leave me alone. I've had enough of them. By the way, why did nobody claim Lilith's body? You and your people know I'm the one who made arrangements for her funeral service, right? As in, I'm the one who paid for it and I'm the only one who attended her service. Which one of those snarky elders do I talk to about that?"

There was a long pause, and then the line disconnected. I looked at the screen a moment before setting it on the bar top.

"Bunch of crazy assholes," I muttered and downed my beer.

I did not believe in psychic ability, or magic, or any of that nonsense, and I damn sure wasn't going to believe in a gypsy curse. But in the weeks and months that followed, I would remember this phone call. I would remember it in my waking moments and in my dreams.

"How about another beer, beautiful?" I said to Marti with a grin, forgetting all about my mental reminder to slow down.

CHAPTER 48

I finished cleaning my grill and filled the hopper with wood pellets at about the time Anna came home. Marti was with her and they had the car stereo blasting, as usual. I don't know how they could stand it. After a moment, they exited the car and walked over. Gracie bounded behind them, only pausing long enough to squat in the grass.

"Hi, girls," I greeted.

"What are you cooking?" Marti asked.

"Garlic and herb-stuffed prime rib roast," I answered.

She inhaled deeply. "It smells wonderful. What's for dessert?" she asked. She had a mischievous grin when she said it and punctuated it with a flirtatious wink.

I tried not to, but I grinned as well. I told myself I wouldn't do it, but the two of us had recently hooked up one night after Mick's had closed. I certainly hoped Mick did not bother looking at the bar's surveillance video, because we not only christened the bar top, but the humidor and one of the couches as well.

It was spontaneous, poorly thought out, but I had to admit I did not regret a second of it. Evens so, the two of us agreed it was going to be our little secret. Since then, we'd hooked up a couple of additional times. I had to admit, she was fun to be with.

Anna, who was oblivious, spoke up and peppered me with questions about the party.

"Do you know if everyone is coming? Do we have enough to eat and drink? What beverages are we serving?"

"Stop worrying. Everyone who matters is coming and we have enough to feed a small army."

"What about beverages?"

I pointed at a blue plastic barrel sitting near the back door.

"There's a quarter-barrel keg in there on ice, and we have various sodas in the fridge. If anyone wants something stronger, they need to bring it."

"Alright, I'll go check on the rest of the food," she said and walked inside. Marti waited before the door closed before speaking.

"I think she's going to spend the night with Percy tonight after the party," she said.

I nodded. "Remind me to disable the cameras, or else Ronald will find out."

Her jaw dropped open. "Do you think he watches the cameras at the bar?"

My face tightened. "I hadn't thought of that. He hasn't said anything, so I think we're okay."

She giggled. Our conversation stopped when my phone rang. I looked at the caller ID. It showed the call originating from the Rutherford County Jail. When I answered, an automated voice informed me an inmate was calling me collect. When it identified the inmate as Flaky, I frowned in concern and hurriedly accepted the call.

"How's it going, Thomas," Flaky greeted.

"Hey, I take it you've been arrested, am I right?" I asked.

"Yeah, I got myself into a little situation," he said.

"Oh, yeah? What's going on?"

"Well, it goes like this. The cops have charged me with murder."

THE END